T0296575

Ancient Magic

Ancient Magic

By Alexandra Ivy

LYRICAL PRESS
Kensington Publishing Corp.
www.kensingtonbooks.com

LYRICAL PRESS BOOKS are published by
Kensington Publishing Corp.
119 West 40th Street
New York, NY 10018

All Kensington titles, imprints, and distributed lines are available at special quantity discounts for bulk purchases for sales promotion, premiums, fund-raising, educational, or institutional use.

Special book excerpts or customized printings can also be created to fit specific needs. For details, write or phone the office of the Kensington Sales Manager: Kensington Publishing Corp., 119 West 40th Street, New York, NY 10018. Attn. Sales Department. Phone: 1-800-221-2647.

Lyrical Press Books and Lyrical Press eBooks logo Reg. U.S. Pat. & TM Off.

First Electronic Edition: August 2024
ISBN: 978-1-5161-1139-8 (ebook)

First Print Edition: August 2024
ISBN: 978-1-5161-1142-8

Printed in the United States of America

Chapter 1

Skye Claremont studied the brick building in front of her. Once upon a time, the Green House Theater must have been an impressive sight. Consuming most of the city block, it had high arched windows on the upper floor and a massive marquee outlined with lights that jutted over the sidewalk. In the center of the building was a glassed-in box office framed by two sets of double doors with ornate handles. Even the roof was decorated with bronzed statues that peered down as if waiting for an invisible crowd to enter.

Now, it was less impressive and more depressing. Even at a distance she could see that the bricks were crumbling and the windows were covered by sheets of plywood that had been spray-painted by vandals. And not even good vandals.

Just crappy initials and gang symbols.

Skye heaved a sigh. The Green House Theater looked...depressed, she decided. As if it were feeling abandoned by the audiences who'd turned their attention to other entertainments.

Maybe it was the gray October weather that was making it look sad, she acknowledged. It wasn't raining, but the clouds hung low in the sky, blocking out the afternoon sun and casting a shadow over New York City. Or maybe it was the empty lots that surrounded the building that emphasized an air of neglect.

Whatever the case, this place had obviously seen better days.

Turning her head, Skye glanced at the woman standing next to her.

Maya Rosen appeared to be in her early thirties with elegant features that were highlighted rather than marred by the spidery web of scars that ran from her left ear down her jawline. Her eyes were a bright green and her silky-smooth black hair was chopped at her shoulders.

Most people first meeting Maya assumed she was a successful businesswoman. And they would be partially right. She did own a wildly popular coffee shop called the Witch's Brew in Linden, New Jersey. But she'd passed her thirtieth birthday several decades ago. Like all mages, she'd stopped aging after her powers had fully matured. It was one of many bonuses to possessing the wild magic that flowed in their blood.

Not that Skye had ever been concerned about aging. At the age of twenty-seven she still looked like a teenager with her mane of pale, corkscrew curls that bounced around her heart-shaped face and deep dimples. It didn't help that she chose her clothes for comfort, not style. Today she'd pulled on a pair of sweatpants and a fuzzy sweater with the Cookie Monster on the front to combat the chilly air.

It was only her black eyes that were framed with long lashes that warned she wasn't as young and innocent as she appeared. Her gaze had unnerved some of the most powerful demons. As well as a vampire or two. Maya had once told her that people could sense the mystic powers that bubbled inside her.

"You're sure this is the place?" Skye asked her companion, her voice barely above a whisper.

Despite the fact they were in Upper Manhattan, the sounds of traffic and pedestrians were muffled, as if this neighborhood was shrouded from the city that hummed with an electric excitement just a few blocks away.

Maya grimaced before touching her temple. "According to the voice in my head."

Skye wasn't reassured. She'd been taken in by Maya almost five years ago when she'd wandered into the Witch's Brew in search of a job. The older woman was not only one of the most powerful mages that Skye had ever encountered, but she was also one of the rare few who wasn't under the rule of a vampire.

Vampires were rare—only the leeches knew the exact number—but they owned the Gyres, where the last of the magic in the world lingered. It was rumored that the hotspots were the ancient lairs of dragons who'd left this world eons ago. Not that it mattered. However the Gyres had been created, they offered demons the ability to touch their primeval powers. And since the vampires controlled the Gyres, they controlled the demons.

Thankfully for Skye, mages didn't depend on the Gyres for their magic. It flowed through their blood. And while her magic might be amped by the power that hummed in the air and thundered beneath her feet, she had no desire to be the slave of a vampire. Or a demon.

Not again.

But as Maya had warned her, independence had a price. For Maya it was the mysterious Benefactor. Skye didn't know much about the elusive creature. It never visited the Witch's Brew or contacted Maya by traditional means. Instead, it spoke directly into the older woman's mind. And while the Benefactor surrounded them in an aura that somehow kept away the leeches, it occasionally demanded they perform small tasks.

Like today.

"So what you're saying is that the Benefactor placed an invisible GPS in your head," Skye teased, trying to ease the tension that had been building since they entered the city.

"Something like that."

"And I thought I was weird."

"You are," Maya assured her.

"True," Skye agreed. Unlike her companion, or Peri Sanguis, another mage that Maya had taken in, Skye didn't have enormous magic. She couldn't brew potions like Maya or call on long-lost powers like Peri, but she was the most unique of all mages. A seer. A rare gift that did nothing to help in their current circumstances, she acknowledged as she glanced back at the theater. "The place looks empty. What now?"

"I guess we go inside." Maya squared her shoulders before crossing the road and heading toward the empty lot next to the building.

Skye struggled to match her friend's long strides. Just one of many problems for a short girl.

"Maybe we should give Peri a call," she suggested.

"It's her day off."

It was Sunday and the coffee shop was closed, meaning Peri would be spending the day with her mate, Valen, the Cabal leader of the East Coast, in his lair near Central Park. A short taxi ride away.

"Yeah, but she's the muscle of our crew," Skye muttered.

Maya arched a brow. "What am I?"

"The brains."

"Debatable." Maya halted in front of a rusty side door propped open a few inches by a broken brick. She turned her head to send Skye a wry smile. "You, however, are most certainly the heart."

Skye leaned forward to peer through the narrow crack. "Very nice, but right now I'd prefer some muscle."

Maya paused, as if communicating with the voice in her head. Then she grimaced.

"We can't wait. It has to be now."

"Okay, then." Skye grabbed the handle and pulled the door wide enough for them to enter. "Are you ready?"

"No," Maya muttered even as she squeezed through the opening.

Skye quickly followed, glancing around the narrow hallway. Directly ahead of them an arched opening led to the main auditorium that was lined with rows of seats. To the left the hallway disappeared into the shadowed wings of the stage, and to the right a wide staircase curved up to the mezzanine.

Skye moved to peer into the auditorium, only to be halted as Maya grabbed her arm in a tight grip.

"We're not alone."

Skye instantly froze. One of Maya's many talents was the ability to sense the presence of demons.

"How many?" Skye whispered.

"Five. Three goblins and two fairies."

In ancient times the demons openly roamed the world. But as the magic had faded, they'd been forced to hide among the humans, usually gathering in the Gyres, where they could still access their diluted powers even if it did mean bending the knee to a vampire.

"Where?" Skye asked.

Before Maya could answer they heard the crunch of footsteps just outside the door. With a startled glance, they scurried forward, jogging up the staircase to disappear in the gloom.

Once on the mezzanine, Maya took the lead, bending over as she headed toward the low wall at the front of the overhang. Skye crab walked behind her, pressing her side against the wall before she cautiously peeked over the edge.

Below her the auditorium fanned upward in a half-circle facing toward the wide stage. The chairs remained intact, but the wallpaper was peeling and the ornate cornices and molding had long ago lost their gilding. Overhead there was a large chandelier that someone had tried to yank out, cracking the plaster and leaving it at a drunken angle, but it didn't look as if it was going to collapse on her head in the next few minutes.

The only good news since Maya had announced they were traveling to the city.

She turned her attention to the demons seated in the front rows, as if waiting for a show to start. The three goblins looked remarkably alike. All were broad and bald and bulging with muscles. All were wearing jeans with gray hoodies. And of course, all of them were surrounded by a red glow that marked them as demons. At least to those who possessed the magic to see the aura. The two fairies, on the other hand, were slender with long reddish hair and delicate features. They wore the same hoodies as if it was a group thing, but the glow around them was green instead of red.

Even from a distance Skye could tell that none of them had particularly strong auras, revealing their blood had been diluted with humans' over the centuries and that they were low on the demon social scale. It didn't mean, however, they weren't dangerous.

As if to emphasize the point, the group of demons turned toward the stage as a large form suddenly appeared from the wings. He was a goblin with the usual muscular body, and like the others, he'd shaved his head and was casually attired. But his aura was twice as bright as the others, warning Skye that he came from a family with considerable power.

"You're late," one of the goblins from below groused.

"Fuck off, Gunther," the man on stage retorted. "I'm here now."

Skye blinked. Someone was grouchy.

One of the goblins, presumably Gunther, rose to his feet, his hands on his hips. "Then let's get this over with. Why are we here?"

The man on stage, who was the obvious leader, glared down at him. "Did you do a sweep of the building?"

"Course we did. We're a professional crew."

"So you keep saying."

"We weren't the ones who were an hour late," Gunther snapped, glancing around the empty theater. "I don't like being out in the daylight. Too many eyes watching."

The leader scowled, as if he wasn't used to being chided. "You'll be out when I tell you to be out. I'm the one paying the bills."

"But you aren't, are you?"

The scowl deepened. "Aren't what?"

"Paying the bills," Gunther groused. "You keep promising that we're going to be living large, but so far we're out there risking our asses with nothing to show for it."

"You'll get what's coming to you." An ugly smile curved the male's lips.

Gunther snorted. "When?"

"Soon."

"The bill is adding up. Are you sure you're going to have enough money to cover it?"

"I told you. You'll get paid."

"Yeah, well, it'd better be in the next couple of days." The demon cupped his hand between his legs. "My bitch needs some new bling or her pretty mouth isn't going to be wrapped around my cock. And then I'm going to get real fussy real quick."

Maya and Skye shared a glance of pure disgust as the demons obediently laughed at Gunther's crude joke. The man on stage, however, appeared less amused.

"If you're unhappy with the situation, I can find another crew." The leader deliberately paused, flicking his hard gaze toward the gathered demons. "Better yet, I could ask your buddies if they want to choose a new leader. I'm betting they'll decide to get rid of you. It's a better option than walking away with nothing after all their hard work. What would you bet?"

Gunther shuffled his feet, smart enough to back down from the threat. "Chillax, dude," he grumbled. "If we're not going to get paid, then why did you call us here?"

The leader folded his arms over his chest. "I need someone who isn't a member of your crew to perform a separate task."

"What's my cut of the pay?"

"That's between you and whoever you hire, but I have rules."

"What rules?"

"If he gets caught or squeals about our extracurricular activity, you all die."

There was a sudden burst of chatter between the gathered crew. Gunther ignored them. "Caught by who?"

"Anyone."

"That's a little vague."

"Make sure they don't get caught."

Gunther hesitated. Was he debating whether or not to accept the responsibility for an outside contractor? Maybe, but he wasn't going to back down.

"Okay, but it's going to cost more," he abruptly warned. "Say...double our normal rate."

"Whatever." The leader shrugged. "Put it on my bill."

Gunther visibly jerked, caught off guard by the male's ready agreement to his demands. Skye wasn't. The demon on the stage possessed a cold brutality she'd sensed before. He would kill the entire crew once they'd completed the job. And he would kill them without remorse. Like a snake striking an enemy and slithering past the corpse.

"Fine." He forced out the word. "Anything else?"

The leader stepped forward, running a dismissive glance over the demons sprawled in the front seats.

"Is this your entire crew?"

"No. I have four others. They're on a job."

The male clicked his tongue, as if disappointed with the answer. "Next time I call for a meeting, I want them all here."

"Why?"

"Because I said so. That's the only explanation you need."

Gunther cleared his throat, as if he was beginning to wonder why the male would want them all gathered in one spot. Skye could have told him it was so it would be easier to kill them.

"About that money you owe us—"

"Shut up." The leader abruptly tilted back his head, sucking in a deep breath. "There's someone here. Humans." He released a feral growl, glaring at Gunther. "You said you searched the place."

"I did. If there's someone here they must have snuck in while we were waiting for you."

"Find them," the leader snapped. "No one gets out of here."

Maya grasped Skye's arm, dragging her toward the back of the mezzanine. Below them the bellows of angry demons echoed through the air, reverberating against the domed ceiling as they charged in pursuit.

"Stay close," Maya commanded as she released her grip on Skye and reached into the purse slung over one shoulder.

Skye knew that her friend would have at least a few bottles of potions stashed in the leather satchel. A good mage never left home without them. Skye, on the other hand, touched the silver bracelet that encircled her wrist. The various charms that dangled from the delicate chain weren't for decoration. She used them to store extra doses of magic.

Extra doses that were going to be handy dandy in the next few minutes.

Reaching the stairs, they headed downward only to halt as one of the goblins appeared at the bottom.

"They're here!" the demon managed to call out before Maya tossed a slender glass tube in his direction.

The male held up his arms, protecting his face as the thin glass shattered and a massive explosion sent him flying backward. He roared in fury as he hurtled down the hallway and smashed into the far wall. The force was enough to knock him unconscious and Maya didn't hesitate as she continued down the staircase. Skye scurried behind her. They had to get out of the theater before their escape was cut off.

They were halfway down the steps when Skye felt a familiar flare of magic spread through her. A vision. Dammit, now wasn't a good time. Not that any time was good. But this was spectacularly bad.

Sadly, she'd learned a long time ago it was futile to try to suppress them, no matter how unwelcome they might be. You might as well try to halt a volcano from erupting. Besides, Maya was still holding her hand. The personal contact meant that the vision was more than likely connected to her friend.

Gritting her teeth, Skye grunted as she was rudely blinded by her powers, and the image of Maya lying dead at the bottom of the staircase seared through her mind. There was a bleeding bullet hole directly in the middle of her forehead, and her eyes were wide open, staring sightlessly at the demon standing over her.

"No, Maya!" Skye wrapped her arm around her friend's waist, yanking her to a halt.

They stumbled, falling backward at the same moment that a gunshot boomed from the hallway and a bullet ripped through the exact spot where they'd been standing.

Maya released a shaky breath, turning her head to send Skye a glance of gratitude despite the fact that the older woman had made Skye swear never to share visions she might have of Maya or Peri while they all lived at the Witch's Brew. Skye understood Maya's rule. Knowing the future without context was worthless. And Skye had always been happy that she had no ability to see her own destiny.

But desperate times called for desperate measures.

And this was about as desperate as it could get.

"I don't suppose the Benefactor is whispering an escape plan in your head?" Skye demanded, scrambling back up the stairs.

Maya once again reached into her purse and pulled out a vial. She tossed it over her shoulder without looking back.

"Nope."

"Typical."

Skye clenched her muscles as she prepared for another explosion. Instead, a cloud of smoke filled the air and she could hear demons choking from the hallway.

The potion had given them a brief opportunity to escape. If only they could find a way out of the building. Back in the mezzanine, Maya headed directly toward the windows. They would have to bust through the plywood, but—

"Stop!"

Skye's thoughts were shattered as the male voice echoed from the other side of the mezzanine. Turning her head she watched the two fairies leap over the low wall and race toward them. Skye touched a charm on her bracelet and whispered a spell, but even as the magic pulsed in her blood, the closest fairy tossed a dagger. Skye dodged to the side, but the blade was enchanted. Curving with lethal precision, it headed straight for her heart. Skye released a hasty spell designed to create a bubble of protection. It deflected the knife far enough to avoid a killing blow, but the blade managed to slice through her upper arm.

Maya muttered in frustration, throwing another vial. It wasn't aimed at the advancing males, but instead it hit at their feet, smashing against the warped floorboards. There was a loud sizzle before flames abruptly appeared, twirling like tiny tornadoes as they headed directly toward the advancing males. The fairies shouted in fear, diving back over the edge.

"Are you okay?" Maya rasped, turning to inspect the wound on Skye's arm.

"I'll be fine," she assured her friend, trying to ignore the throbbing pain. "Let's just get out of here."

"Good plan."

Maya turned back toward the windows, lifting her hand as she released a pulse of magic. It smacked against the plywood, splintering one in half. Not enough to allow them to squeeze through, but Skye was hoping that it weakened the wood enough that they should be able to physically wrench it off.

They rushed forward, Skye holding her hand over the wound that seeped blood down her arm. She would worry about healing the cut later. Right now nothing mattered but fleeing.

Unfortunately, there were still five demons determined to prevent them from accomplishing their goal.

On cue, the leader roared his way up the stairs, his aura flaring with a brilliant crimson as he barreled directly toward them. Maya whirled to face him, but even as she reached into her purse the male was swinging his meaty fist, catching Maya directly on the chin. The mage soared backward, slamming into plyboard that collapsed beneath the impact. With a low cry, Maya flew through the broken window and down to the street below.

Skye lunged forward, terrified her friend was seriously hurt. Mages were far more durable than humans, but they weren't immortal.

She'd managed only a few steps when a massive hand grabbed her by her nape and lifted her off her feet. She struggled to glance over her shoulder to see the demon who was carrying her forward. The instinctive turn of her head saved her nose from being busted as he slammed her face first against the wall.

"Who are you?" the leader snarled, ignoring the white cloud of plaster that floated from the ceiling to layer them in a fine powder. "Why did you follow me?"

Skye ignored the pain that burst through her skull as it connected with the wall. She also ignored the male who continued to slam her into the wall as he asked the same question over and over.

Her ability to glimpse the future or to sense emotions wasn't much help during a fight. And while she had a few spells, they weren't potent enough to combat a full-grown goblin. Thankfully, she had one other skill. A skill she'd discovered by accident and rarely used.

Reaching up, she pressed her hand against the fingers that were currently digging into her neck. Her magic, including her visions, always worked best when she was touching someone. She assumed it had something to do with the sheer intimacy of her powers.

Now she closed her eyes, blocking out the demon who continued to shout at her for answers, the acrid stench of flames, the plaster dust floating in the air, the splintering pain in her head, and the fear that Maya might be injured. Then, focusing her thoughts on the feel of his fingers beneath her hand, she released a tendril of magic, directing it to crawl up his arm and along the broad width of his shoulder.

The demon stiffened as her magic reached his neck and arrowed upward. Did he feel her powers moving through his body? Or was he tired of smashing her into the wall? Nah. He couldn't be tired. Not when he was obviously getting pleasure from her pain. Which meant he sensed the danger.

Realizing she had to hurry, Skye clenched her teeth and concentrated on the magic, urging it to surround his mind in a web of shimmering strands.

"What the fuck? Get out of my head."

The male abruptly released her, allowing her to drop to the ground as he tried to shake off her lingering touch. It was too late. Skye had a firm grip on his mind, her magic tightening and tightening until the demon screamed in agony.

"Stop! You bitch. Stop..."

With a moan the demon fell to the floor, clutching his head in his hands. Skye could have destroyed him. Just another squeeze and his mind would have become mush. Instead, she broke the connection between them and leaped through the window.

Chapter 2

It wasn't easy to attract attention in New York City. Not when there was a plethora of pedestrians who clogged the streets with styles that went beyond flamboyant. Skye had seen a man stroll stark naked through Times Square without getting a second glance.

But not even the jaded citizens of the Big Apple could hide their interest as Skye and Maya limped their way into Penn Station. They certainly had a zombie vibe going on. It might have been their torn clothing, tangled hair and layers of dust and plaster that clung to them. Or the blood that dripped from Skye's arm. Or Maya's swollen eye where she'd slammed through the plywood and hit the pavement two stories below. Or perhaps it was the grim expressions on their faces that warned the world they weren't in the mood to... Well, anything really. Unless it included a hot bath and a bottle of aspirin.

Whatever the cause, they were given plenty of space as they settled in the train that whisked them to New Jersey. Neither spoke during the thirty-minute ride. Skye was too relieved that they'd escaped alive, while Maya no doubt brooded on the reason the Benefactor had sent them to the stupid theater in the first place.

Hobbling off the train in Linden, they crossed the parking lot and zigzagged their way through the narrow streets, backtracking more than once. Skye assumed that Maya was making sure they weren't being followed. No doubt a wise precaution, but Skye wasn't in the mood to be wise. Or cautious.

She was cold, exhausted, and her arm hurt like a bitch. Time to get home.

At last they turned onto the block where they could see the neon sign stuck over the sidewalk with a coffee cup in the center of a witch's hat.

The Witch's Brew. Thank goodness.

Concentrating on placing one foot in front of the other, Skye jumped in surprise as a man abruptly appeared from seemingly nowhere. Instinctively she touched a charm on her bracelet, absorbing the magic. Tired or not, she was ready to fight off an attack.

It wasn't until he stepped closer that she breathed a sigh of relief. Joe was a regular fixture in the area. She didn't know if he had a home nearby or stayed in the local shelter, but he was always hanging around, usually dressed in a velour tracksuit with a fishing hat stuck on his head. His age was indeterminant behind his bushy beard, but she suspected that he was older than she'd first assumed.

"Hey, Joe," she murmured.

The man leaned toward them, his eyes nearly hidden beneath his hat. "You look like you rolled in the sewers. You smell even worse."

Skye managed a weary smile. Joe enjoyed calling out insults whenever they passed. She honestly preferred it to the creepy whistles and catcalls that some men thought were flattering.

Without warning, Maya glared at the harmless man. "Not now."

Joe snorted. "You know what? The smell of you would be an insult to the sewers. You—"

Maya pointed a finger in the man's face. "Not. Now."

"Maya," Skye protested as they limped past Joe. "He's just teasing."

"I don't trust him."

Skye frowned. Since last summer, Maya had grown increasingly suspicious of Joe.

"You keep saying that, but I don't understand why not. He's been hanging around here forever."

Maya's features pinched into a sour expression. "He's more."

"More what?"

"I don't know," the older woman muttered. "But I intend to find out."

Skye didn't argue. She was too tired. Besides, arguing with Maya was like smacking her head into a brick wall. And her head had already been smacked into enough walls for one day, thank you very much.

Reaching the coffee shop squashed between a tanning salon and a falafel restaurant, Skye placed her hand against the door to unravel the protective wards and they stepped inside.

It wasn't a large establishment but to her it was filled with charm. There were small round tables spread around the white-tiled floor and walls that were painted a bright lavender. Skye had recently decorated the large front windows with fall leaves, pumpkins, and black cats in celebration of the Halloween season. And even though they were closed, the air was scented with the rich aroma of freshly pressed coffee and baked pastries that lured customers from miles around to stand in a line down the block. Sometimes for hours.

For those customers who weren't in the mood for coffee and muffins—or just preferred a bit of peace—there was an attached bookstore where you could sink into one of the cushy armchairs and read without distractions.

Of course, there were parts of the Witch's Brew that weren't so charming.

From a small, barren office at the back of the building, the three mages offered their magical expertise. For the right price, a demon could purchase a love potion, a glamour spell, an illusion charm that would last for weeks, and a tonic that could stiffen up a demon's sagging performance in the bedroom.

And if you had deep enough pockets, they could create agonizing curses to punish an enemy.

Coffee, muffins, potions, charms, and curses. A full-service business.

At the point of crossing toward the door behind the counter that hid a staircase to the upper floors, Maya came to a sudden halt.

"Is something wrong?" Skye demanded.

"Peri's here." Maya's brows tugged together as if she was attempting to pinpoint their friend's precise location. "She's in the office."

Skye instantly forgot her weariness, her aching head, and the wound that still seeped blood. There had to be something wrong. Since becoming Valen's mate last summer, the couple had made it a rule that Sunday was the one day a week that they were unavailable. Nothing and no one were allowed to intrude into their privacy.

Clearly as alarmed as Skye, Maya hurried through the attached bookstore and into the back office, where Peri was pacing the floor, her body tense and her hands clenched.

"What happened?" Maya demanded.

Peri jerked as if she hadn't sensed their approach, slowly turning to face them.

"Hello to you too..." Peri's words trailed away as she took in the sight of her bedraggled friends. For a long moment she merely stared at them, as if wondering if she was hallucinating. Then she shook her head in disbelief. "Holy crap. You're asking me what happened? Look at you guys." Her eyes widened with horror. "Skye. You're bleeding."

"I'm fine."

Skye managed a weak smile as she edged around Peri and headed toward Maya's desk at the back of the room. Pulling open the bottom drawer, she pulled out one of the emergency healing potions. They were nothing if not prepared. Acutely aware she was being watched, Skye tugged off the stopper and poured the thick green liquid over her wound. It didn't instantly heal, but the bleeding stopped and the worst of the pain eased. Replacing the vial, she grabbed a disposable wipe and cleaned off the dried blood and dust.

Once she was finished, she returned her attention to her friend, who was watching her with a lift of her brows. Peri was wearing a casual pair of jeans and a Chicago Cubs sweatshirt, but she still managed to look elegant. The mage was just a couple years older than Skye with long dark curls and glorious blue eyes and a stark beauty that had softened with happiness since she'd mated with Valen.

"Are you going to explain why the two of you look like you spent the day with a horde of demons?" Peri demanded.

"Because we spent the day battling a horde of demons," Skye admitted.

Peri's mouth dropped open. "Why?"

"A request from the Benefactor that went sideways," Maya answered, moving to stand next to Peri. "We can discuss our spectacular failure when you come to work tomorrow. For now I want to know why you're here."

Peri grimaced, wrapping her arms around her waist. "It's nothing really. I'm sure I'm overreacting—"

"You're worried," Skye abruptly broke into Peri's attempt to act casual.

Peri stiffened. "Skye."

Skye held up her hand. "I wasn't peeking into your mind," she assured her friend. "But I can sense your fear."

"Is it Valen?" Maya snapped. The older woman was as protective as a mother hen when it came to Skye and Peri. Especially when vampires were involved. "Skye and I have sensed for weeks that something's bothering you. You might pretend to be happy, but you can't fool your family. You're worried and it's only getting worse."

"What are you talking about?" Peri tried to sound surprised, but she had to know her friends had noticed the darkening shadows in her eyes.

"You can tell us," Maya insisted. "Has Valen done something to you? I warned you that leeches couldn't be trusted—"

"Valen is perfect," Peri swiftly defended her mate.

Maya narrowed her gaze, her silvery scars seeming to glow in the stark light. "Perfect?"

"Okay, maybe not perfect, but he makes me happy."

"Are you sure?" Maya pressed. "If he's done something—"

"Tell us what's bothering you," Skye interrupted before a squabble could break out.

The three of them were closer than sisters. Which meant they had a genius talent for annoying the crap out of each other. Peri hesitated before squaring her shoulders. She had come to the Witch's Brew with a purpose, and she wasn't happy about it.

"The Cabal showed up in New York last night," she abruptly announced.

Maya and Skye released mutual sounds of shock. Only the most powerful vampires were invited to become members of the exclusive group who ruled over the demon world.

"The whole Cabal?" Skye breathed in horror.

Peri shook her head. "Four of them. Gabriel from Denver, Micha from New Orleans, Kane from St. Petersburg and Ambassador Azra. He's some sort of assistant to Sinjon, who's the current head honcho of the Cabal."

"Four of the most lethal leeches invaded Valen's territory?" Maya's magic tingled in the air, brushing over Skye's skin like an electric current. "Are they plotting a rebellion?"

Peri grimaced. "TBD."

Maya blinked. "What?"

"To be determined," Skye clarified for her friend.

Maya sent her a frustrated glare. "I know what it means. I want to know why it's yet to be determined."

Skye shrugged. "Then that's what you should have asked."

It was Peri's turn to head off a squabble. "The rumors of my wild magic have made their way through the demon world. The Cabal is here to determine if I'm a danger to the demons."

Skye felt a sudden stab of unease. Unlike regular witches who could manipulate magical items and create spells with the proper ingredients, mages were born with wild magic flowing in their veins. Usually that manifested in a nuclear blast of power that ignited their magic when they reached adulthood—like gas being poured on kindling—before the magic retreated to a low simmer. Except for Peri. Her magic had always been amazing, but during a battle a few months ago with an ancient evil, the raw magic had once again blasted through her and stayed, giving her a power that was off the charts.

The sort of power that didn't go unnoticed by those in charge.

"I don't believe that's why they're here," Maya growled in dangerous tones. "They aren't worried about demons, they're worried your power might be great enough to pose a threat to their supreme rule."

Skye blinked. "Seriously? You think they're a threat to Peri?"

"Absolutely. Leeches consider themselves superior to the rest of us. If Peri threatens their dominance, they'll do whatever is necessary to destroy her."

"I don't threaten anything," Peri argued.

"Of course you do," Maya insisted. "Just having the power in your hands is a threat."

Skye studied Peri, absorbing the pulses of apprehension that she couldn't control.

"You're worried," Skye murmured.

Peri offered a grudging nod. "I don't know exactly what they want from me. It's not like there are specific reassurances I can offer to prove I'm not going to hurt anyone. At least, I would never hurt anyone on purpose." She grimaced. "Plus, having four of the most powerful vampires in the world staying at our lair is a lot. Even Valen is uneasy."

"You should stay here until they leave," Maya announced, sounding as if the decision had been made.

Peri shook her head. "Tempting, but I refuse to be driven from my home. Even if they are the Cabal."

Skye moved to grasp her friend's hand. "What can we do to help?"

Peri offered her a grateful smile. "Valen and I are hosting a formal dinner party tomorrow night to welcome the Cabal to our Gyre. Not that we're in the mood to entertain, but we don't want anyone to think we have anything to hide." She looked like she'd rather have her teeth pulled than to roll out the red carpet for her unwanted guests. "We've invited a few demons, along with the servants who've traveled with the vampires. And I want you both to be there."

"Of course we'll be there," Maya said. "What time—"

"No," Skye interrupted.

Maya narrowed her gaze. "No?"

Skye gave Peri's fingers a squeeze. "We love you, Peri, you know that. And we would do anything to help you. But Maya can't be trusted around vampires."

The older woman sucked in a harsh breath. "That's not true."

Peri was clearly blindsided by Skye's stark refusal. "It's just for one evening."

Skye kept her gaze focused on Peri. "Do you remember when Maya and I traveled to Paris to take pastry lessons at the Le Cordon Bleu?"

"Yeah, I stayed here to keep the shop open."

"We were there less than a week before we were on the verge of being thrown into the local dungeon."

Peri arched her brows. "I didn't hear this story. What happened?"

"The vampire in charge of the local Gyre discovered we were staying in Paris and requested that we join him for dinner at his chateau," Skye said. "Most people would have been honored."

Peri's lips twisted. "But not Maya?"

"She told his messenger to shove his invitation up his ass and threatened to shrink his balls to the size of grapes if he returned to our hotel." Skye leaned toward Peri to whisper in her ear. "Spoiler alert. He didn't return."

Maya clicked her tongue. "It wasn't an invitation. It was a royal decree with enough of a threat to piss me off."

Skye ignored Maya's protest. The invitation might have been worded in a way that sounded like a command, but it hadn't been that obnoxious.

"We were told to leave Paris and not return. And then last year we went to China to taste a selection of teas we wanted for the shop and—"

"That's enough, Skye." It was Maya's turn to interrupt, obviously not anxious to have Skye share the story of the spectacular fire she'd caused when a vampire at the airport insisted on searching their luggage in search of ancient artifacts he implied they'd come there to steal.

Peri grimaced. "I could really use someone there who has my back."

Maya heaved an audible sigh. "Skye should go, but she's right. I'm not sure I would be an asset. I'm not very good at hiding my opinion of vampires. Although..."

Both Skye and Peri glanced at Maya in confusion as her words faded. "What are you doing?" Skye demanded.

Maya tapped her temple. "Waiting for interference."

"Ah. The Benefactor." Skye belatedly realized why her friend hesitated. "Anything?"

Maya shook her head. "Nope."

"Okay. I guess I'll be flying solo," Skye said, not unhappy that the Benefactor had kept his opinion to himself.

She was still aching from head to toe from their disastrous trip to the theater.

Peri cleared the lump from her throat. "Drinks start at seven o'clock, but if you don't mind coming a little early I could use your help to get ready. I'm not sure my hands will be steady enough to put on makeup. Or manipulate a zipper. Or open a door."

Skye wrapped her friend in her arms. "I'll be there. I'll *always* be there."

"I know." Peri leaned into the hug before she was pulling away to grab the satchel she'd left on one of the wooden chairs. It was no doubt brimming with various potions. Better safe than sorry. A mage's motto. "I love you guys."

With a wave, Peri disappeared from the office. Maya watched her leave, with her hands on her hips.

"If those vampires try to hurt her I'll burn Valen's lair to the ground."

"I'll light the match," Skye agreed.

* * * *

The next morning most of Skye's injuries had healed. She still ached from head to toe and she had to use an illusion spell to hide the bruises on the side of her face, but she counted herself lucky that nothing had been broken. Thankfully, Maya seemed equally recovered, although her expression was grim as they served the crush of customers who were stretched down the block despite the icy drizzle that escaped from the sullen clouds.

Skye assumed the grim expression was caused by the knowledge that several members of the Cabal were currently gathered in New York City. Having vampires hanging around was not only dangerous for Peri, but any demon or mage who refused to accept their authority.

Of course, it was also possible that her pissy mood was a direct result of the Benefactor sending them to the theater for no rational reason. Skye assumed the mystical patron had been bored and decided to brighten his Sunday by tossing them into a nasty demon nest to battle for their lives. It was the only thing that made sense.

Whatever the cause, Maya wasn't ready to discuss the epic failure at the theater or the arrival of the Cabal. Which was fine with Skye. If being a seer had taught her nothing else, it was to live in the moment. There was no point in brooding on the past or fretting about the future.

It was the *now* that mattered.

Besides, she had enough on her plate without fretting over Maya's bad temper, she wryly acknowledged.

Before tonight's dinner she still had to replenish her charm bracelet with magic, dig through her closet for something halfway presentable to wear to a formal dinner, and hopefully sneak in a nap.

But first she had an important duty that demanded her attention.

Removing the apron she'd slid on before her marathon morning of grinding and brewing coffee, Skye replaced it with a bright yellow rain slicker before she opened the walk-in cooler and grabbed a wicker basket.

"Where are you going?" Maya demanded as she completed the cleansing spell that not only sanitized the shop from any germs and bacteria but purged it of any hexes that might have been cast when they weren't looking.

Their side business of bewitching, beguiling, and occasionally cursing demons meant they made a lot of enemies.

"It's Monday," she reminded her friend. "I'm going to take Clarissa some goodies."

Maya glanced toward the large windows with a frown. "It's raining. If you'll give me a minute, I'll drive you."

Skye had never bothered to learn to drive. Her visions hit without warning, momentarily blinding her. It wouldn't be safe to be behind the wheel when that happened.

"It's only a couple of blocks away," Sky said, heading toward the front door. "Besides, I like walking in the rain."

Maya clicked her tongue. "I hope that woman realizes how lucky she is to have a friend like you."

Skye shrugged. She'd befriended the local fortune teller not long after she'd settled in New Jersey. Both Maya and Peri assumed it was because she felt sorry for the woman who struggled to make a living. And she did, but the truth was that she'd sought out the older woman because her own mother had been a fortune teller in a traveling carnival. At least until she'd died of cancer when Skye was just a child.

"She's an old woman on her own," Skye reminded her friend. "It's what neighbors do."

"Not all neighbors," Maya muttered, still glancing out the window.

Skye frowned as she noticed the man leaning against the light pole a few feet away from the shop. He was hunching forward, as if trying to keep the rain out of his face, but there was no mistaking the velour tracksuit and oversized fishing hat.

"What is your problem with Joe?" Skye abruptly demanded. "He's harmless."

Maya's jaw tightened, emphasizing the silvery scar. "There's nothing harmless about him," she insisted. "I don't know who or what he is, but he's not another homeless man wandering the streets. In fact, I don't think he's human at all."

Skye considered the accusation. When she was very young she'd been like any other kid. She had no idea there were vampires or demons or even mages. And while she'd known her mother was clairvoyant, she hadn't known that she was a practicing witch. Not until her visions started to appear.

Since then, she'd discovered there was a huge magical world surrounding her. Why wouldn't there be creatures she hadn't encountered yet?

"Neither are we," she pointed out.

"True." Maya shook her head, visibly dismissing Joe from her thoughts before she glanced toward Skye. "Call if you want a ride back."

"I will."

Skye exited the building, not bothering to pull up her hood as the drizzle dampened her curls. She'd nearly reached the light pole when Joe lifted his head, his eyes briefly glowing with a deep green fire before he covered them with his hand, as if he were protecting them from a blinding light.

"Yikes. You look like a lemon exploded."

Skye glanced down at her slicker with a smile. "It's new. Do you like it?"

"Like it?" His voice was low, but it held a distant thunder. "It gives me a headache."

"Thank you." She smiled, reaching into the wicker basket to pull out a muffin. "Here you go."

Joe snatched it from her fingers, holding it to his nose to take a deep sniff. "Blueberry? Probably tastes like dog piss." He scowled over the top of the pastry. "Where's my cappuccino?"

"You'll have to ask Maya for one." Skye nodded toward the shop. "She's inside."

"Huh. I'd rather stick a fork in my eye."

"She'd probably hand you the fork," Skye assured him, snapping shut the basket as a stiff breeze swept down the street. She didn't mind the rain but she hated the cold. "Have a lovely day."

Skye hurried up the street, skipping over the puddles and the bits of trash that swirled out of the gutter. The area went from charming to crumbling in the span of three blocks, but she wasn't worried. She could deal with any human threats and most demon ones when they weren't in the Gyre.

At last reaching the narrow strip mall, she slowed to study the buildings that were nothing more than a smear of gray in the misty rain. An improvement really. The stark, industrial cement blocks wedged together to create a laundromat, an auto parts store, an Indian takeout, and an insurance agency would never win architectural awards.

At the very end of the strip mall was a store with a wooden sign hung over the doorway: *The Lunar Pathway*. A shop that catered to the local mystics as well as those who wanted Clarissa to read their future.

Prying open the glass door, Skye stepped inside and shook off the clinging raindrops. At the same time, she wrinkled her nose as she was hit by a cloud of smoke from the bronze burners hung next to the window.

The incense was used as a deterrent to evil spirits, as were the numerous satchels filled with dried spices that lined the walls. There were also crystals and charms that the local witches used to connect to their earth magic. And a table with candles that filled a home with calming scents. At the very end of the store was a glass case filled with oils and trinkets that were supposed to improve a sagging sex life.

Skye occasionally wondered if they would improve a *nonexistent* sex life. Not that it mattered. Even if she wanted a man in her bed—and she was currently just fine without one, thank you very much—the various cures would have no effect on her.

This shop catered to humans, not mages. Which made sense because the owner had no idea mages existed.

"Hang on, I'll be right out," a voice called out from a back room.

Skye grimaced at the hopeful note in the older woman's voice. No doubt Clarissa was scurrying to pull on the colorful shawl and silk scarf she used to cover her thinning gray hair. For years Madame Clarissa had traveled with carnivals to ply her trade as a fortune teller, but her advancing years and encroaching arthritis had made it painful to continue her life as a vagabond. She'd decided to open this shop in Linden, New Jersey, hoping that the locals would be anxious to have a glimpse into their future.

Turns out, the locals were more interested in paying their electric bill.

Which was why Skye had started dropping by with a basket to ensure the woman had a couple of good meals a week.

"It's just me, Clarissa," Skye said in a loud voice.

"Oh. Come on back, dear."

Skye ignored the hint of disappointment that was combined with pleasure at her visit. Times were tough for the older woman.

Reaching the back of the narrow store, Skye pushed aside the thin sheet that covered the doorway and entered the cramped room that was technically an office, although Skye suspected Clarissa slept on the narrow couch more often than not.

In the center of the room was a round table covered with a blue silk cloth embroidered with silver stars. Clarissa was seated on a wooden chair wearing a flowing caftan that matched the tablecloth and heavy bracelets that rattled as she closed the book she'd been reading. Next to her was a crystal ball and stacks of tarot cards ready to do a reading if a customer happened to show up.

"What are you doing out in this weather?" Clarissa chided.

Skye moved forward with a smile. Clarissa was in her mid-sixties although she looked older with a round face and gray hair that she pulled into a tight knot at the back of her head. Her blue eyes, however, still sparkled and her smile held a sweet sincerity that encouraged her customers to trust her.

At a glance, she looked like a cheerful grandmother who could offer wisdom and comfort to those in need. Skye, however, could sense the weary defeat just beneath the surface. This woman had struggled her entire life to survive. Now it was an effort to make it day to day.

"I brought you a goody basket," Skye said, placing the hamper on an empty chair next to the table.

Clarissa clicked her tongue. "You shouldn't have. Especially not today. Look at you. You're all wet."

Skye shoved her fingers through her damp curls. "I like walking in the rain."

"You would tell me you enjoy crawling through a blizzard so I wouldn't feel guilty."

"Why would you feel guilty?" Skye demanded, opening the basket to pull out the fresh salad and crusty loaf of bread. "I'm here because I want to be here."

"Spending the afternoon with an old woman?" Clarissa protested. "You should be with a boyfriend."

"I'm happy." Skye concentrated on arranging the fresh fruit and warm muffins on the table. "Why spoil my life with a man?"

"Why do you assume a man would spoil it?"

"Why do you assume one would improve it?"

The older woman grabbed the fork Skye had provided and dug into the salad. No doubt it was her first real meal in days. "I had a special one."

Skye arched her brows in surprise. They'd discussed Clarissa's colorful past a hundred times, but she didn't remember her mentioning a man in her life.

"Really?"

Clarissa continued to work her way through the food spread in front of her. "It was a long time ago."

"Did he work in the carnival?" Skye was genuinely curious.

The older woman shook her head. "We both worked at a small Renaissance fair. I told fortunes and he juggled fire. We were dirt poor and outrageously happy."

Skye paused, absorbing the echoes of joy that filled her friend at the memory. "What happened?" she finally forced herself to ask.

Clarissa sighed. "We'd just celebrated our first-year anniversary when he died in a car accident."

"I'm sorry."

"Me too." Clarissa glanced up, her expression wistful. "But the time we had together was wonderful. I want that for you."

"Perhaps one day," Skye said, even as she silently dismissed the possibility. Her ability to sense emotions, along with her visions, made it difficult to maintain an intimate relationship. Nothing like knowing your date is lusting for the woman at the next table to put a damper on the evening. "Right now I want to make sure you eat a decent meal." Skye studied the circles beneath Clarissa's eyes. "You look tired."

"I haven't been sleeping well," the woman admitted, nibbling on a muffin.

"Is something wrong?"

"I'm not sure. It feels like..."

Skye leaned forward as the woman hesitated. "Feels like what?"

"A thunderstorm."

"In October?" Skye considered the possibility. There were some witches who were sensitive to the weather.

"I'm sure it's nothing." Clarissa broke into her thoughts, clearly embarrassed she'd shared her concern. Then, with an obvious effort to change the conversation, she gathered up the empty dishes and placed them back into the hamper except for the fruit and bread that would no doubt be her dinner. "Thank you for this, but you should get back home."

Skye nodded, grabbing the basket. Today she couldn't linger. "I'll be back in a few days."

Clarissa reached out to grasp Skye's hand. "You're a good girl, Skye. I..."

Without warning, the woman's eyes widened and her grip tightened until she was crushing Skye's fingers.

"Clarissa." Confused, Skye tried to pry her hand free. "Clarissa, you're hurting me."

"Thunder," the woman rasped. "Do you hear it?"

"What thunder?" Skye demanded, her heart racing as a green fire briefly consumed the woman's blue eyes.

"It's under our feet. Rumbling. Stirring."

"Clarissa!"

The woman blinked, and as abruptly as it'd appeared, the green fire was gone. "I'm sorry." Clarissa released her hold on Skye's hand, her expectant expression revealing she had no idea anything unusual had happened. "Did you say something?"

Skye licked her dry lips. "Are you okay?"

"Just tired." Clarissa managed a weary smile. "I think I should lie down for a little while. Will you lock the door on your way out?"

"Yes, of course."

Skye waited until Clarissa was stretched on the couch before she headed out of the shop, double-checking the lock and then placing a protective spell on the door. She didn't know what had happened to Clarissa, but she suspected that the older woman had been dabbling with a magic that went beyond her powers. Or perhaps she'd accidentally gotten ahold of a demon talisman that had infected her.

Tomorrow she'd return and do a thorough sweep of the store.

Just another job on her to-do list.

She heaved a sigh and plowed through the rain that had gone from a drizzle to a gully washer.

Perfect.

Chapter 3

The sleek glass-and-steel building that towered toward the star-splattered sky in central Manhattan was an impressive sight from outside. It was even more impressive for the rare few who were allowed beyond the heavily guarded lobby.

Valen, Cabal leader of the northeast sector of North America, understood that his personal lair was required to project an image of success and impenetrable strength. Centuries ago he would have built a sprawling castle and surrounded it with a moat and armed knights. Now he chose high-tech gadgets and designer furnishings.

Standing in a corner, Valen allowed his gaze to skim over the formal salon of his penthouse. The soft glow from the recessed lighting revealed low couches and comfy chairs upholstered in soft grays with charcoal accents. One wall was devoted to bookshelves loaded with rare first editions, and on the far wall were several framed oil paintings that were worth an astronomical figure. Everything in the salon had been purchased through a professional decorator. Valen preferred to keep his public rooms a statement of wealth, not an insight to his personal taste. Besides, the jewel of the room was the floor-to-ceiling windows that offered a view of the park.

Currently the salon was overflowing with a flood of guests who were mingling in groups that melted and reformed as if dancing a waltz to the classical music that played in the background. The most powerful goblin and fey families had arrived in force, wearing their most expensive attire and dripping with jewels. It was a long-standing tradition to try to outshine each other whenever they had an opportunity to enter Valen's lair. At the same time they cast nervous glances toward the five vampires spread around the room.

Not surprising. It was rare for one vampire to enter the territory of another, let alone to have four of them arriving at the same time. The power currently gathered in the room was sending shock waves through the city. As one of the dominant members of the Cabal and the local leader, Valen had anticipated being the center of attention, which was exactly why he'd chosen a black Ralph Lauren tuxedo with a crisp white shirt. The classical style emphasized his stark features and the molten silver of his eyes. It also contrasted nicely with the golden shimmer of his hair, which was smoothed from his narrow face. His mate, Peri, assured him the expensive suit made him look like an arrogant ass who expected the world to bow at his feet.

Which was exactly the vibe he was going for.

At the point of glancing at the Rolex strapped around his wrist to determine the exact number of minutes he was going to have to endure the unwelcome guests, Valen was distracted by the large male striding toward him with a grim expression.

Gabriel Lyon.

Like Valen, he was wearing a tuxedo, although his was a pale gray with a black shirt and matching tie. His silver-streaked dark hair was long enough to reach his shoulders, but his face was chiseled with distinguished features and his gold-flecked hazel eyes held a calm trustworthiness that gave him the appearance of a wealthy banker. As long as you didn't catch a glimpse of the tattoos on the side of his neck. The thin, barbaric lines were the slave marks from his ancient past.

"Gabriel," Valen murmured. This male held a territory that took in a large swath of the western states including a powerful Gyre centered near Denver. "Is something wrong?"

"Smile," Gabriel commanded as he reached Valen's side. "You don't want them to smell your fear."

Valen abruptly smoothed the scowl from his face, but a smile was beyond him. "Better?"

Gabriel didn't appear to be impressed. "At least you don't look like you'd rather have a hot poker stuck up your ass than spend another second with your guests."

"Ah." Valen's lips twisted. "Peri calls that particular expression my I'm-about-to-kill-the-next-creature-who-gets-on-my-nerves face."

"That sounds like something your mate would say. She's a unique creature."

Both men glanced toward the tall woman wearing a shimmering Chanel gown with her dark curls piled on top of her head. She appeared glamorously confident, but Valen was painfully aware of the unease that darkened her eyes and her instinct to hover near the closest exit. She was a woman battling her urge to flee.

"She's a stubborn, quick-tempered woman who can bewitch or destroy with equal ease. I'm terrified of her." He stilled as Peri glanced in his direction, his unbeating heart melting. Vampires were eternal, but his human host could be destroyed, forcing the inner demon to be resurrected in a new body. Each resurrection erased the memory of the vampire and stole their powers. Valen had been in his current form for almost two thousand years, an impressive length of time, but Peri was his first and only mate. A familiar mixture of joy, adoration, and wry disbelief jolted through Valen. "And she's the reason I was created."

Gabriel folded his arms over his chest. "You failed to mention she's also the first mage in endless centuries to be able to tap into her wild magic."

Valen snapped his attention back to the man standing next to him. He'd known that Peri's shocking ability to use the ancient powers would disturb a few of his fellow vampires. But he hadn't been prepared for the melodramatic response.

"Her magic is a blessing," he insisted.

"A little more than a blessing," Gabriel countered. "She blasted a crater in the middle of Central Park and nearly caused a riot when she opened the cages at the Bronx Zoo. Humans tend to get upset when there are tigers roaming the streets."

Valen managed to disguise his discomfort at the direction of the conversation. He had no intention of revealing there'd been a dozen more disasters that hadn't been quite as public.

"We all had our growing pains when we came into our powers. Some more uncomfortable than others."

"Agreed. But stepping out of line means harsh punishments for vampires."

"No one is punishing Peri."

Gabriel held up a hand as Valen's anger created tiny ice shards that floated in the air. "Then you need to convince the Cabal she's not a threat."

The ice abruptly disappeared as Valen regained command of his composure. Gabriel was right. He couldn't force the Cabal to accept his mate was harmless. Mostly because she wasn't. All he could do was try to convince them that she was an asset, not a danger.

Something easier said than done, especially with the vampires who'd been sent to decide Peri's fate.

"An interesting delegation," he murmured, his gaze sweeping around the room. "How was it chosen?"

"A few weeks ago a sealed petition was sent to Sinjon, demanding that Peri be labeled as a threat," Gabriel revealed, referring to the current head of the Vampire Cabal, who had remained in Greece. "The invitations were sent out to start an investigation into her powers, and here we are." Gabriel shrugged. "Investigating."

"I assume I can trust you?" Valen demanded.

"Only as far as you can trust any member of the Cabal," the male warned. "But I will promise to inform Sinjon of the fact that I've spent time with your mate and while she's outspoken and unwilling to submit to vampire authority, including your own—"

"No shit."

"I've never detected any ambition in her to challenge our place as rulers of the demon world."

"Ruler?" Valen snorted. "Her precise words were that she'd rather be dipped in honey and fed to ants than be involved in Cabal business."

"More importantly, I have nothing to gain by undermining your control of this Gyre," Gabriel continued, his gaze moving toward the vampire with pale hair pulled into a braid and a massive body stuffed in tight gray slacks and a white silk shirt unbuttoned halfway down his massive chest. Kane, the current Cabal leader of northern Asia. "I might not be as powerful as you, but I'm satisfied."

"Unlike others."

Gabriel nodded. "Civilizations rise and fall, just as the magic of the Gyres ebbs and flows. You currently hold the prized Gyre. That puts a target on your back."

"It makes sense that Kane is hoping to kick me out and take my place," Valen agreed, his attention moving from Kane toward the male with light brown hair trimmed short and dark eyes that surveyed the room with a visible intensity. He was wearing a blue suit with a yellow shirt. "And Ambassador Azra might say he's only here to make sure that an outbreak of violence doesn't threaten the stability of the Cabal, but it's possible he has his own ambitions. He's older than I am and has never had his own Gyre."

"Doubtful."

Valen frowned at the soft warning. "Why do you say that?"

"My contacts in Greece have told me that the ambassador has the ability to directly share his thoughts with Sinjon. Whatever he sees or hears while he's visiting your Gyre is passed directly to our king."

Valen grimaced. "A rare talent."

"Yes. It makes him a perfect spy. Plus, Sinjon is wise enough to pay him a king's ransom to remain loyal." Gabriel shrugged. "And honestly, Azra's never had the strength to become a leader. Not even of a small Gyre."

"I can't argue with that." Valen turned his gaze to the remaining vampire, who stood alone next to the windows.

He was as tall as Valen, with lean muscles beneath his cashmere sweater and silk slacks. His curly black hair was buzzed close to his head to emphasize the chiseled beauty of his face, and the golden glow of his eyes contrasted with his light brown skin. If Valen was handsome and Gabriel was distinguished, this male was painfully beautiful. Like an ancient god brought to life.

"What about Micha?" Valen demanded.

Gabriel turned his attention toward the younger male. "What about him?"

"Is he hoping to expand his territory?"

"That's a question you're going to have to ask him."

Chapter 4

Micha hated parties. It baffled him why anyone would want to be stuffed in a room with a bunch of demons and humans who yammered about subjects that they either knew nothing about or subjects they knew *too* much about. And worse, he was expected to pretend he was interested in whatever entertainment was provided, when he really wanted to find a quiet corner and read a book.

Or set himself on fire.

Anything was preferable to standing around, waiting for the opportunity to escape.

This party was no different. In fact it was worse. It was bad enough to have a horde of demons clamoring for his attention, but he didn't usually have to deal with his fellow vampires. The Cabal was wise enough to realize that the only means of keeping the brotherhood from destroying one another was to separate the most powerful of them into individual Gyres and create brutal consequences for any attempt at invasion.

Tonight was a reminder of the tense violence that thundered in the air when they were forced to gather in one spot. One misstep and New York would be bathed in blood.

"I can offer to show you my private art collection if you want an opportunity to escape to the rooms I've prepared for you."

Micha had sensed Valen's approach from behind, but he kept his attention locked on the crowd that swirled through the room. Valen wasn't the threat. At least not an immediate threat.

"Is that a bribe, Valen?" he asked the male who appeared at his side.

"Do I need one?"

Micha's gaze moved to take in Peri Sanguis, Valen's mate. "Presumably that's what we're here to discover."

"I can promise you that Peri isn't a threat."

"Her magic and the damage it's caused in a short amount of time says otherwise."

"She's still learning to control it. In a few months—" Valen cut off his words, as if realizing he was offering a promise he couldn't keep. "Or maybe a few years," he amended. "There won't be any more unfortunate accidents."

"And her magic will be even more dangerous."

"She has no desire to rule the world."

Both Valen and Peri had traveled through Micha's territory when they'd battled a mysterious evil months ago, but he hadn't invited them to his private lair. It hadn't been personal. He simply valued his privacy.

Micha reluctantly turned his head to meet his companion's gaze. There was no missing the concern that simmered in the depths of his eyes.

"And you?" Micha asked.

"What about me?"

"You control a powerful Gyre and now you're mated to a mage who can unleash a torrent of wild magic that is capable of destroying a vampire. Maybe more than one. It tends to make the Cabal twitchy."

"You're never twitchy," Valen protested.

"No."

"So why did you agree to come? I've heard rumors that you hate traveling away from your territory."

"It's no secret," Micha readily admitted. "I hate people. And demons. And especially vampires."

"Fair enough." Valen paused before repeating his question. "Then why are you here?"

"As I said, I don't like vampires, but some are worse than others," Micha conceded, turning his head until Kane came into view. He had a long, painful history with the Cabal leader. "You've been a decent neighbor who minds your own business and rarely intrudes into my territory. It's in my interest to allow you to maintain your position."

The temperature abruptly dropped. "*Allow* me?"

"Don't underestimate the threat," Micha warned, his attention returning to Valen's mate.

"Trust me. When it comes to protecting Peri, I never underestimate the threat," Valen said between clenched fangs. "Or my response."

About to remind the male that violence was exactly the response Kane was hoping to provoke, Micha forgot how to speak as Peri was joined by a woman with golden curls and the face of an angel.

Micha thought a strangled sound was wrenched from his lips, but he couldn't be sure. He was too busy trying to understand what had just happened. He'd seen beautiful women. Some of the most beautiful women in the world. And he'd been in lust countless times over the past fifteen hundred years. But he'd never felt like he'd just been smashed headfirst into destiny. This wasn't attraction or passion or enchantment. No, wait. That was a lie. Attraction and passion and enchantment bubbled through his veins like the finest champagne, but it was more. So much more. In the span of one moment to the next, his life had changed beyond recognition.

"Micha?"

Still disoriented, Micha battled to clear his stunned thoughts, reminding himself of the need to act normal. Even demons freaked out when a vampire neglected to blink and breathe as if they were normal.

"Who's that?" Micha was surprised his voice sounded the same as usual. Low and steady with a hint of a Creole accent.

"Peri?" Valen asked in confusion.

"No." It was an effort not to snap as Micha vibrated with a worrying need to discover everything possible about the stranger. "The woman next to her."

"Oh. Skye Claremont."

"The seer," Micha murmured, feeling a tiny stab of surprise as he recognized the name. "She's one of the mages from the Witch's Brew."

"You've done your research," Valen murmured.

Of course he had. Once he'd discovered that Peri had unleashed wild magic during her recent battle, he'd searched through his considerable library to read through the manuscripts and texts devoted to the ancient power, as well as doing a thorough background investigation of Peri and her closest friends.

"I'm a recluse. What else would I do with my time?" he asked, allowing his gaze to glide over the gauzy white gown that swirled around the woman like an enchanted mist and the ballet slippers encrusted with pearls.

She looked nothing like the other women in their designer dresses that clung to their curves and the sky-high heels. She was a seraph floating in the clouds.

"Let me think," Valen said in mocking tones. "Perhaps run a multimillion-dollar empire that includes several casinos, hotels, and oil refineries? Collect ancient artifacts? Write essays on the evolution of demons and their decline after the retreat of the dragons?"

Micha held up a silencing hand as Valen listed off his latest business and scholarly activities.

"I'm obviously not the only one to do my research."

"Anything to protect Peri." Valen squared his shoulders, as if preparing to face an unpleasant task. "I suppose I should mingle with my guests. Feel free to return to your rooms when you're ready. The lower floors are off-limits to everyone but members of the Cabal. You won't be disturbed." His lips twisted into a wry smile as he stepped past Micha. "Lucky bastard."

Micha briefly considered the offer to escape. Five minutes ago he wouldn't have hesitated. He was all peopled out. But now that he'd seen Skye Claremont, there was nothing on this earth that could drag him away.

Considering the best way to approach her, Micha frowned as the woman consuming his thoughts abruptly turned away from Peri and weaved her way across the room. Was she leaving?

The sight spurred him into motion. He wasn't one of those vampires who assumed every woman was his prey, but the fear she might disappear before he had a chance to speak with her was unacceptable. He had to hear her voice, catch the scent of her skin, feel the warmth of her body brush over him.

Skimming along the edge of the crowd, Micha's tension eased as the woman entered a shallow alcove and disappeared. She wasn't leaving the penthouse. She was escaping the noise of the party.

Ah. A smile of anticipation curved Micha's lips. Obviously, they had a lot in common.

Pausing as he entered the alcove, Micha leaned forward to peer into the attached room. It was small compared to the main salon, but there was a warmth and comfort that was far more inviting. Best of all, Skye Claremont was alone.

With a silence only a vampire could achieve, Micha stepped inside and closed the door behind him. Then, crossing the thick carpeting, he circled around the worn leather couch and low coffee table to approach Skye from the side.

He could tell the second she sensed she was no longer alone. Her spine stiffened and her hands curled into tiny fists. But she didn't turn. Instead, she stepped closer to the framed painting hung on the paneled wall.

Micha didn't blame her fascination. The masterpiece was a museum-grade artwork with exquisite brushstrokes and mesmerizing talent for capturing light and shadow. It was an expensive acquisition, but since it'd been tucked in this private room, he assumed that Valen treasured the beauty of the painting, not the price tag. Otherwise it would be hanging in the main salon where people could ooh and aah over it.

Still, he didn't think Skye was admiring the brushstrokes. She was hoping that by ignoring his presence, he would politely go away. Micha smiled. She didn't know him at all. At least not yet.

Moving to stand at her side, Micha's smile abruptly vanished as the scent of laurel leaves wafted through the air, the tendrils wrapping him in a spell of bewitchment.

Laurels. The scent of oracles.

Of destiny.

Micha shivered as a voice in the back of his mind whispered for him to flee. He hadn't traveled to New York to be distracted by a woman, no matter how tempting she might be. All he wanted was to ensure that this Gyre wasn't stolen by a treacherous rebel and then return to the welcome privacy of his lair.

But he didn't flee. In fact, he took a step closer, savoring the heat that radiated around her. Mages were warmer than mortals, intensifying the sensation he was being well and truly beguiled.

"Beautiful," he murmured in soft tones.

She slowly turned her head, revealing her delicate features and a midnight gaze. Shock jolted through Micha. Skye might look as innocent as an angel, but there was an aching, primordial knowledge contained in those eyes.

"It is lovely," she agreed.

Micha swept his gaze over her upturned face. "And priceless."

She met his gaze without flinching. "I'm not here to steal it, if that's why you followed me."

Startled appreciation seared through Micha at her bold courage. Most creatures melted in fear whenever they were in the presence of a vampire. This woman might look fragile, but her spine was made of steel.

"That's not why I followed you," he assured her. "I have no doubt that if you wanted it, Valen would hand it over without any need for an art heist."

"Doubtful," she argued, nodding toward the masterpiece. "Valen is generous, but according to Peri this is one of his favorite paintings."

His gaze remained tangled with her mesmerizing eyes. "And according to Valen he would do anything to please his new mate. Including giving away his favorite painting to her closest friend."

Her brows lifted in surprise. "You know who I am?"

Not as well as I intend to know you.

"Skye Claremont. A mage, seer, and one of Peri's partners at the Witch's Brew," he said out loud, pressing a hand to the center of his chest as he prepared to offer her an old-fashioned bow. "I am—"

"Micha. Cabal leader from New Orleans," she cut short his introduction.

"Ah. I suppose Peri warned you about the various vampires invading her lair?"

She shrugged. "There was no need. Vampires rarely need introductions. Even the ones who prefer to stay out of the spotlight."

Unfortunately, she was right. Even when he preferred to avoid the human press, it was impossible to amass his enormous fortune without attracting a considerable amount of attention.

"I'm not sure if that's a good or a bad thing," he muttered.

"It's universally accepted that it's good to be the king."

"I'm not technically a king."

"Leader? Chief. Big kahuna?"

Micha chuckled. He'd never encountered anyone like this woman. "Did you come in here just to admire the Rembrandt?"

She hesitated, as if she was considering whether to answer his question. Then she glanced toward the closed door with a small sigh.

"I needed a few minutes away from the crowd."

"Wise decision. A horde of demons jammed in one room is enough to give any sane creature a panic attack," he said dryly. "Me included."

"It's not that they're demons. At least not entirely," she clarified. "But I'm tired and my shields are weaker than usual. It makes it more difficult to block out the emotions of the guests."

"Is sensing emotions a byproduct of your gift?"

"Gift." Her jaw tightened, as if she was clenching her teeth. "I suppose you could call it that."

"You don't?" Micha asked, genuinely interested. He had two mages who lived in his territory and provided services when needed, but their relationship was purely business.

He suddenly realized he knew very little about the rare creatures. And even less about seers.

"Sometimes," she conceded. "And yes, my magic allows me to sense the emotions of others, especially when I'm in the Gyre. The power intensifies everything." She turned back to meet his curious gaze. "But usually I don't have any problems in blocking them out. As I said, I'm tired."

"Does my presence bother you?"

She shook her head. "I can't sense a vampire's emotions." Her lips twisted into a wry smile. "Although your power can be smothering."

"And our arrogance is insufferable," he added.

"Those are your words, not mine."

"Maybe I'm the mind reader."

"You are," she readily agreed. "But not my mind."

"True." A vampire could enter the minds of both humans and demons to manipulate them, although the result was rarely worth the effort. It was easier to intimidate or pay them to do what you wanted. Now, however, he was frustrated by his inability to peer into this woman's thoughts. Ironic, really. He was usually the one considered to be mysteriously elusive, but Skye was a master of hiding her emotions. On the surface she was confidently charming, but he sensed that was a well-rehearsed façade. "It's a shame. I would like to know what's in that mind of yours, Skye Claremont," he admitted with blunt honesty.

"Nothing of interest."

"Now that I very much doubt." He stepped forward, frowning when she took an abrupt step backward. "Are you afraid of me?"

She wrapped her arms around her waist as if unconsciously trying to protect herself. "I prefer to avoid physical contact."

Micha studied her tense expression. He couldn't detect fear, but unease was laced through her scent.

"With men or demons or people in general?"

"With everyone."

"Everyone?"

"A touch can set off a vision."

Ah. Relief surged through him. He'd been concerned that she might be repulsed by him. There were mages who considered vampires the enemy.

"Have you ever had a vision for a vampire?" he asked, genuinely curious.

"Vampires live multiple lives in multiple forms," she said, not actually answering the question. "It disrupts a seer's magic."

"Have you ever tried?" he pressed.

"No." The word was clipped, effectively ending the conversation. "I should return to the salon before Peri sends out a search party."

Micha resisted the urge to halt her determined retreat. This wasn't the time or place to discover more about the fascinating Skye Claremont. But soon...

"I'm not a threat," he promised, his low voice echoing through the room. "At least not to you."

She halted at the door, glancing over her shoulder. "And Peri? Are you a threat to her?"

"Time will tell," he said, unwilling to lie.

Her eyes suddenly burned with a black fire, the scent of laurel leaves thick in the air.

"Valen isn't the only one who would do anything to keep Peri happy. Or to protect her," she warned. "I might not possess great magic, but if you hurt my family, I make a very dangerous enemy."

Micha dipped his head in acknowledgment of her threat. "I'll keep that in mind."

Chapter 5

Skye wasn't sure how she managed to stroll casually back into the formal salon. Inside she was a seething stew of... Actually she didn't know what was stewing inside. What she was certain of was that she'd never felt anything like it.

Micha.

She'd glimpsed him at a distance, of course. When she'd come out of Peri's private rooms and joined the party, she'd seen the vampires dotted around the salon like aloof statues, surveying the crowd with a hint of disdain. Or maybe they'd been pretending to survey the crowd as they kept a wary eye on each other. Whatever the case, she'd been focused on calming her friend, not paying attention to the unwelcome intruders.

It wasn't until Micha had followed her from the salon and she found herself up close and personal with the leech that she experienced the full impact of his presence. And what an impact it was.

Like all vampires, he was gorgeous. But it wasn't the elegant beauty of Valen or the dignified perfection of Gabriel. Micha's presence was like a punch to the gut, demanding a stunned sense of awe. In ancient days he had no doubt been worshipped. And even now she suspected he would cause riots on the street if he wasn't a recluse.

Barely remembering to breathe, she had allowed her gaze to roam over the angular lines of his features. The proud thrust of his nose, the full, sensuous lips, the chiseled cheekbones, the wide brow, and the golden eyes that studied her with a terrifying intensity.

This was the face of a warrior. A predator. A hunter who'd discovered his prey and was patiently waiting to pounce.

She should have been frightened. Vampires might pretend to be civilized, but they considered themselves above laws and basic morality. As far as they were concerned, they were the chosen species and everyone must bow to their will.

But it wasn't fear that scoured through her, stripping her nerves until they felt raw. It was fierce, brutal awareness.

Thankfully, she'd spent her whole life hiding her emotions. First from her father and then from the demons who'd held her hostage. That experience allowed her to share a conversation with the magnificent male that had included more than dumbfounded grunts and sighs of pleasure.

She was taking that as a win.

Heading directly toward Peri, Skye ignored the demons who chatted in loud voices and shoved one another aside in an effort to get closer to the vampires. Their antics were understandable since they depended on the goodwill of the leeches to maintain their ancient homes in the Gyre. And of course, many of them were hoping for a chance to become a meal for one of the vampires. Becoming a blood donor meant large amounts of cash and added social status. Or at least, that was what Skye had always heard.

With a grimace, she halted next to her friend. She'd been honest with Micha when she said that it usually wasn't this hard to shield herself. But then she usually wasn't squished in a relatively small space with dozens of royal demons and five members of the Vampire Cabal, who sent out pulse waves of thunderous power. It was no wonder she was on edge.

"You look pale," Peri said, lifting her hand toward a uniformed servant standing across the room. The male with dark eyes and a brilliant red aura nodded before he promptly disappeared. "Valen promised to start clearing out the guests within the hour," she assured Skye. "You should get home."

"What about you?" Skye demanded, trying not to reveal her relief at the thought of escaping from the party. "Are you okay?"

"I don't know." Peri swept a resigned glance over the mingling crowd. "Would you define okay as fantasizing about jumping out the nearest window and finding a sunny beach where no leech could ever find me?"

"Just another Friday night in the big city," Skye murmured.

"Something like that." Peri paused as the demon servant shoved his way through the crowd and handed Skye her long white cape that matched her gown. "Mercado can drive you home."

"No need." Skye hastily declined the offer, unable to bear the thought of spending any more time in a confined space. "I need the fresh air and open sky."

"But—"

"I can take care of myself," Skye interrupted, leaning forward to sweep a kiss over her friend's cheek before Peri could argue. Then, with grim determination, she battled her way to the door. She would return tomorrow to make sure Peri wasn't being bullied, but first she needed a good night's sleep. And maybe one of Maya's calming potions, better known as a margarita...heavy on the tequila.

Once at the door, Skye retrieved the phone she'd dropped in the pocket of her cape. She wanted to pull up her transit app before leaving the building. She preferred to take a leisurely stroll to Penn Station, but she was willing to dash through the backstreets if there was a chance of getting an earlier train to Jersey. Her thumb hovered over the screen when she realized that she'd missed a dozen texts. All from an unfamiliar number.

With a frown she pressed the top message, a chill running down her spine as she read the words.

I'm in the city. Need to see you. Come to
the pub Under the Bridge ASAP.

Love, Dad

Dread crawled through Skye, leaving behind a nasty taste in her mouth. It didn't matter that it'd been fifteen years since she'd last laid eyes on Howard Claremont. Or that she was no longer the vulnerable young girl that he'd bartered off like a piece of property. Just the thought of him was enough to make her nauseous.

An icy awareness abruptly shattered the suffocating sense of doom. Skye lifted her head to discover Micha studying her with an unwavering intensity from across the room. Her breath tangled in her throat as she allowed herself to sink into the hypnotic power of his eyes. A portion of her unease faded and she brushed her fingers over the charms she'd coated with potent spells before leaving the Witch's Brew.

She'd not only survived her past, she silently reminded herself, but she'd gained the sort of power that meant she no longer had to fear men like Howard Claremont. Not to mention the fact that she had friends who would destroy him without blinking an eye.

Squaring her shoulders, she stepped out of the apartment and headed for the private elevator. If she could face down Micha—one of the most powerful creatures in the world—then she could confront her father and tell him to crawl back under the rock he'd been hiding under.

Refusing to contemplate whether she was being an idiot for giving in to her father's demand for a meeting, Skye stepped out of the building and waved down a passing taxi. As much as she wanted to enjoy the night air, Under the Bridge was a notorious demon pub located near the base of the Brooklyn Bridge. It was too far to walk. Plus, it had the reputation of erupting into fights on a nightly basis and selling dragon scale powder to the more adventurous customers. She wanted to get in and out before the place descended into a messy brawl.

Less than an hour later, she was standing in front of the narrow redbrick building surrounded by broken asphalt and weeds. It wasn't directly beneath the bridge, but during the day it was shrouded in the shadows from a massive pier. And she assumed the demons liked the play on the old nursery tale about the troll under the bridge.

Forcing herself to walk forward, Skye ignored the loud music and coarse shouts that spilled through the open doorway. With any luck she would be in and out of the pub before she was noticed by the locals. Then finally she could head home and tumble into bed.

The image of being snuggled beneath a pile of blankets was beginning to form when a shadow abruptly detached from the side of the building to reveal a male goblin. He was dressed casually in jeans and a flannel shirt with a New York Yankees ball cap. He was tall enough that Skye had to tilt back her head to take in his massive form that towered over her, but the aura that surrounded him was a pale red. His ancestry was diluted with human blood, weakening his powers.

Assuming he was the bouncer who was there to intimidate the customers into taming their most violent tendencies, Skye ignored his lingering gaze as she stepped around him.

Without warning, his arm shot out to block her path. "Sorry, babe, this is a private club."

"I'm meeting someone."

"Meet them somewhere else." He took a slow survey of the expensive cape that swirled around her and the pearl-encrusted shoes. "We don't serve your kind here."

She heaved an impatient sigh. He thought she was a human. "I don't want trouble," she assured him. "Just move aside."

The demon narrowed his eyes as he leaned down until their noses were nearly touching. "Are you deaf? You can't come in."

"Demons," she muttered, arching away from the nasty smell of cigarettes that clung to his skin. "Always the hard way."

"You want it the hard way?" The man reached down to cup the front of his jeans. "I'll give it to you hard."

Sexual threats were always the go-to favorite for bullies with more brawn than brains. Skye slowly smiled. It was luck more than foresight that urged her to load a curse onto one of the charms on her bracelet. It wasn't as nasty as the ones that Peri could brew, but it would cover him in painful hives for the next few hours. Long enough for her to do her business and be safely back at the Witch's Brew.

Brushing the crow-shaped charm, Skye was on the point of releasing the curse when another male suddenly appeared in the doorway. This one was several inches shorter and fifty pounds lighter, but his aura pulsed with a deep rose color. He was several steps above the bouncer in the demon hierarchy.

"Miles," he growled, obviously in charge. "Stop."

"Why?" The demon's square face flushed with annoyance at being interrupted. "I'm going to teach this bitch a lesson."

With a shocking speed, the smaller male had Miles slammed against the side of the building, his forearm pressed against the broad chest to keep him pinned in place.

"She's the mage we were expecting, you idiot."

"Seriously?" Miles glared over the smaller man's shoulder at Skye. "She doesn't look like a mage."

"I gave you the photo to memorize."

Skye grimaced. She assumed her father had mentioned he was waiting for someone, but it was creepy to think the demons passed around a picture of her.

"That was hours ago," Miles whined. "How was I supposed to remember?"

The older demon muttered a few foul words before lowering his arm and stepping back.

"Return to the kitchens and tell Gorman that I made a mistake in promoting you."

Miles stared at him in disbelief. "But—"

His words were cut short as the leader deliberately turned his back on him to offer Skye a tight smile.

"Follow me."

Skye waited for the male to enter the pub before trailing behind him at a cautious distance. Was this a trap? It was hard to imagine that anyone would be foolish enough to risk Valen's wrath by trespassing into his territory and attacking his mate's best friend. You might as well put a target on your back and wait to be executed.

Then again, her father hadn't been overly blessed with brains. And there was a real possibility that he had no idea what she'd been doing with her life since she'd escaped her prison.

Glancing around the narrow room, Skye counted a dozen demons leaning against the bar that ran the length of the space, their attention focused on guzzling the mugs of ale the bartender was serving as fast as he could move. All of them were low-ranking goblins, with a couple of fairies hidden in the gloom at the very back of the room.

Music blared from the speakers set in every corner, and a dim light spilled from the open-beamed ceiling, giving the illusion it was just another dive bar in the city. It was only the glowing auras and the sharp intensity of the emotions pounding through the air that assured her she was surrounded by demons.

Shuddering at the effort of once again protecting herself from the onslaught, Skye allowed herself to be led to a booth on the opposite side of the room. The demon stepped aside, and clenching her teeth, Skye reluctantly slid onto the wooden bench and glanced at the man who sat across from her.

Howard Claremont was a tall, slender man with light brown hair that matched his eyes and movie star features. Once upon a time, that face had made women sigh in pleasure. Including Skye's mother.

Tonight, he looked older than his fifty years. Even in the shadows Skye could see that his eyes were bloodshot and a haggard weariness stooped his shoulders. With an obvious effort, he curved his lips into a smile and reached across the table, as if hoping she would grasp his hand.

Deliberately she leaned away, pressing her back against the wall behind her. "Howard."

He winced at her cold tone. "Howard? Is it so hard to call me Dad?"

She blinked. Was he joking? "Impossible," she assured him. "Why are you in New York? And how did you get my number?"

The smile faltered, but Howard Claremont was a born showman. He'd run away from his home when he was sixteen to join a circus and risen through the ranks from cleaning the animal cages to becoming the ringmaster. At one point he'd even been contacted by an agent to audition for a film in Hollywood. It was only his love for gambling that had destroyed his profitable career. Kicked out of the circus, he'd joined a traveling carnival where he'd met a beautiful young fortune teller. Skye doubted her father had intended to stay with the carnival, or her mother, until she announced she was pregnant.

"I wanted to see my daughter." Howard broke into Skye's dark thoughts, not answering her question of how he'd managed to get her private number. Instead, he pointed toward the bottle of cheap wine that was half-empty. "Drink?"

Skye wrinkled her nose. "No."

"Tea?"

"No."

Howard leaned back, his fingers tapping on the top of the table as he studied her. Was he trying to decide the best way to convince her to do what he wanted? Because that's what he did. Manipulate people.

"You're not going to make this easy, are you?"

"Why should I?" she demanded.

"I did raise you after your mother died." There was a hint of censure in his voice. "Surely I get some credit for that?"

"Credit?" She blinked. "Are you serious? Why would you get credit for raising your own child?"

"I could have dumped you into foster care."

She shook her head in disbelief. Howard Claremont took first prize in worst father ever. He really did.

"Instead you sold me to a horde of demons," she reminded him in sharp tones.

He stuck out his lower lip in what was supposed to be a charming pout. "I didn't know they were demons," he protested, only to shrug when she narrowed her eyes at the blatant lie. "At least not right away."

"I was twelve."

"They needed your services," he said, as if that explained why any parent would hand over their child to a gang of violent criminals. "And they promised you wouldn't be hurt."

"They held me prisoner and forced me to use my gift for their personal profit."

A flush crawled over Howard's face. Was he capable of feeling shame for what he'd done to her? Or just embarrassed at being called out for his sins?

"No one's perfect," he muttered.

Skye bit back her sharp retort. This man was a narcissist who saw the world from his own narrow vision. Nothing mattered beyond his comfort and pleasure. Not even his daughter.

She couldn't change that, but that didn't mean she couldn't keep him out of her life.

"I paid your debt," she informed him in icy tones. "And in return I told you I never wanted to see you again. It was a simple transaction."

"I have left you alone," he insisted, grabbing the bottle of wine to pour himself a large glass of the dark liquid. He drained it in one gulp before returning the empty glass to the table. Then, clearing his throat, he finally got to the point of why they were sitting in the noisy demon pub. "But now I'm in trouble."

Skye rolled her eyes. Of course he was. "And?"

"And I need your help."

"What sort of help?"

There was a tense pause before Howard leaned forward. "I'm having some money problems and I need—"

"I knew this would be a waste of time," Skye sharply interrupted his plea for a handout, scooting out of the booth.

She had plenty of money, but she wasn't stupid. The minute her father believed she could be a steady source of income was the minute he would become a perpetual intruder in her life. Like a barnacle she couldn't scrape off.

"Skye, I'm serious," Howard rasped, hurriedly wiggling his way across and off the bench to stand next to her.

"So am I," she warned, stepping back as he tried to grab her arm.

His bloodshot eyes glittered with his first genuine emotion. Fear. "They'll kill me."

"A shame, but I have no doubt you brought on whatever terrible fate is waiting for you."

He blinked, as if caught off guard by her stubborn refusal to be swayed by his dramatic claim.

"You don't care if I die?"

Did she? Skye took a moment to consider the question. It was true that he'd kept her with him after her mother's death. At least until he found a way to make money off her. Maybe she should feel some grief at the thought that he might be in danger. But honestly, he might as well be a stranger.

She had no feelings for him, one way or another.

"As I said. It's a shame." She shrugged, preparing to bring an end to the unwanted meeting. "But it's not my problem. The only reason I came here was to make sure you understood that I don't want you in my life. Don't ever contact me again."

"Skye." Without warning, her father lunged forward and grasped her upper arm. "I'm so sorry."

Skye eyed him in confusion. "Sorry for what?"

He didn't answer, but he didn't need to. A prickle of heat wrapped around Skye. A demon was approaching. One who possessed enormous power.

Cautiously she turned her head, discovering the two fey she'd spotted at the back of the pub had crossed the narrow space to stand directly behind her. One was short, barely taller than herself, with deep-red hair chopped short and green eyes. He was wearing a black sweatshirt and jogging pants, as if he was trying to blend into the shadows. His aura was green, but no more than average strength.

It was his companion who was giving off the pulse waves of power. Allowing her gaze to skim over the taller male, Skye took an instinctive step away. Most fey creatures were lovely. This male was exquisitely beautiful with satin-smooth skin and pale green eyes with flecks of jade. His golden hair was long enough to brush his shoulders and he had a golden stubble on his chiseled jawline. His lean body was shown to perfection in a tight, emerald-green turtleneck and black jeans that molded to his long legs.

There was something oddly familiar about the elegant features, but she didn't think she'd seen him before. This wasn't the sort of male you would forget. Still, there was something in the manner he peered down the narrow length of his nose and the half smile that played around his lips that stirred her memory.

Skye didn't bother to try to pinpoint the vague sense of recognition. She was far more interested in the aura that surrounded the fairy. It was a deep green, revealing his bloodlines were royal, but it was the jagged streaks of silver running through the glow that captured her attention. It looked like lightning dancing around him.

She'd never seen anything like it.

Unease trickled down her spine as she turned back to glare at her father.

"This was a trap?" she demanded.

He tried to look apologetic, but he couldn't disguise his relief that his part in the nefarious plot to lure her to this pub was presumably coming to an end.

"I had no choice."

"We always have a choice." She shook her head in disgust. "You consistently make the wrong one."

Glancing over her shoulder, Howard abruptly released her arm, then without bothering to say sorry or goodbye or hope you don't die, he was ducking his head and power walking his way to the front door.

Jerk.

It was only as she reluctantly turned to face the two fairies that Skye realized her father wasn't the only one who was fleeing for the exit. Obviously there had been some sort of signal. One that abruptly cut off the music and slammed shut the front door as the last of the demons scurried into the dark.

The unease intensified to anxiety as she realized she was alone with the strange males. Not that she was helpless. She might not be the most powerful mage, but she had the spells loaded onto her charms, along with a can of pepper spray in her purse. Plus, she had a phone she could use to call Valen if things got crazy.

Always assuming she wasn't dead before he could rush to the rescue, a voice whispered in the back of her mind.

Grimly refusing to panic, Skye tilted her chin to a defiant angle. "Who are you?"

"Forgive me, I forget we haven't been formally introduced." The taller male who was obviously the leader bowed his head, his odd scent of copper cutting through the thick stench of sweat and beer that tainted the bar. "I'm Lynx."

Skye frowned. "Should I know you?"

"Not personally. But you were a treasured guest of my horde when you were younger."

Red-hot anger joined the anxiety that vibrated through her. There was only one horde she'd spent time with, although she hadn't been a guest. She'd been their captive for ten long years.

She glared at Lynx, not bothering to hide her aversion to his presence. "I don't remember you."

"You wouldn't. I didn't absorb your demons into my horde until a couple of years ago."

"They weren't *my* demons," she snapped.

Lynx shrugged. "Don't underestimate your worth to them. Once you left, the demons lost their main source of income and spiraled into poverty. Eventually they decided they needed a change in leadership."

"And Dexter?" Skye asked, referring to the large goblin who'd been in charge while she was a prisoner.

"He was offered the opportunity to join me or have his head chopped off. He went with the head-chopping-off option."

Skye sucked in a sharp breath. She shouldn't be shocked by the fairy's casual indifference to beheading a competitor. Most demons relished the opportunity to crush an opponent. Whether in the gladiator-style battles that flourished in underground clubs or in business. And really, she should be happy at the knowledge Dexter was dead, right? The creep had made her life a misery. But it wasn't relief that was creating icy chills that inched down her spine.

She didn't know anything about Lynx, but she was absolutely certain he was a thousand times more dangerous than Dexter had ever been.

Absently brushing a finger over her charms, Skye mentally judged the distance to the front door and the time it would take to reach it. She needed to get out of there, the sooner the better.

"What do you want from me?" she demanded, keeping the male distracted as she took a step to the side.

"I have an offer."

"No." She took another step.

Lynx arched a brow in surprise. He was no doubt used to having women fall all over themselves in an effort to please him.

"You haven't heard the offer."

Another step. "I have a job."

Lynx smiled, oozing charm. "Perhaps I wasn't clear. My fault. Let me rephrase my words. This is more a demand than a request."

Skye snorted. Arrogant ass. Did he assume that her lack of magical firepower made her an easy victim? He was about to discover that was a serious mistake.

"You can demand all you want. I'm not interested."

His smile remained, but his eyes narrowed with annoyance. "Your father's life depends on your cooperation."

Ah. He was stupid enough to think that she gave a crap what happened to Howard Claremont.

Skye took another step to the side, giving her a clear path to the door. "I came tonight to give my father a warning. I've told him what I needed to say. Now I'm leaving. With or without your permission."

A silence filled the pub as Lynx studied her with a hint of curiosity. "I was told you were as meek as a mouse and willing to do anything to protect your father," he mused. "Instead I find a hissing kitty who refuses to behave. Interesting."

Meek as a mouse? Skye continued to stroke her charms, magic dancing over her fingers as she was forced to recall the years she'd spent in an isolated prison, her only visitors the clients who'd paid a fortune in the hopes she could offer them a glimpse of the future. She'd accepted that she had no choice but to work until she could pay off her father's debt, but there'd never been anything meek about her.

"This kitty has claws and I promise you that I'll never be a slave to the demons again."

There was throbbing sincerity in her voice that Lynx couldn't miss.

"Slave?" Lynx clicked his tongue, as if offended by her words. "I don't need a slave," he assured her.

"Then what do you want?"

"I need an escort."

Skye was confused. "An escort for what?"

"Come with me and find out." A gentle power drifted over her, as if Lynx was using his fairy magic to try to compel her to bend to his will.

"Thanks, but no thanks."

"I suppose we'll have to do this the hard way." Lynx shrugged, the silver lights in his aura shimmering with a sudden pulse of power. "A pity. I prefer us to be friends." He ran a slow survey over her delicate features. "Perhaps more than friends."

"Gah." Skye tossed her curls. "Never in a million years."

Lynx chuckled, as if amused by her disgust. "You truly are a fascinating creature, Skye Claremont." He held out a slender hand. "We don't have to be enemies. Let's work together."

Okay. Enough was enough.

She was tired from her recent battle in the theater, not to mention the night spent in a crowded room with demons and vampires. Her psychic powers were drained, leaving her unable to use her most potent weapons.

Which meant she had to depend on her brains to escape.

"Hell will freeze over before that happens." Lifting her arm, Skye murmured ancient words of power, tapping into the magic of a charm.

The magic sizzled through her veins, the scent of laurel leaves wafting through the air. Her curls danced on the power that swirled around her, and feeling the spell snap into place, she slashed her hand toward Lynx's smug face.

With a muttered profanity, the fairy instinctively ducked as the magic sizzled over his head. It was exactly what Skye had been expecting and with a stab of satisfaction she heard the sharp shattering of glass. Sprinting across the narrow space, Skye prayed the demons were caught off guard by her unexpected decision to use the window rather than the front door.

It was her best hope of escaping.

"Yugan, stop her!" Lynx called out.

Skye didn't glance back. Her slippers were slick against the wooden floor, but thankful she didn't have on high heels, she grabbing the gauzy material of her long gown and hiked it up to her waist as she made the last mad dash. Just a few more steps and...

There was a blur of movement before the shorter fairy landed directly in front of her, his arms spread wide.

"Stop."

Skye skidded to a halt, once again raising her arm. This time she spoke the words in a loud voice, using a burst of magic to create a shimmering glow around her charms.

The male threw up his hands, protecting his face from the incoming spell. The instinct left him wide open to a more mundane attack, and Skye didn't hesitate as she lifted her foot and kicked him square between the legs.

Maya had trained both Peri and Skye in the art of self-defense. Magic was all well and good, but there were times when you needed to be able to protect yourself without it.

Yugan gasped as her blow landed with enough force to drive him backward, his hands lowering to cover his injured balls as his face flushed with a combination of pain and fury.

Skye didn't hang around to enjoy his agony. Already she could feel a prickle of power forming behind her. Lynx was going to take matters into his own hands.

Still holding up her skirts, Skye darted around the male who was groaning in pain and, for the second time in two days, leaped through a busted window, landing on her back with enough force to drive the air from her lungs.

Crap.

Chapter 6

It had been fifteen hundred years since his latest resurrection, but Micha had a vivid memory of the moment he'd entered his first Gyre. Unlike many of his brothers, he hadn't been reborn with an obvious talent. He didn't have the brutal strength of Valen or Kane, or the Zen confidence of Gabriel. For nearly a century he assumed he would never acquire the power needed to rise to become a ruler. And honestly, the knowledge hadn't bothered him.

He was a scholar at heart. An eternity spent in the peace of the massive library he intended to build was a lot more appealing than trying to keep hordes of fiercely ambitious demons under control. But then he'd reached an age where he was allowed to leave the secluded sanctuary where all vampires stayed during the century of their rebirth and stepped into his first Gyre.

It hadn't been a particularly large pool of magic, but a thunderous connection had sparked inside him, igniting his ability to touch the ancient power in a way that no other vampire had ever done. It wasn't the same magic as a mage. Or even a witch. It came from the deepest bowels of the earth.

Suddenly he was on the radar of every Cabal leader. No one understood his powers or knew if they might prove to be a danger to them. Micha did his best to ignore the attention, at least until Sinjon had ordered him to claim a territory. A vampire with his power would be a constant threat to the other leaders until he was settled.

Now he used that power to touch the magic vibrating beneath his feet as he watched in astonishment as Skye Claremont flew through a nearby window and landed on the hard pavement.

"Stop her!" a voice shouted from inside the pub.

Micha flowed forward and scooped her up in his arms. Concentrating on the shadows, he willed them to thicken around them, obscuring them from view as a half dozen demons leaped off the roof and scurried toward the nearby street.

Micha cradled Skye in his arms, backing into the line of shrubs at the edge of the parking lot. He was acutely aware of how perfectly Skye's delicate body fit against his chest, and the scent of laurel leaves swirling around him with an intoxicating sweetness. His lips twisted as he realized just how easily he was distracted by this woman.

My very own kryptonite...

The word whispered through the back of his mind even as the last of the demons disappeared from the area and Skye shook her head, as if trying to clear the fog from her brain.

"You can put me down," she whispered.

Reluctantly, Micha lowered her until her feet touched the ground and even more reluctantly loosened his arms and stepped back. It felt like he'd lost a piece of himself as the warmth of her body was abruptly replaced by the chill of the late-night air.

"Are you okay?" he asked.

She grimaced, lifting a hand to touch the scrape on her temple that seeped a few drops of blood.

"A pounding headache. Not my first this week." She lowered her hand, her expression wary. "Did you follow me?"

"Yes."

"Why?"

Micha considered his answer. He'd never been impulsive. Most of his brothers and even his servants would call him tediously cautious. But tonight, he hadn't hesitated when he'd seen Skye Claremont scurry out of the party. For the first time in centuries, he'd allowed his instincts to overrule his logic.

Not the most comforting thought.

"You were obviously upset when you left Valen's lair."

She studied him in confusion. "Even if I was, why would you care?"

He folded his arms over his chest. He wasn't going to admit that he'd felt an impulsive need to discover what was troubling her. Not when he had a perfectly legitimate reason to keep track of her movements.

"I hate politics, especially vampire politics, but there's no way to ignore the threat to Valen's position," he pointed out in smooth tones. "Or the threat to the stability of the entire Cabal. If there's a challenge to the leadership of this Gyre, it will affect all of us."

"What does that have to do with me?"

"I'm not sure. But we already know someone is using Valen's mate to try to weaken him—"

"Peri doesn't weaken him," Skye snapped.

Micha shrugged. "She makes him vulnerable."

"Because he loves her?"

"Because she's an unknown threat." He held up a silencing hand as her lips parted to argue. "Unless Valen can prove that she has gained control of her magic and has no intention of using it to challenge the Cabal, then she's going to put him in a perilous position." He deliberately glanced toward the pub, which had shut off the lights. "What better way to force her to do something reckless than to lure one of her best friends into a trap?"

She considered his words for a long moment, then slowly nodded. Was she willing to accept he was there to protect Valen? Or was she just trying to appease him because she thought he was a weird stalker?

Micha's brows arched. He'd never had a female consider him a threat. Not to be a gigantic ass, but he was used to them doing everything in their power to attract his attention. He didn't know whether to be insulted or amused.

"What just happened in the pub has nothing to do with Valen," she insisted. "Or Peri."

"You're sure?"

"Yes. It's a..." Her words faded as a shudder raced through her slender body. "A family matter."

She ground out the last words, as if they threatened to choke her.

"Interesting family," he murmured.

"Not really." She glanced down at her lovely gown that was now coated in dirt. "I have to go. It's late and I'm tired."

Micha wanted to argue. She still hadn't told him what had happened inside the pub and why she'd left through the window. Or why the demons were currently hunting for her. They couldn't be her biological family. Mages came from human men and witch mothers. But she wasn't lying when she said that she was tired. He could feel the weariness that pressed against her with a physical force.

At the moment, she could barely stand. Tomorrow would be soon enough to continue his questioning.

Remaining silent as she walked away with a stiff spine and her head held high, Micha held on to his shadows as he silently followed her across the wide bridge. The demons had disappeared, but that didn't mean they weren't still searching for this woman. He wanted to make sure she got out of the city without any further trouble. Why? A question without an answer. At least not one he wanted.

Eventually they reached Madison Square Garden and she disappeared down the steps to the lower platform of Penn Station. If she sensed his presence, she didn't give any indication as she stepped onto the waiting train and disappeared.

Micha released the shadows, distantly aware of the stirring interest as the humans suddenly noticed his presence. His appearance always created an unwelcome commotion.

With a grimace, Micha shouldered his way through the gathering gawkers, eager to escape from the crowded space. Was it any wonder he preferred to remain in the solitude of his lair?

Managing to disappear before he could be followed by the herd, Micha circled around Times Square and crossed through the park. It was late enough that the trails were empty except for the die-hard joggers who wouldn't notice a vampire, a horde of demons, and a fire-breathing dragon unless they blocked their path. At last turning onto the street in front of Valen's building, Micha came to an abrupt halt at the sight of the large vampire who blended into the darkness.

Kane.

He was pacing the sidewalk with his phone pressed to his ear. Even at a distance Micha could sense the male's tension. Not only was there a layer of frost on the cement, but there were small tremors shaking the ground with each stomp of the male's massive feet.

Someone was in a mood...

Micha strolled forward, watching the older vampire stiffen as he realized he was no longer alone. With an urgent volley of conversation, Kane abruptly shoved the phone into the pocket of his slacks and turned to face Micha.

"What are you doing out here?" the vampire demanded in sharp tones.

Micha shrugged. "I haven't visited this Gyre in several decades. I wanted to do some sightseeing."

The male folded his arms over the width of his chest, his expression suspicious. "Sightseeing? Or surveying the territory in hopes it might become available?"

Relief blasted through Micha as he halted directly in front of the vampire. He didn't want the male to realize he'd been following the seer. Or that he had any interest in her. Honestly, he didn't want *anyone* discovering his fascination with Skye Claremont.

He should have known there was no need to worry. Kane was a male with a one-track mind. Power. Who had it. Who didn't. And how he could get more.

Until a few centuries ago, Kane had commanded one of the most powerful Gyres in the world. He'd been treated with deference by every vampire who crossed his path. But as the magic had shifted, his position in the Cabal had faded, igniting a fierce frustration within the ambitious male.

"This territory belongs to Valen," Micha retorted, a bite of warning in his words.

Kane shrugged. "For now."

"You intend to challenge him?"

"I intend to keep open to all my possibilities." Kane deflected the direct question. "A smart vampire is prepared to grasp opportunity when it presents itself." Kane peeled back his lips, revealing his elongated fangs. "Unless he prefers rotting in the swamps."

"As I recall, you were anxious to claim those swamps."

Kane jerked in surprise. He hadn't realized that Micha knew a couple centuries ago he'd been plotting to travel to New Orleans and challenge Micha for the right to the expanding Gyre in the southern expanse of America. Or that he'd sent endless petitions to Sinjon, insisting that Micha's preference for isolation was wasting the potential of such a rich territory and that he would be better suited to Siberia, where no one expected him to be a strong leader. It was only Sinjon's warning he would be branded as a traitor that had put an end to his maneuvering to steal Micha's territory.

"My ambitions have changed over time," Kane scoffed, acting as if he wouldn't snatch the opportunity to take Micha's place. "St. Petersburg might be cold enough to freeze my balls in the winter, but at least I'm not up to my ass in gaters and slime."

"You forgot the beignets. And the jazz. And the magic," Micha taunted in soft tones. "So much magic it pulses in the air."

Kane's jaw clenched, the air chilling as he struggled to leash his anger. Kane's strength had never been questioned. He undoubtedly was one of the biggest, toughest, most aggressive members of the Cabal. But his inability to control his emotions meant he was always vulnerable. It took more than muscles to be a good leader.

"I forgot nothing," Kane ground out. "And I forgive even less."

Micha met the male's furious glare without flinching. "Be content with what you possess, Kane, and return to your lair in peace."

"Or?"

"Or lose everything."

With a visible effort, Kane squashed his burst of temper. Then he stretched his lips into a tight smile.

"What's that human saying?" He pretended to consider his words before sending Micha a taunting smile. "No pain. No gain?"

Micha refused to be provoked. Unlike his companion, he never allowed his passions to overwhelm his logic. Or at least, he'd always assumed his self-control was impenetrable, a voice whispered in the back of his mind. But that was before he'd encountered Skye Claremont.

He ignored the silent warning. Nothing had changed. The woman was a fascinating distraction, but she wasn't the reason he was in New York.

Parting his lips to warn the older male that doing anything to try to force Valen out of his territory was going to cause considerable pain, he abruptly snapped them together when Azra pressed open a glass door and stepped out of the lobby of Valen's building. The ambassador was silent as he studied them with his dark gaze, and Micha wondered if the ultimate leader of the vampires, Sinjon, was currently staring through those eyes.

A shiver inched down his spine. The thought was creepy as hell.

"Is there a problem?" the ambassador at last demanded.

Micha nodded toward Kane. "That's what I'm trying to discover."

"No problems. At least as far as I'm concerned." Kane shoved his hands into the pockets of his slacks and strolled past the ambassador. "I'm headed to my rooms. Always assuming Micha has no complaint?"

Micha waved his hand in a dismissive gesture. "Be my guest."

Kane's body vibrated tension as he entered the building, leaving behind a sour scent. As if there was something inside the leech that wasn't entirely healthy.

"Be careful, Micha," Azra murmured. "There are rumors that Kane is increasingly frustrated with his dwindling power."

Micha kept his gaze locked on the glass door, watching Kane storm across the lobby. "I'm always careful."

* * * *

Skye was well and truly dead to the world when the smell of blueberries, bananas and a potent dash of magic led her out of the darkness. Forcing open her eyes, she discovered Maya perched on the edge of her bed, staring at her with a worried expression.

As usual the older mage was immaculately groomed. This morning she'd chosen ivory slacks and a soft sweater in a lovely shade of buttercup. Her black hair was smoothed into a bun at her nape, and her sculpted features were so perfect they looked as if they'd been carved from marble. Only the spidery web of scars highlighted in the late-morning sunlight proved she was a real-life woman.

With a groan, Skye scooted up the mattress to lean her back against the headboard. She felt like she'd been hit by a truck. The result of stress, depleted magic, and landing on her head—not once, but twice—after being forced to jump through a window.

And then there'd been her dreams. They'd been dominated by a glorious male vampire who stalked her through the dark. She hadn't been afraid as she'd fled in panic. At least not that she would be hurt. But she was terrified she might give in to his sensual temptation.

Was it any wonder she was weary to the bone?

Maya tilted her head to the side, as if sensing her exhaustion. "Are you okay?"

"I'm fine." Skye pushed her tangled curls out of her face. "Sorry, I didn't mean to oversleep."

"You had a late night. Here." Maya pressed the chilled glass into Skye's hand. "My world-famous smoothie."

Maya wasn't bragging. The smoothie truly was world famous. It also explained the scent of blueberries and bananas and magic that perfumed the air. The smoothie could cure everything from hangovers to the flu.

Skye took a deep drink, sighing as the magic tingled through her, driving away the lingering fatigue.

"Yum. Just what I needed." She smacked her lips before polishing off the last of the smoothie. "Thanks."

Maya reached to take the empty glass, her gaze continuing to monitor Skye's face with motherly concern.

"Did something happen last night?" She at last asked the question that had no doubt been nagging at her for hours.

"Nothing that we didn't expect," Skye said, keeping her answer vague. She wasn't ready to discuss her father's unwelcome arrival in New York City or her intense attraction toward Micha. "The vampires were polite, but most of the night they stood in opposite corners, glaring at each other. I don't know if that's typical leech behavior or if they were angry about something."

Maya's lips tightened. There was nothing that pissed her off more than the mention of vampires.

"And Peri?"

"Tense, but determined," Skye assured her friend. "She's not going to let the Cabal intimidate her."

"Good." Maya paused, narrowing her gaze. "And that's all that happened?"

Skye shrugged. "What did you expect?"

"I'm not sure, but I do know you were so weary when you came home last night, you could barely climb the stairs."

"I underestimated the intense emotions of dozens of royal demons jammed together in one room." It was the truth, although not the full truth. "And it didn't help that my shields were already weak."

Instant regret softened the older woman's features. "I shouldn't have let you go alone."

Skye reached out to touch Maya's arm. "Trust me, you wouldn't have wanted to be there. Plus, I'm fine. All I needed was a good night's rest and some of your super-duper smoothie."

Thankfully reassured, Maya rose to her feet. "Stay up here today and rest."

Skye shook her head. "You need help in the shop."

"Actually, I don't. I brought in our part-time staff for the week. Both Erin and Joyce have been asking for more shifts to make extra money for their Christmas shopping," Maya said, referring to the two older women who'd been working at the shop for years. They were humans who had no idea they were employed by mages. Or that they were selling stuff enhanced with dollops of magic. They just knew that everyone loved the pastries and coffee and that the tips were great. "I want you to concentrate on protecting Peri."

Skye wrinkled her nose. "I'm not sure how much protection I can offer."

Maya clicked her tongue. "You have more power than you realize, Skye Claremont, but your greatest gift will always be your heart." She abruptly leaned down to brush a kiss over the new wound on Skye's temple. A simple gesture that revealed her suspicion that there was a great deal her friend hadn't told her about the events of last night. "And your greatest weakness," she murmured before she straightened and headed for the door. "Rest up."

"Yes, ma'am."

Waiting until she heard Maya's footsteps on the stairs, Skye threw aside her covers and headed into her private bathroom. She'd been too tired last night to wash off the grime from the parking lot, not to mention her father's corrosive touch. Now she felt an urgent need to scrub herself clean.

An hour later she pulled on a comfortable tunic dress that brushed the tops of her ankles. The plain beige linen was embroidered with tiger's eye crystals along the vee neckline. Gathering her curls, she pulled them into a knot on top of her head and settled on the window seat to soak in the sunlight.

This was what she needed, she silently decided. A few hours of peace in the place that had become her home.

The thought barely had time to form when the buzz of her phone shattered her momentary sense of goodwill. Just for a second she considered ignoring the interruption. She wasn't in the mood to deal with any potential problems. But then the knowledge it might be Peri seared away her reluctance.

With a sigh, she shoved herself upright and crossed to the desk, where she'd left her phone the night before. At least she'd had enough sense to plug it in before tumbling into the bed, she realized as she yanked off the charging cord and glanced at the screen.

Surprise replaced her vague annoyance at having her peace interrupted as she recognized the name that popped up. It was Clarissa's private number. The older woman rarely called her. Only if it was an emergency.

She quickly connected the call, putting it on speaker.

"Hello? Clarissa?"

There was a muffled sound before a male voice floated through the air. "I'm afraid she's tied up at the moment, my dear. Quite literally."

Skye sucked in a sharp breath, shock jolting through her as she easily recognized that soft drawl.

"Lynx," she hissed.

"You remembered my name. I'm flattered."

"Don't be." Fear pounded through Skye. She didn't have to be a seer to know that Lynx was currently at The Lunar Pathway and that he had poor Clarissa physically tied up. But the least helpful thing to do was panic. She had to keep a clear head if she was going to save her friend. "What do you want?"

"Nothing more sinister than a conversation."

"We already had a conversation and I told you I won't be a slave to demons." Skye's fingers tightened on the phone, but her voice was steady. "Never again."

He clicked his tongue. "And I assured you that I have no need of a slave."

"As if I would believe anything you say," she scoffed.

In the background, Skye could hear the sound of grumbles, as if Lynx's companions were outraged by her lack of respect. Lynx, however, merely chuckled.

"Do you not trust me because I'm a demon?"

"I don't trust you because you tried to kidnap me last night," she snapped.

"Fair enough. Let's start over."

"No."

"I really am going to have to insist."

Skye's mouth felt as dry as a desert. She wasn't fooled by Lynx's casual amusement. Beneath his banter, he was deadly serious.

"And if I refuse?" she demanded even as she shoved her feet into a pair of comfortable shoes.

"I'm betting you care more about the welfare of Madame Clarissa than you do your father," he drawled.

Skye ground her teeth in frustration. "If you hurt her."

"Her fate is in your hands." There was a short silence before Skye heard Clarissa cry out in pain. "Join us at this lovely establishment. Oh, and come alone," Lynx continued. "If you tell anyone about me, you won't like the consequences."

The connection was abruptly ended and Skye dropped her phone back on her desk. She wasn't going to bother taking it with her. The demons would only destroy it. Just as she wasn't going to take any traditional weapons. They would be a waste of time.

And she most certainly wasn't going to tell anyone where she was headed.

Maya would lock her in her room if she knew what was happening, while Peri would march down to the magic shop and destroy anyone who threatened Skye. It wasn't that they wouldn't care if something happened to Clarissa, but their first loyalty would be keeping Skye safe. Even if it meant sacrificing the fortune teller.

Not that she intended to go into the meeting without some protection.

Opening the lower drawer of her desk, Skye pulled out a wooden box carved with hexes. This was where she kept her most precious possessions, including a faded picture of her mother, a necklace that Maya had given her their first Christmas together, and a collection of charms that Peri had left for her when she'd moved out of the Witch's Brew to be with Valen.

The charms weren't loaded with common spells. Skye could easily prepare those for herself. These were Peri's specialties. Charms that exploded. Some that could blind an enemy. And a couple of nasty curses that would disable an enemy for days. Peri had brewed them for Skye in the unlikely event that she was in danger.

That unlikely event had just arrived.

Placing the box on the desk, Skye pressed her hands against the top and breathed the words that broke through the hex. There was an audible click and the pungent stench of rotten eggs before the lid popped open and Skye reached in to grab the charms. Quickly she exchanged them for the regular ones on her bracelet, then closing and locking the box, she returned it to the drawer. She didn't know how long Lynx would wait before hurting Clarissa, but she wasn't going to test his patience.

Once she was prepared—or at least as prepared as she was going to get—Skye headed for the window that was at the back of the building. She pushed it open. Then, slipping onto the fire escape, she paused, listening to the loud chatter coming from the front of the building. It was the noon hour and the coffee shop was packed, but luckily there was no way to see into the back alley. There was no one to tattle on her as she scurried down the metal steps.

Jogging past the empty building behind the shop, Skye's thoughts were focused on how she could possibly convince Lynx to release Clarissa and then overpower him—

"Hickory dickory dock. The mage crept through the dark."

Skye slammed her hand over her mouth to muffle her cry of surprise, her eyes wide as she watched a form materialize from behind a rusty dumpster. At the same time, she murmured a low chant, preparing to release a spell. It wasn't until her eyes adjusted to the darkness and she caught sight of a fishing hat pulled low and the familiar velour tracksuit that she realized it wasn't a mugger, or one of Lynx's demons sent to attack her.

She lowered her hand to press it against her racing heart. "Oh, Joe. You scared me."

He wagged a finger in her direction. "I'm not the one you should fear, little one."

Skye studied the bearded face, surprised by the fiery glow of emerald in the man's eyes. She'd always suspected that there was more to this man than just a human down on his luck, but she wasn't like Maya. She didn't think he was dangerous.

"Why do you say that? Do you know something?"

"I know many things."

"Have you met a man called Lynx?"

Without warning, Joe tilted back his head, sniffing the air as if there was something to smell beyond decomposing garbage.

"A false name for a false creature. He's not what he seems to be."

With his cryptic warning delivered, the man stepped back and disappeared. Skye stepped forward and peered around the edge of the dumpster. "Joe?"

Nothing. Skye grimaced, turning away to continue up the alley. She didn't have time to worry about disappearing men in velour tracksuits. Or what he meant with his vague words.

She had a fortune teller to rescue from a horde of demons.

Chapter 7

Reaching the strip mall, Skye pushed open the front door of the magic store and stepped inside. There was no point in trying to sneak around. Lynx knew she was coming. If she tried to take them by surprise it would only put her friend in more danger.

Walking down the narrow row between the glass counter and the shelves loaded with cheap merchandise, Skye forced herself to shove aside the curtain separating the private office. As she'd expected, Clarissa was seated at the table, while Lynx and his buddy, Yugan, were standing next to the back wall, watching her enter with wary anticipation. They were both wearing jeans and matching red leather jackets, as if they were in some sort of badass-demon club.

What she hadn't expected was the third demon, who was poised behind Clarissa, pressing a large dagger against her throat.

Unlike the other two demons, this one was short and broad with the red aura of a goblin. He also was missing the red jacket. Clearly he wasn't in the club.

Fury blasted through Skye at the pure terror on the older woman's face.

"Clarissa." Skye stepped forward, intending to wrench the dagger from the male's hand.

"Stop," Lynx commanded, his tone sharp. "Check her."

Grudgingly, Skye halted, standing in rigid silence as Yugan slowly circled her, holding a large crystal that he waved from her head to her toes. She assumed that it was sensitive to magic and created to detect any hexed weapons or potions she might have hidden. Thankfully, her charms were loaded with spells that wouldn't set off the detector. Not until she was in the process of using them.

And then it would be too late for them.

At last, the demon returned to the wall and Lynx stepped forward.

"Happy?" Skye demanded in a tight voice.

She'd never been a violent person. Not even when she was being held captive by the demon horde. But right now, she desperately wanted to punch the smug grin off Lynx's face.

"You can't blame a demon for being too careful," he drawled.

"Release her, you bastard," Skye snarled, her hands clenched into tight fists.

"Now, now." Lynx sent her a chiding frown. "It's not nice to call people names."

"Nice? You're holding an innocent woman hostage. You call that nice?"

"You left me no choice." Lynx spread his arms as if she was being ridiculously unreasonable. "I preferred to use your father as leverage, but he has proven to be a failure."

"Nothing new in that."

"True." He nodded. Everyone could agree that Harold Claremont was worthless. "Thankfully, I've been following you for a few days. I knew there must be someone you cared about."

"You've been following me? Ew. What a creep."

"I'm thorough."

Skye grimaced. She would chastise herself later for not realizing she was being watched.

"What do you want?" she demanded.

Lynx smiled. They both knew he had her well and truly trapped. "As I said before, I need you as my escort."

"Escort?" Skye narrowed her eyes. "You'd better clarify that term."

"A platonic companion," he smoothly offered.

"Why?"

"First I need your agreement to assist me."

Skye scowled in frustration. She was desperate to save Clarissa, but there was a limit to what she would do.

"How can I agree if I don't know what I'm agreeing to?"

"It does appear you're in between a rock and a hard place."

Lynx glanced toward the goblin standing behind Clarissa. The male grinned, grasping a chunk of the older woman's hair to tilt her head at an awkward angle. Then, holding Skye's horrified gaze, he pressed the knife hard enough to draw a line of blood.

Clarissa's eyes widened until the whites were showing. "Skye," she pleaded.

"Stop!" Skye glared toward Lynx. "Fine. I'll be your stupid escort."

"You'll do as I say without argument or attempting to alert anyone that you're with me against your will," he insisted. "Your promise."

"You believe I'd keep a promise that I was forced to agree to?" His gaze skimmed over her face. "Yes. Now give me your promise." He was right, of course. The bastard.

"I...promise." The words were wrenched from her clenched lips.

"Wise choice," he murmured, holding out his hand. "Come with me." Skye ignored his hand. There was no way she was letting him touch her. Instead she pointed toward Clarissa.

"Let her go."

Lynx's smile faded, revealing the ruthless predator beneath the charming façade.

"Once you've gotten me where I need to go." He marched forward, flicking aside the curtain as if annoyed she wasn't eager to help him. "Until then, she'll stay here with my servant. Consider her inspiration for you to do as you're told."

"You just said you trusted my promise."

He shrugged. "Better safe than sorry."

Skye pinched her lips, forcing herself to follow him out of the office and through the empty shop. She was acutely aware of Clarissa's fear as she was forced to leave her behind, as well as Yugan, who was inches from her back.

Rock and a hard place, indeed.

Stepping into the parking lot, Skye frowned as they headed toward a heavy black SUV with tinted windows that was idling next to the exit. She hadn't noticed it when she'd first arrived.

With a shrug, Skye climbed into the back of the vehicle, her hands remaining clenched as she was sandwiched between the two demons. There was a brief conversation with the driver, who looked vaguely uneasy, before they took off with squealing tires.

For the next hour, Skye ignored any attempts to draw her into a casual conversation. Did they expect her to pretend this was just another drive across the bridge into Manhattan? It wasn't until they were turning onto a street a few blocks from Central Park that she realized their destination.

"Valen's lair?" she rasped. "Are you insane?"

"What's life without risk?" Lynx asked, leaning to the side to peer out the window at the towering glass-and-steel building.

"Peaceful," Skye muttered, deeply regretting the fact she was no longer snuggled in her bed, surrounded by the scent of a banana blueberry smoothie.

"Dull. Average," Lynx countered. "Worse than death."

"For you perhaps. Not for me."

"It doesn't matter." Lynx shrugged. "All I need is for you to get us through the front door."

She made a sound of impatience. She wasn't in the mood for games.

"There's the door." She nodded toward the glass entrance as the SUV swerved toward the curb. "Go for it."

A blast of heat swirled through the vehicle as Lynx's aura flared with streaks of silver.

"Don't mistake my desire to remain polite for weakness, Skye Claremont," he warned in soft tones.

Skye shivered. Clearly Lynx wasn't in the mood for games either. "Why do you need me?"

"You're the best friend of Valen's mate. A welcome guest."

Comprehension crashed into Skye. He wanted her to gain access to Valen. Or more likely to Peri.

Suddenly she remembered Micha's suggestion that the demons had lured her to the pub last night to force Peri into using her wild magic. She'd dismissed the idea. Now, she wasn't nearly so confident the vampire had been leaping to conclusions.

"What do you want with Peri?"

"I swear on my life I won't lay a finger on her."

Lynx leaned forward, shoving his arm over the seats that separated them from the goblin driver. There was an awkward pause before Lynx snapped his fingers and the goblin muttered something beneath his breath before he hurriedly yanked open the glove box to pull out something.

Turning, he dropped a velvet bag onto Lynx's upraised palm before whirling back around to grab the steering wheel in a death grip. As if he expected to be punished for not being prepared. Lynx, however, merely leaned back and opened the bag to withdraw a golden chain with a small amulet attached. He slid it over his head, allowing it to nestle against the hollow at the base of his throat. The smell of cloves swirled through the air, revealing the amulet was infused with a powerful spell. A second later, Skye realized exactly what it was. There was a tingle in the air as the golden medallion touched his skin, then a shimmering cobweb floated around him, altering his features and darkening his hair to black.

A disguise amulet.

It didn't fully change his appearance, but his features were thicker and his face rounded while his body looked fifty pounds heavier. Plus, it muted his aura until it was so dim he could pass as a human. Anyone searching for a demon wouldn't recognize him.

He handed the bag to Yugan, and a second later Skye could feel the same magic coming from the male on the other side of her. Obviously money was no object, she silently acknowledged. A disguise amulet was illegal and cost thousands of dollars on the black market.

Once the spell had taken full effect, Lynx shrugged out of his jacket, revealing a blue denim shirt. Skye's brows snapped together as she caught sight of the patch sewn on the pocket.

Witch's Brew

"Take us past the front desk, and no one gets hurt, got it?" Lynx commanded.

Biting back her demand to know where he'd gotten his shirt, Skye focused on the reason she was sitting in the SUV in the first place.

"I'm not doing anything until you release Clarissa."

His eyes flared with annoyance, but pulling out his phone, Lynx hit a number on the screen. It rang once before the sound of a male voice floated through the speaker.

"Yeah?"

"Wait ten minutes and return to the safehouse," Lynx said.

"What about the woman?"

"Make sure she understands the cost of telling anyone about our visit and then leave her there."

"You're sure?" There was a short pause before the servant realized that it wasn't smart to question the boss. "Right. Got it. I'll see ya at the—"

Lynx cut short the babbling and shoved the phone back into his pocket. "Satisfied?"

"Not even a little," Skye muttered.

With a shrug, Lynx shoved open the door of the vehicle and climbed out. He motioned Skye to follow. Skye ground her teeth, grudgingly obeying as she scooted across the seat and stepped onto the sidewalk. She didn't have time to form an actual plan, which meant she was going to have to improvise.

Shifting through various ideas, each worse than the last, Skye barely noticed as Lynx grabbed her elbow and tugged her through the glass doors into the lobby. It wasn't until his fingers tightened and sent jolts of pain up her arm that she realized a uniformed guard had moved to block their path.

"Oh, hi, Mercado," she murmured, recognizing the tall, muscular demon who studied her with a dark gaze. "I'm here to see Peri." She managed a weak smile as she waved her hand toward the males on either side of her. "They're with me."

His gaze flicked over the strangers, no doubt taking note of the Witch's Brew badges sewn onto the shirts and the lack of an aura. As far as he was concerned they were mere humans who worked at the coffee shop.

"Should I call up and let her know you're here?" he asked.

Skye shook her head. "She's expecting me."

With a nod he turned and led them across the elegant blue-and-silver lobby with fluted columns and a small fountain spewing water in the middle of the marble floor. He pulled out a keycard to open the elevator that was separate from those used by Valen's demon staff who filled the various offices. Once inside the carriage, the guard pressed the button for the penthouse before he stepped out and allowed the doors to slide shut.

Squeezing into the back corner to avoid the two males who consumed more than their fair share of space, Skye brushed her fingers over the charms on her bracelet. She'd done what she promised. Now it was time to fight.

Unfortunately, once they reached Valen's apartment, she would have only seconds to decide which spell to use...

Her silent plotting was disrupted when Lynx reached into the pocket of his shirt to pull out a thin plastic card and swiped it over the electronic panel next to the doors. There was a loud beep before Lynx tapped the button for the basement.

Skye pushed herself out of the corner as the elevator abruptly shuddered to a halt and then zoomed downward.

"What are you doing?" she demanded. "Peri is in the penthouse."

Lynx sent her a mocking smile. "I'm not here for Peri."

Fear crawled through Skye, along with a blast of recrimination. It hadn't occurred to her that they might be at this building for any other reason than to stir up trouble for Valen and Peri. Which was stupid. Every Cabal member had hundreds of powerful enemies. Not to mention fellow vampires who were constantly maneuvering to gain power. It was *Game of Thrones* on an epic scale.

What better time to strike than when they were away from the protection of their lair?

Of course, everyone knew that Valen was a fanatic when it came to security. Not only did he have private rooms in the basement for his guests, but no one was allowed on that floor. Not Valen's staff, not the visiting vampires' staff. Only Valen, who had access to entire building, plus the four visiting vampires were permitted.

Kane. Gabriel. The ambassador. And Micha.

"Where did you get a key?" She spoke her confusion out loud.

Lynx winked. "I'm not just a pretty face."

Skye shook her head. She couldn't argue about his pretty face. He was gorgeous. But the fact that he was willing to risk the fury of four of the most powerful vampires in the world made her question his sanity.

"You must have a death wish," she muttered.

"What I have is ambition and the courage to grab opportunity with both hands."

With his arrogance on full display, Lynx strolled out of the elevator as the doors slid open and headed down the brightly lit hallway to the door at the end. He walked with the confidence of a man who knew exactly where he was going and without fear he was going to be challenged.

Skye watched him go, debating whether to scream or shut the elevator doors and go in search of help. The decision was made for her when Yugan wrapped an arm around her waist and clamped a hand over her mouth before dragging her down the hallway.

She didn't bother to fight against his tight grip. The demon not only had a hundred pounds on her, but he was as strong as an ox. Her strength didn't come from muscles. Closing her eyes, Skye whispered a quick spell. She couldn't kill the fairy, but she could make him wish he was dead.

Releasing a burst of magic, Skye opened her eyes, expecting her captor to drop her as a crippling pain ripped through him. Instead, there was a weird popping sound in her ears as the spell fizzled and died.

Crap. Valen had some sort of dampening shield that squashed any attempt to use her magic. Her hasty plans were now worthless. Without her spells she didn't have a chance of stopping Lynx. No wonder he hadn't been worried about having her along.

She was shoved inside a vast bedroom that looked like something out of Versailles, with a fancy canopied bed, a carved wooden armoire and several matching chairs arranged around the Parisian carpet. It even had a chandelier dangling from the ceiling.

Lynx came to an abrupt halt in the center of the room, his confidence faltering as he glanced around.

"He has to be here," he muttered, turning in a slow circle.

"Look out!" Yugan shouted, releasing his hold on Skye as he lunged forward to deflect the blow from the vampire who appeared from the shadows.

The fairy grunted as a fist hit him directly in the face and he flew sideways through the air, slamming into the bed with enough force to snap one of the wooden posts. The canopy drooped, and the scent of blood filled the air.

Skye barely noticed as her gaze locked on Micha. He'd obviously used his mysterious powers to disguise his presence, along with his scent that suddenly flooded through her.

She sucked in a deep breath, as if she'd been starving for that crisp, icy fragrance. *And maybe I have*, a voice whispered in the back of her mind. There were some creatures who believed in destined mates...

With a muttered profanity, Skye sternly squashed her bizarre thoughts and rushed toward Micha, who was preparing to attack Lynx. She had to stop him before he did something impulsive. Micha might be twice as strong as the fairy, but Lynx had obviously planned this intrusion into his private rooms. He wouldn't have come in here if he didn't have a nasty surprise up his sleeve.

"Micha!"

His head jerked in her direction, as if startled by her presence. He was wearing nothing more than a pair of black running shorts that hung low on his hips, revealing his corded muscles that clenched in shock as he watched her run toward him. She grabbed his arm, intending to warn him he had to flee, but as soon as her fingers touched his bare skin, she recognized there was more than one danger.

She had a brief moment to savor the cool satin of his skin before the magic being suppressed by the dampening spell abruptly bubbled through her. It hissed as if annoyed at being repressed, and digging her fingers into Micha's arm, she tried to battle back the surging magic.

A wasted effort, of course. This wasn't just a spell. It was a deeper, darker power that came from the very depths of her soul.

Skye shuddered. The impending vision was like a black hole, sucking her into the center with a gravitational force that was inescapable. She felt a layer of sweat coat her skin as a blinding light exploded in the center of her mind. The world faded, leaving her defenseless in the hands of the lethal demons. Demons who were currently on the cusp of violence.

This was what it meant to be a seer.

The glorious gift of the future, combined with a terrifying vulnerability.

With grudging reluctance, Skye relaxed her coiled muscles, allowing the vision to form. The sooner it happened, the sooner she could return to reality. Or at least that was the hope.

As expected, the image of Micha burned in the center of the light. She was touching him, so it only made sense this vision would include him. But as the light expanded, she realized that Micha was wearing the running shorts he had on now, which indicated that the future she was seeing was happening within minutes, hours, or days from now. No more than a week.

She'd had precog events before. Most notably when her mother died, and another when Peri first came into her powers. Not to mention a day ago, when they'd been under attack at the old theater and she'd seen Maya lying dead on the stairs. But usually the visions peered years into the future. The image expanded even more and Skye's confusion deepened as she watched Micha throw up his hands to cover his face. Was he being attacked? Was it Lynx? No, not Lynx, she abruptly realized as flames suddenly surrounded him. It looked like a volcano had erupted, and she screamed in horror as lava spilled over him, searing the flesh from his body before his bones melted into a puddle of goo.

She kept screaming as the vision expanded to reveal that the fire was not just consuming Micha, it was consuming the world. Everywhere she looked the earth was drenched in fire, the ground cracking as lava poured out to create a hellscape from which there was no escape.

Her heart stuttered back into motion, beating with a sluggish dread as the vision seared through her brain. This was the future not just for Micha, but for the world.

She didn't understand the fire, or how it was going to sweep disaster across the land. It could be actual fire, or it could be a mere symbol of utter devastation, but she did know without a doubt that Micha had to be kidnapped by Lynx. And while she couldn't see herself in the vision, she sensed she had to stay with him.

Grappling to understand the images, Skye felt a stab of panic as the image became dazzlingly bright. She knew what was going to happen even as there was a blinding flash before the vision shattered, like a glass being tossed against the wall.

Pain stabbed through her mind, a pain so fierce she thought someone had stabbed a dagger in her brain. Then thankfully everything went black and she fell to the ground.

Chapter 8

Micha managed to catch Skye as she abruptly collapsed, her eyes rolling back in her head as she presumably fainted.

It wasn't often that he found himself blindsided by events, but he felt as if he was in a nightmare. What the hell was happening? One minute he'd been resting in bed and the next he'd heard the click of his lock. Instinct had him flowing to disappear in the shadows by the armoire, prepared to attack the intruder. He'd known there were others with the tall fairy who halted in the middle of the room, but he sensed this male was the leader.

He'd surged forward, more annoyed than worried as the second fairy blocked his initial blow. The tall fairy was strong, but he was no match for a vampire. Still, he needed to finish the threat as quickly as possible. Who knew if his fellow vampires were being attacked at the same time?

Foolishly focused on what he considered his most dangerous opponent, he barely noticed the human dashing toward him, not until he belatedly caught the scent of laurel leaves and Skye was clutching his arm.

Too shocked to knock her away, he glared down at her, waiting for her to explain what she was doing there. Instead, her lips parted in a silent scream and her eyes glowed as if they were being lit with an inner fire.

Was she being hurt? Had the fairies done something to her? Or was it a vision?

He was still trying to figure out what was happening when she collapsed and he instinctively scooped her limp body into his arms.

At the same time, the fairy leaped forward to snap a thin silver hoop around his neck. Before Micha could react, the demon was scurrying backward, holding up a small metal device with a button in the center.

"You know what this is?" the male demanded.

Micha did. The silver collars had been created centuries ago in an effort to control vampires. They hadn't been particularly successful. Vampires were allergic to silver, and having the metal against his bare skin was creating painful blisters, but it didn't lessen his power or threaten his life. Recently, however, the demons had added a new layer to the collars by installing small explosives that could be activated by the device the fairy was holding. Some were small enough to do damage without killing, but others were specifically designed to blow the head off a vampire.

Micha simply stared at the intruder. He'd had fifteen hundred years in his current resurrection. He'd discovered that silence was far more powerful than any response he could make.

The fairy stiffened, clearly expecting a violent reaction. Then, slowly stepping back, he motioned toward the male standing next to the bed, wiping away the blood that dribbled from his busted nose.

"Yugan, get the seer."

With a caution that revealed he wasn't eager for another blow from Micha, the servant inched forward, only to halt as a low growl rumbled in Micha's throat. It wasn't a conscious warning. Just as his arms tightening around Skye's soft body wasn't a deliberate choice. It'd simply happened. As if some instinct inside him had taken command.

The taller male clicked his tongue, no doubt sensing Micha would happily destroy them if they tried to wrench the woman from his arms.

"Never mind." He glanced at a watch strapped around his wrist. "Gemma should be in place. We need to go."

Waving the device that controlled the collar around Micha's neck in a warning motion, the male turned to head out of the room, obviously expecting Micha to follow him. Micha ground his fangs. He was fairly confident he could move fast enough to disarm the fairy before he could push the button, but he wasn't willing to take the risk.

Not yet.

Instead, he calmly carried Skye out of the room, leaving the shorter fairy to follow behind him. If he didn't allow himself to be taken, how would he discover why he was being kidnapped? And just as importantly, who was behind the outrageous attack. He didn't believe a couple of fairies had the audacity to enter Valen's lair and steal a member of the Cabal. Not without some serious assistance.

Besides, what was the point of escaping if there was going to be another attempt to kidnap him? Whoever arranged the abduction was clearly determined. And the next time, they might be prepared with a weapon that could do serious damage.

All perfectly legit reasons to play along with the demons, and a convenient way to ignore his fierce need to determine how deeply Skye Claremont was connected to the fairies and her precise role in the scheme.

Moving down the hallway, Micha tilted back his head, deliberately glancing at the security camera hidden in the light fixture. Would it be enough to alert Valen to the fact that he was going as a willing prisoner? He hoped so. The last thing he wanted was the male overreacting. Especially when he was beginning to suspect that this was connected to the plot to undermine Valen's authority and wrench this Gyre from his control.

Surprisingly, they turned away from the elevators to move down a narrow corridor before halting in front of a steel door at the end. There was a sign at the top that declared it an EMERGENCY EXIT, and pulling out a keycard from his pocket, the leader swiped it over the electronic reader. There was a loud click before the door swung open.

Micha frowned. It was midday. Not a great time for vampires to be out and about. In fact, he was going to have to insist on staying in Valen's lair if the fairy was leading him out of the building. Even if it meant killing them.

No doubt sensing the sudden chill in the air, the tall fairy glanced over his shoulder. "Don't worry. I went to the trouble of providing you with your own vehicle. I assumed you would feel more comfortable in it."

Micha glanced past him to peer through the open door at the underground garage. As promised, the black van that had been driven to New York by one of his staff was parked near the door. He'd used his private jet to travel from New Orleans, but like all vampires, he always had more than one means of a quick escape ready to go.

Or at least, it was *supposed* to be ready to go in case of an emergency.

"My servant?" he demanded in cold tones.

"He's unharmed." The fairy shrugged. "Although he's still sleeping off a night spent with a lovely demon he met at a fight club last night."

Micha didn't have to ask if the lovely demon had been provided by this male to distract his servant. Obviously this kidnapping was not only well planned but well funded. How many demons had been involved? And did it include vampires?

What about mages?

Only one way to find out.

Cradling Skye tight in his arms, he allowed himself to be led to the van and climbed through the rear doors. He had several safeguards built in, including reinforced panels that blocked the back compartment from the driver's seat, bulletproof shields, and a magical spell that he could activate to keep anyone from opening the doors once they were closed. There were also a dozen weapons and a couple of sunproof blankets hidden in a hatch in the floor. For the moment, the risk of having his head blown off by the silver collar was greater than being sizzled to ash by the sun.

The fact that those dangers were possible, even if unlikely, did nothing to brighten his mood. Lowering himself onto the padded bench that ran the length of the cargo area, Micha waited for the doors to be slammed shut before he placed the unconscious seer on the carpeted floor. He wanted his hands free in case he needed to get ahold of a weapon. Or a blanket.

With an effort, he pretended he didn't notice the sense of aching emptiness as the heat from her body faded. He was already paying the price of letting the woman distract him. Only a fool didn't learn from his mistakes.

Instead, he opened one of the built-in compartments and pulled out a pair of sweatpants and a black T-shirt. There was also a designer suit and Italian leather shoes stashed inside, but that felt a little formal for a kidnapping.

Once he was dressed, he settled on the bench and stretched out his legs. Then, closing his eyes, he concentrated on the magic that pulsed through the ground. The van was currently rattling over a highway heading north. Soon they would be leaving the Gyre. He needed to replenish his powers before then.

Not that his magic was his only protection, he silently acknowledged. He was stronger and faster than any demon and his fangs were lethal weapons. Still, he had things he wanted to take care of before they reached their destination. Starting with the collar around his neck.

Reaching up, he casually stroked the tips of his fingers over the collar locked around his neck. He assumed his captors were monitoring him with the cameras he had installed for his servants to keep a watch on the back compartment if he was asleep or injured. He didn't want them to think he was doing anything but inspecting the thin metal.

Sensing the explosive cord that ran through the center of the wire, Micha skimmed his fingers along the collar until he discovered the blasting cap pressed against his nape. Drawing in the static electricity that hummed in the air, he used his powers to direct it through his fingers. There was a barely audible snap as he short-circuited the detonator.

One problem solved.

Leaving him with a dozen more. Lowering his hand, he folded his arms over his chest and studied the woman sprawled on the carpeting, her long dress pooling around her delicate body and her mass of curls escaping the scrunchie to frame her face like a halo.

She looked heartrendingly fragile. As if she'd been crushed by the brutality of the real world. But Micha wasn't deceived. Some of the most ruthless killers he'd encountered appeared as innocent as babes.

With an effort, he resisted the urge to use his powers on her. He couldn't manipulate a mage's mind, but he could nudge her awake. But why bother? The van had picked up speed, indicating they weren't going to stop anytime soon. He could wait.

And wait. And wait.

In fact, the sun was setting by the time she at last released a low groan and opened her eyes with a visible effort. He remained silent as he watched her stiffen, as she belatedly realized she wasn't tucked in her bed at the Witch's Brew.

"Who's there?" she demanded, her eyes unable to penetrate the darkness of the enclosed compartment.

Micha didn't answer.

Her hands clenched and her lips moved as she cast a spell to create a soft glow that spread through the back of the van. "Micha?"

He arched a brow, holding her confused gaze as she struggled to sit up as the van swayed from side to side.

"Surprised?" he mocked.

"Where are we? And why was I... Oh. I remember." She lifted a hand to shove her curls out of her face, her expression shifting from confused to wary. "How long was I out?"

"Four hours or so."

She grimaced. "I'm assuming Lynx and his friend are driving the vehicle?" He didn't answer and she heaved a noisy sigh. "Can you at least tell me where we're headed?"

She appeared genuinely anxious, but Micha wasn't letting down his guard. "The only thing I know is that you and your demons betrayed the Cabal," he said in a voice edged with icy disdain. "That's a death sentence." He paused, flicking his gaze over her rumpled form. "Although your lover has obviously decided you have outlived your usefulness. Otherwise he would never have thrown you in with the lions. Metaphorically speaking."

"Ew." Her nose wrinkled, as if she'd smelled something rotten. "Lynx isn't my lover."

Relief blasted through him, and Micha ground his fangs. What did it matter if she had a dozen lovers? A hundred?

Then his lips twisted into a wry smile. He was well beyond pretending that he didn't care if this woman was committed to another male. And, just as important, if she'd plotted with that male to threaten the Cabal.

It mattered.

A lot.

He shrugged again. "Then your partner."

"He's not my partner either," she insisted, meeting his steady gaze. Her jaw tightened when he didn't respond. "You don't believe me?"

"I believe that I was sleeping in the supposed protection of Valen's lair when I was attacked by unknown demons and a seer who claimed to be a friend to Peri Sanguis."

She flinched, as if his words had cut her. "Peri isn't my friend. She's the sister of my heart."

"That only makes your betrayal worse."

She leaned forward, her eyes smoldering with a dark fire. "I didn't betray her. I couldn't. Not ever."

Magic tingled in the air. Not a spell. Just the side effect of a pissed off mage.

"She knew about your plan to kidnap me?" he pressed.

"Of course not." She made a sound of frustration. "*I* didn't know about the plan to kidnap you."

Micha spread his arms. "So this is all just a misunderstanding?"

Her jaw clenched, as if she was struggling not to send a spell hurtling in his direction. Then, with an effort, she smoothed her hands down the linen of her dress and regained command of her temper.

"Will you listen if I tell you what happened?"

"Do I have a choice?"

"That's the same question I asked myself," she retorted, clasping her hands together as the scent of laurel leaves filled the air. "Sometimes you have to do what you have to do."

Micha leaned back, annoyed by the sudden urge to wrap his arm around Skye and assure her that everything was going to be okay.

It would be a very bad idea, he sternly told himself.

Not only was he trying hard not to trust her, but he also had no idea if things were going to be okay or not.

"Tell your story, but don't expect sympathy," he warned.

Her lips tightened, but she did as he commanded. "It started last night when I got a text from my father. He wanted to meet at the pub Under the Bridge."

"Your father?" He didn't disguise his disbelief. Demon bars were notorious for their violence, and a rabid prejudice against humans. "A brave choice."

"My father was invited there," she informed him. "He's known about demons since he traded me to a horde of mercenaries to pay off his debt fifteen years ago."

"Fifteen years ago?" Micha was genuinely shocked. "You were just a child."

"A seer isn't like most mages. It didn't take a burst of wild magic to ignite my powers. My visions started when I was very young, although they were mere flashes at first. Just glimpses that were there and gone so fast I didn't know what they meant."

Micha considered her explanation. He hadn't realized that a seer could see the future at such a young age. Most witches came into their powers after they matured enough to control their magic. And if he didn't know, he doubted that it was common knowledge.

"How would the demons know about your visions?" he demanded.

"My mother was a fortune teller in a traveling carnival. She died when I was a baby, but my father realized that I'd inherited her talent, although at the time he didn't realize mine would evolve into something different." Her expression was emotionless, but Micha could feel the sense of betrayal that still festered inside her. "I took my mother's place in the carnival when I was five. Eventually word got around that I was able to read the future despite my young age." She hunched her shoulders. "That's when the demons appeared and Howard traded me off like a used car."

Micha narrowed his gaze. As far as sob stories went, this one was a heart-tugger. Only a monster wouldn't be touched by her terrible fate.

Thankfully, vampires qualified as grade-A monsters.

"So you do work for demons," he accused.

"In the past," she insisted. "I spent ten years paying off my father's debt; then I walked away. Eventually I moved in with Maya and Peri at the Witch's Brew."

"They just let you go?" he asked in disbelief, well aware that the demons would have made a fortune off a genuine seer.

She tilted her chin to a defiant angle. "They could keep me captive, but they couldn't force me to share my visions."

Micha studied the stubborn expression, slowly allowing himself to believe she was speaking the truth. It would be next to impossible for a demon to force a seer to reveal the images in her mind. Especially when she was also a mage who could punish anyone stupid enough to try to force her.

He was guessing that she possessed a rigid sense of integrity that had forced her to complete the deal her father had made with the demons, but when the contract was fulfilled, she'd felt free to leave.

"But the demons returned last night?" he demanded, turning the conversation to the reason Skye had invaded his private rooms with the suicidal fairies.

"Sort of. I went to the pub to tell Howard I didn't want anything to do with him, but of course it was a trap." Her features scrunched as if she'd bitten a lemon. Or maybe it was the memory of her father. "The demons were there, but they weren't the same ones who'd held me hostage. The leader, Lynx, said he'd taken over the horde a couple years ago. Somehow he'd heard about my previous connection and was under the mistaken belief I would care when he threatened to hurt my father." She snorted in disgust. "I informed them I couldn't care less what happened to Howard Claremont and tried to leave. That's when you showed up."

That explained why she'd jumped out of the window. "You should have warned me then that I was in danger."

"I didn't know what they were planning," she protested. "I had no intention of helping them, so there wasn't any need to ask questions."

He glanced around the back of the van. "Obviously they managed to change your mind."

"Only because they kidnapped Clarissa and threatened to slit her throat."

"Clarissa." Micha tested the name. It didn't stir a memory. "Mage or demon?"

"Neither." Skye's features hardened with anger. "She's an innocent human who owns a magic shop and tells fortunes to make a few extra dollars. Her only mistake was being friends with me."

Her voice broke, revealing how much she cared about Clarissa. And the guilt she felt for placing her friend in danger.

"That's why you agreed to kidnap me?"

She vehemently shook her head, the golden curls bouncing. "No. I agreed to help them get past the security guards in the lobby of Valen's building. I never dreamed they would be foolish enough to threaten a member of the Cabal."

Micha found himself struggling to keep track of her story. So far he knew that Skye had been bartered off by her father, held hostage by demons, blackmailed by a new horde, and forced to sneak them into Valen's lair. She surely realized the fairies hadn't been there to welcome the vampires to New York?

"What did you think they were going to do?"

"Honestly, I assumed they'd been hired by a vampire to attack Peri."

"Why?" The story continued to take unexpected turns. "If a vampire wanted Peri dead, they wouldn't have to hire demons to take care of her."

"If they killed her, then they'd have to deal with Valen, and I assume face some uncomfortable questions from the Cabal. You were the one who said that forcing her to use her wild magic would compromise Valen's position," she reminded him, her tone indicating she thought he was being excessively dense. "Even if it didn't flare completely out of control, they could claim that she posed a danger to the vampires sleeping in the basement. There would be no retribution from Valen, and the Cabal could get rid of a threat to their dominance with the pretense they were only protecting themselves."

Okay. She had a point. He had suspected the attack at the demon bar last night might be connected to Peri and her volatile magic. Still, her explanation only created more questions.

"You were willing to put your friend in danger?"

She clicked her tongue, as if offended by his words. "I'm not completely helpless. I'd prepared my spells before I went to meet Lynx. Once we reached the penthouse, I intended to disable them before they could hurt Peri." Her defiance abruptly faltered, replaced with uncertainty. "But then we went downstairs instead of up and my spells were suddenly worthless."

Micha didn't answer. Instead he focused his attention on their surroundings as the van veered off the highway and rattled over a dirt path that challenged the expensive suspension system that he'd spent a fortune to have installed. There was a sense of emptiness that stretched for miles, revealing the remoteness of their location. And a fresh scent of fir trees. They were in the mountains, he abruptly concluded. And isolated from the nearest civilization.

The van briefly stopped, as if waiting for a gate to open, then it rolled forward at a cautious pace. They drove in what felt like a wide circle before it was put in reverse and they backed up until the bumper banged into something metal that made a clanging noise. Micha frowned. There was a heavy sense of weight hanging over them, indicating they'd entered a cave that was dug deep underground. A prison? That's what it felt like.

"Exit the van." The voice floated through the intercom system and Micha tilted back his head to stare directly into the camera overhead. The bastard had the nerve to laugh. "Do I have to say pretty please?"

Accepting he had no choice if he was going to get his answers, Micha shoved open the back doors, unsurprised to discover that the van was parked in front of a large cell made out of silver bars.

With a motion too fast to track, Micha had his fingers wrapped around Skye's upper arm and was pulling her out of the van.

"You're coming with me," he growled.

They'd barely hit the roughly carved stone floor when the van peeled away and a heavy door slammed shut.

"Welcome to the Resistance Stronghold," a voice called out as the van disappeared into the thick darkness that surrounded the cell.

"Idiot," he muttered, walking along the edge of the bars to detect any hidden guards.

The cell was large enough to fit a dozen prisoners and placed in the center of the barren cave that stretched deep into the mountain. There were piles of rubble on the floor that revealed the holes for the silver bars were a recent addition. As if the cell had been hastily constructed within the past few weeks.

Interesting.

He returned his attention to his companion, who was standing in the middle of the prison, attempting to look as if she wasn't terrified.

"I have one more question," he said.

"What?"

"How did the demons get past the security in the elevators?"

"They had a keycard."

"Yours?"

"No." She looked confused by his question. "Peri told me that the lower floors were off-limits. Even to her."

It was the answer Micha was expecting, but he still felt a chill creep down his spine.

"Then who gave them access?"

Chapter 9

Valen smiled as he felt a delectable warmth wash over him, a light floral scent teasing his nose. Peri had entered the room. And even better, she was approaching the bed where he'd spent the daylight hours, protected from the sun by the heavy shutters that covered the windows.

"If this is a dream, don't wake me," he murmured as her fingers brushed his bare shoulder.

"Valen."

His name didn't come out as a husky invitation that promised infinite pleasure. In fact, there was a sharp edge that had him pushing himself into a seated position to study his mate with a worried gaze.

"Let me guess. You're not here to make me the happiest vampire in the world?"

"Not now. I have to leave."

He belatedly realized that she was wearing a quilted jacket over her jeans and sweatshirt and that she had her satchel slung over her shoulder. She was carrying potions. Never a good sign.

Shoving aside the silk comforter, Valen headed for the vast walk-in closet. "What's wrong?"

"Maya called to say that Skye is missing."

Valen swiftly pulled on a pair of gray slacks and a charcoal sweater. Then, sliding his feet into leather loafers, he stepped out of the closet.

"How long?"

"A few hours." She held up her hand as his brows arched. "I know, it's not that long, but it's weird. She snuck out of her bedroom window while Maya was working in the coffee shop. She's never done anything like that before."

Valen didn't know the young seer that well, but he was certain she would never do anything to worry her friends. The three of them were closer than sisters.

"I'm assuming you've tried to call her?" he asked.

"She left her phone in her room."

Valen's vague unease sharpened to genuine concern. Skye might have wanted to sneak away for a dozen reasons. A lover. A break from her duties at the Witch's Brew. A movie...

But there would be no reason to leave behind her phone.

"I'll organize my staff to start a search," he reassured his mate. "They can be spread through the area in five minutes."

She managed a weak smile. "I'm going to Jersey. I might be able to follow her trail with magic."

He moved toward her, wrapping her body in his arms. She was trembling, clearly far more worried about her friend than she wanted to admit. Valen clenched his fangs in frustration. No doubt she didn't want to share her concern when he was dealing with their unwelcome guests.

On cue, a loud ding interrupted his attempt to offer her comfort. With a grimace, Valen reluctantly loosened his hold on Peri and moved to the intercom system mounted on the wall next to the door. Expecting to see the familiar face of his assistant on the monitor, he clenched his hands at the sight of the pale-haired vampire glaring at him.

"It's Kane." He muttered the name like it was a curse. And that's exactly what he was, as far as Valen was concerned. A curse. He forced himself to push the button beneath the monitor to open the microphone. "Can this wait? I'm in the middle of something."

"Bed your mate later," Kane snapped. "I want to know what the hell is going on."

Valen managed to hold on to his temper. Unless you counted the ice that coated the expensive carpet.

"You're going to have to be more specific."

"You swore no one could breach the security of your guest floor."

Valen's anger faded as he stared at Kane's furious expression. Was the bastard trying to imply he couldn't protect guests in his own lair? It was the worst insult a vampire could offer.

"They can't."

"Then why does Micha's room look like he was in a battle and smell of demon blood?"

"Demon blood?" Valen blinked. If Kane wasn't a vampire, he would think he was drunk. "What are you talking about?"

"See for yourself."

Kane stepped aside, revealing that he wasn't in the guest quarters that Valen had prepared for him but instead was in the suite at the back of the building. He'd deliberately chosen the most remote rooms for Micha, assuming the male would prefer not to be squashed between Kane and Gabriel and the ambassador.

"Where's Micha?" he demanded.

"How the hell should I know?" Kane growled.

Valen leaned forward, his brows drawing together as he studied the image that filled the monitor. The view was limited. The intercom wasn't intended to be a security system. But it allowed him to see the broken bedpost and distinct drops of blood on the white comforter. Unless Micha had spent the day indulging in sex that was rough enough to cause someone an injury, then something bad had happened.

He was still processing what he was seeing when there was movement and the monitor was filled with the worried face of Ambassador Azra.

"Valen, we need to speak."

No shit.

"I'll be down."

"No, Valen, we'll be up," Azra surprisingly insisted. "I'm not sure what's happened, but we should check the security tapes. The sooner the better."

"I can take care of that," Valen said. "There's no need for anyone—"

"You'll wait for us," Azra interrupted, his voice hard with an unexpected warning.

Valen stiffened, more ice spreading over the carpet. He was going to have to replace the stupid thing by the time his guests finally left. Of course, that was the least of his worries for now.

"You're giving me orders? In my own lair?"

Azra stepped close to the monitor, revealing his dark eyes that held a power far more ancient than the ambassador. He was looking directly into the gaze of Sinjon, the ultimate ruler.

"There's not just the scent of demons in Micha's room," Azra informed him. "I smell the seer that was at the party last night. It's possible she spent the day at Micha's invitation, but I prefer to avoid any hint there's a less pleasant possibility."

Without warning, the monitor went blank and at the same time there was a rush of footsteps and Peri was grabbing his arm in a grip tight enough to dig her nails through his sweater and into his flesh.

"Skye is with Micha?"

Valen turned to meet her disbelieving gaze. "They did spend time together during the party," he reminded her. "Maybe they planned for Skye to return to finish whatever they started."

Peri was shaking her head before he finished speaking. "She would have told Maya if she planned to come here to be with Micha. There wouldn't be any reason to sneak out."

"Maya isn't a huge fan of vampires," he wryly reminded her. "Skye might have wanted to avoid a lecture."

Peri grudgingly considered his words, then shook her head again. "That doesn't explain why she left behind her phone. Or where she is now."

Valen moved to his desk to grab his own phone, pressing Micha's number even as he led Peri out of the bedroom and into his private office. They didn't have much time before Kane and Azra arrived demanding answers.

Answers he didn't have.

It was no shocker that his call was dumped into Micha's voicemail. The male probably left it packed in his bags. He wasn't big on technology. With a low swear word, Valen shoved the phone into his pocket.

He desperately wanted to believe this was all no more than a misunderstanding, but Peri was right to be suspicious. Everything about the situation felt...off.

Crossing to the desk in the middle of the long room, Valen had opened the laptop and managed to pull up the security footage when there was a soft tap on the door.

"Enter," Valen commanded, watching as his assistant pushed open the door and stepped into the office.

Renee was a powerful fairy with short, bleached-blond hair and dark gold eyes. Before Peri's arrival, she'd run Valen's life with rigid perfection; now the two women coexisted with a wary, armed truce.

She remained silent as the two male vampires swept past her, neither bothering to acknowledge her presence. Many of his brothers were snobs. To them, demons, as well as humans, were lesser beings. Why bother to be polite?

"Make sure we're not interrupted," he said to his assistant, nodding for her to leave.

He wished he could send Peri out of the office as well, but he was wise enough to know he would be wasting his time. Not only would Peri refuse to leave, but it might look as if they had something to hide. That was the last thing he wanted.

Motioning the intruders forward, he waited for them to stand on either side of him before he pointed toward the laptop.

"I have the video ready to start when Micha entered his guest rooms." Grinding his teeth, he waited for Azra's nod before he leaned forward to press a button on the keyboard. He'd been the leader of this powerful Gyre for a very long time. He was the one who gave orders. End. Of. Story. A choking silence filled the room as the video flicked into motion. He'd chosen the footage from the street in front of the building. If no one entered, then they would know whoever had made Micha disappear was already inside.

The silence stretched as they watched the dawn spread over the street and Valen's cleaning crew arrive. They were followed by the various demons who had offices in the building and oversaw his vast commercial empire. It was all business as usual.

It wasn't until the lunch hour had passed that Peri abruptly sucked in a shocked breath. She was standing a few feet away from the desk, as if hoping to avoid the tension spilling from the males, but still at an angle to see the video.

"Stop," she muttered. "That's Skye."

Valen tapped the button to freeze the image. She was right. He leaned forward to study the delicate, golden-haired woman who'd just climbed out of a car that was double-parked next to the front doors.

"Do you recognize the men with her?"

"Can you zoom in?" Peri asked, reluctantly inching forward to peer at the screen.

At the same time, Kane stabbed a beefy finger at the man standing next to Skye.

"He has on a Witch's Brew uniform," he growled, turning his head to glower at Peri. "They're your people."

No one could blame Peri if she'd melted into a puddle of fear. Valen had seen members of the Cabal cower when Kane towered over them. Of course she didn't. Instead she squared her shoulders and met the icy glare with one of her own.

"The Witch's Brew has never had uniforms," she said in tones that skirted the edge of antagonistic. "And if we did, they wouldn't be those ugly things. Besides, Maya would never hire men..." Her words trailed away as she returned her attention to the image on the screen. "No, wait," she breathed. "Not men."

A growl rumbled in Kane's throat, but Azra held up a warning hand, his gaze locked on Peri.

"Have you noticed something?" the ambassador demanded.

"They're not men, they're demons." She leaned forward, pressing the tip of her finger against the taller of the two males. "Look. That's a disguise amulet."

Valen pressed the key to enlarge the image, focusing on the small medallion visible at the base of the stranger's throat. His enhanced vision allowed him to make out the rune scratched onto the surface, although it was meaningless to him. Only a mage could have ignited the illegal magic.

Skye?

He exchanged a worried gaze with Peri before switching to the security footage. There was a flicker on the screen before the lobby came into focus. Valen silently took note of the guards dotted around the vast space. He would interview them later. For now, his attention was locked on the two demons who flanked Skye as they entered the building. The senior guard moved forward, exchanging a few words with the young mage, his suspicious gaze lingering on her companions, but with a small nod he led them to the elevators and the doors slid shut, blocking the trio from view.

Valen pulled up the next video of Skye forced out of the elevator by the shorter male, her eyes wide with fear as she was hauled to the back of the building where Micha's room was located.

"They have keycards," Kane burst out, his anger creating tiny quakes that rattled the expensive Waterford crystal vase on his desk. "So much for your promise no one could enter."

Valen was genuinely baffled. Not just because the intruders had managed to get their hands on one of the four keycards that he'd removed from his security vault, but they knew precisely where they were going.

If they'd just wanted to grab a vampire, Kane would have been the closest. So why Micha?

The question was whirling through his brain when there was movement on the video and the two males stepped out. The tall one was holding a small device in his hand, and the shorter one was limping, as if he'd been injured. Micha was walking with them, wearing a pair of shorts that he'd no doubt been sleeping in when the intruders had entered the room. And shockingly, he was carrying an unconscious Skye.

What the hell had happened in there?

Peri made a sound of distress, clearly worried about Skye, who didn't have any visible wounds but was hanging limply in Micha's grasp.

As they headed down the corridor, Micha looked up, staring directly into the camera. Valen froze, recognizing there was a warning in that glance. But what? A plea to rescue him? Or a command to let events play out without his interference?

He was guessing it was a demand to let him handle whatever was happening. Valen straightened as the group entered the short hallway that led to the emergency exit and disappeared into the underground parking lot. He would, of course, send someone to search for them, as well as to interview the guard on duty, but he didn't have much hope of locating the demons.

It'd been infuriatingly easy for the creatures to waltz through his lobby, acquire keycards to a supposedly impregnable area, and then kidnap and sneak away with an important member of the Cabal.

This went beyond well organized. Only someone with detailed knowledge of his lair could have known how to get to the lower floor and then to the precise location of where Micha was sleeping...

His thoughts were shattered as the Waterford vase abruptly burst into a spray of glass shards.

"Betrayal," Kane snarled, leaning his barrel chest toward Valen in a blatant attempt at intimidation.

Valen met the male's fierce accusation with a lift of his brow. He wasn't going to give the male the satisfaction of knowing how troubled he was by the events of the day. Not when it was quite likely Kane was involved up to his arrogant ass.

"I'm not sure what happened," he admitted in icy tones. "But I do swear I'll get answers."

"Like I would trust you," Kane snapped. "It's obvious you and the witches will do anything to protect your mate. Including attacking a member of the Cabal. What happened? Did Micha decide that your female was too dangerous to leave out in the wild? Were you afraid we'd have to lock her away to prevent—"

"Kane," Azra smoothly interrupted, stepping between the males as Valen's fangs lengthened in warning. Valen didn't care what'd happened to Micha. Anyone foolish enough to threaten his mate was going to die. The ambassador moved to stand directly in front of Valen, eyeing him with an apologetic expression. "I'm sorry, Valen, but this does need to be investigated, and we need to do it in a way to avoid any appearance of tampering with the evidence."

"Exactly." Kane thumped his fist against his chest. "*My* servants will take care of the investigation."

Valen hissed, but once again the ambassador headed off the brewing battle.

"I will have *my* staff make any inquiries. They are all handpicked by Sinjon." His gaze moved from Valen to Kane. "I'm sure neither of you will question their loyalty to the Cabal?"

It was a direct challenge. If they refused, then they were indicating that Sinjon couldn't be trusted. A lethal mistake.

"Very well." Valen offered a stiff nod.

Kane took a grudging step back, his feral gaze locked on Valen. "They can investigate all they want, but my people are going to keep an eye on you, Valen, along with your witch," he growled, unable to concede defeat.

Or perhaps this was deliberate. His response was certainly melodramatic enough to be an act. How better to convince everyone he wasn't involved in the kidnapping. "I don't trust either of you."

Azra held up his hand, indicating the conversation was over. "We will begin our questions at the Witch's Brew. We'll need to speak with the owner and search the seer's room. I want both of you—" He glanced from Kane to Valen before turning his attention to Peri. "And you. To remain here."

Peri grimaced. "Maya isn't going to be happy."

* * * *

Accustomed to long hours of inactivity, Micha stood motionless in the corner of the cell as the minutes ticked past, stretching into an hour. He assumed this was a deliberate ploy by the fairies to gain the upper hand.

Lock up the leech and then watch him sweat...

Micha wasn't going to give them the satisfaction.

Skye, on the other hand, was pacing from one end of the cell to the other, her expression distracted, as if she was troubled by something beyond being locked in the cell with a vampire.

Micha should have been insulted. Even if she wasn't terrified to be alone with him, she could at least acknowledge they were sharing a cell. He wasn't used to being so completely ignored. Instead, he took the opportunity to savor the delicate grace of her movements and the sparkles of magic that danced in the air.

She didn't seem real, he silently acknowledged. More like a fantasy that had been plucked from the depths of his soul.

It was the scent of fairy that eventually intruded into his fascination with the young seer. Seconds later a tall male crossed the cavern to stand next to the cell. He looked marginally different now that he'd removed the disguise amulet. His face was thinner and his body several pounds lighter, but there was no mistaking this was the fairy who'd attacked him in his rooms. The one who'd snapped the collar around his neck.

A growl rumbled in Micha's throat as he moved to place himself between the demon and Skye. It was pure instinct, but he didn't try to halt the impulse.

The fairy smiled, as if entertained by the revealing reflex. He was, however, smart enough to keep his amusement to himself. Pressing a hand to the center of his chest, he performed a formal bow.

"Allow me to introduce myself. I'm Lynx, leader of the largest demon horde in the world."

The name wasn't familiar to Micha, which meant it was doubtful his horde was larger than a few dozen demons.

"Why am I here?" he demanded in cold tones.

The pale green eyes flared with anticipation, as if he'd been eagerly awaiting the question. "You, my friend, are going to give the demons what we've always wanted."

"And what's that?"

"Our freedom."

"Freedom?" Micha abruptly realized where this conversation was heading. Not that he was going to make it easy. He deliberately glanced toward the silver bars that separated them. "You're standing next to my cell complaining about freedom? A little ironic, don't you think?"

Lynx narrowed his eyes at Micha's deliberate taunt. "You are temporarily being held against your will. It's nothing like being forced to bend the knee to an oppressor just for the privilege of living in the Gyre."

"Oh, is that it?" Micha lifted his hand as if he was stifling a yawn. "I should have guessed."

"Guessed what?" Skye demanded, moving to stand next to him.

Micha kept his gaze trained on the fairy. "Demon rebellions roll around like clockwork. Every five hundred years or so, a particularly ambitious demon decides that they're the one destined to overthrow the evil Vampire Cabal. Some uprisings are more costly than others, but they all end in the same way. With hundreds, sometimes thousands of demons dead, and the Cabal still firmly in charge."

The scent of copper swirled through the air even as Lynx forced a mocking smile to his lips.

"At least you're honest. Vampires *are* evil."

"And you're not?"

"I care about my people."

Micha wasn't impressed. He'd lived through rebellions before. They'd never been started by leaders who gave a shit about their people. It was all about power.

"You care so much that you'll sacrifice them in a rebellion just to feed your ego?"

"Of course a vampire would want us to meekly accept our place as your slaves," Lynx sneered. "If you lost control of the Gyres, the Cabal would collapse."

"Without the Cabal, the demons would descend into constant warfare. Anyone who has read history knows that centuries after the dragons retreated and the demons were left to fend for themselves, they created utter chaos. The hordes nearly destroyed one another before the vampires took control."

"All they need is a strong leader to unite them."

Micha studied the male's arrogant expression. Lynx was using the arguments expected from a power-hungry demon who was intent on leading a rebellion. It sounded too perfect. It felt like he was reading a script, not offering a passionate debate for his cause.

Micha folded his arms over his chest. "And naturally you're the leader who can do what no one else could do?"

"Naturally."

"And how do you intend to accomplish such a miraculous feat?"

"The Tempest."

Micha's suspicions were forgotten as he shook his head in resignation. "That's why you kidnapped me? The Tempest?" he drawled. "Couldn't you have chosen something a little more interesting? Now you're just a cliché."

"What's a tempest?" Skye demanded as Lynx fisted his hands.

Had Micha's words hit a nerve, or was he pretending to react? It was annoyingly difficult to determine.

Turning his head, he met Skye's baffled frown. "The Tempest is the demon equivalent of Excalibur."

Her confusion deepened. "A sword?"

"Not just a sword," Lynx intruded into the conversation. "A vessel that holds ancient demon magic. The sort of magic that even vampires fear."

Micha returned his attention to the fairy. "The supposed magic he's talking about is nothing more than a nursery story," he retorted. "Not to mention the fact that it's impossible to break the curse that surrounds it."

Lynx planted his hands on his hips, his expression defiant. "If you're so confident that it's harmless, then why have you wrapped it in layers of protection?" he challenged. "Why not allow the demons to try to claim it?"

It was true that Micha had created several barriers around the temple that held the Tempest after he gained control of the Gyre. Honestly, if he could have dug up the stupid sword and had it transplanted far away from his home, he would have done it in a...well, not a heartbeat, since his heart didn't beat, but as quickly as possible.

"I have it off-limits because I'm tired of demons invading my territory in an attempt to claim the sword," he said, his voice hard. "It's disgusting to have their corpses littering the area, polluting the land, and poisoning the water. I used to have to send staff out regularly to clean up the mess."

Lynx harrumphed. "A convenient excuse."

Micha deliberately coated the silver bars with a layer of ice. A small warning of his power.

"I don't need an excuse. The sword is in my Gyre, which means it's my property."

"It belongs to the demons." Lynx touched his fingers to the center of his chest. "It belongs to me. And before the night is over, I intend to retrieve it."

* * * *

"Are you about done?" Maya demanded, vibrating with fury as she watched the vampire rummage through the drawers of her desk.

The male was attired in a black suit with a white shirt and gray tie. His light brown hair was neatly trimmed and his features handsome without possessing the punch of beauty most of his brothers possessed.

It would be easy to underestimate his power, but Maya hadn't been fooled when he'd shown up at her door, demanding entry to the Witch's Brew. There was a smoldering power in that dark, knowing gaze as he'd swept past her along with two goblins, who were obviously his servants.

There'd been another vampire that she'd recognized as Gabriel from the western Gyre, but he'd remained near the door as if ensuring no one interrupted the sanctioned invasion.

The vampire who'd introduced himself as Ambassador Azra straightened as he slid shut the drawers.

"Forgive me, mage, but you must realize this is a precarious situation for all of us," he smoothly apologized.

"Actually, you haven't told me anything beyond the fact that you suspect that Skye was involved in some mysterious kidnapping and that she's disappeared."

"I'm afraid that's all I can say at the moment." His words were polite, but there was an unmistakable warning in his tone. "If you know anything that would assist us in tracking down the location of the seer, it's vital you share that information with us."

Maya forced herself to count to ten. Being so close to vampires in a confined space was scraping her nerves raw. She had a long history of hating the creatures. And to have them claiming that her sweet Skye was somehow involved in a convoluted attempt to destroy the Cabal was threatening to push her toward the edge.

When she went over, very bad things would happen. She lifted her hand to touch the scar that marred the side of her face. A reminder of the cost of losing control.

"I've told you everything I know," she said, her voice carefully stripped of all emotion.

There was a stir of movement before the two goblins stepped into the office. They were both large, both bald, and both surrounded by a bright red aura.

"Well?" Azra demanded.

Both servants shook their heads, indicating that they hadn't managed to find any damning evidence.

Azra moved toward the door, pausing to turn and send Maya a last, warning glance. "If the seer returns or contacts you—"

"You'll be the first to know," Maya interrupted. She needed the leeches out of her home. Immediately.

The male turned to lead the goblins through the bookstore and into the attached coffee shop before Maya could hear them pulling open the front door. About to release the swear words that had been gathering on the tip of her tongue, Maya snapped her lips together as the second vampire silently stepped into the office and crossed to stand directly in front of her.

He was tall and gorgeous with silver streaks in his dark hair and a smile that could melt the sun. No doubt, most women found him irresistible. Maya, however, was a mage, not a woman, and she very much wanted to smash her fist into the center of that handsome face.

"Mage." His lips twitched, no doubt able to read her thoughts. Then, with a bold lack of concern for the magic that prickled through the air, he reached to grasp her hand, raising it to his lips. "Peri wanted me to personally reassure you that the Cabal will do everything in their power to discover the truth," he murmured. "She hopes you'll put your usual trust in them."

Fury thundered through Maya. Peri knew exactly how much faith she had in...

Her anger shattered as she felt Gabriel press a small object between her fingers. She didn't have to look to know it was a computer memory chip. Her brows arched as Gabriel offered a small dip of his head before releasing her hand and stepping back.

"Tell her not to worry," she said, assuring the male that she understood.

Peri was warning her not to trust the Cabal and had sent along some sort of information that was intended to help Maya discover what was going on.

"She also wants you to know that you can contact me directly if you have any questions or concerns about the investigation," Gabriel continued in a smooth voice. "*Only* me."

Maya slowly nodded. Peri was more than likely being carefully watched by the Cabal, she silently conceded. She obviously didn't want them getting their hands on any information that Maya might discover.

Waiting for the vampire to leave the office, Maya moved to close the door and slid her hand over the panels. Magic danced over her fingers, seeping into the worn wood to create an impenetrable barrier. Nothing could get in or out until she released the spell.

Once assured she wouldn't be interrupted, Maya crossed to the desk and sat down. Then, opening her laptop, she slid the chip into the port and opened the file. She wasn't sure what she expected. Maybe a coded message from Peri. Or a map to Skye's location. Not security footage from Valen's lair.

It wasn't until she clicked on the video that she realized that it'd captured Skye arriving at the building along with two strangers. Then shockingly, it jumped to an image of Skye being carried out of a basement area in the arms of a vampire.

"What the hell happened to you, Skye Claremont?" she muttered, watching the video a dozen times until she had reassured herself that there were no visible wounds on Skye as she was cradled in the vampire's arms.

Then, forcing herself to take a calming breath, she studied the video frame by frame. She zoomed in, taking in the uniforms with the Witch's Brew badge as well as the necklaces hanging around the throats of the males. Disguise amulets. Which meant that there was no point in trying to figure out who they were. The only thing that mattered was that Skye looked angry as she marched between them. Whoever they might be, they weren't her friends.

Deciding that she'd learned as much as possible from Skye's companions, Maya turned her attention to the vehicle that had delivered Skye to Valen's lair. It was a boring midsized car without any distinguishing features, but thankfully the security camera had managed to capture the license plate number.

When Maya had settled in New Jersey years ago, she'd developed a vast circle of acquaintances. Some rich, some powerful, and many who lived in the shadows, using their wits to survive. Then, wisely, she made sure that each and every one of them owed her a favor. It was her personal spiderweb of information that she could tug on to acquire whatever information she might need.

Now she grabbed her phone off the desk and typed in a quick text. A minute passed, and then ten. She was about to send another message when her phone pinged and the information she wanted popped up on the screen.

Goblin who goes by the name Long Jong. You can find him hanging at the Dead Badger.

Shutting down the computer, Maya surged to her feet and shattered the spell that protected the door. The Dead Badger was a demon bar in the Bronx. It was going to take her at least an hour to get there, and she needed to gather a few potions and reload her spells.

It was closer to two hours by the time she strolled into the shabby bar squashed between a bodega and a transmission garage. It was a long, narrow space with wooden booths along the walls and a U-shaped counter in the middle where a large goblin with a mohawk and a dozen piercings was doling out mugs of traditional grog for the smattering of customers.

Maya walked confidently toward the bar, her heels clicking on the wooden planks. She'd chosen to wear a pair of black slacks and a white cashmere sweater, knowing the elegant attire would allow her to stand out in such a neighborhood. She'd also pulled her dark hair from her face to emphasize the scars.

As the most powerful mage in the area, she was both hated and feared among the local demons. Which meant she had two choices. A disguise spell to hide her identity, or she could use her reputation to her advantage.

Reaching the counter, she smiled as the bartender froze, his gaze locked on her scars.

"Is there a contract?" he rasped.

She shook her head, assuring him that she hadn't been sent by a rival to curse him.

"I'm looking for Long Jong."

She waited for him to point toward a male slouched in the back booth. He wasn't large for a goblin and his aura was barely more than a flicker of red. Wearing a leather jacket, he was absently eating his way through a bowl of peanuts and nursing his mug of grog.

Maya held up two fingers, and the bartender swiftly pulled a couple of large grogs from the tap and placed them on a tray before shoving them across the counter. Maya reached for her purse, but the male waved her away. Smart demon. He was more worried about getting rid of her than collecting her money.

Mages were never good for business.

Grabbing the tray, Maya turned away, pausing to pretend to rearrange the mugs. With a flick of her wrist, she dumped the potion she'd hidden in a large opal ring into the grog. Then, ignoring the anxious glances from the handful of customers, she headed to the back booth, sliding onto the opposite side of the table from the goblin.

"Can I join you?" she murmured.

The male jerked up his head, as if he'd been verging on sleep. He blinked, his eyes blurry. "You gotta job? Wait..." He furrowed his brow, trying to clear the grog-fog from his brain. "Don't I know you?"

"Perhaps." Maya placed a mug on the table in front of him. "Drink?"

Without hesitation Long Jong grabbed the mug and drained it in one greedy gulp.

"So whatcha want." He slammed the empty mug on the table, releasing a loud belch. "I got some crank, grit, moon rocks." He paused, eying her expensive clothing. "I can get my hands on some dragon scale, but it'll cost you—"

"I have a few questions," Maya smoothly interrupted.

The male snorted. "Then you're talking to the wrong guy. I ain't got no answers. Not for nobody."

She slid the second mug toward the male. "Here."

"Thanks."

This time, Long Jong tried to pace himself. He took a gulp and set the mug back on the table.

"These are simple questions," she assured him.

He scowled. "About what?"

"About the passengers you drove to Valen Corporate Headquarters this afternoon."

A shimmer of crimson rippled over the muddy brown eyes. Her question had struck fear in the male.

"I don't talk about my customers. It's bad for business. And worse for my health."

Maya leaned forward. "It will be our secret."

"Look, I don't know who you are, but...but..." The words faltered as the potion flowed through him. Maya hadn't bothered with a truth serum. The demons who'd hired him had been bold enough to stroll into Valen's lair in broad daylight. They were either suicidal, or more likely well organized.

It was possible they'd given their servants a potion that would erase their memories if someone tried to force the truth out of them. Instead, she'd slipped him a love potion. It was short-term, but for the next few minutes he was going to worship her. "Who are you?" he breathed.

"My name's not important."

His jaws bulged, as if he was instinctively battling against the compulsion. "I should go."

"Stay." Maya reached out to touch his beefy fingers that still gripped the mug. "I insist."

There was a low grunt, his broad face flushing as the potion finally took full effect. Then, leaning back, his resistance visibly melted.

"Okay."

"Look at me," she commanded.

His gaze latched onto her face. "You're so beautiful," he breathed.

"Do you think so?"

"The most beautiful woman in the world."

"And you want to make me happy?"

"More than anything," he rasped. "Tell me what you want."

Maya smiled, trailing her fingers over the wood of the table as she whispered a spell. The air tingled and the sound of the increasingly noisy bar faded to a dull thud. She didn't want anyone trying to overhear their conversation.

"Tell me the names of your passengers from this afternoon."

"I didn't get any names," he said, his expression drooping as if he was disappointed he couldn't give her what she wanted.

Maya kept her smile intact. She'd already suspected that the demons weren't going to make it easy to track them down. That only made her more determined.

"Are they friends of yours?"

"Naw. I never seen them before. Not until I picked them up."

"How did they contact you?"

Long Jong hunched a shoulder. "A dude came into the bar a couple of weeks ago and mentioned he had some friends visiting the city and they were looking for volunteers."

"Volunteers for what?"

"He didn't give details, but he promised that anyone chosen would be cashing in big." The demon took another drink of the grog. "I gave my number but I didn't hear nothing. I forgot all about him until this morning when I got a text with an address and the order to be there at one this afternoon to drive his friends into the city."

"Pick them up from where?"

"A place in Jersey." Long Jong pursed his lips, trying to dredge up something from his memories. "The moon something or other. No wait. Or Lunar..."

"The Lunar Pathway?" Maya suggested, her heart missing a beat as she abruptly understood how Skye could be forced to do something against her will.

The demon snapped his fingers. "That's the place."

Maya licked her lips that were suddenly dry. "Tell me what happened when you got there."

"Nothing. I pulled into the parking lot and waited ten minutes or so. Then they came out and got in the back seat."

"Who came out?"

"A couple of fairies and a woman."

It matched what she'd seen on the security video. An indication that Long Jong was telling the truth. Still, Maya wanted to make certain that she didn't leap to conclusions.

Not when Skye's life might very well depend on her ability to discover what the hell was going on.

"Describe her."

"Blond hair." The male paused, as if painting a mental picture. "Nice tits. Tasty ass."

Maya rolled her eyes. The male barely rated on the demon scale. His teeth were rotting and he was in dire need of a bath. He should at least try to develop a decent personality. Instead he was just...gross.

"There wasn't an older woman with them?" she asked. "A human?"

"Nope. Just the fairies and the pretty chick."

Maya took a moment to visualize what had happened. Somehow the fairies had connected Skye to Madame Clarissa and used the fortune teller to force her to do what they wanted. Maya didn't think the older woman was involved, at least beyond being a pawn. When Skye had first taken the human under her wing, Maya had done a thorough investigation of Madame Clarissa and her magic shop. No one was allowed to be a part of her friends' lives until they'd been given the Maya seal of approval.

Well, not until Valen had stolen Peri away.

Maya shook away the aggravating memory. This was about Skye and how quickly she could find her.

"You drove them straight to Valen's office building?"

"Yep. I pulled in front of the building and they got out. I took off and came back here and waited to get paid." He glanced toward the phone, his expression petulant. "I'm still waiting."

"Did you notice anything special about them?"

"Just the smell."

Maya arched her brows. This male was complaining about someone else's stench? That was ballsy.

"What about the smell?"

"The one who acted like the leader smelled like a fairy, but there was something more."

"Human?"

"No. Something..." He shuddered. "Scary. I was glad when he got out of the car."

Interesting. Maya didn't know what had frightened Long Jong, but she tucked the information into the back of her mind.

"Anything else?"

"Not that I can remember."

Maya stroked her fingers over his arm, the potion was beginning to wear off. She had only seconds left.

"You're absolutely certain?" she pressed. "They didn't say where they were going? Or why they were at Valen's lair?"

He started to shake his head, only to hesitate. "Wait. I gave them the bag that I picked up from the weird dude."

Maya clenched her teeth. She wanted to shake the idiot until the truth spilled out of him. Instead she forced a smile.

"What sort of bag?"

He scratched the end of his nose. "After I agreed to do the pickup, I got another text telling me to stop by and pick up an item before heading to Jersey. It was a few blocks out of my way, but they promised it would pay extra, so I made the stop."

"What was in the bag?"

"Do you think I'm stupid?" Long Jong wisely didn't give her the opportunity to respond. "I didn't ask and I didn't peek. Nothing good comes out of poking your nose into demon business."

"Where did you pick it up?"

"The pawnshop two blocks north of here. A demon with long hair and a tattoo on his face was waiting by the curb." His shoulders drooped as he widened his mouth in a loud yawn. "I'm tired."

She patted his arm. That was all she was getting from Long Jong. At least for tonight.

"Rest and forget. This is all a dream," she murmured, waiting for him to lean forward and lay his head on the table.

In an hour he would wake up with no memory that they'd ever spoken.

Breaking the bubble of silence around the booth, Maya slid out and headed for the door.

The night was still young.

Chapter 10

A thick silence spread through the cavern as Lynx strolled away, presumably preparing for the next stage in his plan for demon domination. A shiver inched down Skye's spine as Micha stood next to her, watching the male disappear, an eerie stillness settling over him.

This was a vampire in his natural state.

She could see Micha. She could reach out and touch him. But she couldn't sense him. It was as if he'd retreated to a place she couldn't follow.

Icy, remote, impregnable.

Why that bothered her was a question she probably didn't want to answer.

Time for a distraction. Moving a step closer to Micha, she studied the piece of metal that circled his throat. Micha hadn't mentioned the collar, but it was obviously a deterrent of some kind that Lynx had placed on him. A means to control a vampire who could rip apart the fairy with terrifying ease.

"I'm not sure if my magic can open the lock on your collar, but I can try," she murmured softly.

"No." Micha took a sharp step back, his expression impossible to read.

"You don't trust me." Skye flinched, hurt by his rejection. Of course, she couldn't deny that he had reason, she silently reminded herself. "Fine. Tell me about the Tempest and why Lynx would go to so much trouble to get his hands on it."

The silence stretched, and Skye accepted he wasn't going to answer. Then he slowly turned to face her.

"The demons have an ancient story that they hand down from one generation to another." He shrugged. "There's a few different versions, but at the heart of each one is a blade that can supposedly tap into the power of the Gyre."

"Don't demons already do that?" Skye asked, genuinely confused. "I thought that was why they swore allegiance with the Cabal. To live in the vampires' territory."

"The magic of the Gyre allows them to touch the power of their ancestors, but its limited. They're no longer the giant goblins who bash their way through the world, or the elusive fey who can enchant creatures with a brush of their fingers."

He spoke of times long forgotten by most species. Before humans had crawled out of their caves and mages had ignited the wild magic.

"Does the sword give them back their powers?"

He shrugged. "From what I could discover, the sword was supposedly forged in the flames of a dragon to preserve the original demon magic in its purest form. It doesn't give them back their primitive powers, but the demons believe it can end the life of a vampire."

Skye remained confused. "There are other weapons to kill a vampire."

"This one doesn't just destroy our host but the spirit that lives inside us," he insisted. "The ultimate death."

"Seriously?" Skye had never heard of anything that could prevent a vampire from resurrecting. Not even magic. "A dangerous weapon. No wonder you keep it locked away."

His expression remained aloof, but something flickered in the stunning golden eyes.

"I'm not worried about the sword being stolen. It's been stuck in the rock for thousands and thousands of years despite the hordes of desperate demons trying to pull it out," he informed her.

Ah. He was annoyed. Interesting.

"So why do you protect it?"

He shrugged. "I have no way of knowing if the blade works or not, but the hex is very real. I wasn't exaggerating when I said that the ground was littered with the bodies of demons who were lured to the sword by tales of glory. Not even my own staff was immune. The only way to halt the carnage was to create a protective barrier to keep out trespassers."

Skye tried to imagine a hex that was not only powerful enough to kill hundreds of demons but capable of lasting for so many years. Honestly, the mere thought boggled her mind. She'd never heard of any spell with that sort of potency. Not unless it was being replenished by something. Or someone.

"Who hexed it?" she probed.

"The story I read said it was a mage named Zara. It was claimed that thousands of years ago she was in love with a powerful demon who used the sword to unite the clans. Her lover managed to destroy several vampires before he was betrayed by one of his top warriors and literally stabbed in the back with a cursed dagger. As he lay dying, Zara used her powers to bind the sword to the stone so no other demon could use it. Then, romantically, she joined him in death."

Skye wrinkled her nose. "That doesn't sound very romantic."

His brows arched, as if she'd managed to surprise him. "Agreed," he finally said.

Feeling oddly vulnerable as his searching gaze swept over her face and down her wrinkled, dust-coated dress, Skye turned to pace across the cell. She'd never cared about her appearance. She had, after all, spent a large chunk of her life enslaved by the demons. And now, she just wanted to be comfortable. It was strange to accept that she didn't want Micha to see her looking like she'd been wrestling with a rabid bear.

Weird and annoying. She had more important things on her mind.

Like the flames from her vision that were threatening to destroy the world.

Yep. That was more important than a lot of stuff.

Reluctantly Skye forced herself to recall as much of the vision as she could. Had there been a sword? Or an object that might represent a weapon? Yes. There had been something... Not a physical sword, but a core of power at the center of the fire.

It was possible the mysterious Tempest was involved.

She whirled around, discovering that Micha was still watching her with that unwavering intensity.

"There's something different about Lynx," she warned, needing him to understand that the fairy was more than just another overly ambitious demon on a suicide mission.

"He's an arrogant ass." Micha pointed out the obvious.

"That's every demon." She deliberately paused. "And vampire."

His lips twitched, then pressed together. "What's different?"

"His aura."

"Because he has royal blood?"

"It's more than that. I can see silver streaked with the green."

"Silver?"

"Like lightning." Skye lifted her hands. She didn't have the words to explain the jagged shards that flared through Lynx's aura.

"Why can't I see it?"

Micha sounded more curious than disbelieving and Skye felt a knot in the center of her belly loosen. The glorious male might not fully trust her, and he most certainly would never forgive her, but he was willing to listen. That was better than she expected.

"I think it has something to do with my gift."

"Like a premonition?"

She shook her head. "It's more a sense that he's hiding something beneath the surface. I don't think anyone has seen the true Lynx. Not even his companions."

He considered her words. "I've never heard anyone mention silver in an aura."

"Me either." She grimaced. "But it's there."

"Anything else?"

She started to shake her head, only to hesitate. "Yes, there's something weirdly familiar about Lynx," she admitted. "I keep thinking he must be related to one of the demons who held me captive, but I can't place the face."

Micha's lips parted, but before he could continue his questioning, the sound of returning footsteps cut through the air. A moment later, Lynx reappeared, along with Yugan. Both fairies had changed into casual jeans and long-sleeved T-shirts. Yugan had also added an assault rifle to his ensemble.

"Ready or not, it's time to go," the fairy drawled, motioning toward Yugan to unlock the door to the cell.

Without warning, Micha moved to stand in front of her. "The seer stays."

She stepped to the side in time to see Lynx shrug. "Fine with me. I'll have her released once I get my hands on the sword."

Skye scowled in annoyance. First off, she didn't believe a word that came out of Lynx's lying mouth. There was no way he was releasing her. Not unless she was a corpse. Second, she didn't need a vampire to decide if she was staying or going.

Even if he was yummy.

"I'm coming with you," she announced, the words bouncing off the distant walls of the cavern. It might have come out a little more emphatic than she'd intended.

"No." Micha and Lynx said the word at the same time.

She rolled her eyes. The two males couldn't be more opposite, but in some ways they were painfully identical.

Stubborn. Arrogant. And convinced they were always right.

She had no choice but to share a portion of her fears.

"I come with you or the world burns."

She'd softened her voice, but the words still managed to echo through the cavern. As if she'd struck a gong of doom.

Micha whirled to face her, his aloof composure replaced with concern.

"Is that a guess or a warning?"

"A promise."

Lynx clicked his tongue, a mocking smile curving his lips. He was pretending that her warning didn't trouble him, but he couldn't disguise the silver that was suddenly flaring through his aura.

"Come or don't come. It doesn't matter to me." He motioned toward his servant to lead them out of the cell. Waiting until Skye was walking past him, Lynx leaned toward her. "If you do anything to interfere with my plans, I'll kill you," he murmured, reaching out to stroke a finger down her cheek. "Which would be a shame. I plan on spending some time together once I have what I need."

Skye ignored the sudden drop of temperature as Micha growled a low warning. She could take care of this obnoxious fairy.

"There's no we." She knocked his hand away. "Not ever."

His smile widened. "A seer can't predict her own future. I might surprise you."

"I don't need my magic to know how I'll feel about you in the future."

"Mm." He sucked in a deep breath, as if savoring her scent. "Spunky."

Skye shivered. Not from fear. The air had gone from frigid to painfully cold and there was a prickle of violence that warned Micha was on his last nerve. She didn't know why Lynx was deliberately provoking the vampire.

"Are you going to stand here boring me?" she demanded. "Or do you actually want to get your stupid sword?"

Lynx pressed a hand to the center of his chest, as if she'd hurt his heart. "A direct hit." He smiled. "Although, I very much doubt you're bored. Still, it's time for us to go." As if flipping a switch, the smile disappeared and Lynx reached into the pocket of his jeans to pull out a small device. He held it toward Micha. "Nothing stupid, leech. Yugan, keep an eye on the seer."

Taking the lead, Lynx crossed the cavern and went into a wide tunnel that burrowed through the depths of the mountain. The construction felt relatively new, and there was a jagged lack of polish, as if it'd been dug with speed rather than care.

Was this a new stronghold? Had Lynx recently relocated? Or maybe the revolution wasn't as old as he was trying to pretend.

Skye shrugged away the suspicion, concentrating on the small hum of power beneath her feet. It wasn't the magic of a Gyre, but this spot had a trace of lingering enchantment. She assumed that was the reason Lynx had chosen the mountain to create his lair.

Eventually the tunnel angled upward and they stepped out of a cave onto an empty field that stretched for acres.

Night had settled in and there was a stiff breeze that cut through the thin material of Skye's dress. If she'd known she was going to be kidnapped, she would have worn something more suitable.

There was a soft tread of footsteps and suddenly Micha was standing next to her. He didn't touch her, but he was close enough that he was able to use his unique talents to wrap her in an invisible cloak of warmth. A dangerous pleasure swirled through her along with the welcome heat.

A silly woman might think that Micha was bothered by her discomfort...

Belatedly noticing Lynx studying them with blatant curiosity, Skye sent him an impatient glare.

"Are we going to wait here for the sword to appear?"

Lynx snapped his fingers, thankfully distracted. On cue, a blinding light flooded the field. "I might not have the casual luxury of a leech, but my horde has acquired enough wealth to provide a few modern-day conveniences, including a private airport."

Skye blinked, struggling to see through the blinding brightness. Eventually she managed to make out the shapes of several demons clustered around a sleek private jet parked at the beginning of a long runway. In the distance she could see the outline of a metal hangar that gleamed in the industrial-grade spotlights.

Wow.

Too stunned to speak, Skye watched in silence as a uniformed goblin approached them and performed a deep bow.

"Master, we're ready to take off when you give the signal."

"Master?" Micha drawled, his voice thick with disdain.

"Better than Your Excellency," Lynx countered.

"If you say so."

With a deliberate motion, Lynx stepped next to Skye and wrapped his arm around her shoulders, pulling her tightly to his side.

"This tempting creature, however, can call me whatever her little heart desires."

Skye started to struggle, only to freeze when the smell of death spiked the air. Not the death of a rotting corpse. This was a cold, steel-edged promise of a swift end to existence. Lynx dropped his arm and stepped back, but a pleased smile touched his lips. He'd gotten the response he wanted. He glanced at the waiting servant.

"We'll board now."

The servant nodded and turned to scurry toward the plane to pull down the stairs. Lynx followed behind at a slower pace with Skye behind him and Micha bringing up the rear. Yugan had disappeared, but she assumed he was like a bad penny, showing up when he was least wanted.

In silence they walked to the runway, climbing the narrow steps and entering the cabin. Predictably, the interior was sleek and modern with a table in the center of the small space with a U-shaped couch surrounding it. The door closed and the engines revved as they moved to take their seats on the couch. Skye swallowed a sigh as she was sandwiched between the two males. Lynx on one side, who was manspreading as if trying to consume more than his fair share of space, and Micha as cold and rigid as a marble statue on the other side.

Great. She didn't know where they were headed, but it promised to be an uncomfortable flight.

There was a small jerk before the jet was rolling down the runway, picking up speed before they hurtled upward with enough force to press Skye into the soft cushions. She hastily grabbed her seat belt and wrapped it around her waist.

Once strapped in, she turned her head to study Lynx's profile. He was staring out the porthole across the cabin, his expression brooding. Not as brooding as Micha's on the other side. But close.

"How long have you been following me around?" she asked, needing to shatter the tense silence.

Lynx shrugged. "A few days."

She gave a dramatic shudder. "Creepy."

"Practical," he corrected. "Your father was confident you would do whatever was necessary to protect him, but I'm a demon who always has a backup plan. Usually more than one."

His boast reminded her of a far more important question. "How did you get the key to the lower floor of Valen's lair?"

His jaw tightened, but he answered with a well-rehearsed ease. "Not all his staff are as loyal as he assumes."

Skye snorted. "Valen isn't careless. Even Peri says that he's a pain in the ass when it comes to protecting his lair. He would never hand out keys to his staff willy-nilly."

Lynx arched a taunting brow. "Willy-nilly?"

She ignored him. "The only ones who would have access to keys would be his guests. So who gave it to you?"

"Valen is arrogant. Like all leeches, he doesn't believe anyone could outsmart his security. It makes it much easier to do whatever the hell I want without getting caught."

He was being deliberately provoking. A sure sign he didn't want to answer her questions. All the more reason to keep pressure on him.

"Did the traitor also tell you which room Micha was using?" she demanded. "You went directly to his door despite the fact it was at the back of the building."

"You're a seer. You of all people should understand the past is meaningless. Only the future matters." He abruptly shoved himself to his feet, his expression hard with warning. "Behave yourselves."

In two long steps he disappeared into a room at the back of the cabin. A bedroom? Or maybe an office. A second later a door snapped shut.

Skye pursed her lips, considering the exchange. She hadn't pried out the name of a coconspirator, but she was convinced that they were currently staying at Valen's lair. Either one of the visiting Cabal or a servant who he trusted without reservation.

That should narrow down the list of suspects. If only she could get word to Peri...

Her thoughts were disrupted as her lips parted in a wide yawn. She was too exhausted to think clearly. After a couple of days of constant tension and restless nights, she could barely keep her eyes open. If she was going to find a way to prevent the world being burned to the ground, she needed to replenish her strength.

Snuggling into the soft cushions, she cast a quick glance toward the vampire seated next to her. He was once again in his statue form, no doubt contemplating the various forms of revenge he intended to enact on Lynx and his pals. Including her.

With a sigh of regret, Skye allowed the weariness to swallow her. Micha was a worry for another time and place.

Two hours later she woke as the jet made a sharp descent and hit the runway at a speed that made the aircraft shudder in protest. Skye was jerked awake, but thankfully she wasn't tossed from her seat. Not because her seat belt protected her. That had mysteriously disappeared while she was asleep. But because she was wrapped tightly in Micha's arms.

A heat touched her cheeks as she tilted back her head to meet his unreadable gaze. She wanted to believe that he'd pulled her close to protect her. Or even because he was overcome with the desire to feel her pressed against him. Unfortunately, she had a memory of her vivid dreams that'd included unhooking her seat belt so she could cuddle against the sexy vampire. Her only comfort was that she hadn't actually tried to strip off his clothes. At least she hoped not.

Pulling out of his arms, Skye shoved her riotous curls away from her face and futilely attempted to smooth the wrinkles from her dress. A lost cause, of course, but it gave her something to do as Lynx reappeared to shove open the door of the cabin and lead them onto yet another secluded airfield.

She had a brief glimpse of a narrow runway hidden by tall rows of cypress trees before she was bundled into a van that pulled next to the jet. Micha crawled in behind her and they were driven a short distance before they were unloaded and forced onto an airboat waiting at the edge of a swampy canal.

There were two other boats waiting in the thick weeds, loaded with a variety of demons, including Yugan still wearing his big gun.

They all had grim expressions that matched Micha's bleak mood, and the air was so thick it was hard to breathe. To be fair, she was almost certain they were in the bayous of south Louisiana. The air was always hard to breathe. But the sullen atmosphere didn't help.

Wrapping her arms around her waist, Skye concentrated on blocking out the varied emotions that battered at her. Fear, greed, anticipation, and a barely leashed hunger for violence.

These males were ready for battle. And she wasn't sure they cared who they killed.

The humid wind tugged at her curls as they skimmed and skipped their way out of the canal and into the open water of the gulf, headed directly for a nearby island. The area was shrouded in a darkness so intense that it was obvious no one lived there. Skye felt a stab of relief. She didn't doubt that Micha was simply biding his time until he decided it was time to end his captivity. And when that happened, things were going to get very bad.

Probably best to keep the humans out of the looming carnage.

The boats navigated onto a crescent-shaped beach and Skye climbed out. Beneath her feet was hard-packed sand covered with driftwood and rotting vegetation. Ahead of her was a line of thick trees draped in Spanish moss that gave the impression of an impenetrable barrier.

She glanced toward Micha, who was standing a few feet away. A dozen demons were spread around them, but none were brave enough to get close to the vampire, leaving him standing alone in a pool of moonlight.

"Where are we?" she asked him.

"My private island," Micha said, his gaze locked on Lynx, who was strolling toward them. "I keep it protected for the local wildlife."

Lynx clicked his tongue as he halted next to Micha. "Lies. It's a baited trap created to punish any demon who wants to challenge the Cabal."

Micha looked bored. "Are you always so dramatic?"

"It's part of my charm." Lynx winked at Skye. "Isn't it, sweetness?"

Sweetness? Gag.

"It's part of something," Skye muttered.

Lynx's mocking expression faded, leaving behind the ruthless determination etched on the overly handsome features.

"Lead us to the temple," he commanded.

Micha folded his arms over his chest. "Lead yourself."

Yugan aimed his gun at the stubborn vampire. It wouldn't kill Micha, but it could weaken him.

"No, Yugan." Lynx held up his hand. "I have a better way to encourage our companion's cooperation."

Micha parted his lips to expose his lethal fangs. As if anyone might have forgotten about them.

"Doubtful."

Without warning, Lynx lunged toward Skye, wrapping his hand around her throat as he pressed his chest against her back.

"Hey," Skye protested, exaggerating her annoyance as she reached up to try to pry his fingers loose. At the same time, she breathed a soft chant, releasing one of the curses stored on her charm bracelet.

She felt the magic sink into his skin as he tightened his grip, threatening to snap her neck.

"I don't want to hurt her, but I will," Lynx warned.

"Nice," Skye chided, dropping her hand. She wanted the fairy to think she'd conceded defeat.

Micha's response was a little more dramatic. With a low hiss, he pointed toward the nearby trees, a thunderous pressure filling the air and bending the foliage until it revealed a narrow pathway.

"You want to prove you're some magical leader and not another idiot with a death wish, knock yourself out," he growled.

Skye felt Lynx's muscles clench. He hadn't expected Micha to give in so quickly. Now he obviously suspected a trap.

"You go first," he commanded.

Micha sent the fairy a mocking glance as he headed toward the pathway. "Coward."

Releasing his hold on Skye's throat, Lynx poked her in the center of the back, obviously wanting her to go ahead of him. Skye snorted. He really was a coward.

Not that her nerves weren't affected by the darkness that slithered over her as she stepped onto the pathway winding through the trees. This wasn't natural. The shadows were alive with magic. As if it was a living creature that hungered for blood. Or maybe flesh.

Skye reached out with her senses, absorbing the power that pulsed in the air. It came from the Gyre, but it wasn't like the one in New York City. This one was deep and primitive and wild. It was as if someone had tapped into the most ancient well of magic and allowed it to spill across the island.

Had it been Micha?

Lost in her musings, Skye barely noticed the vines that glided next to the path, occasionally striking out as if trying to capture the intruders and drag them into the tangled undergrowth. They didn't appear to have any interest in her. Either because Micha was in control of them, or more likely, they assumed she was a creature like them. Created out of magic.

Behind her, however, Lynx was forced to dart and dodge the vegetation that lashed out, muttering a string of expletives in a language that Skye didn't recognize. The fairy was more unnerved than he wanted to admit.

Slowly they neared the center of the island and Skye shivered as she was bathed in a pulsing enchantment. The lush power called to her like a siren's song, beckoning her to sink into green depths and forget the world. It was tempting. Too tempting. If she hadn't been a mage, she would never have sensed the venomous undertones if imbibed too freely.

Malice dipped in honey.

Behind her a scream abruptly pierced the heavy silence. Skye didn't have to look back to know that one of the demons had fallen victim to the vines. By the time they reached the clearing, three more demons had screamed.

Unfortunately, Lynx wasn't one of them. He remained inches behind her as Micha crossed the soggy ground to lay his hand against the rusty door set in a square building made of cinder blocks.

It looked like a bomb shelter, not a setting for a mystical sword.

Curious, Skye readily followed Micha through the opening, her breath catching in her throat.

The outer shell was constructed with a spell that disguised the lavish beauty of the true temple. Once inside, her wide gaze skimmed over the pure black marble floor. The walls were covered with rich tapestries stitched with silver thread, and overhead the ceiling was painted a dark blue and splattered with silver stars.

There was a light, ethereal quality to the space that should have been a relief after the oppressive atmosphere they'd just left, but Skye wasn't fooled. The barriers that protected the island were woven out of nature.

This was something different. It was almost metallic, but not human technology. It was...

She didn't know.

She'd never sensed anything like it.

Instinctively she halted near the door as Lynx swept past her with an avid anticipation. Behind him, Yugan forced his feet forward, looking as if he'd bitten into a lemon. They were headed toward the center of the space where a large sword was stuck into the marble floor.

Skye narrowed her gaze, finally able to pinpoint the source of her unease.

The weapon looked like something out of a fable. It was big with a shiny blade. At least what she could see of the blade was shiny. The rest was hidden by the marble. The only thing unusual was the large chunk of red glass that was inlaid in the pommel and the weird aura that surrounded it.

It wasn't the aura of a demon. It was more like the blurred shadow around a mirage. As if it was an illusion, not a real sword.

Skye inched to the side, moving until she was standing next to the grim-faced vampire.

"What is this place?" Her voice was barely a whisper. She didn't want to attract the attention of Lynx, who was slowly circling the sword.

Micha glanced toward her, his expression impossible to read. "This was the temple created by the mage. It's a monument to the demon she loved."

Skye scrunched her nose. It wasn't that she'd forgotten the details of the ill-fated love story, but she was suddenly certain that there were a few important details missing.

"You're sure?" she pressed.

"That's the legend the demons have passed through the generations." He turned until he was facing her. "Why?"

"I don't know what hexed the sword or built this temple, but it wasn't a mage."

Micha flicked a glance toward Lynx, who was slowly reaching toward the sword, his expression triumphant.

"At last," the fairy breathed.

"Wait, Master!" Yugan abruptly pleaded, rushing toward Lynx. "Don't touch it. This could be a trick. Allow me to try first."

"Stop," Lynx snarled, halting his servant before he could interfere. "This is my duty. You wait outside."

Yugan's face twisted with genuine fear. "But—"

"Now."

The warrior battled against his urge to protect his master and the compulsion to obey his command. At last his desire to please Lynx overcame his need to shield him from danger. He whirled around, stomping out of the temple.

"Arrogant ass," Skye muttered.

Lynx sent her an amused glance, his tension vanishing as he allowed his fingers to curl around the hilt of the sword. He clearly wasn't worried about the hex.

"You're right, seer," he drawled.

"About what?"

"I heard your whispered disbelief that the poor mage and her tragic lover created this temple." The fairy cast a disdainful glance toward the tapestries. "The cheesy story is nothing more than a romantic fantasy conjured by demons to hide the truth."

An icy chill inched down Skye's spine. Not a premonition. Not even a reaction to Micha's burst of anger that was dropping the temperature. It was fear.

"The truth of what?"

"Of this place. And this..." With a dramatic jerk, Lynx pulled the sword out of the marble.

Only he didn't pull it out. The blade remained stuck as the hilt popped off, still clutched in Lynx's fingers.

"You broke it," Skye muttered in confusion.

Next to her, Micha made a sound of disgust. "It's a fake."

"Of course it's a fake." Lynx laughed as he strolled toward them. "Despite overwhelming vampire opinion, demons aren't stupid." He paused, as if considering his words. "Well, let's say not *all* of us. There is a real sword called the Tempest. And it does everything that has been promised. Not only allowing demons to tap into the magic that still flows in our veins, but killing leeches. Permanently." He shrugged. "Unfortunately, it's a fickle weapon and it will only respond to the hand of a demon it considers worthy of being a king."

Skye pointed toward the middle of the room. "Then what's that sword?"

"A diversion. The Tempest was famous ten thousand years ago. Every demon in the world knew of its magic and secretly lusted to carry it." Lynx smiled, as if relishing being at the center of attention. "But there was only one true master of the sword." He paused, adding drama to his story. "Lynx."

"You?"

Lynx shook his head. "It's a family name."

Skye rolled her eyes. "Predictable."

The fairy ignored her, continuing with his monologue. "The story is also true when it claims that the original Lynx was betrayed by his most trusted warrior. The bastard stuck a cursed dagger in his back. My grandfather used his dying breath to wrap it in a powerful magic that would keep it hidden until his true heir could retrieve it." He tapped the center of his chest. "Me."

"Then who created this place?" Skye demanded.

"Lynx. He always knew there was a chance he would be deceived, so he planted the story about the lovers and built this temple." He looked excessively pleased with himself. "He paid a mage to hex it and keep his secret safe. Until I could get my hands on it."

"Then why are we here?"

"The location of the sword remains hidden by the magic." Lynx held up the hilt, using his fingers to wiggle the decorative crystal out of the pommel. "I need the compass to locate it."

"A chunk of glass?"

"Not to me. Watch."

Lynx tossed aside the hilt and balanced the smooth crystal on the palm of his open hand. For a moment nothing happened and Skye quickly whispered the words to a magical snare. If she could trap him before he could call for his waiting servants, they could bring this to an end. But even as the magic tingled through her, the fairy's aura began to pulse, the silver streaks zigzagging through the green until it was almost blinding.

As the silver surrounded Lynx's fingers, a glow abruptly appeared in the depths of the red crystal, as if a fire had been stroked to life by Lynx's touch.

"Micha," Skye breathed in warning.

She didn't know what was happening, but she knew it wasn't good.

With a low roar, Micha reached up to rip off the wire around his neck. Skye felt an irrational stab of annoyance. Aggravating leech. He could have let her know he'd managed to disable the device. Instead he made her think he'd rather have his head blown off than let her help him.

Lynx's eyes widened, clearly blindsided by the realization that Micha was off the leash, quite literally, but he didn't panic. Not even when Micha launched himself forward. Pulling a metal object from his pocket, he tossed it in Skye's direction. She frowned as the thing rolled across the marble floor, halting as it hit the toe of her shoe.

"Choose, vampire," Lynx warned as he raced past Skye, heading toward the door.

On the point of running after him, Skye's air was knocked from her lungs as a freight train smashed into her back, slamming her to the ground. A second later she realized that it wasn't a freight train that pinned her to the marble, but a very heavy vampire. Trying to process what the hell was going on, her thoughts were shattered when a large explosion rocked the temple.

Shards of marble blasted through the air like miniature daggers, slicing and stabbing into Micha as he covered her with his large form. If he hadn't been on top of her, Skye knew that she would be in serious danger. Unfortunately, he couldn't protect her from everything. The vibrations from the explosion were still shaking the ground when the roof abruptly collapsed and a cinder block smacked her on the back of the head.

For the second time in less than twenty-four hours, Skye was knocked unconscious.

Chapter 11

Hexx's Pawnshop didn't look special. It was a one-story brick building squashed between a liquor store and a pet grooming salon. There was a large front window stuffed with the usual watches and gold chains, and a glass door had a neon sign that promised easy credit loans.

It wasn't until Maya had entered the cramped space that she could feel the distinct tingle of magic. Not an active spell but the residual hum from having a lot of magical items stored in the same location. The Witch's Brew felt like a nuclear reactor when she opened their heavily warded safe.

Assured she was in the right place, Maya weaved her way past the open bins filled with used toys, sunglasses, and old DVDs. At last she spotted a girl who barely looked old enough to be out so late at night seated behind a wood-paneled counter. Her hair was short and dyed a deep purple that matched the heavy liner that circled her eyes. She was wearing a fishnet top with a black bra underneath and was perched on a high stool, her attention glued to the phone in her hand.

Maya halted several feet from the counter. The girl was a human and she didn't look dangerous, but only a fool allowed themselves to be deceived by surface appearance. Usually a dead fool.

The girl continued to stare at her phone, and Maya loudly cleared her throat. "Excuse me."

"Can I help you?" The girl didn't bother to glance up.

Maya swallowed a sigh. Good help was hard to find.

"I'm looking for something special," she said.

"Then you've come to the right place." The girl waved her hand toward the glass cases on the far side of the room. "Lots of special stuff here. Jewelry—"

"I don't want jewelry," Maya interrupted, her voice sharp enough to force the girl to at last glance up.

She wrinkled her nose as she took in Maya's black slacks and expensive cashmere sweater. Was she offended by the elegant outfit? "The knockoff clothes are over there," she waved her hand toward the opposite side of the shop where a few wrinkled blouses and a fake fur coat were hanging on the wall. "There are some purses in the bins, but you're better off checking out the street sellers around Times Square. They have more stuff."

Maya ground her teeth. Was the girl being deliberately annoying, or was it her natural personality?

She stepped toward the counter, deliberately turning her head to reveal the spiderweb of scars.

"I said something special."

The girl dropped her phone. "Yikes. That's bad. Did you put your face on the stove?"

Maya smiled. The girl had at least cleared up any confusion. Annoying was her natural personality.

"I heard you had magic that can get rid of blemishes," she said.

"Maybe. I don't know nothing about that hocus-pocus stuff." The girl turned her head to yell toward an open door at the back of the room. "Hexx!"

A minute passed, then another before a goblin with long stringy hair and crimson flames tattooed along the line of his jaw stepped into the shop. He was wearing a sleeveless T-shirt and jeans that looked as if they hadn't seen a washing machine in several weeks, but Maya was more interested in the pale red aura that pulsed around him. A low-grade demon.

"What now?" he snapped, clearly irritated at the interruption.

The girl nodded toward Maya. "You have a customer."

"Buying or selling?" he demanded, his bored gaze swinging toward Maya. Instantly his eyes widened. Unlike his human assistant, he recognized the scars on the side of her face. "Oh shit." Reaching up, he grabbed a small crystal hung around his neck, yanking it off the leather strap and throwing it in her direction.

Maya waved her hand, releasing a burst of power that deflected the crystal. It careened toward the shelf of bowling balls and exploded. There was a loud crash as the balls collapsed to the ground, some shattering beneath the impact and others rolling crazily across the cheap Formica tiles.

"What's happening?" the girl cried out, ducking behind the counter. "Should I call the cops?"

"No!" Maya and Hexx roared in unison before the goblin was spinning on his heel and darting into the back room.

Maya raced behind him, but not before he slammed the door and locked it. Dammit. She rolled her eyes, dipping her hand into her purse to pull out a small vial. Centuries of finding herself in dangerous situations had taught her to reserve her magic, preferring to use the potions she could brew at home in her leisure. Spells weakened her and left her vulnerable. Stepping back, she tossed the vial at the door handle, her nose wrinkling as the acid ate through the lock. Melting metal dripped onto the floor, and lifting her leg, Maya kicked the door open. It slammed loudly against the wall, and Maya stepped into a small room that appeared to be a combination office and storage space.

Hexx was currently grabbing the lids off boxes piled in a haphazard fashion, no doubt searching for a weapon to use against her.

"Settle down," Maya commanded, moving to stand in the middle of the room. "I just want to talk."

Reluctantly turning to face her, Hexx licked his thin lips. "You're Maya Rosen."

"Yes."

"I heard what you did to Jada."

Maya frowned. "Jada?"

"She was a friend of mine. She did séances to make some extra money."

"Ah. I remember." A decade ago she'd heard rumors of a witch who'd moved to the area offering to speak to the dead for grieving families. It didn't bother her until she'd discovered the woman was gouging the poor humans by demanding outrageous sums of money and threatening to trap their dearly departed if they didn't pay up. "I did warn her to shut down her business. More than once. She decided she could do whatever she wanted, even if she risked stirring prejudices against magic users. Things could have gone much worse for her."

Hexx grimaced. "Okay, she made a mistake, but shit...she still breaks out in a rash during the full moon."

Maya shrugged. It wasn't her curse that continued to make the witch break out in a rash. It had been a temporary spell that would have dissipated within a few weeks. If Jada continued to have rashes, it was a psychosomatic response. Not unusual and probably a response to her own sense of guilt for taking advantage of vulnerable humans.

"As I said, she was warned."

Hexx stepped back. "I don't want any trouble..." His words faded as he dove toward the nearest box and pulled out a small linen bag filled with various herbs. Maya could smell lavender and mint and cloves. Probably the ingredients for a sleep spell, but the magic wasn't activated. Thankfully,

Hexx didn't seem to know anything about the items he sold, and tossing it in her direction, he watched her with wide eyes.

Maya allowed the linen bag to bounce off her chest before she swayed and lowered her head as if she were going to sleep. At the same time, she reached into her purse to pull out another vial. On cue, Hexx darted toward the door, desperate to get away.

Waiting until he passed, she spilled the contents of the vial onto his shoulder. Instantly he froze in place.

"Argh." Hexx struggled against the potion that held him prisoner. "What have you done to me?"

"Nothing that can't be undone." She strolled until she was standing in front of him. "Answer my questions and you might survive."

"I...yeah, okay." He did more lip-licking, a fine layer of sweat coating his tattoos, as if his face really was on fire. "What do you want to know?"

"Earlier today you gave two disguise spells to a demon who goes by the name Long Jong."

He sucked in a sharp breath. It wasn't what he'd been expecting. "Who?"

Maya reached into her purse, pulling out a small crystal. It was nothing more than a healing gem, but Hexx wouldn't know it wasn't a dread curse.

"Don't even start with me," she warned.

His eyes darted from side to side, but he was stuck. And he knew it. "What about him?"

She dropped the crystal back into her purse. "Who told you to give him the amulets?"

He hesitated, obviously reluctant to reveal the identity of the buyer. "No one told me," he eventually said. "Long Jong came by the shop to buy them."

"A lie," she snapped.

"If Long Jong told you a different story, he's the one who's lying," he insisted. "I swear."

Maya ground her teeth. Skye was out there somewhere, obviously in trouble. And this idiot was wasting her time.

"You're starting to piss me off," she snapped. "There's a simple way to discover who's telling the truth."

Hexx made a strangled sound, his eyes wide with terror. "No magic. Please! I don't want a rash."

She rolled her eyes, nodding toward the desk across the room where a small monitor was set on top of an old-fashioned DVD player. Even from this distance she could see it was a security camera monitoring the store.

"There's no need for magic. We can watch the security video."

"Oh. Right. The security camera." His fear remained, but it was threaded with an unease that had nothing to do with her. "Sorry, it's not working."

Maya narrowed her gaze. Enough was enough. "Tell me, Hexx. Do I look stupid?"

"No."

She pointed a finger at the center of his face. "Do you think I won't turn you into a hamster?"

He blinked, his mouth falling open at the threat. "You can do that?"

She released a trickle of magic. Just enough to make his greasy hair float on an invisible breeze.

"Let's find out, shall we?"

"No! Wait!"

"Talk," Maya commanded, emphasizing her request with a sharp yank on his hair.

Hexx's face paled to a pasty gray. "Okay, okay. Earlier today I got a text telling me to have two disguise amulets in a bag and to be waiting by the curb at noon for someone to pick them up."

"Who sent the text?"

"I don't know."

Maya clicked her tongue. It was like dealing with a five-year-old. "You honestly expect me to believe you received a random text telling you to prepare two disguise amulets that are not only forbidden in Valen's territory but extremely expensive and then to stand next to the curb to hand them over to a stranger? And you thought...yes, that's a fantastic idea?"

"I was going to delete the text," Hexx protested. "I get all sorts of crazy messages. Some dude last week came in looking for a corpse. What kind of shop does he think this is?"

Maya deliberately glanced toward the stack of crates shoved against the back wall. A few of them had a familiar logo stamped on the side.

"One that sells black-market magical items," she stated the obvious. "No doubt you also dabble in illegal drugs, including dragon scale—"

"Well I don't trade in dead bodies," he interrupted. As if that excused his criminal behavior.

"Who sent the text?" she pressed.

"I truly don't know." His expression tightened, the muscles of his neck bulging as if he was struggling against her spell. When he failed, he sent her a glare of frustration. "Look, I was going to delete the text but a second later I got an alert from my bank showing a very large amount of money was just deposited into my account. The sort of money that was as good as a threat. Whoever sent it didn't intend to take no for an answer."

Maya believed he'd gotten a large sum deposited in his account. Whoever was funding the attack on the Cabal wasn't counting pennies. But she didn't believe he'd felt threatened. At least, not by taking the money. He most certainly was terrified to reveal who had deposited it.

"Was anyone with Long Jong when he stopped to get the amulets?"

"Not unless he had someone hidden in the trunk."

"Did he say anything?"

"Nope. He rolled down his window and I threw the bag to him. End of transaction."

Maya lowered her hand and stepped back. She was wasting her time. Hexx was obviously nothing more than a pawn. He didn't have the information she needed. Her only hope was that he could lead her to someone who knew what was going on. And where she could find Skye.

"I won't turn you into a hamster. At least not tonight." She sent him a warning frown. "But I will be back to discuss your habit of selling black-market items."

"No discussion needed," Hexx stammered, torn between relief he wasn't going to suffer any immediate repercussions and fear that she might destroy his lucrative trade. "I'm sure all of this can be cleaned out."

"I'll be back," she insisted.

"Okay, yeah, sure. Gotcha." He forced a stiff smile. "Now if you can just... Hey, wait!" His voice cracked with fear as Maya turned on her high heels and headed for the door. "You have to release me."

"The spell will fade." Maya halted at the door to give him a finger wave. "Eventually."

His loud pleas followed her through the shop that was now empty after his young employee wisely decided to bolt, but Maya didn't slow her steady march until she was out of the building and halfway down the street. Only then did she step behind a lamppost and turn back toward the pawnshop. She was betting that Hexx was going to scurry to his employer's lair and warn them that a powerful mage was asking uncomfortable questions. And plead for mercy at having revealed his connection to Long Jong.

Ten minutes later her wager was rewarded as he stepped out of the shop and glanced nervously around before he locked the door and headed south. He was going to plead for mercy.

Satisfaction surged through Maya as she followed at a safe distance. One way or another she was going to get answers.

They jogged a couple of blocks before Hexx thankfully darted into the subway. Maya had more stamina than a human, but her heels were made for beauty, not durability. She lingered in the shadows until the train stopped and Hexx jumped on without looking back. Maya quickly slid on behind him, not worried she was being led into a trap.

Hexx was the sort of demon who had zero impulse control. It wouldn't have occurred to him that he might be followed. His only thought was getting to someone who was stronger, smarter, and hopefully willing to protect his black-market business.

They'd reached Upper Manhattan before Hexx pushed his way through the commuters and off the train. Maya waited until the last second before darting through the doors and losing herself among the gathered crowd. There was always the chance Hexx was meeting someone and she didn't want to spook them into fleeing.

Hexx paused, glancing around, but with long strides he was heading up the stairs and out of the station. Maya had no choice but to trail behind. Where was he going? There weren't any demon clubs in the neighborhood. At least none that she knew of—

Her speculations churned to a halt as they turned a corner and she realized where they were headed.

The Green House Theater. The spot where she and Skye had blundered into the top-secret demon meeting a few days before. The air was squeezed from her lungs as she watched Hexx stop in front of the box office, his hands shoved in the pockets of his jeans and his shoulders hunched.

He just stood there for several minutes, shifting from foot to foot in a nervous dance. Then the door to the theater was shoved open and a large form suddenly appeared, stepping on the sidewalk to stand directly in front of Hexx.

Maya released a string of swear words, recognizing the goblin with a shaved head and muscular form stuffed into a leather jacket and jeans. Or more specifically she recognized the aura that was bright enough to spill through the streets.

This was the head goblin commanding the others to perform some mysterious task a few days ago.

Hastily she reached into her purse to grab her phone. There was no way she could get close enough to overhear the heated conversation, but she could make sure this wasn't a wasted opportunity. Careful to stay hidden in the shadows, she took several photos of the two demons. She couldn't put a name to the goblin, but there was an excellent chance that Valen or one of his staff might recognize him.

The males ended their conversation and Hexx turned to scurry away. A second later the demon disappeared into the theater, slamming the door shut behind him.

Maya tucked the phone back in her purse and grimly headed toward Valen's lair. It couldn't be a coincidence that the Benefactor had ordered her to travel to this theater. He'd wanted her to see the male demon. Probably because he was going to be involved in Skye's disappearance. Not to mention the attack on the Cabal.

Dwelling on the Benefactor and the reasons he might have sent her to this location, Maya abruptly found herself lifted off the ground by an invisible force and pressed against the side of an abandoned pool hall. It wasn't a spell. Or magic. But she recognized the smell of unyielding power that swirled through the air.

The Benefactor.

Her mysterious patron possessed a scent that was utterly unique.

The invisible bonds pressed against her with a force that wrenched a small groan from her lips. There were times she wasn't sure the Benefactor knew his own strength. Or perhaps he didn't recognize her fragility in comparison to his overwhelming powers.

Knowing better than to struggle against the magic, Maya flinched as the image of the Witch's Brew seared through her mind. She was clearly being commanded to return home.

She hissed in annoyance. She desperately wanted to speak to Peri and share what she'd discovered. If Valen could identify the goblin from the theater, then they might be able to track down Skye. They would at least know where to get answers.

Now she would be forced to send the pictures to Gabriel, who was presumably acting as the liaison between her and her friend, and hope they would follow up on the clues.

Maya's frustrated fury boiled through her like acid, nearly causing her to miss the shadowed form standing directly across the street. Even when she forced back the anger and cleared her mind to call on her magic, she could make out nothing more than a vague man shape and the strange outline of something on his head.

Wait. Shock jolted through Maya. Was the man wearing a fishing hat? He stepped away from the wall into a pool of light. Suddenly she could see the bushy beard and the velour jogging suit.

"Joe," she breathed, struggling against the crushing grip of magic. "Did you follow me?"

With a shrug, he turned to stroll down the street.

"Wait!" Maya commanded. "Why are you here?"

Stopping beneath the lamppost, Joe slowly turned and Maya braced herself to ignore his usual insults. She wasn't going to let him distract her. Not this time.

But he didn't toss out some rude comment; in fact, he didn't say anything. He stood, staring at her as if he was contemplating some deep thought. Or perhaps communicating with an alien spaceship. Anything was possible with the insufferable man.

Then, without warning, there was a strange distortion in the air around him. As if he were suddenly going out of focus. Maya snapped her lips together, wondering if the Benefactor was blurring her vision. She wouldn't put it past him to temporarily blind her to keep his secrets. But it wasn't her eyes that were being blurred, she realized, as Joe was replaced with a tall, broad-shouldered male with burnished copper hair framing perfectly sculpted features.

He was gut-wrenchingly gorgeous. Even from a distance his striking beauty hit her like a punch. The smooth bronzed skin, the angular features that had been chiseled by the hands of a master, and the eyes that glowed with a brilliant emerald fire.

For a moment...or an eternity...Maya couldn't think. She didn't know where she was or why. She could barely recall her own name. Her brain had short-circuited and she was fairly certain that she was being given a glimpse of something no mortal should ever see.

She was still gaping at the vision when it flickered and abruptly disappeared and Joe was once again a solid form. Maya made a strangled sound, struggling to figure out if the vision had been real or a figment of her raw nerves. It'd been a rough couple of days. Maybe her brain was fried.

As if sensing her bewilderment, Joe bent over in a mocking bow before he straightened and strolled away.

Chapter 12

Micha could sense each tick of the clock, frustration boiling through him as he was forced to waste precious seconds recovering from the explosive blast, followed by the collapse of the temple. The wounds hadn't been life-threatening, but they'd been numerous, breaking bones and smashing vital organs that had to be restored.

And worse, he'd finally managed to get Skye Claremont in his arms, and they were both too damaged to appreciate the moment.

Later...he promised himself as he shoved upward, knocking aside the crushing pile that buried them in rubble. He no longer doubted that she had been a victim in Lynx's plot to get his hands on the strange crystal, but until he stopped the demented fairy, he couldn't allow himself to be distracted.

Not that it was easy, he grimly acknowledged, reaching down to pull Skye to her feet. Even coated in a layer of dust and her golden curls tangled in a messy halo, she was the very essence of temptation. A succulent treat he ached to taste.

Holding her hand in a gentle grip, he swept his gaze down her tiny frame, ignoring the bits of debris and flecks of blood that marred her clothes. He was searching for open wounds that would need immediate healing.

"How badly are you hurt?"

She tugged her hand free, wrinkling her nose as she futilely attempted to wipe away the dirt.

"I'm fine." She glanced up through her lashes. "Thanks to you."

Another wave of desire smashed into Micha, wrenching a low growl from his lips. The need to cup her face in his hands and kiss her until they both melted in pleasure was overwhelming. Only the distant sound of croaking frogs and the pungent scent of moss kept him from giving in to his hunger. This wasn't the time or place.

He stepped back, in dire need of space to clear his mind. "Can you walk?"

"Yeah."

"Good. We need to get away from here."

She grabbed the skirt of her dress to climb over the busted cinder blocks before he led her down the pathway, her gaze warily glancing toward the undergrowth that seethed with remnants of magic. He didn't smother the dangerous traps he'd laid around the area. He'd made assumptions and believed in rumors, and his lack of diligence had come back to bite him on the ass. Until he knew beyond a doubt that the sword and surrounding hex were destroyed, he wasn't going to take any chances.

They traveled back to the shoreline in silence, both too weary and battered to make small talk. And honestly, he doubted that Skye was in the mood to discuss the past few hours. For now it was enough to put one foot in front of another.

Stepping out of the thick foliage, Micha wasn't surprised to discover that the airboats had vanished. It'd been less than ten minutes since the explosion, but that was more than enough time for Lynx to disappear. He had to act quick if he was going to pick up their track.

Thankfully, he could already make out the whomping sound of an approaching helicopter.

"They're gone," Skye muttered. "I don't know whether to be happy that I don't have to spend any more time with Lynx and his goons, or sad that we're going to have to swim to get back to civilization."

"No swimming," he assured her, pointing at the flashing lights growing brighter by the second. "That's my helicopter."

She sent him a wary glance. "How did they know you were here?"

"They don't, but I have guards who monitor this area of my territory. They wouldn't have been overly concerned by the airboats. The wards I've placed around the temple are usually enough to run off any intruders. But they would have been alerted when the temple exploded. Heads would have rolled if they didn't come to investigate what the hell was going on."

She breathed a soft sigh of relief. "Thank God. I have to get back to Maya and Peri. They're probably out of their minds with worry."

Micha studied her relieved expression. Of course Skye's first thought would be concern for her friends. Not that she'd been kidnapped and hauled halfway across the country. Or nearly squashed by an enchanted temple.

Was it any wonder he was bewitched?

Such a unique, fascinating creature.

Unfortunately, as much as he admired her tender heart, he was going to have to convince her to keep their location a secret. Along with the fact that Lynx had his hands on the crystal. "My servants can take you to New Orleans." He moved to stand directly in front of her as the helicopter swooped downward. The pilot had no doubt caught sight of him standing at the edge of the water and was preparing to land. The blades were already picking up debris and tossing it through the air. "But I'm afraid you'll have to stay at my lair."

She frowned, but she didn't look angry. A better start than he'd expected. "Why?"

"Until we figure out who gave Lynx a key to get past Valen's security and revealed the location of my private rooms, we can't trust anyone," he reminded her. "If they know we're alive, they'll realize that they need to destroy any evidence that connects them to the demons. Including the traitor."

Her frown deepened. "My friends aren't involved."

"No, but they are vulnerable. If, however, my servants put out word that the temple has exploded and they're searching for survivors, the traitor will assume we're dead or missing. It will give us at least a few hours to figure out what's going on."

Skye slowly nodded. "Okay, I'll go to New Orleans. But we can't just wait for Lynx to find the sword. Or whatever it is he's really seeking." Her expression was grim. "We have to stop him before he gets his hands on it."

Micha nodded. She didn't have to tell him that the vision of a fiery future hadn't changed. It'd probably become more likely since he'd allowed the bastard to escape with the strange crystal.

Frustration bubbled through him. "I'm going to have the helicopter drop me off at the spot we picked up the airboats. That's the most logical place for him to return to shore. I'll try to pick up his scent there."

She sent him a worried glance. "It's almost dawn."

"Then I have to catch him quickly. I'm not going to risk losing his trail."

She sent him a strange glance. "Actually, I don't think you have to worry about him going too far."

Micha eyed her in confusion. "A new vision?"

She shook her head. "A curse."

"What do you mean a curse?" Her words did nothing to clear up his confusion. "Lynx was cursed?"

"He is now," she said with a shrug. As if she went around cursing people on a regular basis. And maybe she did. He'd always heard it was Peri Sanguis who was in charge of the hexing and cursing side of the business, but that didn't mean Skye wasn't involved. "I detonated it when he grabbed me on the beach."

Micha had gone endless centuries without being blindsided. He was a male who was meticulous in planning his existence precisely because he didn't like being caught off guard.

Since traveling to New York City, there had been one shock after another. Most of them nasty. His gaze swept over Skye's delicate face. And some earth-shattering.

His life would have been far more peaceful if he'd ignored the command from Sinjon, he wryly acknowledged. And not just because he'd been swept up in a brewing demon war. Even if he did manage to halt Lynx and his mysterious partner in crime and return to his lair, he suspected Skye Claremont was going to continue to disrupt his life for a very long time.

At least...he hoped she was around to disrupt it. The possibility of spending the next thousand years without her was too awful to contemplate.

"I'm almost afraid to ask what's going to happen to him," he murmured. "According to my research there are mages who can make body parts fall off for the right price."

"At the Witch's Brew we don't usually contract for body parts to actually fall off." She pursed her lips as if considering the unfortunate recipients of the powerful magic. "But you might wish they would."

"And Lynx?"

"Nothing awful." There was a hint of regret, no doubt wishing she'd caused several body parts to dissolve. "A simple sleeping spell."

The air buffeted them as the helicopter lightly settled on the beach. Micha stepped closer, speaking directly in her ear as the thumping sound of the blades created a deafening roar.

"How long will it last?" he asked.

"It's hard to say," she admitted. "When I got the call they were holding Clarissa hostage, I didn't have time to prep my charms, so I grabbed the emergency spells that Peri left for me. Her magic is always off the charts, so I would usually estimate that he'd be out for days." She glanced toward the shoreline where the airboats had landed. "But Lynx is more powerful than most fairies. He might be able to fight through the spell a lot quicker."

"Twenty-four hours?" he suggested.

She wrinkled her nose. "Give or take a few hours."

"Okay." For the first time since he'd awakened to sense Lynx sneaking into his private rooms, Micha didn't feel as if he was two steps behind. Just maybe he could get ahead of events before they bit him on the ass.

"Then I can send my guards to try to discover where he's sleeping while I go to New Orleans with you."

"What are you going to do?" she asked as he grasped her upper arm and urged her toward the waiting chopper.

"Lynx can't search for the sword if he's unconscious, which gives me time to do some research." His lips twisted as he bent low to avoid the blades that continued to spin. "I prefer not to repeat the same mistake."

"What mistake?"

"Accepting myth and legend as truth." Self-disgust jolted through him at the memory of watching the sword he'd wasted centuries protecting being revealed to be nothing more than a tarnished bit of steel. "I want to know exactly what crystal Lynx took from the sword, who created it, and what it does."

"He said it was a compass," she reminded him as they climbed into the back seats.

Micha motioned toward the pilot, who pressed the thrust lever to lift them off the beach and soar toward the star-splattered sky. The servant would realize that Micha wanted to return to his lair unless he gave him specific directions to fly in another direction.

"Lynx said a lot of stuff that proved to be a load of shit," Micha muttered, still furious with the arrogant fairy. And himself.

"True."

"I also want to do more research on the Tempest," he said, speaking loud enough for Skye to catch his words without allowing the pilot to overhear the conversation. He trusted his staff, but right now he intended to treat everyone as a potential traitor. "I never bothered to study the history of the sword when it was protected by a hex, along with my own layers of security. A lapse that might cause a new demon war if Lynx manages to get his hands on it."

She reached to lay her hand on his arm. "You couldn't have known what he was plotting."

Her touch was as light as a butterfly wing, but Micha reacted as if he'd been scalded. Was she offering him comfort? It should have been amusing. He was a member of the Cabal. The leader of a powerful Gyre. He had thousands of demons who had pledged their loyalty and would readily lay down their lives to protect him.

But would any one of them care if he was injured or even destroyed? Would anyone mourn his passing? It wasn't a thought that had ever entered his mind. He had associates and servants, but no one close enough to fret over his welfare. He'd never felt the need to create intimate connections.

Not until now.

Gazing down at her upturned face, he desperately wanted to believe that she was concerned for him. Micha. Not the Cabal leader.

Unable to resist temptation, he covered her fingers with his hand, giving them a soft squeeze, even as he forced his thoughts to return to the danger of allowing Lynx to accomplish his mysterious plans.

He had twenty-four hours, maybe less, to stop him. And the clock was ticking.

"The sword was in my territory, along with the mysterious crystal, which makes it my responsibility," he insisted. "I can only hope we can discover what Lynx is truly searching for and destroy it before he ever wakes."

"Where are you going to do this research?"

"I'll start with my personal library and go from there."

She lifted her hand to impatiently shove her curls out of her face. The wind had whipped them into a glorious halo of gold.

"Do you have research books that focus on magic?"

"Several thousand," he assured her. "Why?"

"There was something strange about the spell that held the sword in place. I think it's important we find out who placed it there," she told him. "If we do figure out how to locate the sword, or whatever it is that Lynx is searching for, it's probably best we know exactly what to expect."

Hard to argue with that.

Chapter 13

The large antebellum house looked like it'd been plucked off a movie set. The central building was painted white with black shutters and had a wide porch with fluted columns. There were two wide wings with balconies that overlooked the carefully tended grounds and a shingled roof with brick chimneys that Skye would bet her last dime had never been used. Vampires and fire were never a good combo.

Stepping through the double doors, Skye halted in the center of the vast foyer. The impression of walking across a movie set was only intensified, she silently acknowledged, taking in the black-and-white tiled floor and the sweeping staircases that led upstairs. Overhead a crystal chandelier bathed the room in a soft white glow that reflected off the polished wood paneling.

Micha halted next to her, his expression tense, as if he were bracing himself for an attack.

"Is something wrong?"

"No," she assured him, her gaze lingering on the marble statue set in a shallow alcove. She suspected it was an original Greek sculpture. "It's beautiful."

"But?"

She held up her hands, trying to explain her reaction to the boringly perfect house without being rude. "It doesn't seem like your style."

"I hired someone to design and decorate it." He shrugged. "I use the public area when I'm forced to deal with human authorities, and there are offices on the upper floors for my staff as well as cottages spread around the area for the servants who stay here full-time. Most of my employees live in New Orleans or Atlanta or Mobile to oversee my businesses."

Skye smiled wryly. That made much more sense than Micha surrounding himself with this cheesy elegance. Of course, in her defense, she wasn't accustomed to spending time with anyone who owned multiple homes, office buildings, clubs, casinos, restaurants, and who knew what else?

"So where do you live?" she asked.

"In the basement."

"Seriously?" She stared into his painfully beautiful face, wondering if that was some sort of joke. First of all, basements in Louisiana were a disaster waiting to happen. Eventually any hole was going to fill with swamp water. And second, this male might not fit the stiff perfection of the house, but she couldn't imagine him crouched in a dark, moldy basement.

He nodded toward one of the wide openings. "Follow me."

Micha turned to stroll across the tiled floor, ignoring the female goblin who'd appeared on the upper landing and was glancing over the carved railing. Skye assumed the woman was one of Micha's numerous assistants, but while she appeared mildly surprised that her employer had made a sudden appearance when he was supposed to be in New York City, she didn't say a word. No doubt she was trained to stay in the background unless her services were required.

Skye's lips twitched. She would have been pounding down the stairs demanding to know what the hell was going on and who was the strange woman and how long they were going to stay. Along with a hundred other questions.

Which was why she worked in a coffee shop where her insatiable curiosity was an asset.

Stepping into the dimly lit kitchen, she had a vague impression of French-style white cabinets and lots of stainless steel appliances before Micha led her into a pantry. More confused than ever, she reluctantly stepped into the cramped space and watched as the back shelves swung open. Ah. A hidden passage. Just like the Batcave.

Micha bent down to avoid knocking his head on the low doorframe and was swallowed by the thick shadows. Skye followed behind, her steps a lot more cautious. She could see better than most humans in the dark, but she didn't have the vision of a demon or a vampire.

She was inching down what felt like a dirt ramp when Micha reached back to grasp her hand, as if belatedly realizing she couldn't see through the gloom. The cool touch of his fingers not only guided her through the darkness, but it also offered a strange assurance that nothing bad could happen to her. A silent promise that she was safe.

Skye swallowed a sigh, trying to concentrate on the sensation that they were headed down to the center of the earth instead of shivers of pleasure at his touch. What was the point of dwelling on her intense awareness of Micha? It wasn't like she had an overabundance of gorgeous, sexy, powerful males in her life. What woman wouldn't want to strip him naked and lick him from head to toe? And lots of places in between.

It was much more unnerving to realize that every moment she spent in his company, he was stealing another chunk of her heart...

The treacherous thought was just forming when Micha hit a switch and a soft glow spread through the cavern that stretched in front of her. Skye's lips parted as she released a soft gasp of shock.

The vast opening was carved stone with a flat bedrock floor and a coved ceiling that towered above them, but there was nothing natural about the space. It was all too smooth and polished, without a hint of mildew or decay. She closed her eyes, attempting to pinpoint the spell. It had to be powerful to create such a vast space and maintain it against the pressures of Mother Nature. There was nothing.

She opened her eyes to discover Micha watching her with an unnerving intensity.

"How's this possible?"

His eyes glowed like molten gold as he stepped toward her. "My powers are intertwined with nature."

"You?" She blinked, genuinely shocked. "You created these caverns?"

"Yes." A slow smile curved his lips, revealing the tips of his fangs. Yum. No, no, no. Not yum. She silently chided herself. She was alone with a dangerous predator. She shouldn't be wondering if the rumors were true that those fangs could cause an orgasm with one bite. And if the bigger the fangs, the more pleasure they could give a partner. And if he'd ever fed from a woman's inner thigh... A flush stained her cheeks.

"Skye?"

Micha's voice shattered her X-rated thoughts and Skye cleared the lump from her throat. Was it warm in the cavern? Or was it just her?

"What if something happens to you?" She blurted out the first question that her fuzzy brain could latch onto.

The gold in his eyes shimmered, easily catching the scent of her desire on the air. Thankfully, he allowed her to pretend that she wasn't hot and increasingly bothered.

"I hired several local mages and spent a fortune to create the perfect atmosphere for my collections, as well as providing lights throughout my lair. I purchased an additional layer of magic to protect the irreplaceable items." He waved a hand toward the tall glass cabinets that lined the length of one wall.

It took a minute but at last Skye could make out the shimmering forcefield that surrounded them. She didn't doubt that the magic would cause a painful response if anyone was stupid enough to touch them.

He turned to point toward the heavy steel vault that took up a portion of the opposite wall. "And the ones that are too dangerous to fall into the wrong hands are triggered to self-destruct if I'm destroyed or if someone tries to steal them." He paused, his jaw tightening as if he was struck with an unpleasant thought. "Although, I spent a fortune on manpower, not to mention using a large amount of my own powers, to protect a hexed sword that was basically useless. I'm not as confident in my ability to distinguish genuine artifacts from illusions as I used to be."

She grimaced. She didn't blame him for his annoyance. Before today, she would have assumed it would be suicidal to attack the Cabal.

A bad time for assumptions, obviously.

Turning toward the other side of the cavern, Skye strolled toward the sturdy shelves that displayed a variety of gem-encrusted weapons and marble busts of various human royalty and military leaders. Micha had no doubt met them all during his long life, but to her they were figures out of history.

She'd reached the middle of the cavern when she came to an abrupt halt. She'd caught an unexpected scent. Lilies? The sweet aroma drifted past her at the same time she felt a brush of electricity prickle over her cheek. An invisible touch that made the hair on her nape rise.

"Do you live here alone?" she asked, glancing over her shoulder.

Micha arched a brow as he sauntered to stand next to her. "I don't have a lover, if that's what you're asking."

Yes.

She shook her head even as satisfaction flared through her. She truly hadn't been asking the question, but she wasn't sad to be reassured he didn't have a roommate. Especially a roommate who shared his bed.

"I wasn't," she insisted, reaching up to touch her cheek. It still tingled. "I just sense..."

"What?"

"A presence."

The finely chiseled features appeared more intrigued than worried by her revelation.

"This lair appears to be a barren cavern, but it's at the very heart of the Gyre. The power pulses in the air."

She cautiously lowered the barriers she'd built over the past twenty years. They not only protected her from the emotions of others, but they muted the magic that flowed through the world. A necessary precaution considering not all powers were benign. She didn't want to get hit by a blast of evil before she could protect herself.

A second later she gasped. It was one thing to be braced for the power that thundered beneath her feet, but nothing could prepare her for the magic that rolled over her like a tidal wave.

It wasn't the same as most Gyres. It didn't have the raw power of Valen's territory. Or the delicate enchantment of the European Gyres. And it most certainly wasn't the lingering echo of a dragon lair.

This was...arcane magic. Ancient powers that had formed the world out of dust and starlight.

"Older," she whispered in awe.

"Older than what?"

"It's older than magic."

Micha's brows lowered, his gaze sweeping across the cavern as if searching for a hidden enemy.

"Is it dangerous?"

Skye considered the question. The brush against her cheek hadn't been painful, but it hadn't been comforting, either. More of a desire to be noticed.

"It doesn't feel threatening," she assured him, then frowned as the air thickened, as if the spirit was sending a warning. "Not to us," she amended.

Micha slowly nodded, his brief unease replaced with a rueful acceptance. "This is Louisiana. It would be a shame if my lair wasn't haunted."

"True."

Micha waved a hand toward the opening between the bookcases. "I'll show you to your rooms."

She nodded in agreement, not sure what to expect as they moved through a wide tunnel that branched off in every direction, giving the sense of a vast spiderweb running beneath the bayous. The caverns were stark, but they didn't feel inhospitable. It was more a feeling of an empty space waiting to be filled.

Pushing open the wooden door at the end of the tunnel, Micha waved for Skye to enter. As she stepped over the threshold, a soft light spilled from an overhead globe connected to a magical spell that ran through the caverns. Micha hadn't exaggerated when he said he'd spent a fortune on mages. The glow revealed a surprisingly cozy room with a large four-poster bed and a polished wood armoire that was left open to reveal the satin robes hanging inside. There was also an opening on the far side that offered a glimpse of a bathroom complete with a walk-in shower. Skye released a sigh of pleasure. Exactly what she needed.

"You can rest here while I—"

"I'm not tired," she cut off his words, then ruined her claim with a wide yawn. She held up her hand as he started to protest. "Really, I'm fine," she insisted, well aware there would be no way she could sleep. No matter how tired she might be. "A shower, maybe something to eat, and I'll be ready to figure out what magic was protecting the crystal."

The golden gaze swept over her stubborn expression before Micha offered a grudging nod.

"I'll have fresh clothes and dinner delivered while you shower," he promised. "My staff has access to the finest restaurants in New Orleans. They can have whatever you desire in less than an hour. What are you hungry for?"

Skye pressed her hand against her stomach as it rumbled, licking her lips in anticipation. There was nothing better than Cajun cuisine.

"Everything."

Micha made a strangled sound at her response. Or maybe it was the whole lip-licking thing. He stepped closer, his icy power wrapping around her. Skye shivered. Not from cold. Oddly, the closer he stood, the hotter her blood ran. No, it wasn't odd, she silently conceded, tilting back her head as he loomed over her. He was so devastatingly beautiful. The sculpted features with a bold nose and sharply carved cheekbones and sensuous lips. His dark skin as smooth as satin and his eyes shimmering with a vibrant golden glow.

A lush, magnificent god that stirred her deepest fantasies.

He reached out to stroke his fingers through her curls. "Everything?"

"Yes," she agreed without hesitation.

"All you have to do is ask and I'll make sure it's yours."

She moved forward, arching against his hard body. "That's a bold promise."

Micha hissed in pleasure, wrapping her tight in his arms as his gaze skimmed over her upturned face.

"You make me bold, Skye Claremont," he said, his voice harsh with hunger. "Until I caught sight of you in Valen's lair, all I wanted was to hide in the shadows."

"Why?"

His hands slid up the curve of her spine, his touch igniting sparks of delight that tingled in all the right spots.

"I've never been plagued with the restless ambitions of my brothers," he admitted, his hands continuing to explore her willing body. "I don't need to conquer and rule to satisfy my ego. All I truly wanted was peace and the opportunity to savor my vast collections."

Skye could sympathize. She loved spending time with Maya and Peri and the customers who came into the Witch's Brew, but there was a cost to being surrounded by people. She was forced to constantly keep up her shields, even when she was alone in her rooms. Being alone with Micha in these caverns was the first time she'd ever been able to truly relax.

"So why are you a member of the Cabal?" she asked.

His jaw tightened even as his fingers traced the curve of her shoulders and down her arms. The touch was as light as a feather, but it continued to spark a desire in Skye that was threatening to rage out of control.

"Those in power always fear that someone is plotting to steal it away from them," he murmured, his nostrils flaring as he caught the unmistakable scent of her need. "And my talents are quite unique. It made me a threat whether I wanted to be or not."

She held his smoldering gaze, not remotely surprised the Cabal would be eager to control this male. The vampires ruled the world by maintaining a unified alliance. Any rogue would threaten their image of invincibility.

"I would guess your talents aren't only more unique, but they're stronger than most vampires," she said dryly, unable to imagine how much power it must have taken to carve the cavern out of pure bedrock. "Not even Valen could create this lair."

He shrugged. "Just as you're unique." His hands slid up to cup her face in his palms, his gaze lowering to her mouth. "We have a great deal in common." His brows arched as she abruptly laughed at his claim. "What's so funny?"

"The thought that we have anything in common," she retorted. "Your unique talents gave you a seat on the Vampire Cabal and a fabulous lair filled with treasures. Mine gave me years of imprisonment by a horde of demons and a kidnapping by yet another demon who is determined to start a war," she reminded him. "That doesn't include the vision of watching the world burn."

He flinched, as if her words caused him physical pain. "I'm sorry. I didn't mean to remind you of the bastards who held you captive."

She reached up to press her fingers against his lips. "I'm not trying to get sympathy. My life hasn't been that bad; in fact, the past few years have been wonderful," she said. And it was true. Since moving into the Witch's Brew, she'd discovered that it was possible to wake each morning with a sense of anticipation that it was going to be a great day. And to know that she would always have her friends at her side. It was a gift that she never took for granted. "But I'm not sure we have much in common."

His fingers circled her wrist, pressing his lips to the center of her palm before he allowed his fangs to lengthen, scraping them down sensitive flesh to rest against the vein of her inner wrist.

"Then I'll have to convince you."

Skye's heart thumped against her ribs, her stomach quivering with a fevered yearning. She wanted to be convinced. Over and over and over...

"How would you do that?" Her voice was a rough rasp, her breath coming out in jagged pants.

He'd done nothing more than touch her with the tips of his fangs and she was on fire. What would happen if he actually bit her? Spontaneous combustion?

It was a real possibility.

"I could start with this." He grazed his fangs up her forearm before lifting his head. His expression was stark with hunger. The same hunger that pulsed inside her. "Or maybe you prefer this?"

He bent down to claim her mouth with a blatant need. Skye grasped his shoulders as her back curved beneath the pressure of his kiss, but she didn't protest. In fact, she met him kiss for ravenous kiss. She hated being treated like a china doll, especially when she was in a man's arms.

Micha muttered something in an ancient language, his hands cupping her backside to haul her tight against his thickening erection. Skye had a moment to savor the sheer size of his arousal before she was distracted as his tongue dipped between her lips.

She moaned in pleasure, the urge to tug him toward the nearby bed thundering through her. She wanted his powerful hands ripping off her dress and spreading her legs before his heavy body was pressing her into the mattress and his fangs were sinking deep into her throat.

As if able to read her mind, Micha turned his head to glide his fangs down the curve of her neck.

"You taste of destiny," he murmured in a thick voice.

Destiny...

The word whispered in the back of her mind, setting off tiny bells of alarm. Skye stiffened, the unwelcome memory of flames and doom intruding into the dreamy sense of bliss.

Dammit.

Why couldn't her visions be of buttercups and puppies? Or bathing in chocolate? Or spending endless centuries devouring the male who was nuzzling the pulse at the curve of her throat?

Heaving a heavy sigh, Skye pressed her hands against his broad chest. "Speaking of destiny," she reluctantly said.

Slowly Micha lifted his head, frustration boiling deep in his eyes. "Are you reminding me that we're wasting time?"

Skye smoothed her hands over his hard muscles. "It doesn't feel wasted." An insatiable craving throbbed in the air between them, but Micha forced his arms to lower as he stepped back.

"No, but you're right," he agreed. "We need to concentrate on stopping Lynx." His gaze continued to smolder with desire. "But soon."

An aching regret tugged at her heart. What if they couldn't halt the coming flames? What if she never discovered the intense pleasure of having this male moving inside her...

No, she couldn't think like that.

She had to believe they were going to turn fate and save the world.

"Soon," she whispered.

His fangs remained fully extended, but regaining his composure, Micha pointed toward the door.

"My library is the second door on the left."

"I'll find you." He turned to leave, but Skye impulsively reached out to grasp his arm. "Micha."

He glanced back, his brows arched. "Yes?"

"You still didn't explain why you live alone."

A slow, devastating smile curved his lips. "I hadn't met you."

The breath was knocked from Skye's lungs as he turned and smugly sauntered away.

I hadn't met you.

Such simple words, but they had the potential to change Skye's life forever. Always assuming they'd survive long enough to discover if they had a future together, she wryly reminded herself.

Grabbing one of the robes, Skye headed into the bathroom and closed the door. Then, stripping off her dress that was torn and filthy, she tossed it in the trash and stepped into the shower. It was an hour before she forced herself to switch off the hot water and dry off. Not only had the pounding water eased her aching muscles, but it was the first decent shower she'd had in years. As much as she loved the Witch's Brew, it wasn't blessed with water pressure.

Leaving her damp curls to bounce freely down to her shoulders, she returned to the bedroom to discover a pair of jeans and a fuzzy yellow sweater folded neatly on the bed along with a tray that was filled with gumbo, dirty rice, shrimp scampi, and a platter of beignets.

Her mouth watered at the scent of garlic and butter and rich spices. Micha must have sent the helicopter to pick up the food to have it there so quickly. Not about to let his generosity go to waste, she perched on the edge of the bed and ate her way through enough food to feed a football player. She didn't have Peri and Maya's ability to absorb the magic that leaked from the auras of demons. She needed a more ordinary burst of energy.

With an effort, she managed not to lick the plates, although she did stick her fingers into her mouth to clean off the powdered sugar from the beignets. It would be a sin to wipe away that ooey goodness. Then, dressing in the jeans and sweater, she went in search of Micha.

Not that it was much of a search. She could have closed her eyes and easily looped her way through the complicated tunnel system. His power pulsated through the air like the steady beat of a drum.

Strolling the short distance down the corridor, she stepped into his private library and came to an abrupt halt. Her mouth fell open as she allowed her gaze to roam over the floor-to-ceiling bookshelves that consumed three of the walls. They towered high enough that it would take a ladder to reach the top and were lit by spotlights hidden in the bedrock overhead.

She turned in a slow circle, thoroughly enchanted. There had to be thousands of leather-bound books. Many of them so old the bindings would no doubt have crumbled to dust if the climate in the cavern wasn't carefully controlled. Like a museum for knowledge. And on the far wall a glass case displayed ancient maps. Many of them revealing a world that was barely recognizable.

A deep sigh escaped her parted lips and without warning a cool wash of power spilled through the room.

"Is everything okay?"

Skye glanced over her shoulder as Micha entered the room behind her wearing a black cashmere sweater that clung to his broad chest and a pair of silk slacks. His hair was damp as if he'd just stepped out of the shower, and his eyes glowed like molten gold.

She blinked, and then blinked again.

Oh no. She most definitely wasn't okay.

Every time she caught sight of this male, his beauty set off an explosion of awareness. And that didn't even include the thunderous impact of his power that made the earth tremble beneath her feet.

Still, now wasn't the time to share her struggle to concentrate on anything but the awareness scraping her nerves raw. Once the passion between them was ignited, she had no doubt it was going to burn out of control.

They had other fires to fight first.

"I'm drowning in envy," she instead murmured, waving her hand toward the nearby shelves. "When you said you had a library, I had no idea it would be this."

"These are the books that I share with interested researchers," he said. Skye blinked in shock. "There's more?"

Micha nodded toward the opening on the far side of the library. "Through there."

Skye eagerly crossed the floor to enter the inner chamber, instantly feeling the thick layers of protection that had been laid over the cupboards that lined the walls.

"Inside the cabinets are the scrolls and manuscripts that are too rare or too fragile to be handled by anyone but an expert, as well as the more dangerous artifacts I've collected," he told her, not bothering to give a tour as he headed toward an opening on the other side of the space. "And through there—"

"Magic," she whispered, lured through the open doorway like a bee to honey.

It was a smaller space than the other rooms, with a low ceiling and an atmosphere thick enough to choke her. Maya had a vault beneath the Witch's Brew where they kept the spell books and artifacts that were too powerful to leave lying around. And it felt just like this when she entered it.

A buzzing in the air that prickled over her skin. Like electricity. Or standing in a thunderstorm.

"Yes, magic," Micha murmured and Skye glanced back to discover his gaze locked on her with unnerving intensity.

She sent him a rueful smile. "I'm starting to understand why you never wanted to leave here."

"Maybe I didn't realize what I was missing," he admitted, strolling to stand directly in front of her.

She studied his elegant features, wanting nothing more than to step forward and wrap her arms around his hard body. When she was this close to him it didn't feel as if anything bad could happen.

Unfortunately, her vision had been a warning that she couldn't ignore.

"There are some wonderful things. And some not so wonderful things," she said. "But I would miss it if it was gone."

He stroked his finger over a bouncy curl. "It's not going to be gone."

She smiled wryly. "More bold promises."

His hand cupped her cheek. "Eventually I intend to make them come true."

"A vision?" she teased.

"A hope." His fingers tightened, as if he was battling the urge to kiss her. Then, with a small shake of his head, he dropped his hand and stepped back. "I'll start my search in the main library. If you need me, just give a shout."

She watched him leave with a pang. Just because her brain understood they couldn't be distracted until the threat had been eliminated didn't mean that her body had gotten the memo. It sulked like a petulant child denied a cookie.

And what a cookie...

With a click of her tongue, she shoved away the erotic image of nibbling Micha from head to toe and forced herself to focus on her surroundings. Closest to her were glass cabinets filled with a variety of items. As she moved toward them she could see that each of them glowed with power. Some were hexed, others held curses, and a few were bespelled with traps intended to harm whoever was foolish enough to pick them up.

She moved to the next cabinet. Inside were a dozen vessels. A few were ceramic, others were glass, and some were molded out of pewter. She assumed that each of them held a potion, but she wasn't going to check. At least not on this visit.

She had high hopes she was going to be invited back for a more thorough inspection of the collection.

Reaching the shelves at the back, she hesitated. There were nearly a hundred leather-bound books that appeared to be arranged by age, from oldest to newest, and honestly she didn't know where to start.

Probably because she didn't have a clue what sort of magic had been protecting the sword. It wasn't fey, or goblin, or mage. Unless the hex was so old that it'd transformed into something completely new and different. Peri had discovered the dangers of ancient magic entombed too long in the depths of the earth.

And there was something different about the magic that smoldered in this Gyre. It might have altered the original spell.

With impeccable timing, the smell of lilacs swirled through the air, and one of the books from the top shelf toppled forward to land on the floor. Skye released a small squeak as she instinctively danced back. She loved books, but these were filled with magic. There was a real possibility that they contained spells, curses, hexes, and other nasty surprises. There was also a real possibility that the mysterious spirit was trying to drive her away.

There was a blast of icy air before Micha rushed into the room. Obviously he'd heard her tiny squeak. A reminder that this male possessed super-duper senses. It would be impossible to hide anything from him. Including her habit of singing off-key in the shower and eating copious amounts of chocolate when she was stressed.

His smoldering gaze swept around the room, his fangs fully exposed. "What's happening?"

The words had barely left his lips when the book flipped open and a ball of mist rose to hover in midair.

"Either this is the start of a horror show, or the book was triggered with a spell," she muttered, touching the charms on her bracelet as she prepared to try to contain the magic the spirit had unleashed.

Micha hissed, his power thumping through the room. "Are we in danger?"

Skye's fear eased to curiosity as the mist expanded until it was taller than her and twice as wide. It didn't feel threatening. There was nothing tangible about the fog as it began to thin and fade. In fact, it was remarkably familiar.

"I don't think so," she finally decided. "This feels like a vision..." She struggled to pinpoint exactly what was happening as an image slowly formed in the center of the mist. It was like a doorway had been opened and they were peering inside. "But different," she lamely finished.

"Is it the future?"

She shook her head, studying the cavern that was being revealed. For a second, Skye thought it might be Micha's lair, but then she noticed the mosaic tiled floor and fluted columns that held up a ceiling embedded with precious gems. In the very center of the floor was a heavy white pedestal that appeared to be carved from white marble threaded with gold.

"It's the past," she finally concluded. Skye couldn't explain the sense of age that pressed against her, but she was absolutely certain that she was glimpsing a place from the far distant past. "A memory."

He sent her a confused glance. "Whose memory?"

"I'm not sure, but it was deliberately captured and stored in the book," she explained. "I've heard of the spell, but I've never seen one or known a mage capable of creating one."

A minute passed and then another and another as they stared at the image that hung in the air.

"Intriguing, but I'm not sure it's going to help us." Micha abruptly broke the silence.

As if his words had prompted the spell to reveal its secrets, a shadow flickered at the edge of the cavern and a tall, slender woman wearing a fur cape that brushed the mosaic floor appeared. Her red hair was curled in an elaborate braid that looked like a crown and held hints of fire in the soft lighting. Odd. Even more odd, her face glowed with a metallic bronzed sheen.

But it was the fire that surrounded her that captured Skye's attention. Not the aura of a demon. It blasted around her like solar flares around the sun. A fiery, ruthless power.

"Dragon," Micha muttered in shock.

"Really?" No wonder the magic felt old. Although she'd been surrounded by demons most of her life, she hadn't spent much time or effort studying their history. Her secluded childhood meant she had a lot of catching up to do to learn how to be a mage. She didn't have time for anything else. But she did have a vague idea that the latest dragon hibernation had started around thirteen thousand years ago, prompting the beginning of the last ice age, but honestly, it could have been even longer ago. "Are you sure?"

"I have no memory of the beasts in my current form, but I've done enough research to recognize one."

Skye nodded. "That explains her outrageous aura. If she was standing in the room I would be blinded. And she's not even in her natural form."

"There are writings that claim that earthquakes shook the ground when they walked and a flap of their wings could cause typhoons," he added.

A sudden realization smacked into Skye like a freight train. The spell might be revealing the past, but it was connected to her vision. She was absolutely certain.

"And breathe flames that could destroy the world?"

Micha stiffened at her soft words. "It's possible." Then he shook his head. "But only if they were wakened."

A shiver inched down Skye's spine. "Yes."

A shadow flickered in the image and the dragon turned as she was joined by a male. He wasn't much taller than the female, but he was twice as wide with heavy muscles that rippled beneath a leather tunic that left his arms bare and ended at the leather boots laced up to his knees. His skin was a rich brown and his head was shaved to reveal an intricate tattoo that swirled from his brow to his nape. The fact that he had no aura revealed he was either a human or a vampire, then he came into sharp focus and Skye didn't have to guess what species he belonged to.

His fangs could rival a saber-toothed tiger's.

"Tatis," Micha said, a hint of wonderment in his voice.

"You know him?"

"Only through the stories that were passed down. He was killed during the last demon wars."

The name didn't mean anything to Skye. "I assume he was famous for a reason?"

"He negotiated the treaty that ended the reign of the dragons. Which means the female must be Zanna, Queen of Dragons."

Skye arched her brows, watching as the dragon and vampire stood in the center of the cavern, their lips moving as if they were having a heated exchange. She couldn't hear what they were saying, but the flares of fire that danced around the dragon and the layers of ice that coated the rock floor warned they weren't exchanging pleasant chitchat.

"I'd heard there was some sort of treaty, but I thought that was a myth," she admitted.

He sent her a baffled glance. "The dragons?"

"No, that a vampire managed to convince them to go into hibernation." She shrugged. "I figured it was time for the dragons to sleep, like a bear during winter, and a vampire decided to take credit for their disappearance."

His lips twitched even as he shook his head at her audacity. "Not an unreasonable hypothesis, I suppose, but according to vampire lore, it was a joint decision to prevent our mutual extinction."

"You were at war?"

He hesitated, his expression smoothing to unreadable lines. Her lack of education wasn't the only reason she wasn't overly familiar with demon or vampire history. They were notoriously secretive. Vampires rarely shared anything about the inner workings of the Cabal or how they'd gained power over the Gyres.

And they most certainly never discussed how they were resurrected after they died. Skye didn't even know how a new body was chosen or where they went while they were in between human forms.

Then with an effort he answered her question. "The war wasn't organized, but there was a constant battle for who would control the various territories."

"Who was winning?"

"For countless eons, dragons controlled the world," he conceded. "There weren't many of them, but dragon fire is the one certain way to destroy a vampire."

Skye widened her eyes. "Forever destroyed?"

"Yes. There was a time in the long-distant past when there were thousands of my brothers roaming the world."

Yikes. Thousands of vampires? That was...horrifying. She shuddered, happy she hadn't been around when there were an overabundance of vampires roaming around and dragons were belching fire at them.

"If dragons could destroy the vampires, then why would they agree to a treaty?"

"The vampires discovered that dragon scales could be pierced by iron. Once they created weapons that could slay the beasts at a distance, my brothers went on a killing spree." Micha grimaced, as if troubled by the savagery of his people. "Eventually the dragons were forced to accept they had no choice but to negotiate with the vampires and find a way to exist without exterminating one another." He nodded toward the male and female still arguing in the mist. "They eventually concluded if they couldn't live in peace, they would have to take turns sharing the world."

"Were the demons involved?"

"At the time, most of them were enslaved by either the vampires or the dragons. At least until the dragons went into hibernation. From the artwork and scrolls that managed to survive from that time period, it seemed there was a lot of chaos. Not surprising. There would have been a major power vacuum before the vampires managed to gain control. Plus, for many goblins and fairies it was the first time in their existence that they'd been free. Eventually they started forming their own hordes." His lips twisted into a wry smile. "It was inevitable it would lead to the first demon war."

There was a movement from inside the mist and Skye returned her attention to the silent tableau that was unfolding. Tatis and Zanna stared at each other with a tangible loathing, but they both managed a stiff bow.

"They must have come to some sort of agreement," Micha said.

"Zanna doesn't look happy," Skye retorted, watching the flames dance around the dragon's slender body as if she was struggling to restrain them.

"There's someone else coming," Micha murmured as there was more movement, and a tall male with long reddish-gold hair and blue eyes so dark that Skye initially thought they were black strolled to stand between the two powerful creatures. He was wearing a long, silvery robe threaded with gold that shimmered as he walked. His hood was up, but she could make out the delicate lines of his profile.

Skye studied him in confusion. She felt as if she'd met him before. But where?

"A demon?" she asked in confusion.

Micha shook his head. "Back then there was no mistaking a goblin or fairy," he reminded her. "Most goblins stood over seven feet tall and fairies still had wings. Plus, there's no aura."

Lifting a hand, the unknown creature pushed back his hood, and Skye could make out an arrogant expression and a familiar half smile.

"Oh. He looks a little like Lynx," she said, although that didn't fully satisfy her sense of recognition.

"That must be his relative. The original Lynx."

"And the reason this spell was triggered."

"You think someone wanted us to see this particular memory?" he asked. She nodded. It was the only thing that made sense, unless it'd been the most amazing coincidence in the history of the world. Her thoughts had been focused on the crystal and the mysterious spell that had protected the temple. The spirit must have activated the magic to reveal the memory.

"I do."

His golden gaze swept over her face, as if searching for a secret. "There's something bothering you."

She clicked her tongue in frustration. "I feel as if I can almost recognize the male. Not just because he looks a little like Lynx, but..." She shook her head. "I can't think of who it is."

The male they assumed was Lynx reached into a hidden pocket of his robe and pulled out a scroll. Then, with a flamboyant motion, he unrolled the document and spread it on the pedestal, revealing the glyphs etched on the parchment. Minutes passed before the vampire and dragon nodded in grudging agreement and Lynx covered the scroll with his hand. Seconds later the middle of the pedestal seemed to melt into a puddle and the scroll sank out of view. Skye arched her brows. She didn't know what sort of magic the creature possessed, but it was powerful. Had his great-times-ten-grandson inherited the same magic? Skye grimaced at the thought.

Trying to shuffle through the spotty history she'd learned of magic users in an attempt to identify the male, Skye nearly missed the conclusion of the treaty. It wasn't until the vampire lifted his hand to press his thumb against the lethal point of his fang that she realized that the dragon was already shaking blood on the pedestal where the scroll had disappeared. Sparks exploded and Skye imagined she could hear the sizzle as the blood hit the marble. A puff of smoke was starting to rise, only to instantly freeze as the vampire's blood hit the marble in the exact spot. The two splatters of blood darkened and spread across the pedestal, bubbling as if it was brewing into some sort of toxic amalgamation.

And maybe it was. Even as she watched, a mist formed above the blackish liquid. It thickened, pulsing with a crimson glow. It continued to pulse and thicken, shrinking to the size of a...

Skye sucked in a sharp breath. "That's the crystal that Lynx took from the sword," she rasped.

In the vision, the original Lynx grasped the crystal and slid the large gem into his pocket.

Only it wasn't a gem, she reminded herself. It was the mixed blood between a dragon and a vampire that had hardened into a shiny rock. So what did that mean?

"Did you see that?" Micha abruptly demanded, his gaze locked on the fading image as the dragon and vampire marched out of view, both clearly unhappy with the situation.

"See what?" she asked.

"Can you replay the vision?"

Skye considered his request. "I'm not sure," she finally confessed, "but I can try."

Closing her eyes, Skye concentrated on the lingering scent of lilacs. The spirit seemed to be the bridge that connected her to the magical memory. Nothing happened and she opened her eyes to tell him that it was impossible, when the fog abruptly returned with the image of the empty cavern.

Skye remained silent as the scene played out, her attention locked on the strange demon who was obviously the negotiator between the vampires and dragons. If he wasn't a demon, then what was he?

"There." Micha broke the silence, pointing toward Zanna as she halted next to Lynx and leaned forward. She placed her fingers on his neck as she whispered in his ear, then pulling away, she scraped her nails over his flesh. "She marked him."

Skye leaned forward as if it would help her to see the faint lines of magic that formed an intricate pattern before sinking into Lynx's skin.

"It looks like some sort of binding spell," she said.

"What does a binding spell do?"

"Lots of things." She shrugged. "It can be used in a love potion or a curse or something as simple as luring customers back to the shop to enjoy my yummy lemon and blueberry scones."

"Could it force someone to obey you?"

"Like a compulsion spell?"

He nodded and Skye tried to imagine the amount of magic it would take.

"I suppose it's possible, but it would be an extremely short-term compulsion, and it would swiftly drain the magic of any mage."

"What about a dragon?"

"I honestly have no idea," she admitted. "Do you think that Lynx was somehow forced to place the crystal in that sword and send his ancestor to retrieve it thousands of years later?"

His lips twisted as the vision once again faded. "Put like that, it sounds like a ridiculous theory."

"We're grasping at straws. All we have are ridiculous theories," she reminded him. "Still, the memory spell did reveal why I didn't recognize the magic that surrounded the hexed sword. I'm not sure what species the original Lynx was, but I suspect it's something I've never encountered before. And we know now that the crystal isn't a compass."

Micha turned toward her, silently considering her words. "Maybe not a compass in the traditional sense, but there's a chance it might lead the owner to the location of the treaty," he suggested.

She slowly nodded. The crystal was formed out of the mixed blood of the vampire and the dragon, intended to seal their treaty. It made sense it would lead the owner back to that spot.

What didn't make sense was why Lynx had gone to such an effort to get his hands on the thing.

"Why would anyone want to go there?" She spoke her confusion out loud. "Unless the magical sword that Lynx claims he's looking for is hidden in the same location?"

"There's only one way to find out."

She blinked. Was he suggesting that they travel to the location of the treaty? "You know where it is?"

He stepped toward her. Close enough his icy power brushed over her like a soft caress.

"I have a general idea of where it is hidden. Plus, there's several books that have hints to help us pinpoint the precise spot."

She tilted back her head to meet his golden gaze. "Us?"

He threaded his fingers through her damp curls before he angled his head down to touch her lips in an achingly sweet kiss.

"We're partners, aren't we?" he asked against her mouth.

She trembled in pleasure, ready, willing, and eager to join this male's team. "I suppose we'll find out."

* * * *

Valen was reviewing the security footage for the thousandth time, futilely hoping he would notice something he'd overlooked, when the door to the office was shoved open. Surging to his feet, he gathered his power like a thundercloud. He'd warned his staff he wasn't to be interrupted. Not by anyone.

But even as he prepared to strike the intruder, he was forced to leash his temper as Gabriel entered the room. The male's expression was wary as he glanced around, and he was wearing black silk pants with a charcoal sweater and suede jacket, as if he was preparing to go out.

"All alone?" he asked Valen.

"For the moment." Valen stepped around the desk, his jaw clenched at the memory of his latest clash with Kane. If the ambassador hadn't been in the room it most certainly would have ended in bloodshed. "Thank God."

"Is Peri sleeping?" Gabriel demanded.

"Yes. I finally convinced her to lie down an hour ago. She's terrified for her friend, but she's so tired she can't keep her eyes open. The stress is going to make her ill."

"Kane?" Gabriel pressed.

The books rattled on the nearby shelves as Valen struggled to keep his temper. "The bastard followed the ambassador down to the guest suites. He's still complaining that Maya and Peri should be imprisoned until we discover what happened to Micha."

With a nod, Gabriel moved to stand directly in front of Valen, his voice barely above a whisper.

"Fortunately for us, Maya isn't locked away."

"Why do you say that?"

Gabriel hesitated, glancing around as if he was worried they were being watched. And it was possible, Valen acknowledged with a stab of frustration. Until he discovered who'd given the fairy the keycard to get to the guest rooms, he had to assume there was a traitor in the building. One that might have planted hidden cameras.

Motioning the male to remain silent, Valen led him across the room to press his fingers against the bookshelf. It swung inward and they stepped into his private office. Only Peri was allowed in there. It was the one place he could work without interruption. Which meant no servants or random guests would have access to this location to hide a bugging device.

Valen waited for the door to close behind them before he led Gabriel past the glass cases displaying his collection of Ottoman artifacts and Roman daggers on one wall and the high-tech monitors that displayed images of his various clubs, spread from Boston to Washington, DC, on the opposite wall. It wasn't until he reached the massive desk angled to take in the stunning view of the park through the floor-to-ceiling window that he halted and turned to face his companion.

"What did you discover?"

"Maya sent me some interesting photos." Gabriel pulled his phone from the pocket of his pants. He touched the screen before he turned it so Valen could see the image he'd pulled up.

A growl rumbled in Valen's throat as he easily recognized the long-haired demon with a weasel face.

"Hexx. He runs a pawnshop in the Bronx."

"Maya sent a text that claimed this is the demon who provided the disguise amulets that the kidnappers used."

"Dammit." Valen snapped his fangs together. "I suspected he was dealing in the black market, but he's never stepped over the line far enough for me to interfere. Obviously a mistake."

Gabriel didn't try to make him feel better. Instead he turned the phone to pull up another image.

"She also said that she saw this demon." He turned the phone so Valen could make out the large goblin with a shaved head and bright red aura. "He was at the same spot a couple days ago. He was meeting with a demon named Gunther and his local horde. She didn't know why, beyond the fact that he'd hired them for some mysterious task."

Valen studied the image. "He looks familiar, but I can't place him."

"Maybe this will help."

Gabriel brushed his fingers over the screen, pulling up yet another image. This one was obviously from a newspaper article and blurry, as if it had been taken at a long distance through a zoom lens, but it was clear enough to reveal Kane in formal attire as he entered the Kremlin. And two steps behind was a goblin with a shaved head wearing a military uniform.

"Igor Triton. Kane's top lieutenant," Valen hissed, belatedly realizing he'd seen the male during his occasional visits to the Winter Palace in St. Petersburg over three hundred years ago. "When did she send the photos?"

"Fifteen minutes ago."

"Where?"

Gabriel slid the phone back into his pocket. "Green House Theater in Upper Manhattan. I have the address."

Valen headed toward the door. "We need to get to that theater."

Valen moved in a blur of motion before Gabriel abruptly blocked his path. "You should stay here. I'll go."

"No." Valen clenched his fists. He hated to leave Peri alone, but right now it was vital to discover who was behind the kidnapping and where they'd taken Micha and Skye. The sooner the better. "Kane threatened my mate. I'll do the questioning."

Gabriel wisely stepped aside as Valen plowed forward, heading out of the office and across the outer salon to the elevator. His assistant, Renee, appeared before she hastily ducked out of sight as she easily sensed his emotions that rolled through the penthouse like a tide of doom.

Fury. Frustration. And grim determination to bring a brutal end to the threat against his mate.

They reached the lobby, but before Valen could decide the quickest way to get to the theater, Gabriel pushed open the glass door and nodded toward the black SUV parked next to the curb.

"This is mine."

In silence they climbed into the waiting vehicle and settled into the plush leather seats. The driver waited for Gabriel's tap on the back of the seat before he pulled away from the building and began weaving his way through the nearly empty streets. They managed to reach the theater at a speed that would have been impossible if it wasn't so late. Or so early, depending on whether you were a night or a day creature.

Valen was definitely in the night creature category and his senses were already warning him that he had to be safely tucked in his lair in less than two hours.

The knowledge added an extra edge to his impatience, but Valen forced himself to point toward an alley a couple of blocks from the theater. He wasn't going to do Peri any good if he rushed into a trap. Or worse, spooked the enemy into flight.

"Stop here," he commanded, his voice harsh. "I don't want to give him the opportunity to escape."

Gabriel nodded as the driver glanced into the rearview mirror. A second later they were stopped in the alley and climbing out of the SUV to silently glide through the shadows.

"He might already be gone," Gabriel warned as they cautiously circled the aging theater, making sure there were no hidden demons waiting to ambush them.

"If he was here I can track him," Valen assured his companion. He wasn't being arrogant. Locating and following both demons and vampires was one of his specialized talents. "As long as he doesn't have magical help disappearing," he conceded.

If the demon was dabbling in black-market items, there was always the possibility he possessed a spell to cover his trail. The thought shattered his fierce determination to use his brain, not his unbeating heart, to confront the enemy. Heading to the side of the building, he kicked the rusty door off its hinges and stepped inside.

Valen moved through the darkness, searching for any hint of demons. "I caught the scent of Hexx on the front sidewalk, but he never entered the building," he finally concluded.

"Wait. I smell demon," Gabriel warned, moving across the wide foyer to push open the doors to the auditorium.

Valen was instantly hit with a potent stench. "Demon blood," he growled, aware of Gabriel pulling a dagger from a hidden sheath beneath his jacket even as his gaze moved to the body dangling by its feet from the chandelier overhead. The wide torso had been gutted, spilling blood and guts over the rotting seats. The grisly sight was magnified by the realization that the demon was missing his head.

Already knowing what he was about to see, Valen braced himself as he glanced toward the stage. He'd spent a lot of years surrounded by feral barbarian warriors and ruthless Roman legions. The depths of depravity during times of war were bottomless. It didn't matter if it was humans or demons or vampires.

Evil was just beneath the surface.

As he expected, he discovered the head of the demon planted in the center of the stage, face grinning at him with a ghoulish horror.

"Shit," he muttered as he recognized Kane's faithful servant.

Igor Triton.

Gabriel stepped next to him, the dagger still clutched in his hand. "We're too late."

Chapter 14

After gathering every book he possessed on the Dragon Treaty, Micha had spread them across the long wooden table in the center of the main chamber and started his search for the location of the original meeting. Just a few feet away, Skye did the same, her brow furrowed as she absently chewed on the end of one golden curl. The knowledge she was so near, looking gloriously adorable, not to mention exquisitely edible, should have been distracting. Instead, there was an easy comfort as the two of them worked side by side as they shared information and separated myth and legend from genuine history.

A merciless certainty settled in the center of Micha's chest. He'd known beautiful, sexy, intelligent women in his long life. But Skye was the only one who fit into his lair as if he'd created it just for her. And maybe he had, he wryly acknowledged. Perhaps when he'd been arrogantly deciding to create a lair where he could retreat from the world, he'd unconsciously wished to discover that one, unique creature who could share it with him.

And he was going to do everything in his power to make sure that she spent her future at his side.

Everything in his power.

Now, Micha stood at the back of the space, studying the top map that was framed and protected by layers of glass and magic. It was his oldest map that he'd discovered buried beneath tons of hardened lava. It'd been protected by layers of fey magic and hidden from the world for countless centuries.

Lifting his hand, he pressed a finger against the glass, pointing at a location in the center of Panama.

"These caves are the most likely location."

Standing close enough to envelop him in her scented warmth, Skye nodded. "I agree."

Micha slowly turned. He'd devoted enough time and attention to solving the mystery of Lynx and his weird-ass crystal. He wanted to concentrate on this mage who'd bewitched him with a glance.

"I knew that we would make a good team," he murmured.

She arched a brow. "Not always. You accused me of kidnapping you."

"You did kidnap me."

She pretended to consider his response. "I suppose that's true."

He grimaced as he recalled his shock when she'd arrived with the fairies to force him out of Valen's lair and into the van.

"And worse, I was dreaming about you when you snuck into my private rooms," he confessed.

She blinked. "You were not."

He stepped closer, using the tips of his fingers to trace the delicate sweep of her jaw.

"Why are you surprised? It wasn't an accident I followed you into Valen's private study during the party. You caught my interest from the moment I glimpsed you across the room." He smiled as a rosy heat tinted her cheeks and the scent of lush laurel leaves swirled through the air. Desire sizzled and snapped between them, creating an electric current that threatened to set him on fire. In the best possible way. "It wasn't just your beauty, although I'll admit I was fascinated by these lush curls," his voice roughened as he threaded his fingers into her satin hair and tugged her head back. "And the darkness of your eyes that promised the mysteries of the world." Slowly he lowered his head to press his lips against each of her eyes before sweeping his mouth over her brow. "And of course, there was the desire to rip off that gauzy bit of fabric and discover if your skin was as satin smooth as it appeared." With a growl, he lifted his head to study her with a blatant hunger. "And then you looked me in the eye and warned me not to harm your friend and I was lost."

A bemused expression emphasized her sweet features. "You dreamed about me because I threatened you?"

"Because you were fiercely loyal and willing to face down a member of the Cabal to protect someone you love," he clarified. "And then I witnessed you getting tossed out of the window of a demon bar and that was that. I became a victim of your allure."

She snorted, a hint of amusement shimmering in the depths of her midnight eyes. "Hardly a victim."

"Hmm. Let's say I was a *willing* victim," he conceded. "But it was entirely your fault that I was lost in my fantasies when I was so rudely interrupted by the kidnappers." His gaze lowered to the lush temptation of her lips. The memory of her addictive taste rushed through him, lengthening his fangs until they throbbed for a taste. "Even after I was attacked I thought the scent of laurel leaves must be a product of my imagination. I couldn't imagine why you would be with the fairies."

Without warning she reached up to place her fingers against his lips, a stricken expression twisting her delicate features.

"Please don't say that," she pleaded. "I was terrified they were going to hurt you."

Micha remembered watching her dash toward him. At the time, he hadn't been worried that she intended to hurt him. Just baffled at her presence.

"Is that why you grabbed me?"

"Yes. I didn't even consider the possibility of a vision." She grimaced. "Careless."

"Fate," he said in firm tones. He was a dedicated scholar who believed in what he could see and touch. But he was also a vampire who'd lived a very long time in the unfathomable magic of the bayous. Logic was all well and good, but it didn't explain everything. "The same fate that brought me to New York City to discover what I was missing."

She allowed her fingertips to brush lightly over his face, as if savoring the feel of his skin.

"Your life would have been a lot more peaceful if you'd stayed home," she murmured.

"Or I would have perished when the world was consumed with fire," he reminded her.

"There's that."

Before she could dwell on the dark visions plaguing her, Micha leaned down to kiss her with a fierce urgency.

"And I refuse to believe that destiny wouldn't have found a way for our paths to cross," he said against her lips. "Not when you were meant to be a part of my future."

She trembled, arching against him as if the thought of a life without him was terrifying. Or at least, that's what Micha told himself. He wanted to believe she couldn't bear the thought of not having him around.

"How can you be so sure?"

He scraped the tip of his fang over her lower lip. "Perhaps I'm an oracle."

Her eyes darkened in anticipation. "You see the future?"

"I feel it." Grasping her hand, he pressed it against his chest. It didn't matter if his heart was beating or not. It was where his complex, and yet startlingly simple, emotions for this woman were hoarded. "Here."

Her breath faltered, as if her lungs were suddenly too tight. Then she made a visible attempt to dampen the desire smoldering between them. "Shouldn't we be concentrating on finding Lynx?"

Probably, he silently conceded. They still didn't know the meaning of Skye's vision, and if it was connected solely to him or if it had something to do with Lynx and his mysterious search for the Tempest. Hell, they didn't even know if the Tempest existed.

Just as importantly, they didn't know who had betrayed Valen to help the fairies kidnap Micha or if they were a danger to other members of the Cabal.

All of them were potential disasters waiting to explode, but in this moment, Micha couldn't force himself to concentrate on anything but the woman standing close enough to wrap him in her scented warmth.

"My servants will continue to search for Lynx and I'll have my plane prepared to take us to Panama, but there's no way to reach the caves before sunrise. I'm trapped in this lair until then." He wrapped his arms around her waist, and a groan wrenched from his lips as she pressed against his thickening erection. "Although, it doesn't feel like I'm trapped."

She trembled. "What does it feel like?"

"Paradise."

The air tingled with enchantment. Not just the primitive pulse of the Gyre but a light, exquisitely delicate tingle of magic escaping from his beautiful seer. It swirled through Micha with an addictive promise of bliss.

As if overwhelmed by the ruthless tide of need, Skye gently pressed her hand against his chest and stepped out of his arms. Then, turning away, she wandered toward the center of the stone floor.

"I can understand why you are happy to spend your nights lost in these caverns," she murmured, clearly determined to lighten the atmosphere.

Micha didn't bother to try to smother his desire. He was beginning to realize it was a perpetual state of being when he was with Skye, but his passion was only a part of why he enjoyed being in her company. Simply listening to her voice brought him indescribable pleasure.

"They certainly provided me with a legitimate excuse to ignore the world," he confessed, moving to stand beside her as she studied his towering bookshelves.

She sent him a confused glance. "Why would you need an excuse?"

"It took me longer than most vampires to come into my powers," he said, careful not to reveal the hidden sanctuaries that were used to protect newly resurrected vampires. The heavily protected locations were known only to vampires. Just as mages hoarded their own secrets. "For most of my brothers, that was the worst fate imaginable. They craved the power struggles and political backstabbing in their battles to become members of the Cabal." He shrugged. "It didn't trouble me at all. I preferred to spend my time traveling the world and gathering knowledge rather than negotiating and battling my way up the vampire hierarchy." He swept his hand toward the collections that lined the edges of the cavern. "It was a habit I kept even after I was granted this Gyre."

Something flared in her dark eyes. An ancient wound that hadn't fully healed. "It's hard to overcome your past."

He studied her fragile profile, a stab of anger slicing through him at the thought that she'd been hurt and betrayed by the people who were supposed to protect her.

"My past was nothing more than avoiding the petty arguments between my brothers," he conceded. "Not like yours. You were forced into slavery and yet you refused to be broken."

She looked surprised at his fierce words. "Because of Maya and Peri. If I hadn't found them—"

"You would have found another home and created a wonderful life," he interrupted, his brows drawing together. He was accustomed to dealing with vampires and demons who were eager to boast of their accomplishments. Usually exaggerating them beyond recognition. It was aggravating that this woman who had overcome ruthless odds couldn't appreciate her amazing gifts. "You're a survivor."

She stubbornly shook her head. "You wouldn't say that if you knew what my friends went through."

He sent her a chiding frown. "Why do you dismiss what you've achieved?"

"Because I'm not sure what I *have* achieved."

"You were forced to support your father when you were barely more than a baby and then sold off to a horde of demons who abused your gift for their own profit. You could have let them crush your spirit or taint you with bitterness. Instead you molded yourself into a strong and independent and terrifyingly courageous mage."

She paused, clearly not convinced that she was special. "I like to think that I'm independent," she finally conceded. "But I'm not sure I'm courageous. It's more likely I'm too stubborn to admit when I'm in over my head. And I'll never be strong," she insisted.

Micha parted his lips to argue, only to snap them shut. Abruptly he understood. Skye had never been exposed to mages until she'd escaped the demons who held her captive. Not until she'd joined her friends at the Witch's Brew. It was no wonder she considered her magic less than astonishing. Her roommates were two of the most powerful mages in the world. And Peri might very well be the most powerful mage in several millennia. Tough to compare yourself to that.

Reaching out, he grasped her fingers in a light grip and tugged her toward the opening across the cavern.

"Come with me."

"Where are we going?" she asked even as she readily followed his lead.

"I want to show you something."

"Seriously?"

He sent her a baffled glance at her dry tone. "What?"

"This is not the first time I've heard that line."

He chuckled at her unexpected teasing. "I promise. It will be magical."

She shook her head. "You're not helping your cause."

"Trust me," he urged, entering a side tunnel that was wrapped in layers of illusions. It would be invisible to anyone searching the cavern. Even the mage who'd created the opening.

Her steps never faltered as they entered the vast bedroom that was the complete opposite of the outer chambers. There were no stark lines or empty space. This room was lit by the glow of a thousand crystals embedded in the walls, and rich tapestries covered the stone floor. The furniture was a baroque explosion of lavish décor with a four-poster bed draped in crimson and gold and several ebony chests that held his most personal possessions.

Overhead the domed ceiling was painted with bright blue skies and puffy clouds where angels danced.

Angels that had a remarkable resemblance to Skye Claremont, he acknowledged with a stab of surprise. As if he'd already known exactly who he wanted sharing this room.

"Oh," Skye breathed, spinning to take in the vibrant colors that spilled from the crystals. "This is beautiful."

Smugly pleased with her reaction, Micha moved to touch the electronic pad hidden behind a large bronze vase. A second later the soft sounds of a waltz hummed through the air.

He walked toward Skye with a determined step. She watched his approach with arched brows.

"You're not going to strip, are you?"

"Only if you ask very, very nicely," he assured her, stepping close enough to wrap his arms around her waist. "For now I want you to dance with me."

She looked skeptical. "I'm not very good."

"I don't believe that." He gazed down at her. "You're the most graceful creature I've ever seen. Including the elder fairies."

She blushed but stubbornly shook her head. "Not when I'm dancing. Maya says I have the elegance of a drunk rhino."

"Don't worry," he murmured. "I've got you." Tightening his arms around her waist, he began to sweep her in a wide circle. He continued until he could feel her slowly relax and she was matching him step for step. "You've seen the results of my powers, right?"

She tilted back her head, her hair tumbling over her shoulders in a riotous halo of gold. His fangs throbbed. Stunning.

"Do you mean the horrifying vines on your island of death that tried to eat the demons? Those are going to give me nightmares. Or this room that makes me feel like I'm in a palace, even though I should be drowning in swamps and gators?"

"Those might appear to be a symbol of my strength," he agreed, not adding that the flesh-eating vines he'd created to protect the hexed sword were one of his favorite endeavors. "But they didn't save me from certain death. This did."

They continued to circle the open space in the center of the room, as Micha focused on the magic that vibrated around them. They were smack in the middle of the Gyre, and the power was a tangible force. Spreading his powers, he concentrated on condensing the magic until it was squashed into a layer beneath their feet. At least that was how he envisioned what he was doing. Since he'd never encountered another vampire with his gift, he had to make it up as he went along.

The hit-and-miss method had led to a few disasters, but now he could feel the air thickening beneath their feet, creating a platform that allowed them to defy gravity.

It took several seconds of twirling with buoyant ease before Skye gasped in shock. "Are we floating?"

"We are."

"Oh." She smiled in pleasure. "I like this power. But how did it save your life?"

"It was when I was first traveling the world on my own. I'd heard rumors of stone etchings from the earliest days of fairies that revealed them in their true form. Of course, it had to be hidden in flooded caves beneath a remote island. I'd been there less than a week when the local volcano rudely decided to erupt. Before I could escape I was surrounded by rivers of molten lava."

Her smile faded, as if she sensed that his amusing story hadn't been amusing at the time. Honestly, Micha had been inches from a painful death.

"So you floated away?" she asked.

"It was more of a lurching meander just an inch above the liquid magma, but I managed to make it to the nearby sea where I'd left my boat."

She studied him with a searching gaze. "I'm very happy you survived, but I sense you're making a point."

Micha's hands spread across her lower back as he continued to hold them above the ground.

"I am," he assured her. "I wanted you to understand that strength comes in many forms. You might not possess the raw power of your friends, but that doesn't lessen your gifts." He twirled faster, pressing her tight against his hard body. "And..."

"And what?"

"And I wanted a legitimate reason to hold you in my arms," he confessed.

She wrapped her arms around his neck, deliberately nestling against the hard thrust of his arousal.

"So it was a pickup line to lure me into your bedroom?"

"Literally," Micha groaned, tilting his head down to scrape the tips of his fangs along the curve of her neck.

"I feel like I have wings," she whispered.

Micha was drowning in the dizzying scent of sweet desire and laurel leaves, his soul molding and realigning as it created a space for his destined mate.

"I suspected you were an angel from the moment I saw you."

Chapter 15

Valen swiftly gathered his composure and took command of the situation. This wasn't a random act of violence. Someone was either sending a message to Kane or, more likely, Igor had outlived his usefulness and was disposed of before he could reveal his master's secrets.

"You search the body. I'm going to look for a trail," he commanded Gabriel. "We need to know who did this and where they are now."

Not waiting for his friend's nod of agreement, Valen zigzagged his way through the auditorium before heading through the outer lobby and up to the mezzanine. There were layers of scents to follow, but none of them fresh enough to be the killer.

He was studying the busted window when he felt Gabriel cautiously climbing the broken stairs to join him.

"Anything?"

Gabriel shrugged. "He's been dead less than an hour. I couldn't see any defensive marks, which makes me think he knew his attacker." He paused as if considering a new thought. "Or he triggered a very nasty trap."

"I'm going with the knowing-his-attacker theory," Valen said.

"Me too."

"Any indication who that might be?"

"Vampire."

Valen clenched his hands. He didn't have to ask if Gabriel was certain it was a brother. He wouldn't have made the claim if he wasn't one hundred percent sure.

"Who?"

"They were careful not to leave their scent."

"A rare talent," Valen muttered in frustration. He'd heard of vampires who had the ability to disguise their presence, but it was the sort of talent that they were careful to keep a secret. Who knew when it might come in handy?

"Did you have any luck?" Gabriel asked, his gaze sweeping over the broken window.

"Maya and Skye were here," Valen told him.

"In the theater?"

"Here." He pointed toward the scorch marks in the carpet. Signs that a powerful potion had been activated. "They were attacked by demons coming from that direction."

Gabriel glanced back at the shattered stairs. They looked as if they'd been hit with a grenade.

"Impressive."

"Peri isn't the only dangerous mage in my territory," he conceded.

Gabriel turned back, studying the mezzanine that had obviously been shabby and coated in dirt before the battle started.

"What were they doing here?"

"I'm not sure, but Igor attacked them from the balcony. I'm guessing they escaped by jumping out of the window."

"What does this tell us?" Gabriel sounded like a professor prodding his student to think through a problem.

Probably because the older male had once been a mentor at the sanctuary for newly resurrected vampires.

Valen forced himself to shuffle through the few facts they'd managed to discover. It didn't take long.

"Maya and Skye came to the theater, I assume willingly since they didn't lodge a complaint with me or Peri about being kidnapped and forced to the city. They were attacked by unknown demons, including Kane's pet servant."

Gabriel continued the review of the facts. "Next, Skye Claremont attends your reception for the Cabal leaders and speaks privately with Micha before leaving the building, only to return hours later with two fairies to kidnap Micha."

Valen frowned as he realized that their story was taking them in a circle. "Then Maya traces the disguise amulets worn by the fairies to a demon named Hexx who led her back to this theater. This place must have some significance."

"Agreed." Gabriel grimaced. "But we don't know what significance, and we still don't know who is behind the plot or why they targeted Micha."

Valen abruptly reached out to grasp his friend's arm. "Someone's here."

ANCIENT MAGIC 167

"Goblin," Gabriel muttered, heading toward the edge of the balcony. Valen joined him and they peered down at the bald male with broad shoulders and bulging muscles. He was wearing a gray hoodie and jeans and was surrounded by a red glow that marked him as a demon. A grim smile curved Valen's lips as he recognized the male.

Gunther.

In silence they watched the goblin study the body hanging from the chandelier before he turned his attention to the head planted on the stage.

"What the hell?" Gunther muttered, stumbling back even as Valen and Gabriel vaulted over the brass railing of the balcony to land lightly in the middle aisle.

"My exact question," Valen drawled.

With a warning snarl, Gunther spun around, a gun clutched in his hand. At the sight of Valen and Gabriel his eyes widened in fear.

"Your Excellency." Dropping to his knees, Gunther tossed away the weapon and bent his head.

"Gunther." Valen stepped forward, sensing Gabriel moving toward the side door to make sure the demon was alone. "Get to your feet," he commanded, waiting for the male to struggle to surge upright, his head still lowered. "What are you doing here?"

"This is the headquarters for my horde." He struggled to swallow, as if he had a lump in his throat. "I have squatter rights."

Valen ignored the claim, pointing toward the body hanging above their heads. "Are you responsible for this?"

"No way." Gunther gave an emphatic shake of his head. "I couldn't do that even if I wanted to."

He had a point. Gunther was a local bully, but his power was at the low end for demons. In a head-to-head battle, Igor Triton would have ripped him to shreds without breaking a sweat.

This time, Valen pointed at the head on the stage. "Do you recognize him?"

Gunther paused. Was he debating if he could get a lie past Valen? At last deciding it wasn't worth the risk, he offered a grudging nod.

"He calls himself Igor, but I don't know if that's his real name," Gunther said. "He came to New York last month."

Last month? Shock jolted through Valen. Kane's most trusted servant had been creeping around his city for a month? Why the hell hadn't he known? The question burned through his brain, but he already knew the answer. His attention had been consumed with Peri and their mating.

Nothing else had mattered.

Now his distraction was coming back to bite him on the ass.

Valen was careful to keep his expression unreadable as he glared at the nervous demon.

"How do you know him?"

"He started showing up at the clubs around the city flashing lots of money and promising to share it with anyone willing to work for him."

"Doing what?"

"I think he had different jobs for everyone. When he found out I had one of the biggest hordes in the city he hired us to..." The words faltered as Gunther shifted from foot to foot, the scent of his sweat tainting the air.

"To what?"

"A few odds and ends," he muttered, the old-fashioned phrase exposing his age. Demons weren't immortal, but their lives were counted in centuries, not years. When they were nervous or upset they allowed past clichés, or even long-forgotten words, to slip into the conversation.

Valen narrowed his gaze. "'Odds and ends' is a little vague."

Gunther licked his lips. "You know. We ran some errands and introduced him around the neighborhood."

With a blur, Valen's arm snapped out and he had his fingers wrapped around the male's thick neck. He squeezed just hard enough to make Gunther's eyeballs bulge in terror.

"Listen very carefully," he commanded, his voice a mere whisper. "I claimed this Gyre centuries after I'd matured and learned to control my emotions. Before then I was known as a butcher. A leader who was always willing to kill first and ask questions later." It wasn't an exaggeration. There'd been vicious stretches of history when his name had inflicted terror among the demons. "Don't ever mistake my desire for peace for weakness."

"Please." The word came out as a pained grunt. "What do you want?"

"The truth. What did the demon pay you to do?"

"Cause trouble."

Valen peeled back his lips to reveal the lethal length of his fangs. "You're pissing me off, Gunther. Tell me what he paid you to do. Exactly."

"Okay." More lip licking. "He hired us to tear shit up."

Valen loosened his grip on the male's throat. That wasn't what he'd been expecting. "Why?"

"We'd trash houses or set buildings on fire and then tell people that we'd seen your mate losing control of her magic. Stuff like that."

Valen should have laughed. It was inconceivable that anyone would believe such bullshit. But he didn't laugh. Because at least a few of his people had believed. At least enough to cause a low hum of prejudice against Peri.

"There had to be more," he said in cold tones, knowing that Kane wouldn't have snuck his servant into New York City just to set a few fires and spread gossip.

Gunther hunched his shoulders, as if preparing for a blow. "I hired a witch who looks sort of like your mate and filmed her in the park pretending to drink demon blood and sacrifice babies. Then I put it out on social media saying I'd witnessed her trying to use her evil magic to take over the Gyre."

Valen hissed as he suddenly understood the animosity that had been brewing for weeks.

Ice coated the nearby seats as he struggled to retain control of his temper. "You were behind the rumors."

"Igor wanted people afraid of your mate."

"Why?" he growled.

Gabriel returned to the auditorium, obviously satisfied there were no hidden dangers.

"So that Kane could claim Peri is a threat to the Cabal and that you should be replaced," Gabriel said, revealing he'd been listening to the conversation. "Preferably by him."

"Shit." Valen clenched his hands, infuriated by the nights he'd chased one empty threat after another while Kane played him like a puppet on his strings. It was embarrassing. "Why didn't I suspect from the start that I was being sabotaged? The destruction was too organized to be random."

"Because you feared that your people wouldn't accept Peri as your mate." Gabriel offered his blunt opinion. "Especially when they discovered her ability to tap into ancient magic."

Valen flinched. Gabriel was right, of course. There'd been a part of him that had been prepared for the local demons to protest against Peri. Not only because they had vied for centuries to lure him into choosing a mate from one of the royal families, but demons didn't trust mages. Especially one who had the power to destroy a skyscraper.

"Kane's greatest skill has always been to divide and conquer," he snarled, recalling the male's scheming during his short time in St. Petersburg.

With an effort, Valen shoved away his seething emotions. Later he could wallow all he wanted in shame and self-reproach. Nothing mattered now but discovering why Micha had been kidnapped. And more importantly, his current location.

And if the answers led to Kane being banished or even forced to walk into the sunlight, so much the better.

Reaching into his pocket, Valen pulled out his phone and scrolled to the picture of Lynx he'd copied and enlarged from the security tape.

"Tell me about this male." He turned the phone so Gunther could see the screen.

The demon started to shake his head, only to hesitate. "Wait. I think I've seen him around the city."

"What's his name?"

"I don't know. Just a fairy hanging around—"

The words were cut short as Valen once again grabbed the male by the throat and squeezed. He very much wanted to keep squeezing. This male had deliberately provoked hostility toward Peri. A hostility that had wounded her feelings and put her life at risk. Worse, it would take years to reverse the damage.

But as much as he wanted the pleasure of crushing the male's throat, he needed information. Later he would enjoy his revenge.

"Think very carefully about your next answer," he warned. "The fairy attacked a member of the Cabal. Tell me what you know about him."

"Nothing. I swear." The demon struggled to breathe, the stench of his fear polluting the air. Any violence directed toward a vampire was a death sentence for demons. A slow, painful death sentence. "I saw him a few times in the local demon clubs but I never spoke to him."

"Someone was helping him," Valen hissed.

"Not me."

"How many of your horde work at my lair?"

Gunther stared at him in confusion, as if he didn't understand the simple question.

"Work at your lair?" he repeated, his lashes lowering over his bloodshot eyes. "None of them. We're just street thugs. We sell some dope and occasionally shake down the local businesses for offering them protection." He squeaked as Valen's fingers tightened. "Shit, I'm being honest." The demon turned his head enough to glare toward the head on the stage. "I was out of my fucking mind to let that bastard convince me to cause trouble. I might not be a devoted citizen, but I'm not an idiot. I would never have attacked the Cabal. And I don't know nothing about the fairy."

Frustration crashed through Valen. Gunther was telling the truth. Or at least the truth as far as he knew it.

"Other members of your horde might not have been so reluctant to make money on the side," Valen suggested, more out of desperation than genuine hope.

"That's true, I suppose."

The demon looked doubtful. Valen didn't blame him. He carefully interrogated the staff who were allowed access to his lair, no matter what their job title. It seemed doubtful that a street thug had managed to sneak their way past his layers of security. But someone had given Lynx the key to the private guest rooms, he grimly reminded himself.

"I want them gathered in my office within the hour," he commanded. It was past time that he interviewed everyone in the building.

Gunther's mouth opened and closed, like a fish out of water. "I can't," he finally forced himself to admit.

Valen hissed, lifting the demon off his feet until they were nose to nose. "You're playing a dangerous game."

Gunther wheezed in desperation, his square face turning a weird shade of puce. "It's no game," he rasped. "I haven't been able to contact any of them."

"Since when?"

"I..." Gunther's eyes started to roll back in his head, and with an impatient click of his tongue, Valen released his grip and allowed him to drop awkwardly to the ground.

"When was the last time you met with your horde?" Valen repeated his question as Gunther massaged his thick neck.

"We were all at the theater a couple days ago," he said, his voice hoarse. "Why?"

"Igor demanded we meet with him. I thought we were going to get paid but he said he had more jobs for us to do. None of us were happy about that. You can't spend promises, and my bitch was starting to complain—"

"Get to the point," Valen sharply interrupted.

"Yeah, okay." Gunther coughed, his hand still rubbing his bruised neck. "Igor had only been here a few minutes when we realized there were a couple of mages hiding in the balcony. I don't know if they were pissed about us causing trouble for your mate, but they took out three of my crew and the rest of us scattered." He glanced around the empty auditorium as if hoping they might suddenly appear. "I've been trying to get in contact with them ever since then, but...nada. It's like they just vanished."

Gabriel took a step forward, sending Valen a worried glance. "Or someone made them vanish."

Valen nodded, equally worried. The list of questions kept growing. The list of answers did not. It was enough to infuriate the most patient vampire.

"So why are you here?" Valen snapped.

"I've been coming back here every few hours, hoping one of them might be hanging around," Gunther explained, his voice edged with genuine loss. He might be a criminal, but the horde was obviously the only friends and family he had. "Or at least someone might have left a message telling me where they're hiding." His gaze returned to the rotting head. "The last thing I expected was a mutilated demon and two leeches."

"Is it unusual for them to disappear?"

Gunther spread his hands, his expression baffled. "One or even two of them might go off the radar for a few nights. But they're usually holed up with some bitch or sleeping off a bender. The whole crew doesn't fall off the face of the earth."

"Someone's getting rid of the witnesses," Gabriel said, pointing out an obvious explanation for the missing demons.

"Kane," Valen growled.

Gabriel nodded. "He either got spooked and is cleaning up his mess, or he's confident his plot has succeeded and is preparing to challenge you for the Gyre."

The words sent a blast of fear through Valen. He still didn't know why Kane would kill his most loyal servant or what he'd done to Micha, but the thought that he was clearing the way to take over the Gyre was enough to have him rushing toward the door.

"I have to get back to Peri." Reaching out, he grabbed Gunther by the arm as he passed by. "Let's go."

Gunther tried to dig in his heels as he was roughly dragged down the hall. "Actually, I need to get back to my bitch." He yelped as Valen tightened his grip until the demon's arm threatened to break. Abruptly he stopped trying to get free and instead scurried to keep up with Valen's long strides. "Yeah, sure. No problem."

In silence they made their way back to Gabriel's waiting vehicle. Then, squashing the nervous Gunther between him and Gabriel in the back seat, Valen motioned for the driver to return them to the lair.

The cresting dawn pressed heavily against Valen, warning him how close he'd come to losing track of time. Something that hadn't happened since... never. An indication of just how distracted he was by Kane's lethal games.

Thankfully, Gabriel's vehicle was custom designed and the tinted windows kept out the rosy glow spreading over the horizon. And of course, the towering buildings kept the sidewalks shadowed as they reached his lair and they climbed out and hurried through the glass doors.

It was still early enough that Valen expected the lobby to be empty. The offices didn't open for another hour, and beyond the on-duty guards, there was no reason for anyone to be there. Instead, he walked in to discover a crowd gathered in the center of the floor.

On one side were three of his guards half circled around a familiar woman, and on the other side were four of Kane's servants, visibly bristling as their red auras pulsed with the threat of violence.

"Peri," he rasped, the earth shaking and the massive glass windows threatening to shatter as he took in the sight of the largest demon grabbing his mate's arm.

"Valen!" She tried to step forward, only to be halted as the demon tightened his grip.

Valen's fury continued to vibrate through the lobby despite the fact Peri was clearly more annoyed than terrified. Typical of his mate. She had no concept of fear.

"Release her," he commanded.

The demons turned to face him, his own staff appearing relieved to avoid an unpleasant confrontation with no clear idea of whether they were allowed to kick the asses of the visiting demons. Even Kane's men appeared uneasy. As if equally unsure what the rules of engagement were.

Jerking out of the distracted demon's grasp, Peri rushed toward him, throwing herself against his body and wrapping her arms around his waist.

"Thank God. I was so worried. I woke up and I couldn't find you and those..." She turned her head to glare back at the guards, who paled as she released a spell that created tiny flames spinning through the air. "Those jerks refused to let me leave the building."

The demons stumbled back and Valen hid his smile as the nearest demon lifted his hand to bat away the swirling flames, sweat dripping down his square face.

"We were told to keep her in the building," the male protested, continuing to fight the flames until Peri grudgingly extinguished her spell. "Even the ambassador said no one was to leave."

Valen glanced toward the tallest of his guards. Mercado had been with him since he'd first taken control of this Gyre and was one of his most trusted servants.

"Take them to the dungeons," Valen ordered, shoving the silent Gunther forward. "Including this one."

A smile of anticipation curved Mercado's lips even as Kane's demons exchanged horrified glances.

"What the hell?" the seeming leader of Kane's crew sputtered. "You can't do that. My master told us—"

Mercado stepped forward and smashed his fist into the back of the male's head. The male grunted before flopping to the floor like a bag of wet cement. "Thank you," Valen muttered.

Mercado's smile widened, revealing that Valen hadn't been the only one infuriated by the arrogance of Kane's servants who'd strutted around the place like they already owned it.

"My pleasure," he assured Valen.

Not bothering to wait for his staff to gather the prisoners and haul them down to the cells built far beneath the building, Valen headed toward the elevators.

"What's going on?" Peri demanded, easily keeping pace. "Do you know where Skye is?"

"I'm hoping to find out," he promised, gripping her shoulders as the steel doors whisked open. "Wait for me in the penthouse."

"Absolutely not."

"Peri, this is Cabal business."

His soft tone did nothing to persuade her to obey his request. Shocker.

"We're in this together." She planted her fists on her hips, glaring at him. "Besides, it's not just Cabal business. Skye is a mage. And more importantly, she's my sister."

"This could get ugly," he insisted. "I intend to get answers from Kane no matter what I have to do."

"I hope it does get ugly. I have several curses loaded and ready to go." Her face was grim as she held up her arm to reveal the jade bracelet that glowed from the magic pulsing in the green depths. "If you can't beat the answers out of him, then I'll make him wish he had never been resurrected."

Pride swelled in Valen as he gazed down at the woman who'd stolen his unbeating heart. She would move heaven and earth for the people she loved.

"Fine." He conceded to the inevitable. "But don't kill anyone until I get some answers."

She clicked her tongue, stepping into the elevator. "I'm not making any promises."

"You have an interesting life, Valen," Gabriel murmured as he stepped past Valen to enter the lift.

"You have no idea," Valen agreed, joining them before he pulled out his keycard to send the elevator dropping to the lower floor.

Once they reached the guest floor, he stepped out and glanced toward his companion.

Valen possessed a skill in tracking both demons and vampires, but Gabriel was able to sense their presence even when they were miles away.

"Is Kane here?" he asked the older vampire.

"No."

"Can you follow his trail?"

Gabriel tilted back his head, as if testing the air for various scents. "There's nothing," he at last announced. "It's like someone scrubbed away any hint of his presence."

Valen snapped his fangs together. Okay, it'd been a lot to hope that Kane would return to the lair and hang around long enough to be tortured into revealing his devious plans. Or better yet, left an easy-to-follow trail to where he'd stashed Micha and Skye.

Still, he could have left behind something to help them figure out what the hell was going on.

"The ambassador?" he forced himself to ask.

Gabriel shrugged. "Not here."

With a frown, Valen headed to the double doors that led to the ambassador's suite. He'd deliberately given the male the best rooms in the hope that Sinjon would appreciate the gesture and give Peri the benefit of the doubt.

Laying his hand against the smooth wood, he gently pushed on the door, grimacing when it easily slid open. He didn't need Gabriel's skills to sense that the suite was empty, so it was no surprise when he walked through the elegant living room and into the bedroom not to discover Azra waiting for him. What was a surprise was the fact that there was no indication the male had been there at all.

The bed was neatly made, the closets were empty, and the leather suitcases gone. There wasn't a trace that he'd ever been there. Not even a stray scent.

"Where did he go?" Valen muttered.

Gabriel stood at his side, his expression troubled. "I don't know, but it's not good."

"We need to look at the security footage." Valen turned and headed back through the suite.

He was near the door when he was brought to a sharp halt as Gabriel grabbed his shoulder.

"Wait," he commanded, nodding toward the intercom system that had been ripped out of the wall, the cords charred as if they'd been set on fire. "I don't think it's going to help."

Valen clenched his hands. "Dammit."

Chapter 16

Skye stepped out of the thick vegetation and halted in surprise. They'd arrived in Panama less than four hours after sunset and taken a short helicopter ride to be dumped in the middle of a mangrove forest. It'd felt remarkably like they were still in Louisiana with lots of green mossy plants and soft swampy ground until she stepped into the unexpected clearing. She turned in a slow circle, amazed by the abrupt change in scenery. The swampy ground was replaced with slick craggy rocks, and directly in front of her the mouth of a vast cave rose like a beast from the age of dragons, ready to swallow the unwary. The moonlight spilled from a sky that appeared close enough to reach up and pluck a silvery star from the dark velvet, reflecting in the water that pooled in low areas.

"Oh, it's beautiful," she breathed, then instinctively she clapped her hand over her mouth. "Sorry."

Stepping next to her, Micha studied her with a searching gaze. "Why are you apologizing? It is beautiful."

Beautiful...yes. Skye melted as she tilted back her head to absorb the sight of the male's outrageous splendor. From the start she'd thought he looked like a god. Now, surrounded by the lush primitive landscape, he was even more divine. A dark, mysterious deity too perfect to be real.

"We're here to stop the world from going down in flames, not to admire the scenery," she said, not adding that Micha was enough of a distraction.

"We can do both, can't we?" he asked in confusion.

Skye wrinkled her nose. The apology had been instinctive. Over the years, she'd developed an ability to isolate the visions from her day-to-day life. It was the only way to keep her sanity, and for the most part, the visions didn't affect her on a personal level. It didn't mean she'd forgotten the visions, just that she was able to keep them contained so they didn't overwhelm her.

"Most people wouldn't think so," she said. "They don't understand how I can see someone's imminent death and then spend the day baking muffins."

An eerie stillness settled around Micha. When he was distracted he forgot to look human.

"Damn. I just realized how hard it must be for you not to allow the visions to taint your life," he said in soft tones. "They must be overwhelming at times."

"Crushing," she agreed. If Micha truly intended to spend a future with her, then he needed to know that her magic had a cost. "That's why I try to limit contact with people I don't know."

With an ease that made Skye's heart skip a beat, Micha grabbed her hips and tugged her close, gazing down at her with a stark intensity. She lifted her hands to smooth them over his chest, reminded of long daylight hours they'd spent stretched on his mattress. They hadn't shared more than slow, drugging kisses, but it had been glorious. And wrapped tightly in his arms, she'd eventually fallen into a deep sleep that had restored her badly depleted magic.

"Which means more contact for me," he said in a husky growl.

Anticipation curled in the pit of her stomach as she became lost in the rich golden gaze. "You triggered my last vision, remember?"

"Never again." He leaned down to press a lingering kiss against her lips. "I promise."

Skye curled her fingers into the soft fabric of his jacket. They were both dressed in black jeans and matching black windbreakers. They couldn't hide themselves from the demons, but they hoped to avoid attracting the attention of any local humans.

"You make a lot of bold promises," she reminded him.

"I'm attempting to convince you that I should be a part of your life."

Going onto her tiptoes, Skye kissed him hard enough to feel the delicious press of his fangs.

"I'm already convinced."

"Skye..."

Her name died on his lips as Micha jerked his head up, the encircling vegetation swaying as if he was using his powers to search the area for intruders.

"You sense something?" she demanded, touching the charms attached to her bracelet. They glowed in the moonlight, the echo of Peri's wild magic tingling in the air.

"Copper." Micha at last identified the scent that had captured his attention.

"Lynx." She sent Micha a tight smile. They'd taken a risk to trust the memory spell might be connected to the fairy's current quest for the mysterious sword. It was a relief to know that the gamble had paid off.

"Yes. And there's five other demons with him." He nodded toward the far side of the clearing. "They're headed this way. Let's see where they go."

Silently retracing their steps, Skye and Micha disappeared in the lush plants even as Lynx stepped into the open.

He'd pulled his golden hair into a braid and had changed into a spandex shirt and pants that clung faithfully to his lean muscles. He looked like he was about to hit the gym. Then the moonlight coated him in silver, revealing the bleak determination etched on his features.

This was a fairy on a mission.

"Stop," he said, his tone sharp as he held up a hand. "I want you to wait for me here."

The ever-faithful Yugan came to a startled halt. "You're going alone?"

"You're not allowed to follow me into the sacred chamber," Lynx told him smoothly.

"But—"

"And I need you to watch my back. I'm too close to have that damned leech interfere."

Without waiting for his crew to agree, Lynx marched forward, his back stiff as he entered the cave. Was he afraid?

Watching as the fairy disappeared from view, Skye was distracted as Micha leaned close enough to speak directly in her ear.

"The servants don't trust him."

Skye studied the five demons, who exchanged glances as they shuffled from foot to foot. Micha was right. It wasn't just that they were nervous about being at the cave. She could smell the distrust that prickled in the air between them.

"Maybe not," she conceded, nodding toward the shorter male with chopped red hair and a green aura. "But Yugan isn't going to let us get past him."

Micha hesitated, as if debating with himself, then he reached to cup her hands in his palms.

"I'll take care of the guards. You follow Lynx."

"There's five of them." Skye blew out a sigh as she realized what she was saying. A vampire of Micha's strength could destroy a dozen demons. But that didn't mean it wasn't dangerous. Over the past few days the unpleasant surprises just kept piling up. "Okay, but don't show off."

"I might show off a little." His thumb brushed her lower lip. "Just to impress you."

"Micha."

He kissed away her protest before lifting his head and regarding her with a somber gaze.

"I'll lead them away. You follow Lynx, but don't try to stop him." The muscles in his jaw bulged, revealing how hard it was to encourage her to walk into a potential trap. "Wait for me."

"I thought I was a powerful mage," she teased, trying to lighten the mood.

"You are." An emotion that seemed too vast to be contained darkened the golden eyes. "You're also precious. If something happened to you—"

She pressed her fingers against his lips, her heart thudding. "Nothing's going to happen to me."

With an effort, Micha leashed his emotions, allowing the tip of his fang to press into the pad of her finger.

"Now who's making bold promises?"

"You must be rubbing off on me."

He grasped her wrist, pressing a kiss into the center of her palm. "Be careful."

"Same," she commanded, her heart lodging in her throat as Micha rose and boldly strolled into the clearing.

"I thought I smelled something rotten," he drawled, crossing to stand directly in front of Yugan. "The swamp stench really lingers, doesn't it?"

The demon hissed, yanking a silver dagger from a sheath at his hip. "You should know, leech."

"Me? I smell as fresh as a daisy." Micha leaned forward. "Want a sniff?"

Yugan growled, swinging the blade toward Micha's chest. "Sniff this, you cold-blooded reptile."

Micha easily dodged the strike, spreading his arms in a taunting gesture. "You're a walking, talking cliché. Do you even try?"

Yugan glanced over his shoulder at the demons who were gawking at Micha in horror.

"Look for the mage. She has to be close by."

Micha took a step back, luring the demon away from the mouth of the cave. At the same time, Skye breathed a soft spell, wrapping herself in the scent of the surrounding plants.

She couldn't entirely disguise her presence, but she could make it more difficult for the demons to locate her. Then, bending low, she inched her way around the edge of the mangrove forest.

"You honestly believe I would bring a vulnerable young woman into the middle of a demon revolt?" Micha asked in a loud voice, keeping Yugan distracted.

"She's not a woman. She's a mage."

Skye's brows arched at the bitter edge in the male's voice. There were plenty of demons who didn't like mages, but Yugan sounded as if his aversion was personal.

"She's still mortal. There's no predicting what will happen if Lynx gets his hands on the Tempest." Micha allowed a loaded silence to fill the clearing. "Assuming it even exists."

Skye continued to creep forward, dodging the demons trying to battle their way through the thick foliage in search of her.

"It exists," Yugan growled, taking another stab at Micha. "And what's going to happen is you're about to be destroyed."

"Along with you," Micha taunted.

Through the tufts of ferns, Skye could see Yugan jerk, as if Micha had managed to strike an open wound.

"What?"

Micha clicked his tongue. "You're not stupid enough to think Lynx will leave any witnesses alive, are you? Not when they can reveal the source of his brand-new power."

Yugan lunged forward, swearing as Micha easily danced away. "He wants demons to know he has the Tempest," the fairy snapped, regaining his balance. "It's legendary. Everyone would unite behind him."

Skye picked up her speed, approaching the cave from the side. She wanted to be in position to dart inside as soon as Yugan was far enough away.

"It's also a warning to all vampires," Micha insisted. "If they suspect the sword has been found, they'll attack and destroy Lynx before he can organize his revolution. He needs time to prepare, and for that, he needs secrecy. And the only way to make sure you won't spill the proverbial beans is to kill you."

"You're full of shit." Yugan's voice was harsh, but he couldn't entirely disguise his uncertainty. This wasn't the first time he'd considered the possibility that he was demon fodder. "Lynx needs us."

The demon lunged again and Micha leaped backward, nearly at the edge of the clearing.

"Every leader needs sacrifices to the cause. That's you." Micha continued to mock the demon, keeping his attention focused on him as Skye inched out of the cover of the undergrowth. "If he truly thought you were going to be a part of his revolution, he would want you with him to witness his moment of glory. That way you could spread the word. Instead you're stuck out here."

"To keep out the trash."

"He could just kill me with his new sword, right? No need for you to risk fighting me. Not unless he wants me to take care of his dirty work. Which is fine with me. It's been centuries since I had a decent fight."

Micha peeled back his lips to expose his fangs, and Skye darted forward. If Yugan wasn't fully distracted by the vampire about to rip out his throat, then he was never going to be distracted.

Plunging into the darkness of the cave, Skye gasped as she skidded on the slick stones. Windmilling her arms, she managed to remain upright but wisely slowed her pace. She was there to save the world, not fall on her ass.

Struggling to see through the gloom, she at last spotted the narrow crack on the back wall. She hurried forward, not giving herself time to consider the wisdom of what she was doing as she squeezed into the narrow tunnel. She could smell the lingering trace of copper in the air. This was where Lynx had gone.

She placed her hand on the stone wall, using it to guide her through the darkness. It felt as if she was angling down, but she couldn't see more than a few feet in front of her. Two things were certain, the air was getting thicker and the temperature was rising. As if she were headed into a sauna.

Even the stone beneath her hand was heating enough that she wondered if there was a fire on the other side. Or maybe a hot spring nearby? Or a volcano? The warmth felt natural, not magical. Which she assumed was a good thing.

Clinging to that hope, Skye stepped out of the end of the tunnel and into another cave. This one was smaller, with a low roof and sharp stones protruding from the floor. Oh, and an angry fairy glaring at her with murder in his eyes.

"Hello, Lynx," she murmured, acting as if she'd expected to find him there instead of accidentally stumbling across him.

With a visible effort, Lynx smoothed away his annoyance and forced a stiff smile.

"Seer. You just can't take a hint, can you?"

Too late to wait for Micha. Skye stepped forward even as she kept the tunnel blocked. Unless there was a hidden doorway, that was the only exit.

"Are you implying you're not happy to see me?" she demanded.

"I'm always delighted to have a beautiful woman following me around, but you're bordering on stalking." He flicked a knowing glance down her body. "Isn't the leech satisfying your itches, my dear?"

"Itches?" Skye sent him a chiding frown. "Really?"

Lynx shook his head, as if regretting his lame response. Then, seemingly convinced she posed no immediate threat, he turned his back to her to investigate the wall.

"I'm preoccupied," he muttered. "My banter might not be at its sparkly best."

She watched as he ran his hands over the rocks. Did he think the sword was stuck in the stone? Or was there a hidden key?

She didn't bother to ask. He wasn't going to willingly give her information, even if he didn't think she was a threat.

Instead, she concentrated on keeping him distracted. Micha would soon get rid of the demons. The longer she could keep Lynx from locating the sword, the better.

"Did you enjoy your nap?"

Lynx hissed in anger, but he never turned around as he continued his search. "That wasn't a very nice thing to do."

"You threatened to slit the throat of my friend and then kidnapped a member of the Cabal. I don't think you get to be the nice police."

"Fine. But in my defense I didn't realize you had a crush on the vampire when I kidnapped him."

"Neither did I," Skye admitted in wry tones. "No one's more shocked than I am."

Lynx made a gagging noise and Skye inched closer, her brows lifting as she caught the glint of ruby red between the male's clenched fingers. He was using the crystal to locate the sword. She didn't know if it would work or not, but it was probably best to try to convince Lynx to give up his hunt before they found out.

"Do you know what that crystal is?" she demanded.

"I told you." He skimmed his hand from side to side, the tension in his body visible as his futile search continued. "A compass."

"No."

"You need the proof?" Lynx abruptly whirled around and held out his arm. Then, with a grim smile, he jerked up his sleeve to reveal the bright red lines that marked his skin. "As soon as I touched the crystal, this map appeared."

From a distance it was impossible to see the intricate details, but it certainly explained how Lynx had managed to find the cave.

"Nice trick." She shrugged, hoping she looked unimpressed. "So where's the sword?"

It was a genuine question. If the crystal was the same as the one they'd seen in the memory spell, then it was the combination of vampire and dragon blood that sealed the treaty, not a mystical map to a demon sword.

"It will be in my hand soon enough," Lynx assured her, returning to his search without fear she might be a threat. Jerk.

She took another step forward. If Micha didn't show up soon she was going to have to take matters into her own hands. A prospect that didn't bother her at all. She knew Peri well enough to suspect at least one of the curses on her charm bracelet was pus-filled abscesses that would cover a demon's body for weeks. That would tarnish Lynx's smug arrogance.

"And what if you do get the sword?" she asked, running her fingers over the powerful charms.

"What else? World domination."

"Of course it's world domination. So predictable." Skye rolled her eyes. "What if I tell you I had a vision?"

"About me?"

"You're included."

"Unless it's a revelation of me uniting the demons and conquering the world, then I'm not interested."

"If you do conquer it, there will be nothing to rule." Skye rarely shared her visions. They could be interpreted a thousand different ways, and since there was no way to know what might or might not change them, or if the effort of altering them would make things worse, it was better to let it play out. But not this time. It wasn't just Lynx's fate in the balance. It was the world. "We're all about to be consumed in flames."

"Consumed in flames? Seriously?" Lynx glanced over his shoulder, but he wasn't troubled by her declaration. The bastard was amused. "You must be fun on a date."

"Actually I'm delightful. Everyone says so," Skye ground out. "That doesn't change what I've seen."

"Make up whatever crazy story you want, you're not going to stop me."

Abruptly Lynx stiffened, his hand surrounded by a glowing light as if it'd connected with a hidden power. A second later there was a low scrape and the thick stones began to part.

Skye rushed forward. Any other time, she would be enchanted by the idea of a secret doorway. When she was very young she would dream of stepping out of the shabby camper she shared with Howard to discover she'd been whisked into an enchanted land where her mother would be waiting to greet her with open arms. Now, however, she was quite certain the doorway led to death and destruction.

"Lynx, I'm telling the truth," she called out, her voice shrill. "That crystal brought you here, but it isn't a map to your fabled sword."

Lynx ignored her urgent warning. Of course he did. Stubborn ass. Without glancing back he darted forward and disappeared. Immediately the stones started to swing closed and Skye hissed in frustration. Tapping into her magic, she plaited the air into a thick cushion to keep it propped open. There was a real possibility if it closed, they wouldn't be able to open it again. Not without the crystal.

It wasn't until she was actually tying off the spell that Skye realized the door hadn't stopped. Instead, it continued to inch shut, as if the magic was actively fighting to squeeze through the wedge of air that she'd created.

Who was going to win? Well, Skye wasn't a betting woman despite her ability to peek into the future, but if she was, she wouldn't be placing a wad of money on herself. Not when her magic was fading like dew beneath a scorching sun.

Dropping to her knees, Skye fiercely concentrated to keep the narrow gap open. Still, it wasn't until sweat was coating her face and every muscle was trembling that she felt the cool rush of Micha's presence.

A second later, a large form knelt beside her, and strong arms circled her in a protective hug.

"Skye, are you injured?"

"No, but my magic is wearing out," she rasped between clenched teeth. "Lynx went through the crack in the wall."

Thankfully, Micha could easily sense she was barely hanging onto her spell and, resisting the urge to bombard her with questions, he flowed forward and jammed his fingers into the barely visible fissure. The rocks cracked and popped again, but this time it wasn't magic that was pulling them apart, it was Micha's raw strength.

Sucking in a shaky breath, Skye stared in amazement as Micha gripped the edges of the rock and ruthlessly pried apart the fissure. Or maybe she was staring at the muscles that bulged and rippled at the intense effort. Either way it was a vision that was going to be seared in her mind for a very long time.

"That's as wide as it's going to get," he warned, his voice strained from the effort. "Hurry."

With a shake of her head, Skye scurried forward, turning sideways to squeeze through the crack. She could admire Micha later. Hopefully when he was stretched naked on a soft bed with no worry the world was about to go up in flames.

Until then, she needed to concentrate on staying alive.

At last through the narrow opening, Skye glanced around the cave that was larger than the last one, with a coved ceiling that was lost in shadows. Behind her she could hear Micha swearing as he wiggled his way through the too-small space, no doubt scratching off his top layer of skin. In front of her was...emptiness.

Nothing but barren rock with a hole carved into the far wall.

Lynx was long gone, but she could still smell his coppery scent, so he couldn't have gone far. But oddly, she could also smell lush tropical plants. As if she was standing in the middle of a jungle, not deep underground and surrounded by stone.

Confused by the scent, Skye was vaguely aware of Micha moving to stand next to her, but it wasn't until there was a low, booming thud that sounded eerily like the closing of a tomb that she realized the opening had slammed shut behind him.

Skye shuddered. "I don't like the sound of that."

Micha grasped her hand, his expression grim. "I guess we go forward."

She tilted back her head to study his exquisite features. Suddenly she didn't care if they were locked in the cave or not. She was exactly where she wanted to be.

Next to Micha.

"Together," she murmured.

Lifting her hand, he pressed it against his mouth. "Forever."

Chapter 17

Micha cautiously headed toward the opening across the cave. He could feel the faint breeze coming from the hole in the far wall that revealed it opened into another cave. More importantly, it carried the faint scent of fairy. Lynx had gone through the hole.

Which meant *they* had to go through the hole.

Even if it felt like an obvious trap.

"What happened to the demons?" Skye asked, as if hoping to ease the tension that hummed around them.

Micha shrugged. The demons hadn't been overly powerful, but they'd rushed back to attack him with a furious determination.

It'd taken him longer than expected to convince them to play somewhere else.

"A few refused to accept defeat. The others scattered," he informed her. He didn't feel guilt for ripping the throats out of the ones who continued to fight. He would destroy anyone or anything that was a threat to the woman walking next to him. "They won't be back anytime soon."

"Then it's just Lynx we have to worry about," she said, only to come to a sharp halt when the pungent scent of rotting vegetation swirled through the air. A second later the ground beneath their feet began to tremble as if something very large was about to break through the stone. "Crap. I just jinxed us, didn't I?" she rasped in horror.

Pulling her close, Micha spread his legs as the quakes intensified and the rock started to crumble.

"Is it magic?" he demanded.

She grasped his arm to keep her balance. "I think we tripped a ward."

Micha hissed as the floor crumbled to dust, and large green vines poked through the rubble. At first they were the size of a tree trunk, looking like the arms of an octopus as they waved in the air, seeking something to grab. But as they continued to grow, sharp thorns ruptured through the green flesh.

It looked like a monster out of a nightmare.

And it wasn't alone.

From high above, Micha could hear the sound of the stones popping and fracturing as a massive force pressed against them.

Moving to stand in front of Skye, Micha used his arm as a shield as the vine struck toward them with lightning speed. The thorn sliced through his flesh and he winced in pain. The wound was deep, but on the plus side, he didn't feel any poison pumping through his body. Within seconds his skin was knitting back together.

"Why didn't the creature attack Lynx?" he growled, glancing up as more vines punctured through the ceiling. "The fairy would never have survived."

Skye considered her answer, the scent of laurel leaves filling the air as if she was struggling to determine what was happening.

"It's possible the crystal allowed him to pass," she at last admitted.

"Because this is the place where it was created?"

"I don't know. The power is strange."

Micha felt a blast of energy zoom past his shoulder before the nearest vine shuddered, as if hit by a spell. The vines jerked back with a shrill cry, as if they'd been injured. It was unnerving as hell. Almost as unnerving as watching a crimson glow form around the plant, melting Skye's spell and healing the vines.

"Really strange," Skye muttered. "I don't know how to stop it."

"Then we go through it," Micha announced.

Not giving her the opportunity to protest, Micha braced himself as the nearest vine lashed toward them with a furious intent. The thing was obviously self-aware enough to be pissed off. But so was he. All he wanted was to find Lynx, kill the bastard, and get back to his lair with Skye. Anything getting in the way of that plan was going to be destroyed.

Waiting until the vine was mere inches from his face, he snatched the tip and started to squeeze. The flesh was spongy beneath his grip, easily collapsing. Micha tightened his grip, refusing to allow the creature to slip away. There was another shrill squeal. This time it was fury, not pain, and the remaining vines slithered forward, preparing to strike.

Micha ignored the threat as he focused his powers on the pulp squashed in his hand. The plant was magically enhanced, but it had been created out of nature and he could sense it response to his touch. Plus, they were at the edges of the nearest Gyre. Just close enough to amp up his power. Releasing a sharp burst of energy, he directed it back through the vine. Usually he was attempting to mold the world around him to satisfy his needs. Like creating his cavern out of the wetlands. Or twisting the native vegetation into a lethal defense around the temple. This time, he was trying to kill. As quickly as possible.

As if sensing it was in danger, the nearby vines swung toward him, the thorns now the length of daggers. Micha didn't falter. It was going to be a test of endurance to see if he could kill the creepy thing before it sliced him to ribbons.

Braced for the painful strike, Micha was caught off guard when a large stone flew over his head to smash into the approaching vine with enough force to snap it in two. What the hell?

A quick glance over his shoulder revealed a pale-faced Skye bending down to whisper words over an even larger rock. She hadn't been able to stop the plant with her magic, but she could give him the opportunity to destroy it. As he watched, the rock levitated off the ground and soared toward yet another vine, knocking it backward as the plant screamed in fury.

Grimly, Micha returned his focus to the power he was pumping through the vine in his hand. It wouldn't take Skye long to deplete her magic, and then he would be at the mercy of the thorns. And worse, there were tendrils drilling their way through the ceiling, curling down to wrap around his head.

"We're going to take a very long vacation in the middle of the desert when we get out of here," he muttered.

"Maybe Antarctica," Skye panted. "It's smothering in here."

Micha allowed his icy essence to spread outward, wrapping it around his companion. "Is that better?"

"Not really." Her voice was tight, as if she was in pain. "There's not enough air."

Micha swore as he realized that the magic of the plant was sucking the oxygen from the room. A potent means to kill both humans and demons. But not vampires...

Sending one last blast of power through the plant, he watched in fierce satisfaction as the vines shuddered in agony, swaying back in an attempt to avoid the inevitable. The one in his hand no longer struggled. Instead it went limp as a darkness crawled over the sticky flesh, destroying the plant inch by inch.

Once he was certain the fight was over, he dropped the vine and reached up to jerk away the clinging tendrils. Then, turning, he grasped Skye's arm as she swayed to the side, her face turning blue. He ground his fangs together, resisting the urge to sweep her into his arms and carry her from the cave. They had no idea what new horror was waiting for them. He had to be prepared to fight if they were attacked.

Cautiously leading her past the vines that had curled into tight balls, Micha impatiently knocked aside the tendrils that continued to drop from the ceiling. They were becoming more desperate as he neared the round hole that he assumed was the only exit.

He paused as they reached the back of the cave, debating whether it would be safer for him to go first, and risk a rear attack on Skye or to—

The decision was made as Skye leaned forward and scurried through the cramped opening. Micha rolled his eyes as he followed behind her, wondering why he thought for a second he might be the one in charge. Skye was going to do what Skye was going to do. End of story.

Forced to bend nearly double, Micha awkwardly squeezed into the adjoining cave, instantly shrouded in utter and complete darkness. He hissed in fear.

"Skye?"

Slender fingers brushed over his arm, as if seeking to find him. Then they skimmed down to grasp his hand in a tight grip.

"I'm here."

Instinctively, he wrapped his arms around her waist, tugging her close. He didn't sense approaching danger, but that didn't mean it wasn't there.

"Did we break through the ward?"

"The first layer."

Micha squashed his burst of frustration. He hadn't expected it to be easy. As far as he knew, no one had returned to the location of the Dragon Treaty since it'd been signed and sealed in the earth. Even the crystal that had been created by the mixing of vampire and dragon blood had been hidden beneath layers of a lethal hex that had killed thousands over the centuries.

Still, the caves were scraping his nerves raw. He'd rather battle a horde of demons than stumble from one random disaster to another. At least he could be prepared for what was coming.

"Can you breathe?" he asked.

"Yes, but I can't see."

"Neither can I."

"It must be a blinding spell."

He heard the rustle of movement as Skye lifted her arm. Then there was a ball of light that danced around her slender fingers. A soft glow spread through the space before it was abruptly gone. Like a candle being snuffed out.

Micha had only a brief glance around the cave before it was once again plunged into darkness, but it'd been enough to reveal that it was half the size of the last one with a low ceiling. The good news was that there hadn't been any vines ready to attack them. The bad news was that there were cracks in the floor that were filled with boiling hot lava. And even worse news, the cracks were swiftly widening.

"That's not good," he muttered.

"I used to play the floor is lava when I was bored and waiting for a customer to come into the tent, but I never expected to actually have to navigate one." Micha didn't need the acrid edge to her scent to know Skye was battling a sudden surge of panic. He could hear her heart pounding as if it were threatening to leap out of her chest. "We can't risk stumbling through the dark."

"We can't stay here." Micha lifted her hand and pressed it against his lips. "I'll go first. I can sense the heat and where the lava is spreading. Follow my footsteps exactly."

Turning, he held on to her fingers. Then, reaching back, he grabbed her other hand so he could wrap her arms tightly around his waist. Before he could take a step, however, Skye was burying her face in the middle of his back.

"Micha, no. It's too dangerous."

He hesitated. Should he ask if she'd had a vision? He didn't want to. What choice did they have but to go forward? But while he was willing to take a necessary risk, he would be a fool to deliberately charge into a death trap.

"Skye..." The question died on his lips as there was a pulse of heat against his stomach. Glancing down in surprise, he realized one of the charms dangling from Skye's bracelet was hotter than the others. Much hotter. "Are you using your magic?"

She stiffened in surprise. "No. Why?"

"You're hot."

"Micha," she chided.

Whirling back to face her, he held up her arm to reveal the charm that was surrounded with a dull glow valiantly battling against the oppressive darkness.

"See?"

"Oh, you're right," she breathed.

"Is the magic reacting to this place?" he asked as the glow spread to encompass them, revealing Skye's distracted expression as she stared at the charm.

"Yes."

"That's a good thing, right?"

She didn't answer, her head tilting to the side as if she was lost in her thoughts.

"Right?" he repeated.

She slowly nodded. "I think so. It's reacting to the spell that's stored in that particular charm."

Micha frowned. There was a hint of confusion in her voice that warned it wasn't all good news.

"And?"

"It's not mine. It's Peri's magic," she revealed.

As she spoke the name of her friend, the glow stretched and thinned until it no longer surrounded them but instead weaved itself into a golden strand. Micha instinctively stepped back as the thread arrowed toward the ground. Then, hitting the hard stone, it crawled across the cave toward the distant wall.

The strange magic didn't glow bright enough to light up the room, but as it curved past the cracks in the floor, it revealed the rivers of lava that continued to spread. Micha abruptly realized that the thread offered a safe path through the cave. *Or maybe it's a trick to lure us to certain death*, a voice whispered in the back of his mind.

Hard to guess which one.

"Is Peri aware of what is happening?" he asked.

Skye moved to stand at his side, studying the golden strand. "I don't sense her presence, but her magic is oddly in tune with this place." There was a long silence before he felt her give a sharp shake of her head. "Why would she have any connection to the Dragon Treaty?"

The heat in the room intensified and the sound of popping stones echoed through the cave. The cracks were widening, allowing more lava to pump into the cave. Soon they would be cut off from any hope of escape.

"Maybe we should worry about the whys later," he warned. "I don't think we have much time."

"You're right." She grasped his hand. "Besides, I trust Peri. She wouldn't lead us astray."

Micha didn't possess the same faith. Not when Peri's magic had proven to be as unpredictable as it was powerful. But he trusted Skye. If she believed, then so did he.

Gripping her hand in a grasp that was just short of painful, he inched his way down the narrow path, angling his body to block a portion of the heat that bubbled from the nearby lava. He was fully prepared to snatch her in his arms and toss her across the cave if the lava spilled onto the pathway. Thankfully, his heroic urges were unnecessary as they passed through the lethal maze and reached the far wall. There was no obvious exit, but the golden strand disappeared into the center of the wall. Skye reached out, laying her palm against the rough stones. That was all it took for the hidden door to swing open, allowing them to enter a vast cavern with a towering ceiling.

Behind them the door slammed shut, but this time there was nothing ominous in the sound. In fact, it was a relief to have the screaming heat from the lava trapped behind layers of stone. There was an even greater sense of relief to realize they'd reached the cavern that had been revealed by the magical memory.

There was no mistaking the mosaic tiled floor or the priceless gems that shimmered in the ceiling.

"This is it," Skye whispered, her thoughts echoing his own. "This is where they signed the treaty."

He leaned down to speak directly in his companion's ear. "And there's the fairy," he warned, nodding across the cavern where he could catch sight of the male as he moved between the fluted columns. "Let's have a word with him."

Skye nodded, walking next to him as he crossed the glittering tiles to approach Lynx from behind. As they neared, Micha released her hand, preparing for the fairy to attack.

Lynx hadn't come this far only to have his prize snatched away without a fight.

If there even was a prize.

Halting far enough away to react if Lynx was carrying a weapon, Micha watched the fairy as he ran his fist over the tapestry that covered the wall. He had the crystal clutched in his hand, no doubt using it to try to locate the Tempest. If his stiff back and rigid shoulders were anything to go by, he wasn't having much luck.

"Looking for something, Lynx?" he at last drawled.

Uttering a sharp profanity, the fairy swung around to glare at them, his handsome features twisted with a smoldering wrath. Micha arched his brows. He hadn't been wrong. Lynx was obviously infuriated by his inability to locate his promised key to world domination.

"How the hell did you get in here?" the fairy snarled.

Micha smiled, a portion of his own frustration easing at the knowledge the bastard was suffering.

"Magic," he answered, exposing the tips of his massive fangs.

"Bullshit." Lynx spit out the curse even as he flicked a worried glance toward Skye. "Only the descendent who controls the crystal can navigate the labyrinth."

The words were recited as if he was trying to convince himself he was the hero of the story and not some delusional jackass.

"It wasn't so much a labyrinth as a thick hedge and smelly sauna," Micha taunted, deliberately minimizing the terror of their journey.

Lynx clenched his jaw. "It doesn't matter. You're too late."

Micha arched a brow. "You have the sword?"

"It's here."

"Doubtful."

"Afraid I'll find it, leech?" Lynx ground out. "You wouldn't be so cocky if you couldn't crawl out of your grave like a nasty zombie."

"Zombies are technically different creatures. We don't crawl from our graves." Micha stepped toward the fairy. "We're resurrected in a new form."

"Stay back." Lynx held up his hand that clutched the crystal, a reddish glow appearing to surround his hand.

"Micha, be careful," Skye called out.

"Yeah, be careful," Lynx taunted. "Listen to your girlfriend."

"Always," Micha retorted without hesitation, coming to a halt. It didn't appear that the fairy knew how to use the crystal as a weapon, but that didn't mean it wasn't dangerous. Anything connected to the dragons was a threat to vampires. "I'm wise enough to accept good advice when I hear it. Unlike some."

Lynx snorted at the obvious implication. "The day I take advice from a leech is the day I slit my own throat."

"This place has nothing to do with your precious Tempest." Micha continued to provoke the fairy, hoping to keep him distracted long enough to strike. With a sweep of his arm, he indicated the vast cavern. "This is the place where the Dragon Treaty was signed. It's a shrine to that moment, not to some mysterious demon legend."

Lynx stubbornly shook his head. "The sword is here. It has to be."

"Who told you the location?"

"It was given to me...in a vision." He glared at Micha as he stumbled over the words. "I'm the chosen one."

"A lie." Micha didn't need his skills to realize that Lynx was inventing his supposed vision. "Someone convinced you that you were a mystical hero, and you were so eager to believe them that you were willing to risk everything to claim your precious destiny."

Lynx flushed as Micha's accusation hit him right where it hurt.

His pride.

"I've always known I was special," the fairy hissed.

Micha took another step forward, ignoring the pulsing red glow. "Who persuaded you to steal the crystal and come here?"

"The Tempest is a kids' story fed to every demon," he insisted. "I just didn't know that I was a direct descendent to the original Lynx."

"So how did you find out?" Micha pressed.

Lynx's eyes darted from side to side, as if seeking the nearest exit. Or maybe he was hoping the sword would magically appear so he could get rid of Micha once and for all.

When nothing materialized, he returned his attention to Micha with a sour expression.

"I was given a private diary along with this medallion from my ancestor." Using his empty hand, Lynx reached beneath his shirt to pull out a large metal pendant hanging on a thick chain with an opal in the center. "The diary had an etching of a fairy who looked almost identical to me." The green eyes flared with a fierce satisfaction at the memory. "I suddenly realized my dreams of leading the demon world hadn't been empty fantasies. They'd been a glimpse into my future."

"Ah." Micha abruptly chuckled. "You weren't Lynx. You changed your name to match the story."

"It seemed appropriate."

"And the same mystery person who gave you the diary also told you that the crystal would lead you to the sword?" Micha demanded.

"Eventually." Lynx took a covert step to the side. Then another. Was he going to make a run for it? Behind him, Micha felt a hum of magic surround Skye, as if she had the same thought and was preparing a spell to stop the fairy. "First I had to prove I was the genuine heir," Lynx continued, trying to keep them preoccupied.

Micha didn't care why he was sharing how he'd come to believe he was some chosen warrior. Not as long as he eventually revealed who'd been helping him.

"By deluding a bunch of outcast demons to follow you into a losing cause?" Micha taunted.

Genuine outrage rippled over Lynx's perfect features. "I prefer outcasts. Any demon can survive by kissing the ass of a leech. It takes genuine skill to succeed with your own cunning. My horde is a team of survivors."

"You took over Dexter's horde," Skye abruptly intruded into the conversation. "They're a team of idiots."

Lynx shrugged, conceding her point. "Some are more talented than others."

"So how did you prove your worth?" Micha prodded him to continue his story.

There were more cautious steps to the side. Micha allowed the idiot to believe he hadn't noticed.

"After years of gaining a following among the demons, I wasn't surprised when I was approached by a demon with royal blood and powerful connections," Lynx boasted. "It was inevitable that my brilliance would be recognized and rewarded."

"Lucky you," Skye muttered.

Lynx flushed. "Not luck. Talent."

Micha sent out a pulse of compulsion. Lynx was too powerful to compel an answer, but he could *encourage* him to reveal the name.

"Who was the demon?"

"Igor Triton."

Lynx blinked as the name tumbled from his lips, as if shocked he'd revealed his secret partner in crime. Micha was equally shocked. Not by the fact that Lynx had finally revealed the traitor, but who had betrayed the Cabal.

He wouldn't have been surprised if Igor had been working with Kane to overthrow Valen. That was what they'd suspected from the start. But to be the leader of a demon revolution? No way. The male might have the balls, but he didn't have the brains.

"Igor Triton?" He repeated the name, struggling to accept what he was hearing. "Kane's devoted servant?"

Lynx hunched his shoulders, accepting it was too late to deny the truth. "Not so devoted. He was willing to pretend to be a loyal servant to Kane so he could gain a position of authority, but he was desperate to break free of the leech."

"He wasn't a prisoner. If he wanted to leave he didn't need to sneak around. He could walk out the door."

"Yeah, right." Lynx's features hardened with contempt. "You leeches love to act all civilized when the truth is that you're nothing more than cold-blooded bastards who use your position of authority to oppress everyone around you."

Micha didn't bother to argue. Although most vampires had adapted with the modern codes of decency, there were still many vampires who believed that they were superior to every living creature and resorted to threats or violence to impose their will on those in their care.

Including Kane.

Instead, he tried to reconcile himself to the possibility that the Cabal had been so easily played by a swaggering idiot. Was it possible? No. No way. There had to be something he was missing.

Micha folded his arms over his chest. "How did Igor locate you?"

Lynx shrugged. "He'd been on the lookout for a fairy with the natural talent for organizing and inspiring demons."

"And you magically appeared?"

The smell of copper swirled through the air. Lynx was more than a little touchy at the implication he'd fallen into the role of the chosen one. Obviously it was important to his ego that he believe he'd been chosen by fate.

"Not magic." The gemstone in his hand pulsed, as if reacting to his flare of temper. "Hard work. I created my destiny. I didn't have my inheritance handed to me just because I'm a zombie who won't stay in my grave."

"Again. Not a zombie," Micha reminded him, "but while I might not possess your lofty claim to fame, I've often crossed paths with Igor Triton over the centuries. He does have royal blood and a small amount of cunning, but he doesn't have the intelligence to research the Tempest or how to locate it, let alone track you down to guide you toward your supposed destiny. And he certainly couldn't organize my kidnapping."

Belatedly remembering he was trying to escape, Lynx inched to the side, nearly reaching one of the marble columns.

"I organized that," he insisted.

Micha shook his head. "Someone told you when the Cabal was coming to New York and gave you the keycard to get to the lower floors. They also told you the exact location of my bedroom and how to get out the emergency exit."

"Igor."

"Impossible."

Lynx snorted. "You just can't accept that a demon could outsmart a bunch of leeches."

Micha frowned. His senses told him that Lynx truly believed what he was saying. So that had to mean...

"He's right." A smooth male voice echoed through the cavern. "A demon could never have executed such a glorious rebellion. But I could."

Micha hissed, his fangs fully exposed as he whirled around to confront Kane.

Only it wasn't Kane standing in the middle of the mosaic tiled floor.

In fact, the vampire with light brown hair and dark eyes, wearing an ankle-length black robe, was the last male he expected to see.

"Ambassador Azra," he rasped in shock.

* * * *

Valen watched his mate toss her cell phone on his desk, her body vibrating with frustration.

"Has Maya heard from Skye?" The words tumbled from his lips before he could halt them.

It was a dumb question. One glance at Peri's tense expression and the sparks of magic sizzling through the office revealed that the news wasn't good. But he'd spent most of the daylight hours pacing the floor while he wallowed in endless recriminations for not realizing that his demons were being poisoned to hate his new mate. Not to mention the fact he'd allowed the perpetrator of his troubles to stay in his lair, where he plotted to kidnap a member of the Cabal and Peri's best friend.

The epic mess might not be his fault, but it'd happened on his watch.

Was it any wonder it was increasingly difficult to think through his smoldering guilt?

"Nothing," Peri confirmed, stopping to stare out the window at the darkness creeping over the city. Soon it would be full night and he could return to his hunt for Micha. If only he knew where the hell to start his search. "Maya's going to track down her various contacts in the city to see if they have any information. She's not hopeful."

With an effort, Valen calmed his seething emotions and moved to wrap a comforting arm around his mate.

"We're going to find them."

She leaned her head on his shoulder. "I'm scared. I can feel her, Valen. As if she's trying to reach out to me, but she's too far away."

Valen brushed his lips over the top of her head even as he felt a sharp chill before Gabriel stepped into the office.

"I think we should have a word with the prisoners," the older male announced, his own impatience edging his voice. "One of them has to know where Kane is."

"Agreed," Valen murmured, lowering his arm as Peri turned to regard him with a stubborn frown.

"I'm coming," she stated in tones that defied argument.

Valen didn't bother to try to reason with her. He didn't have the strength to waste on butting his head against a brick wall. There were bigger battles to concentrate on.

Keeping his arm around Peri's shoulders, he headed to his private elevator and used his keycard to open the doors. The three of them stepped into the carriage, dropping to the deepest floor in silence. They'd spent hours debating what they'd seen and heard at the theater. There was nothing left to say. Not until they had new information.

The elevator swooshed to a stop and the doors slid open to reveal a long cement hallway that was lit by bare light bulbs hanging from the low ceiling. It was deliberately designed with a gulag vibe, warning Valen's enemies that they'd truly screwed up if they were headed to this location.

Stepping out of the carriage, Valen was turning in the direction of the cells when Gabriel abruptly reached out to place his hand on Valen's shoulder.

"Wait."

Valen stopped, his senses on full alert. "What's wrong?"

Gabriel sniffed the air. "Are there any other vampires in the area?"

Valen shook his head. He had a couple of vampires who oversaw his businesses at the far edges of his territory. He preferred not to have any in his primary lair. It avoided any unfortunate complications when it came to who was the boss.

"There are none in the dungeons."

"This way." With long strides, Gabriel headed in the opposite direction of the dungeons.

Valen kept Peri close as he followed his friend.

They continued through the hallway before Gabriel abruptly turned into a short passage that was blocked by a massive steel door.

"The WCS," Valen muttered in surprise.

Gabriel glanced over his shoulder in confusion. "The what?"

"Worst Case Scenario." Valen scooted past his friend to place his hand flat on the steel door. "I built a panic room in the unlikely event the lair was ever overrun by enemies or the more likely event of a natural disaster." He nodded toward the red lights above the door. "It's been triggered."

Gabriel stepped forward. "How do we get it open?"

"It can only be unlocked from the inside." Valen slammed his hand against the unyielding steel that was a foot thick. "This is Valen." He waited for the lock to click. Even through the massive barrier he would be able to hear the click. Nothing. He smacked his palm against the steel. "Ambassador? Open the door. You're safe."

Gabriel pursed his lips. "I don't think he trusts you."

Valen hissed in annoyance. "We have to find out what happened before Kane can escape."

"I'll open it."

The soft voice floated from the main hallway and Valen turned around to discover Peri lifting her arm, the jade bracelet around her wrist already glowing with power.

"Peri—"

"I can do this," she insisted, her floral scent mixing with tingles of electric magic.

Valen grabbed Gabriel's elbow and pulled him out of the passageway, giving Peri a clear shot at the door.

"I have no doubt you can do it," he assured his mate, adding a hint of warning to his voice. "I'd just prefer you open the door without turning our lair into a pile of rubble."

Peri shrugged. "I make no promises."

"Wait," Valen commanded. He would survive the building landing on top of him, but he wasn't sure that Peri would.

"I'm kidding," she assured him as she closed her eyes to concentrate on her spell. "Hopefully."

Next to him, Gabriel shook his head in resignation. "I don't envy you."

"It's an adjustment," Valen conceded, only to grunt when a sharp elbow was dug into his ribs. "A *magnificent* adjustment," he clarified.

Peri clicked her tongue, her eyes still closed as she vibrated with the power that surged through her.

"Stand back and don't distract me."

Valen brushed a hasty kiss over her cheek. "Be careful."

She was already lost in the wild magic that coursed through her blood, and Valen hastily moved to press his back against the far wall. Gabriel was wise enough to join him as bolts of lightning danced from Peri's slender fingers. The powerful magic sizzled with a white-hot heat, proving it wasn't just an illusion. And just in case there was any doubt, the ground began to shake and the cement walls cracked from the sheer pressure of the snowballing spell.

Valen felt the hair on his nape rise with an instinctive fear before Peri muttered a word of power and released her magic. With a loud hiss it blasted through the passageway, the lightning weaving together to form a battering ram before it smashed into the door with shocking force.

Valen winched at the painful shriek of ripping metal, but it was impossible to see what happened as a cloud of pulverized cement wafted out of the passageway. It wasn't until the choking fog faded and the ground at last stopped shaking that Valen and Gabriel tentatively stepped forward to inspect the damage.

The older vampire grunted in disbelief. "Damn."

Valen slowly smiled, wrapping his arm around Peri as she sagged wearily against him.

"She never fails to amaze," he murmured, pride in his voice as he took in the steel door that had been blasted off its hinges.

There wasn't a vampire in the Cabal who could have matched her strength. In fact, there was a very real possibility that only the dragons possessed more raw power.

For a second they admired the devastation in silence. It wasn't often they were astonished by the power of another creature. Then there was a flicker of movement from inside the safe room and Valen released his hold on Peri to flow forward.

He sensed Gabriel next to him as they reached the end of the passageway, both halting at the mangled door to peer inside. There was no use in risking Peri's unpredictable magic only to rush into a trap.

He narrowed his eyes against the bright security lights that had been triggered when the door was forced open, sweeping his gaze over the small room that held a wooden chair and table where a laptop was available to keep in contact with the outside world. There were also numerous weapons and a freezer filled with frozen blood, but they were stockpiled behind layers of magic that could only be unlocked with his personal touch.

There was another flutter of movement, and Valen realized there was something or someone cowering beneath the pile of blankets in the corner. Striding forward, he grabbed the covers and tugged them aside, his mouth dropping open in pure shock.

"Shit, Kane," he rasped, barely recognizing the massive vampire.

The long blond hair had been ripped from his usual braid to hang in clumps around his face. A face that was currently twisted in pain. His leather jacket was missing and the T-shirt that covered his chest had been shredded by whatever weapon had gouged deep wounds into his body. Several of them continued to leak blood down his torso and onto the cement floor.

Kane held up a beefy hand, his expression one of sheer terror. "No, no."

Valen stared down at him in confusion. He'd assumed that Kane was long gone from the lair. Not hiding in his panic room.

"What the hell happened to you?"

"Are you with him?" the male rasped.

"Who?" Valen demanded, sensing Gabriel move out of the cramped space as Valen's servants rushed to discover what had happened. He thankfully realized that Valen wanted to question Kane without being interrupted.

"Azra."

Valen glanced around the room in confusion. "The ambassador? Is he here? Has he been hurt?"

"The bastard." Kane released a low snarl, his hand covering one of his deeper wounds. "He tried to kill me."

Valen crouched down, focusing on the male sprawled on the hard cement. It wasn't as easy to read a vampire, but Kane was gravely injured. It should make it easier to detect a lie.

"Why?"

"Traitor." The word ended on a groan.

Valen leaned forward. "A traitor to who?"

"The Cabal." With an effort, Kane's hand reached toward the nearby freezer built into the wall. "I need to feed."

Suddenly Valen realized why Kane had been in this corner. He'd been trying to force his way through the layers of magic to get to the blood.

"Not until I have some answers," he warned the male, struggling to accept he might have leapt to conclusions.

He had convinced himself that Kane was the traitor. Every clue pointed to the ambitious male being behind the endless troubles that had been plaguing them. Including the kidnapping of Micha and Skye. But there was no denying the fact that Kane was the one who'd been severely injured while Azra had disappeared. And while it was possible that Kane had been the one to attack Azra first, it wouldn't explain where the ambassador had gone. Or why he'd taken his belongings with him.

"You're claiming that Azra—Sinjon's most trusted servant—is a traitor?" He needed to be sure he hadn't misunderstood the male.

Kane licked his lips, his face twisted with pain. "I can't..."

"Try really hard." Valen leaned forward, allowing his power to press against Kane. "We already know it was Igor who came to New York days ago to stir up anger toward my mate."

Kane hissed but seemed to accept that he wasn't going to get the blood he so badly needed until he'd answered Valen's questions.

"Why not?" A soul-deep hunger flared in the depths of the vampire's eyes. "This Gyre should be mine."

"If you believed that, you would have openly challenged me to take control of my territory. Instead you were a coward, hiding behind your trusted servant, who was sneaking around, trying to turn my people against Peri."

Kane released a low growl. "Not trusted."

"What?"

"He...he betrayed me. With the ambassador." Kane shuddered, his skin unnaturally pale as his powers visibly drained away. "Give me blood."

"How did he betray you?"

Kane shook his head. "Food."

Valen swiveled to the side, placing his hand flat against the magic. There was a sharp tingle that crawled up his arm, as if seeking to confirm his identity, before there was a loud pop as the spell was broken. With a deliberate desire to torment Kane, he slowly opened the freezer and pulled out a bag of blood, holding it just out of reach.

Kane's fangs protruded, his body trembling with hunger.

"Talk," Valen commanded.

"Fine." Kane's gaze remained locked on the blood. "It's true that I sent Igor to cause trouble."

"Why?"

"I hoped your witch would be provoked into losing control of her magic and the demons would demand a new leader."

"I assume you would be that new leader?"

"Of course."

Valen battled back the surge of fury at the memory of Peri's distress at the fear she'd never be accepted as his mate. Kane was fading. He had to get the information he needed before the vampire became too weak to talk.

"Why kidnap Micha?"

"I had nothing to do with that." Kane swore in frustration as Valen dangled the blood directly over his head. "I swear."

"Then what happened to him?"

"I don't know."

"This isn't a game, Kane," Valen snapped. He was tired of feeling like he was constantly running one step behind a mysterious enemy. The shit stopped now. "You share what you know and I'll allow you to feed. Or you can starve. It makes no difference to me."

Kane groaned. "Please."

"Tell me what happened to Micha and Skye."

"All I know was that last night I tried to contact Igor but he was ghosting me," Kane snarled. "He wouldn't answer my calls or respond to my messages. Finally I tracked him to an old theater."

There was the soft tread of footsteps as Gabriel stepped back into the room. He'd obviously sensed the tension vibrating in the air. Kane was reaching his breaking point. The desperate male would either confess the truth or he'd attack Valen in an attempt to get his hands on the blood.

"And?" Valen prodded.

"And Igor was there. With Azra."

"What were they doing?"

Kane briefly closed his eyes, his jaws tight as he struggled to remain conscious.

"Igor was demanding the reward he'd earned for assisting the vampire in kidnapping Micha."

"What did he do to help?"

"Something about making sure one of Micha's servants was incapacitated and getting a driver." Kane grimaced. "It didn't make much sense."

Valen assumed that it was Igor who arranged the driver that dropped off Lynx in front of his lair and then helped in the getaway. But why? What could Azra possibly gain by kidnapping a member of the Cabal?

Questions for later.

"What did you do?"

"Nothing." Kane paused, and Valen frowned. Had the bastard passed out? Then, with a pained effort, he continued his story. "Before I could confront them, Azra casually reached out and ripped off Igor's head. Just like that." The vampire shuddered, as if genuinely troubled by the memory. "One minute they were talking and the next Igor was headless. Then Azra pulled out a dagger and gutted my servant like a deer. I've seen vampires consumed by bloodlust, but Azra..." Another shudder.

"What?"

"He looked bored. As if beheading and gutting demons was something he'd done a million times." Kane shook his head before wincing as if every movement was agonizing. "That's when I bolted."

Valen studied the male's pale face. The words sounded true to his ears. More importantly, they matched up with the precious few facts he'd managed to uncover. Which meant that Ambassador Azra had been the traitor the entire time, and Valen had been even more blind than he'd first thought.

Anger vibrated through him as he glared down at Kane. The male might not have been the one to kidnap Micha and Skye, but he'd stirred enough shit to distract Valen from the real threat.

Whatever that threat might be.

"How did you get in this room?" he demanded.

"I tried to use the emergency exit to sneak in. I didn't want Azra to know I'd seen what he did. But he must have sensed my presence at the theater. He followed me back to the lair and attacked me when I reached the garage." Kane glanced down at the numerous wounds that marred his chest. None of them were healing in his weakened state. "I managed to get into an elevator and get down here. I knew you'd have a place to hide. That's it. That's all I know."

Kane flopped his head back and Valen straightened. This male had revealed all he was going to. At least for now. And it was time for Valen to turn his attention to tracking down the missing Azra.

Lifting a hand, he waved it toward the waiting Gabriel. Instantly understanding what he wanted, the older male turned to gesture toward the guards, who eagerly rushed into the room.

"Take him to the dungeons," Valen commanded, handing the bag of blood to the demon in charge of the dungeons. "Don't feed him until you have him chained."

The large male nodded and Valen turned to leave.

"Someday we'll finish this, Valen," Kane rasped as he was roughly hauled off the floor by four goblins.

"It's finished," Valen announced with a cold indifference that revealed his utter lack of fear.

Kane might leave his dungeons. Some day. But he would never be a threat again.

Valen headed out of the safe room, glancing toward Gabriel, who fell into step next to him. "Do you believe what he said?"

"I believe he told us what he knows. Whether that's the full truth is yet to be determined." Gabriel shrugged. "What now?"

"We call Sinjon," Valen said. The ultimate leader of the Cabal needed to know he'd been betrayed by his servant.

The sooner the better.

"And if Sinjon is involved in Azra's plot?"

"Then we're screwed."

Chapter 18

Micha instinctively stepped to block Skye from the vampire who was strolling toward them with obvious pleasure at their shocked expressions. He wasn't sure what astonished him more. The fact that the vampire had followed them to the cavern. Or that he'd seemingly appeared from thin air.

"Ambassador?" Lynx appeared equally stunned, his brows drawing together as he stared at the vampire wearing a long black robe. "Sinjon's servant?"

Azra hissed, continuing to move forward. "I'm no one's servant."

Micha struggled to wrap his brain around the realization that the ambassador had arranged his kidnapping.

"It was you," he hissed.

Azra shrugged. "You'll have to be more specific."

"You arranged the keycard to get Lynx into Valen's lair and told him where to find my room," Micha clarified.

The male stopped a few feet from Lynx, a smug smile curving his lips. "Guilty."

"No. That's not true," Lynx burst out, his eyes wide as he stubbornly refused to believe that he'd been used and manipulated by a vampire. "It was Igor."

Azra folded his hands together, looking like a prophet confronting his naughty disciple. Micha, however, sensed a wariness beneath the male's calm demeanor.

It was almost as if Azra was afraid of the fairy...

No. Micha shook his head. It wasn't Lynx he feared, it was the energy pulsing from the crystal clutched in the fairy's hand.

"Igor was a lump of muscle who proved to be a convenient tool, but he didn't have the brains to tie his shoes without a vampire giving him directions," Azra taunted.

"A lie," Lynx snapped. "He was the one who sought me out and revealed my destiny."

Azra laughed at the claim. "You gullible fool. You made it all so easy." Micha narrowed his gaze. Ah. Now he understood. Azra couldn't take the crystal by force. He needed the fairy alive to handle the thing. Was his plan to gain control of Lynx's mind and force him to his will? Was that why he was deliberately provoking him? That seemed the most obvious explanation.

"Was Kane involved?" Micha abruptly demanded, stepping forward. He could try to overpower Azra. He was stronger than the male, despite being a thousand years younger. But he had to get closer. Oh, and pray that the male didn't have any nasty weapons hidden beneath his robe.

"He was, but he had no idea he was being used," Azra conceded, grudgingly glancing in Micha's direction. "As usual, Kane was oblivious to everything but his obsessive fear of losing power. He'd approached Sinjon a dozen times over the past two centuries, complaining that he should be offered a Gyre in the new world. I suspected that it would only be a matter of time before he found an excuse to challenge Valen for his territory, and so I laid my plans. Then Valen conveniently mated a mage with the sort of magic that was destined to strike fear in the Cabal, and I knew it was the perfect opportunity."

"What plans?" Micha demanded.

Azra pursed his lips, perhaps considering his options. The vampire didn't have many, Micha reassured himself. No doubt he could smash his way into Lynx's mind and force him to obey his will, but he still had Micha to deal with, along with a powerful mage.

"First I began with Igor." Azra forced himself to answer the question, pretending they had all the time in the world.

Micha took another step forward. "Why him?"

"I needed someone close to Kane to prod the impulsive idiot into making his challenge to Valen, plus I knew only a demon could approach the fairy." He sent a sneering glance toward Lynx. "He would never have trusted a vampire."

"Damn right I would never trust a leech," Lynx spit out in fury.

"How did you convince Igor to betray his master?" Micha hastily regained the vampire's attention. Azra appeared calm, but there was a layer of ice spreading across the marble floor near his feet.

His control was razor thin.

Azra sent him an impatient glance. "It was simple. I promised to kill Kane and free his mate."

Micha arched his brows. "Why was his mate imprisoned?"

"If you and your fellow Cabal members hadn't been so self-obsessed, you would have known that Kane never earned the loyalty of his people, he forced it," Azra taunted. "He filled his very large dungeons with hostages and kept them for as long as their loved ones were useful. After that..." Azra snapped his fingers. "They simply disappeared."

Micha felt a small stab of guilt. It was true that he'd turned a blind eye to Kane. And a lot of other things. As long as it didn't directly affect him, he was happy to remain hidden in his caverns and allow the world to drift along without his interference.

It had taken his beautiful Skye to lure him out of his self-imposed exile.

Oh, and the threat of the earth being drowned in flames.

"What does any of this have to do with Lynx?" he demanded, refusing to waste time debating Kane's vicious leadership skills.

Azra risked a quick glance toward the fairy, his jaw tightening as the crystal continued to pulse with a crimson glow. His desperate hunger to complete whatever had brought him to this place tainted the air with a sour stench.

Micha released a pulse of power, creating a crack in a nearby column. Just a reminder that he possessed the ability to destroy the cavern and bury them all beneath a mountain of rock.

"You want the truth?" Azra tilted his chin to a defensive angle. "Fine. I've never had any power. No matter how hard I trained or studied, I could never match my brothers. I've been weak my entire existence."

The confession resonated with a blunt candor, making Micha frown in confusion. "You're Sinjon's most trusted companion."

Azra released a bitter laugh. "Companion? That's a joke. I'm a pampered pet who is kept on a very short leash. And if it wasn't for my ability to share my mind with Sinjon, I'd be begging for crumbs."

Micha couldn't argue. Azra *was* weak. And without his ability to act as a spy for Sinjon he would no doubt be a servant who was barely above a demon in vampire society.

Micha shrugged. "We have all endured resurrections that left us at the bottom of our society."

"Yes, and with no guarantee the next resurrection will be any better. For all I know I might be stuck in the gutters for an eternity," Azra snapped, as if Micha had to be reminded that vampires had no idea when or in what form they would be returned to the world. The only thing they knew for certain was that they entered an afterlife and that they would eventually be whisked back into a vessel that had been chosen from among the humans. It could be weeks or endless centuries later. There didn't seem to be any rhyme or reason to the process. "Thankfully, I had a vision," Azra continued, his bitterness replaced with a grim resolve.

"A seer?" Skye demanded from behind Micha.

"Better. Sinjon isn't the only powerful creature who can enter my mind."

"Lynx?" Micha guessed.

Azra made a choked sound of disgust. "A fairy? I'm not that desperate."

"The original one," Micha clarified.

The ice spread across the marble, revealing Azra's shock that they knew about the origin of the crystal and what had happened in this cavern. Then, with a deliberate motion, the male ran his palms down the smooth material of his robe, as if forcibly calming his nerves.

"Very good," he murmured, although it didn't sound as if he thought it was good. Just the opposite. "No, Lynx was an important part of my vision, but he wasn't the one who offered me a new destiny."

"Then who?"

"Zanna."

It was the obvious answer. There had to be a reason they were standing in the cavern that had been lost and forgotten for thousands of years, right? It wasn't like they'd gathered there because they got a thrill out of battling lethal foliage or walking over floors made of lava, although that did sound like something humans would pay to do.

Still, he couldn't keep himself from demanding confirmation. "The dragon?"

"Dragon Queen," Azra chided.

Micha glanced around the empty cavern. "She's in hibernation."

"For now." A creepy anticipation rippled over Azra's face. "Soon, however, she will once again be free to walk the earth."

A dark dread spread through Micha as he glanced toward the fairy, who was glaring at them in confusion. They'd feared that the dragon was somehow involved in Skye's vision. But a vague suspicion wasn't the same as having a demented vampire threaten to waken the Queen of Dragons to destroy the world.

That same dread clenched his heart as he glanced toward Lynx, at last understanding exactly why he'd been kidnapped and why the fairy had been manipulated into believing he would find the vampire-killing sword in this cavern.

"You believe the crystal will wake her up?"

Lynx made a strangled sound, holding his hand over his head to allow the crimson glow to spill around him.

"What are you talking about?" he snapped. "The crystal is a compass to the Tempest and my—"

"Hush," Azra interrupted the fairy's angry words, and Lynx's lips snapped together, as if an invisible force had glued them shut. Then the vampire returned his attention to Micha. "Where were we?"

"Zanna," Micha said, needing to know exactly how he intended to awaken the beast.

"Ah, yes." A strange, almost dreamy expression settled on the male's face. "She came to me, revealing what had happened in this temple."

"The treaty?"

"Exactly. A treaty she never desired and had no intention of honoring."

Micha didn't waste time wondering how a dragon had managed to touch Azra's mind. The creatures possessed enormous powers that had been forgotten over the centuries.

Instead, he shuffled through the images that had been revealed in the memory spell.

"If she didn't want the treaty, then why did she seal it with her blood," Micha demanded.

"An unfortunate necessity. The dragons were weary of war with the vampires and pressured her into negotiating for peace." Azra cast a glance toward the pedestal in the center of the cavern. "But she was wise enough to maintain a link to her captor."

"Captor?" It took Micha a second to realize he was talking about the male who'd witnessed the signing of the document. "You mean the original Lynx?"

"Yes."

Micha ignored the muffled curses from the Lynx-wannabe. "What is he?" he asked. "A demon?"

"She refused to tell me," Azra admitted. "All I know was that it was the only creature capable of compelling both the vampires and dragons into signing the treaty. And that he forced her into hibernation."

Despite the urgency of the situation, Micha found himself overwhelmed with curiosity. The rare manuscripts he'd collected over the centuries had hinted at mysterious powers that could step in and alter the course of history. But he'd never been able to find a text that revealed details about the strange creatures.

The thought that he'd seen one—if only in a memory spell—was dangerously distracting. His scholarly obsession demanded answers.

"So Lynx was more than just a witness to the signing of the treaty," he pressed. "He was some sort of enforcer?"

"His magic created the crystal that holds the blood of Zanna and the vampire," he grudgingly admitted. "And until the crystal is placed on the podium and the treaty destroyed, the dragons are stuck in hibernation. That's why she marked him."

Micha recalled the female dragon running her fingers over Lynx's neck. "What was the mark?"

"A binding spell. Eventually the male would have been compelled to bend to her will."

Micha hadn't spent much time studying dragons. There were thousands of scholars that devoted their lives to probing the history of the oversized lizards. Many of whom concentrated on how best to defeat them when they did waken. He hadn't felt the need to add to the plethora of information filling the libraries.

But what he did know was that dragon magic was some of the most powerful in the world. And it only made sense that the queen's magic would be off the charts. So how had any creature managed to battle against the compulsion?

"So where is the original Lynx? Why use the fairy to bring the crystal here?"

"The creature realized what Zanna had done. After leaving this place he went to a remote location and sacrificed his life to protect the crystal."

"Your temple," Skye said, moving to stand at his side. "That was the magic I sensed."

Micha glanced toward the beautiful mage. "That explains why the curse was so lethal. It wasn't normal magic."

Azra shrugged. "Zanna believed she was doomed to remain trapped in hibernation. Perhaps forever, since no one could touch the crystal. Not until a century ago. Suddenly she could sense his power moving through the world."

Micha arched a brow. "How?"

"Either he possessed the vampire skill of resurrection—"

"Impossible," Micha snapped.

It wasn't that he cared if other species possessed the ability to rise from the dead. But his vast research had never hinted at any other species utilizing that particular form of immortality.

"Or he passed his magic through his bloodline," Azra continued in hard tones. Obviously he didn't appreciate Micha's interruption.

Skye made a sound of surprise. "A child?"

"Yes."

Micha tucked away the knowledge that the strange creatures seemed capable of producing offspring. When all this was over he intended to spend some serious time gathering every scrap of information that had been written about the Dragon Treaty and who had been involved in the creation of the document.

Well, first he intended to devote several centuries to making Skye Claremont the happiest woman on the planet. After that he could spend some time learning about the secretive demons that were walking among them. And if they might be a threat.

"The dragons have been hibernating for at least thirteen thousand years. What took her so long to sense it?"

"Zanna claimed that the power doesn't always manifest. In fact, it's very rare."

Ah. Micha nodded. That explained how they managed to remain so secretive. If there were less than a handful of the creatures in the world, then it would be easy to remain hidden.

"But a hundred years ago it woke her from her slumber," Azra continued.

"A century is a blink of the eye for most immortals, but if Zanna was so eager to leave her prison, why wait to break free?" Micha demanded.

"She was waiting for the best candidate to bend to her will," Azra said smoothly, glancing toward Lynx. "When she found him, she reached out to me."

"Okay. That explains what the fairy is doing here. But why you?" Micha was genuinely curious. It was vital to know if the dragon had reached out to any other demons or vampires. "Why did the dragon queen trust you as her..."

"Colleague," Azra asserted as Micha struggled against the urge to call him a servant. Or more likely a slave. Any vampire who trusted a dragon was a fool. "Because of my very unique skills, of course. Zanna was able to touch my mind, but more importantly, I could join with hers. I could see exactly what she needed and how to waken her from her hibernation. We melded together to forge a partnership that promised to be beneficial for both of us." Folding his hands in front of his waist, Azra deliberately resumed his appearance of the calm, unflappable servant that they'd known for so long. It was a façade that Micha now realized had always been a lie. This male had obviously been a seething mass of resentment for centuries. "Plus, no one would ever suspect me of plotting with the enemy." His lips twisted into a sneer. "I'm just Ambassador Azra, right? A male with no thoughts or ambitions of my own. Invisible."

Micha battled back his surge of disgust at how easily the male had fooled the Cabal. Not to mention Sinjon, who was going to be furious when he discovered how Azra had abused his position of power.

"How did you locate the fairy?"

Azra shrugged. "Zanna could offer me the general location, although it took a few months to make certain that it was the fairy who she was sensing. And even then I continued to monitor him." The male cast a disdainful glance toward Lynx. "I couldn't believe such a pathetic creature could be related to a male who had the power to command dragons."

Micha flicked a glance over the fairy, who was visibly struggling to open his sealed lips. "Why create this elaborate hoax? Couldn't you just tell him the truth?"

"No one was allowed to know the truth, no one but me," Azra snapped. He paused, regaining control of his temper. "Besides, after studying the fairy, I determined he would be easy enough to manipulate. Like most demons he was desperate for glory. And there was the added benefit of his hatred for vampires. I could use both to my advantage."

"By pretending you knew the location of the Tempest?"

"I sent Igor to befriend him first. Then, when I was certain he'd earned his trust, I had Igor offer him the diary."

"Ah yes, the diary. Where did you find it?"

Azra sent him a smug smile. "I didn't."

"It's a fake?" Micha demanded before he could halt the startled words. Then he clicked his tongue, silently conceding the male had been very clever. "Of course it is. How better to get the fairy to believe he was some mystical hero?"

"Exactly. It was a work of art. Truly. I even added a sketch that looked like the fairy to add to the illusion."

"Impressive," Micha conceded.

Azra tried and failed not to ooze conceited satisfaction. "The demons had already created a dozen myths about a legendary sword that could destroy vampires. And conveniently they believed it was the one that was hidden in your territory, despite the fact it had killed hundreds of them. I simply changed a few of the details so the fairy would believe that the myths were true but that the actual sword had been hidden in this temple, and he needed the crystal to find it."

"Is there an actual Tempest?" Micha asked.

Azra blinked, as if he'd never considered the question. "I have no idea."

Neither did Micha. Myths and legends quite often were founded on a kernel of truth, but not always. It could have been a story invented by vampires to lure the more ambitious demons to certain death.

Micha concentrated on more important matters. "You arranged for me to be kidnapped."

"That was entirely your fault," Azra chastised.

"My fault?"

"I tried on several occasions to open the passage to the crystal before allowing the fairy to attempt the treacherous journey. Your security system was formidable. And costly. I sacrificed dozens of my finest warriors trying to discover a way into the temple. It eventually became obvious I needed you to offer him a way through." Azra pursed his lips, as if still counting the cost of trying to get his hands on the crystal. "Thankfully, Kane's petition to Sinjon brought you to New York City. It made everything so simple. I could get my hands on you and eventually the crystal. As a bonus I made sure that Kane was the obvious suspect."

Micha refused to dwell on how easy he'd made it for the bastard. And how eager they'd all been to suspect the Cabal leader of Russia of treachery. Now wasn't the time.

"And the medallion?" he asked, talking as he inched forward.

"The what?" Azra looked confused before he remembered why he'd given Lynx the pendant. "Oh. A simple tracking device. I needed to know where the fairy was and when he was finally headed toward this temple. He wouldn't know to come here until he had his hands on the crystal, so it was an early warning system for me." He looked pleased at his clever scheme while Micha silently acknowledged that Lynx hadn't been wrong. Obviously the crystal had been some sort of compass. "Once I was certain it was time to release Zanna, I cleaned up a few loose ends in New York and headed to Panama."

Micha briefly wondered if Valen knew about Azra's betrayal. It seemed doubtful. The male had been annoyingly cunning.

"How did you get down here?" Micha asked, judging the distance between him and Azra. Not close enough to attack. But close.

"Zanna revealed a secret tunnel."

"Of course she did." Micha rolled his eyes, recalling the lethal maze they'd had to battle through while this male had strolled through a hidden entrance. "And now that you're here, what's supposed to happen? I mean, I know the crystal was created here, but why go to so much trouble to bring it back?"

"The crystal is a—" He cut off his words, as if dredging for the word that Zanna had used to lure him to the dark side. "Lock."

"A lock for what?"

"It keeps the vampires and dragons from breaking the treaty."

Micha abruptly understood. "It's the physical manifestation of the blood pledge that keeps the dragons in their hibernation."

"Exactly," Azra said. "Once it's returned to the place it was created, the treaty is at an end."

They'd suspected that the crystal was connected to releasing the dragons, but it was always good to have confirmation. He'd jumped to way too many conclusions. And paid the price.

"So that's what the dragons get out of your unholy partnership. What about you? What's in this for you?"

"Zanna has promised me a position of power."

Predictable. "And you trusted her?"

"Why wouldn't I? Everything she has told me has been the truth."

"I'm sure it has been," Micha taunted. "She obviously needs you to bring the crystal to this cavern and shatter the magic holding her captive. Once you've freed her, you'll be dispensable. Any childish dreams of becoming leader of the Cabal—"

"There won't be a Cabal. She has promised to destroy you," Azra casually interrupted. "Truly destroy you."

"Who?"

"All of you. Every single vampire. Dead."

Micha flinched as the truth smashed into him with shocking force. He'd already accepted Azra's treachery. The male had not only lied and deceived his brothers, but he'd colluded with a dragon to break the treaty that allowed vampires to walk freely, he'd sacrificed countless demons in his demented quest, and no doubt intended to kill Micha and Skye as soon as he'd completed his evil scheme.

But to wipe vampires off the earth for all eternity? That was demented. Or whatever was beyond demented.

Unhinged. Certifiable. Batshit crazy.

All of the above.

"Genocide?" he finally managed to rasp.

Azra twisted his lips into a cruel smile. "Vampires are true believers in might makes right, aren't they, brother?"

"You're no brother of mine."

"It doesn't matter. Soon you'll be dead along with all the others who underestimated me."

"Including you, you idiot," Micha hissed. "Skye has seen a vision of your glorious future. Do you want to know what your precious dragon is going to actually do to you?"

"No."

"Tough, you're going to hear it anyway," Micha growled, moving until he was close enough to attack the traitor. "She's going to bathe the world in fire," he warned. "She's going to destroy everything and everyone. Including you."

"Shut up." Azra whirled toward the silent Lynx, who was staring toward the pedestal with wild eyes. As if he was seeing something even more terrifying than a crazed vampire bent on destroying the world. "Take the crystal to the pedestal," he commanded. "Now."

Lynx grimaced. Then, with an awkward shuffle, he walked forward like a puppet being jerked by unseen strings. The crystal was still held over his head as the crimson glow pulsed brighter and brighter. Micha lunged toward the fairy, his fangs extending. The pleasure of destroying Azra had to be put on hold. At least for the moment. He couldn't allow the crystal to reach the pedestal.

He was just inches from the male when he felt a pulse of energy push against him. It wasn't coming from the fairy. Or even Azra, who was too occupied with his compulsion to steer Lynx to the center of the cavern to notice Micha's attack.

It had to be the crystal, he belatedly realized, bracing himself for a blast of pain. It was obviously protecting itself. Or perhaps it was protecting Lynx. Either way, Micha sensed it was going to lash out.

Reaching the glow, Micha clenched his fangs, determined to put an end to the threat no matter the cost. But it wasn't pain that sent him flying backward to land in an awkward heap on the marble floor.

The crimson glow was not only an impenetrable shield, but the moment he'd gotten too close, it'd lashed out with enough power to send him flying like he was a twig, not a vampire who weighed a ton.

Micha surged to his feet. Dammit, he had to stop him. But how? He couldn't get close enough to wound him. And he doubted even a physical weapon would get through the glow.

Perhaps he could kill Azra and break the compulsion, but that was going to take time. Time he didn't have. Plus, there was no guarantee that the fairy wouldn't return the crystal to the pedestal even if the compulsion was gone. Lynx had convinced himself he was destined to become a demon savior for too long to easily give up the dream. He was desperate enough to try anything at this point.

What Micha needed was...

Actually, he had exactly what he needed.

Turning his head, he glanced toward Skye, who was concentrating on the fairy with a fierce expression.

"Skye, we have to stop him from reaching the pedestal."

Chapter 19

"I got it," Skye assured Micha, despite the fact that she'd been struggling to enter Lynx's mind since Azra had made his unexpected entrance into the cavern. The strange magic that pulsed around the fairy was not only a physical barrier but also a mental barrier. Thankfully, Azra had unintentionally offered her a small shred of hope. But only if she could keep Micha from giving in to his savage thirst for revenge. She crossed to stand directly in Lynx's path to the pedestal, risking a quick glance toward Micha. "Keep the vampire from interfering—"

"With pleasure," Micha promised.

"But keep him alive," she completed her request.

A growl rumbled on Micha's lips as he halted his advance toward the male, who appeared lost in his mental connection with the fairy.

Good. That should make things easier for her.

Micha wasn't nearly so pleased.

"Why?" he demanded.

"The magic of the crystal is causing interference," she confessed with a grimace. "I can't enter Lynx's thoughts while he's holding it, but I think I can use Azra's compulsion to slip in and take control of his mind."

He turned to study her with a strange expression. Did he sense the uncertainty bubbling inside her? Probably. She didn't doubt for a second that if Lynx managed to place the crystal on the pedestal, the dragons would awaken and release a hellfire that would destroy everything in its path. It was up to her to keep that from happening. But she'd never done anything like this. And certainly not when they were facing an end-of-the-world scenario.

Peri would know what to do. And so would Maya. But she didn't have their power. Or their courage...

Stop it. With a fierce effort, she pushed against her insecurities. Meeting Micha's steady gaze, she squared her shoulders.

"I'm ready," she assured him.

"You got this, Skye," he murmured, his voice low and his gaze steady. "I believe in you."

Closing her eyes, Skye concentrated on her powers that were tightly knotted in the center of her heart. This wasn't the same as using an incantation. Or tapping into the spells that were stored in her charms. This was her own special gift. The magic she'd been blessed with that had marked her as a seer when she was a young girl.

Concentrating on her carefully restricted powers, she peeled away the barriers she'd erected. It wasn't a perfect system. If she was tired or she'd stretched her magic too far, then the barricades would leak. Or if a vision was particularly strong, like when she touched Micha, the power would burst out.

Skye released the last of the barriers and there was a heady rush of pleasure as the magic crashed through her. She trembled, savoring the intoxicating sensation. Sometimes she forgot how glorious it felt to have the full force of her magic flowing through her body.

Then the reminder of why she was so careful to keep it locked away slammed into her.

First was the smell. Not the musty odor of the cavern or the rich, coppery scent that was embedded in the marble. Those were natural scents that she'd noticed from the moment they'd entered the vast space.

No, it was the stench of emotions that wrinkled her nose in regret.

Lynx's panicked desperation. Azra's bitterness layered with a hint of insanity. Micha's grim determination.

Even her own fear of failure.

The next thing to hit her was the tension that pulsed through the cavern. The smothering force squeezed her in a painful vise that tightened with every beat of her heart. It felt like a hurricane about to unleash its fury in a torrential explosion.

Shuddering as the various sensations washed over her, Skye focused her concentration on the fairy, who continued a slow, plodding path toward the center of the room.

He was still protected behind the crimson glow of the crystal, but she could sense the threads of compulsion that Azra had woven through the shield and directly into his mind. She could actually see the connection.

It looked like an inky line power-drilling into the back of the fairy's head. Weird. Her own magic appeared in a shimmer of silver and gold, barely visible as she delicately coiled it around Azra's link. Her touch was delicate, as she sternly resisted the urge to smash through the barriers keeping her out. She didn't want either male to realize what she was doing as she crept along the black thread of compulsion inch by inch.

After what felt like an eternity, she reached the fairy's mind.

"Lynx," she whispered, forming the image of a net wrapping around the male's slender body to reinforce her commands. "Stop."

She breathed a sigh of relief as Lynx's steps faltered, his body stiffening as if he was battling against two separate impulses. And he was. The inky strand of vampire power writhed in frustration, trying to cut through her shimmering magic. Skye tightened her grip on Lynx's mind, coating the compulsion in layers of shimmering gold.

Like smothering a fire.

Engrossed in cutting off the vampire's hold, Skye didn't consider the possibility that there might be more than one danger. Not until the glow from the crystal flooded Lynx's mind, severing Azra's connection and nearly wrenching away her own grip.

Blinded by the abrupt flash of crimson, Skye didn't see Lynx continue his path to the pedestal, but she sensed his movement.

"Lynx." She added another layer of magic. "Turn around."

"He can't hear you," a female voice abruptly drawled. "Can you, my pet?"

With a soft gasp, Skye whirled around to discover a tall, slender form standing in the center of the cavern. No, not standing, she realized as the image faded before reappearing. It was a vision, but not in her mind, it was filling Lynx's brain, and somehow Skye's connection to the fairy was allowing her to see what he was seeing.

She'd never heard of anything like it. Not even in the ancient manuscripts that had been written by various seers.

But then again, most seers had never encountered a dragon. And Skye didn't doubt for a second that was exactly what she was looking at. A real, fire-breathing dragon who could destroy her with a random burp.

She also didn't doubt that it was the same dragon she'd seen in the memory spell. The creature had replaced the fur cape with a floor-length black robe, and her hair was left loose to tumble down her back like a river of red fire, but her skin still shimmered with the same bronzed sheen and she had the same solar blasts of power that surrounded her in a hellish aura.

Skye's breath was squeezed from her lungs, and sweat trickled down her face. Catching a glimpse of one in a memory spell was considerably different than being up close and personal. It didn't matter that the creature was there in spirit rather than flesh. Or even that she was viewing the creature through Lynx.

Without warning, the black gaze settled on her with an unnerving intensity. "Who are you?" the female demanded, not bothering to hide her disgust.

Wait. Could the vision see her? More importantly, could the beast belch fire at her? Raw fear pulsed through Skye and she desperately battled against her natural instincts. No. She had to stay strong, she sternly chided herself. Whatever her urge to flee in terror, she had to keep Lynx from reaching the pedestal. And the only way to do that was to regain her control of his mind.

Which would be considerably easier if she could somehow keep the dragon focused on her instead of the fairy.

An alarming but necessary sacrifice.

"Zanna, I presume." The words came out more like a croak than a taunt, but her effort wasn't wasted.

The female hissed, sounding weirdly snakelike as she continued to glare at Skye. "Queen Zanna to you, human." The dark gaze narrowed. "Ah, no," she breathed. "Not a human. Magic user."

"Seer to you, dragon," she retorted, sending a ripple of magic through her connection to Lynx. The fairy hesitated, the silver in his aura flaring as he was caught between the two powerful forces.

"Well what do you know. A female with a backbone." Zanna moved forward, appearing to float over the mosaic tiles. "Shall I rip it out?"

Skye stood her ground. Oddly, the closer the female approached, the less afraid she felt. Or maybe the stress of the past few days had finally caused her to snap and she didn't have the sense to be terrified. A much more likely explanation.

Still, Skye was willing to indulge her reckless lack of caution. Right now it was exactly what she needed.

"Are you asking my opinion or telling me what you're going to do?" she asked in flippant tones.

"Who are you?" Zanna asked again, this time with something that might have been genuine curiosity.

"Nobody. Just a mage who happens to have visions."

"Visions of what?"

"The world burning."

"Ah." Zanna released a slow breath, the scent of brimstone swirling through the air. "I have those visions as well. Aren't they glorious?"

"Not so much," Skye said dryly.

"Mmm." Zanna pursed her lips. "I suppose a mortal creature wouldn't be as excited at the thought of the world drowning in fire. For some of us it's going to be pure paradise."

Skye refused to be baited. Instead, she tightened her grip on Lynx's mind, forcing him back a step. Satisfaction flared through her, even as a voice in the back of her mind warned she needed a better plan. Eventually she would run out of magic. Or more likely, the dragon would get tired of playing with her. Then she would force Lynx to complete his mission and the dragons would be free to fulfill her visions.

"You signed a treaty," she reminded Zanna, wondering if she could shame the female into backing down. Unlikely, but hey...it wasn't like she had a plan B. "Do dragons have no honor?"

Sparks danced in the dark eyes as smoke curled from one flared nostril. "Careful, seer."

Skye used the female's spurt of anger to tighten her grip on Lynx's mind.

"You made a pledge and now you're trying to break it," she continued. She might not be able to shame the dragon, but her accusations clearly annoyed the beast. It was better than nothing. "Hardly the behavior of a noble species."

"Do you think such powerful beings could be controlled by a piece of paper? We are gods who have no need to concern ourselves with such pettiness."

"Piece of paper?" Skye arched her brows. "It was a treaty that you sealed with your blood."

Zanna dismissed her words with a restless shrug. "A meaningless gesture."

"If it was meaningless, why agree to the treaty at all?"

The vision seemed to ripple in and out of focus, as if the question had caught the creature by surprise. A second later, the dragon had regained her composure to send Skye a haughty glare.

"Dragons traditionally seclude themselves in their lairs to rejuvenate their powers. It was close enough to our natural hibernation to pretend that I agreed with the stupid pledge."

"Lies," Skye breathed, shocked as she managed to peek into the dragon's mind.

The images were fragmented. And they flipped from one to another with a dizzying speed. But Skye was able to see herself sitting on a massive throne, surrounded by acres of marble and gilding and rich tapestries that glowed in the torchlight.

"Excuse me?" the dragon snapped.

"That's not the reason you agreed to the treaty," Skye said, able to determine that there were several forms standing in front of the throne, all of them large and surrounded by the same formidable auras as Zanna. Dragons. And they didn't look happy. "You were afraid of the vampires."

"I fear no leech!"

The ground abruptly shook, the marble cracking as if an immense force was pressing against it. Zanna's temper? Or was something stirring beneath her feet?

A thought that made Skye's stomach clench with dread.

"Perhaps not vampires, but you feared the weapon they created." She forced herself to focus on the images that continued to flicker through her mind. "You couldn't defend against it no matter how many times you promised to protect your people." Suddenly she wasn't in the throne room. Instead she was standing on top of a mountain, watching her mighty warriors tumble from the sky with shrieks of pain. From behind her the whoosh of heavy wings sent a blast of searing heat over her, and a sudden fear pierced her heart. Someone had landed on top of the cliff and the very fact they had chosen to approach from behind meant their arrival was an unspoken threat. "Worse, you refused to stop attacking," Skye continued. "It's no wonder the other dragons started to question if you were such a great queen."

"They adore me," Zanna snapped.

The images faded, as if Zanna was deliberately trying to shut her out, but Skye had one last clear vision. One that was more shocking than all the others.

"No. They banded together and stormed your lair," she said, shuddering at the image of raw, explosive power that had been blasted at the marble throne room. "They were the ones to insist on signing the treaty. You had no choice but to agree or be banned from the..." Skye paused, trying to come up with the proper word. "What is a group of dragons? A lounge? No, wait. That's lizards. A—"

"Get out of my mind," Zanna snarled, the smoke from her nose curling around her head like a halo.

Firmly forced out of the dragon's memories, Skye returned her attention to her connection with Lynx. He was locked in place, caught between the two warring compulsions. Right now, that was the best she could do.

"I don't think so," she muttered, feeling sweat trickle down her spine. "Not when you're threatening to destroy the world."

"Not destroy it," Zanna reprimanded her. "Remold it into what it should have been from the beginning."

"And what's that?"

"A burning landscape that's no longer infested with vermin."

Skye's stomach clenched even tighter, making her feel nauseous. She didn't need to peek into Zanna's mind. She'd seen the vision of flames consuming the world.

"I suppose vampires are the vermin?" she asked, more to keep the dragon talking than any interest in who she wanted to kill. Everyone would die.

"Vampires. Demons. Humans. Mages," Zanna drawled, as if to reinforce Skye's deepest fears.

"You want a world with just dragons?"

Zanna shrugged. "We are the superior species."

"You're certainly the most arrogant of the species," Skye muttered.

"For good reason." A sneer twisted the female's exquisite features. "As you'll soon discover."

She *was* going to discover, Skye acknowledged, terror pulsing through her. There was no doubt that the hellscape she'd glimpsed in her vision was about to happen.

Unless she found some way to stop it.

But how?

"Do the others know?" she abruptly demanded.

Zanna stiffened, as if Skye's desperate stab in the dark had hit a nerve. "Others?"

"The dragons," Skye clarified, even though there was no need. The unease smoldering in Zanna's dark eyes revealed she knew exactly what Skye was asking.

"I'm their queen." Zanna tilted her chin, her expression defiant. "I made the decision that's best for my people."

"To live in a world that has nothing to offer but a barren emptiness?" Skye shook her head. "Who would want that?"

"Dragons adore fire. It's our natural habitat."

Skye frowned. There wasn't a great deal of information about dragons available to mages. They'd been gone a long time, and even when they roamed the world, they were secretive. But she did know that they were the dominant species for thousands of years.

"If that's true, then why didn't you torch the earth when you were awake? It wasn't like anyone could stop you."

Zanna's lips pinched. "We attempted to share our world. Now it's obvious that the only way to get rid of our enemies is to destroy them all."

"Ah." Skye suddenly understood.

This wasn't about the dragons being forced into hibernation. Or the desire to be the lone surviving creatures.

This was about Zanna and her ruthless ambition.

"Ah, what?" the dragon snapped.

Skye narrowed her gaze, pretending she could still read the female's mind. "We've already discussed the fact they have some questions about your ability to rule. And now you realize that when they climb out of hibernation there's a real possibility that they're going to make some hard decisions about who they want sitting on the throne." Skye shook her head. "Are you really so determined to cling to your position of power that you would condemn them to hell?"

"It will be too late," Zanna snapped, confirming Skye's suspicions. "They will have no choice but to approve my decision—" Belatedly realizing she was revealing more than she intended, Zanna balled her hands into fists and glared toward the trembling fairy. "Place the crystal on the pedestal. Now."

"No!"

Skye jerked her hand in Lynx's direction, muttering the words to a hasty spell. She didn't have a hope in hell of defeating a dragon, not even if she was at full power, but she was reacting on instinct, not logic. If she was thinking clearly, she'd have given up the moment she realized Zanna had lured Lynx to this hidden lair.

Thankfully, the charms on her bracelet reacted to the threat in the air, and without conscious thought, a column of power blasted from her wrist and aimed straight toward the fairy. Of course, it was Peri's magic, so it didn't just knock Lynx to the ground. Or freeze him in place.

Instead, it wrapped around his hand like a glove and lifted him off his feet until he was dangling off the ground. Then the magic started to pulse, tightening on Lynx's fingers until the fairy screamed in pain.

Zanna hissed, her eyes widening as the glow from the crystal clutched in Lynx's hand started to dim.

"Stop it."

Skye cut her connection to Lynx's mind, distracted by the male's agony. She wasn't a mage who was cruel or enjoyed causing pain to others, but right now nothing mattered beyond keeping the crystal from the pedestal. Even if it meant sacrificing Lynx. Or even herself.

"I don't think so," Skye ground out, taking a step toward Lynx. Proximity didn't make the magic stronger, but she hadn't forgotten about Azra.

The vampire must have felt his hold on Lynx being severed. It was possible he would try to physically force the fairy toward the pedestal.

Zanna, on the other hand, appeared frozen. As if shock had turned her into a statue.

"You're destroying the crystal," she hissed.

"Yes," Skye agreed, although she didn't have a clue what she was doing. Or rather what Peri's magic was doing.

"No. That's not possible." Zanna stared at her with genuine fear. "Who are you?"

This time Skye had an answer. Over the past few days she'd survived a kidnapping, a crazed vampire, and now a dragon. Micha had been right.

"I'm Skye," she announced in proud tones. "Skye Claremont."

Flames abruptly danced over Zanna, coating her in a dazzling layer of fire. "Time for you to die, Skye Claremont."

Skye ignored the warning. Any other time, the cloak of flames might have been impressive, not to mention scary as hell, but she knew this was the pivotal moment that would determine if her vision was fulfilled or if she could change the fate of the world.

Just another day at the office, she wryly acknowledged, shuddering as the wild magic continued to pour from the charm.

"Perhaps, but I'll destroy the crystal before you kill me," she said between clenched teeth.

"You fool," Zanna rasped, the fire disappearing. "It will trap us for an eternity."

"Good." Skye smiled. "A world without dragons doesn't bother me at all."

"Stop...please." The word sounded as if it had been wrenched from the depths of her evil soul.

Skye continued to send out the magic. Her trust of the dragon hovered around a negative trillion.

"This rebellion is over, sleeping beauty," she informed Zanna. "Crawl back to your lair and stay there."

The dark eyes flared with fury. "You bitch."

"Me? A bitch? Seriously? Talk about the pot calling the kettle black." She rolled her eyes before she sent another pulse of magic to hammer against the crystal. "Leave or I swear I'll destroy it."

A full minute ticked past. Then another. Skye's mouth was dry and her face coated in sweat. If this didn't work, then they were screwed.

Then, with a grudging reluctance, the vision began to slowly fade. Really, really slowly. As if Zanna was still considering some last desperate attempt to force Lynx to haul the crystal to the waiting pedestal. Skye took another step forward, trying to look threatening. Not her greatest talent, especially when her clothes were tattered, her face covered in dust and blood, and her hair tangled so badly it was going to take a powerful potion to unknot it.

Still, it was thankfully enough, as the vision of Zanna at last faded and a grinding pressure that Skye hadn't even realized was pressing against her body abruptly vanished.

Skye swayed, realizing the pressure had been helping her to stay upright. Behind her there was a loud thump and she glanced over her shoulder to see Lynx lying in an unconscious heap, the crystal still clutched in his hands although it was no longer glowing. No surprise. His mind had been grabbed and jerked between competing forces like a fumbled football. There was a real possibility he would remain unconscious for the next century. Or longer.

"Skye." Micha appeared at her side, wrapping his arms protectively around her. "Are you okay?"

It was a simple question, but a thousand answers sputtered in her brain. *No, of course I'm not okay. I just battled a dragon and nearly died. Yes, I'm fine. I just faced a dragon and lived. Maybe I'll decide if I'm okay after I've had a long nap. Like in a year or so...*

"I think so," she finally managed to mutter.

Micha swept a worried gaze over her face, no doubt sensing she wasn't in a place to have a coherent conversation.

"Is it over?" was all he asked.

"It's over," she breathed.

A grim satisfaction spread over his beautiful face. "Are we done with Azra?"

Her gaze strayed toward the vampire who was glaring at them with a hint of confusion. Obviously he didn't understand how or why he'd lost his control over Lynx, but he did realize that he no longer had the upper hand.

"Done," she assured Micha in icy tones.

Micha released her and turned to face Azra, the nearby marble column popping and cracking as if it was being crushed by an unseen power. Micha? Skye desperately hoped so. She couldn't take another enemy making an unwelcome appearance.

The older vampire took an instinctive step back. "Wait. This has all been a terrible mistake," he rasped, holding out his hands even as Skye could sense him mentally reaching toward the unconscious fairy. "I was obviously being compelled by powers beyond my control. None of this was my fault—"

"Micha, he's trying to wake up Lynx!" she called out, tapping into her magic to block the male from entering the fairy's mind.

There was a brief flare of power before it sputtered and disappeared. Damn. She was all tapped out. Thankfully, Micha still retained his strength. Even better, his ability to manipulate the magic of the Gyre allowed him to create weapons out of nearby objects.

"No one forced you to betray your people," he hissed, lifting his arm and pointing a finger at Azra. "It was your own pathetic lust for power that nearly destroyed us all."

"No. I told you. It wasn't me. It was the dragon. She manipulated me until I couldn't think clearly." Azra pressed his hands together, as if pleading for mercy. His eyes, however, remained hard with ruthless determination. He wasn't conceding defeat, he was playing for time. "Listen, now isn't the time or place to make any hasty decisions. Take me to Sinjon. I'm sure he'd understand."

"Yes, I'm sure he will understand."

Micha sounded almost sad as he gestured with his hand, and without warning the air was filled with jagged shards of marble from the column he'd shattered moments ago. Skye hastily backed away, her eyes wide as the lethal projectiles whizzed directly toward Azra.

The male screeched in fury, lifting his arms to try to protect his face. It was a wasted effort. The marble sliced through flesh and bone with sickening ease, digging deep into his skull. Skye gagged at the sound of the shards sawing their way through Azra before they were zooming around to launch another attack.

Azra's screams were no longer anger. They echoed through the cavern with a pain that made the ground shake.

"Stop! Please!"

Micha ignored the pleas, his face grim as he concentrated on the shards currently slicing Azra to bloody shreds. Skye gagged, turning her back to avoid the gruesome death.

It wasn't that she didn't think the vampire deserved his fate. He'd been willing to watch the world burn in a pathetic power grab. He'd gone beyond ambitious into the realms of demented. Which meant he had to be destroyed. Vampires were too powerful to survive if they were unstable. But she was exhausted, queasy, and unable to endure the sight of any more violence.

She would be brave again tomorrow.

An eternity passed—at least that was what it felt like to Skye—before the ghastly screams began to fade, and she released a shaky breath of relief. Was it over? Really and truly over?

She was almost afraid to believe.

For good reason, she immediately conceded, watching as a shimmering black streak appeared near the pedestal. It was nearly three inches long and as thin as a strand of hair. Just for a second, she tried to convince herself it was a trick of the light that glowed from an unseen source in the ceiling. Or a residual effect from Zanna's magic. The dragon might not have physically been in the cavern, but her spirit form had been spewing a toxic brew of power. Skye could still smell the brimstone.

Or maybe it was a protective trigger connected to the pedestal. After all, she wouldn't have noticed the strand if she hadn't been staring in that direction for several minutes. Maybe it was always there, waiting to release a trap if someone came too close.

She was still busy trying to convince herself that she had nothing to worry about when the strand began to lengthen and then to twirl in a circle. Skye instinctively touched a finger to her charms, futilely hoping that there might be a spell left to toss at the latest threat.

There was nothing. She was all magicked out.

A damned shame since the strand had stretched and grown into a large circle that continued to expand until it touched the marble floor just inches from where Lynx was lying unconscious.

"Um...Micha," she breathed in warning.

She'd never seen a portal, but she'd read an ancient manuscript that had described them. Back in the olden days, when magic flowed freely through the world, there were a few of the more powerful mages who could open a doorway from one place to another, even if it was hundreds of miles apart. She was pretty certain that was what she was looking at now.

There was a cool rush of power wrapping protectively around her as Micha moved to stand at her side, at the same moment the outline of a large male form became visible inside the darkness of the portal.

"I smell copper," the vampire muttered.

Skye sucked in a deep breath. He was right. Whoever was coming had the same coppery scent as Lynx. But it wasn't demon. It was something she'd never encountered.

With the confident assurance of a creature who obviously wasn't scared to enter a strange room without knowing who or what might be waiting for him, the male stepped out of the portal. He was even bigger now that she could fully see him with long copper hair that was pulled into a braid to reveal a startlingly beautiful face. There was something almost fey about the emerald eyes and the angular cut of his features, but she instinctively sensed he was unique.

And old.

Mind-numbingly old.

Without warning, the male dipped his head in their direction. "Thank you for your service."

His voice rumbled like thunder, echoing through the chamber.

"Who are you?" Skye breathed.

"You can call me the Watcher."

"Watcher?" Skye shook her head in confusion. "Is that your name or—"

"You need to leave this place," the stranger interrupted, bending down to scoop Lynx into his arms. With an ease not even a vampire could have matched, he straightened, the unconscious fairy draped over his arms. "Now."

Micha stepped forward. "Not until we have a few answers. And not without the crystal the fairy is holding."

"The crystal is back where it belongs," the male promised.

The temperature dropped as Micha called on his powers. "That's for the Cabal to decide."

"Vampires." The male rolled his eyes, clearly unimpressed with the authority of the Cabal. "Go home."

Micha stiffened, prepared to attack, but with the same liquid ease that he'd entered the cavern, the creature stepped back and disappeared into the portal. A second later the opening snapped shut, as if a door had been slammed.

Skye blinked. "Well that was weird."

"He has the crystal."

He did, but Skye wasn't as upset as she should be. It could be that she was just too tired to work up concern for the stupid red stone. But a part of her accepted that the crystal was truly where it belonged.

A low rumble shook the cavern and for a moment Skye thought it was Micha's power being unleashed in a belated attempt to stop the stranger from disappearing. It wasn't until chunks of stone started to fall from the ceiling that she realized the entire cavern was shaking, as if it was about to collapse.

"We really need to go," she rasped, stumbling to the side as the mosaic floor buckled beneath her feet.

Micha didn't hesitate. Grasping her hand, he raced toward a large crack in the wall that had exposed a hidden passageway. Was this how

Azra had managed to sneak up on them? Probably, but right now Skye wasn't interested in anything but getting out before the mountain landed on top of them.

The threat of being buried beneath tons of granite tended to put her priorities in order.

Chapter 20

Seated at a small wooden table that had been arranged in the center of his bedroom, Micha savored the glorious sense of peace.

He had a few fragmented memories of their return trip to New Orleans. He recalled his servants rushing to assist them the second they'd climbed out of the mountain, and being whisked through the air on his private jet. And even being half carried down to his private lair where he'd collapsed into bed with Skye held tightly in his arms.

It was a full twenty-four hours before he had regained enough strength to take a hot shower, although he hadn't bothered to dress, instead pulling on a black silk robe. He planned on staying in his lair for the next month. Maybe year.

Once his brain felt clear enough to hold a coherent conversation, he'd made a call to Valen, revealing what had happened. In return, Valen had shared his confrontation with Kane and the fact that the large vampire was currently a guest in his dungeons.

Eventually he would contact Sinjon and give a detailed explanation of Azra's descent into madness, but he wasn't ready to be forced to travel to Greece to make a full report. Or worse, have the powerful leader of the Cabal and his vast entourage appear on his doorstep.

He had more important matters on his mind.

Far, far more important.

Leaning back in his seat, Micha studied the woman who was busily polishing off a bowl of jambalaya and an entire loaf of garlic bread.

Skye Claremont.

Like him she was wearing a silk robe, although it was several sizes too large, and her hair was a damp mop of curls that framed her face with wild abandon. Micha was convinced he'd never seen anyone more beautiful. More importantly, her deep sleep and an hour soaking in a bubble bath had restored the flush of health to her cheeks and the electric tingle of magic that hummed around her like a forcefield.

It was going to take time for her to recover her full strength, but he could sense she was settling into the lair. A knowledge that filled a place inside him that Micha hadn't realized was empty. And a desperate hope that she intended to stay.

Swallowing the last chunk of bread, Skye pushed aside her empty bowl and reached for the glass of wine, releasing a soft sigh of contentment.

Micha bit back a groan as he was forced to battle the urge to toss aside the narrow table and scoop Skye into his arms. He wasn't a stickler when it came to etiquette but it seemed only polite to let her finish dinner before pouncing.

"Did Maya have any information about the Watcher?" he forced himself to ask.

Skye had been on the phone with her friend when he'd escorted her into the bedroom to reveal the feast he'd ordered while she was in the tub. And once she had hung up, she'd grabbed a spoon and devoured the meal with a gusto that warned she wasn't in the mood for chitchat.

Now he was hoping that she'd discovered some information that would allow them to track down the creature that had disappeared with Lynx and the crystal.

It seemed impossible to believe that anyone—even a demon—could dig a pathway to the cavern. The entire mountain had collapsed as they'd been rushing away. But he wasn't going to take anything for granted. His logical brain wasn't satisfied with the vague certainty that the dragon was safely locked in her hibernation.

Skye wrinkled her nose. "I'm not sure. She was weirdly cagey when I described him. Almost as if she didn't want to discuss who or what the Watcher might be."

"Is that unusual?"

"Maya is like a two-by-four to the face. There's nothing subtle about her."

Micha grimaced. He had deliberately blocked out the private conversation between the two mages, but no one could have missed Maya's shriek of fury when Skye told her friend that she intended to remain in New Orleans.

"Including her opinion of vampires."

"Exactly."

Skye chuckled, not nearly so worried as Micha about her friend's reaction. Of course, she wasn't the one who was going to end up with a boil on her ass if the older mage managed to get close enough to curse him, he wryly acknowledged.

"We can continue our own research here," he concluded, dismissing his concern. "There has to be information about the crystal and original Lynx hidden in one of the manuscripts I've collected."

"I also warned Maya that there might be other Lynx wannabes out there," she said, her brow furrowed as she drained the last of her wine in one gulp.

Micha frowned. "Is something bothering you?"

"Just a feeling that I'm missing something," Skye muttered. "Something important."

"It will come to you." His gaze skimmed over her delicate features, lingering on the dark eyes that smoldered with an ancient power that had prevented the world from being consumed with flames. But that wasn't the only thing he could see. There was also a sweet, utterly vulnerable woman who had been forced to sacrifice her entire life for her gifts. It was time that she be allowed to discover what made her happy, not what others wanted from her. "Right now we have more important matters to discuss."

She stilled as his voice lowered, the air thickening with an awareness he no longer bothered to hide. Just for a second he feared that she might not be in the mood for what he desired. She had, after all, been on a road trip from hell that had ended with a life-or-death battle with a dragon. No one could blame her for needing some alone time to decompress.

Fiercely attempting to reconcile himself to the fact their night together would have to be postponed, Micha was prepared for her to rise to her feet and leave the room. Instead, she leaned forward, her expression softening with an invitation that made his unbeating heart leap in joy.

"What could be more important?" she asked.

Micha smiled as he reached for the Café Du Monde box. "Dessert."

"Oh," she groaned in pleasure. "That smells amazing, but I'm stuffed."

"Who can resist beignets?" he teased, flipping open the lid. "Golden, deep-fried dough smothered in powdered sugar."

She waved them away. "Later, I promise."

"Later is good," Micha assured her, setting aside the box as he held her dark gaze. "Much later."

"What about you?"

"I'm not hungry." His smile widened. "At least not for beignets."

A flush touched her cheeks. "You need to feed."

"When you're ready," he said, sharing his hope that she would eventually agree to become his donor. The thought of tasting blood from anyone but this female was repugnant. "There's no need to rush. We have an eternity together."

Holding his gaze, she reached across the table to grasp his hand. "I'm ready."

Micha trembled. He'd put a lot of effort into bracing for her uncertainty. Feeding a vampire was not only incredibly intimate, but most creatures feared it would be painful. The fact that she sounded eager to offer her vein was making him tingle in all the right places.

"You're sure?" The question left his lips before he could halt it.

Still gripping his hand, Skye rose to her feet. "More than sure."

Her voice was steady, the scent of laurel leaves scenting the air. Micha readily straightened, tugging her around the table so he could scoop her off her feet.

If she was ready, he was more than ready.

In fact, he was starving.

"Let's make ourselves more comfortable," he murmured, using his powers to switch on soft music and dim the candlelight.

"Very romantic," Skye assured him as he perched on the edge of the bed, with her snuggled on his lap.

"Not really." He gazed down at her, engraving each delicate feature in his mind. Before he'd traveled to New York he would have sworn that he was perfectly content with his life. He had no interest in being distracted by lovers who would demand his time and attention. It had taken one glance at Skye Claremont to realize his life would never be complete without her at his side. "I've been a recluse for too long to have any skills in the romance department," he admitted, regretting the lack of luxury. He fully intended to refurbish the entire lair once Skye was settled in.

She reached up to brush her fingers over his cheek. "Then you must be a natural."

He bent his head to brush his lips over her mouth. "Or perhaps destiny formed each of us to perfectly fit together."

"Agreed." Her hand moved to cup his cheek, a sudden shiver racing through her body.

Micha froze, reminded of the first time she'd touched him. They hadn't fully discussed what had happened in the cavern before it started to collapse. Or what it meant for the future. It'd been enough that they had survived. Now he realized he had to know.

Tilting back her head, Skye eyed him with concern. "Is something wrong?"

"I'm trying to find the nerve to ask," he admitted.

"Ask what?"

"Is the vision you saw when you first touched me gone?"

Her fingers stroked over his face, pausing to trace the thrust of his fangs as if fascinated by their razor-sharp edge.

"It is," she murmured in distracted tones.

"And no new ones?" he pressed.

"No visions." She touched her fingertip against the point of his fang. "Just dreams."

Micha shuddered as a ravenous hunger blasted through him. He desperately needed to sink his fangs deep into her soft flesh, sucking her warm blood as his cock slid deep into her body.

"Do they include me," he rasped, his erection hardening to press tight against the curve of her hip.

"Yes, but..." her words trailed away with a deliberate enticement.

Desire clawed through him, joining the gnawing hunger until he struggled to think clearly. The heat and scent of her was enough to cloud his mind, but the feel of her snuggled in his lap was dissolving his thoughts until only his most basic instincts remained.

"But what?" He was proud he managed to form the words.

As if determined to shut down his brain completely, she reached to grasp the lapels of his robe, tugging them apart so she could slip her hands beneath the silken material.

"You didn't have so many clothes on," she said in husky tones, smoothing her palms over his bare chest.

Micha made a choked sound, his muscles clenching as the friction of her warm palms skimming over his body set off sparks of desire.

"That can be rectified," he assured her, brushing his lips over her forehead.

"Can it?"

"With help."

"Ah." She trailed her hands downward to grasp the belt of his robe, easily tugging it away. "I'm a very good helper," she assured him, pushing the slick fabric down his arms.

"Yes, yes you are." Micha allowed the robe to slide away, leaving him naked as he turned to gently lay her in the center of the mattress. Moving to join her, he rolled onto his side and stretched out next to her reclined form. Staring down at her flushed face surrounded by a halo of golden curls, anticipation bubbled through him like the finest champagne. "And a kick-ass mage," he added as he reached for the belt of her robe.

Pleasure danced in her eyes, her arms stretching above her head as he parted the robe to reveal her soft curves. She looked like a sensual cat begging to be petted.

"I did kick some ass," she agreed.

With a low growl, Micha reached to cup a full breast in his hand, his cock twitching as he watched the nipple clench with an eager need.

"Dragon ass," he added, lowering his head.

"Zanna wasn't actually—"

He sealed her mouth with a kiss that warned he wasn't going to listen to any nonsense. Not if she was going to undermine her heroic efforts. Plus, it was the perfect excuse to taste her sweet temptation.

Magic hit his tongue, tingling through him like an intoxicating potion. She'd already bewitched him. Now she was molding him into someone new. A male who would never be the same after this night.

"You kicked her ass and saved the world," he whispered against her parted lips, his thumb stroking her nipple until she melted in desire.

"Perhaps," she murmured.

He turned his head, scraping his fangs along the line of her jaw. "Eventually I'll convince you to believe in yourself," he promised.

Releasing a shaky gasp, Skye wrapped her arms around his neck. "Well you did promise an eternity together." Holding his gaze, she slowly tilted back her head, exposing her throat in a blatant invitation. "That's a lot of time to convince me."

Micha hissed as a soul-deep craving slammed into him. Not just for blood, but for the soft curves that promised pure bliss.

"Should I start here?" he growled, dragging his fangs down her throat, before pausing to stroke his tongue over the pulse that pounded just above her collarbone.

Her fingers dug into his back, the scent of her desire perfuming the air. "It's a nice beginning."

Micha smiled as he felt her heart miss a beat. "There's more."

"Mmm." She pressed against him. "I like more."

He stroked his lips over the curve of her breast, allowing her small gasps to guide him as he used his tongue and lips to tease her nipple while his fingers explored the satin softness of her body. With intense devotion he traced the dip of her waist and over the contour of her stomach. She was perfect, he silently acknowledged, grasping the back of her leg to tug it over his hip. The position not only squeezed her tight against his throbbing cock, but it gave him the best access to provide her pleasure.

With a last, lingering lick of her nipple, Micha lifted his head to gaze down at her features that had tensed with the same need that echoed inside him.

"Are you ready?" he asked, his voice not entirely steady.

"Yes," she hissed. "Please."

Unable to resist another second, Micha parted his mouth and sank his fangs into the side of her throat. Skye flinched in surprise at his swift strike, but her arms tightened around him as if to reassure him that she wasn't hurt.

Micha groaned as her warm blood hit his tongue, a heady sense of power rushing through him. He'd fed from demons, both goblins and fairies, as well as at least one mage, but none of them could compare to the raw strength that flowed through Skye's veins. It was no wonder she'd managed to face down a dragon, he acknowledged, feeling almost drunk as the magic rushed through him.

Drinking deep, Micha ran his hands down her back and over the curve of her hip before he sought the heat between her legs. Easily locating her cleft, he dipped his fingers into the welcome honey, slipping upward to find the perfect spot. She groaned in delight, as he stroked over her bundle of pleasure, moving faster and faster as he sucked her blood. Her hips moved in a rhythm to match his strokes until she raked her nails down his back.

"Micha!" She arched forward, her eyes closed in intense bliss as her orgasm hit. "I can't..."

"Let go," he urged, sliding out his fangs and using the tip of his tongue to seal shut the tiny wounds.

"Yes," she gasped, her body trembling. "Oh yes."

The climax was still convulsing through her as Micha rolled her onto her back and thrust into her with an urgency he'd never felt before. Probably because he'd waited for an eternity for this female to come into his life.

Threading his fingers in her golden curls, he gazed down at her exquisite face, allowing himself to drown in the ancient beauty of her dark eyes. The feel of her squeezed tight around his arousal was just as glorious as he'd anticipated. The pleasure so intense it was swiftly spiraling him toward a looming climax. But it was the tenderness that flooded through him that caught him off guard.

And the absolute certainty that he would never love another woman for the rest of eternity.

"Micha." With a tiny laugh of delight, Skye wrapped her arms tight around his neck while her legs folded around his thrusting hips. "We're floating."

He buried his face in her neck, the climax blasting through him with enough force to send them spinning through the room. "Hold on tight."

"Forever," she swore.

* * * *

Skye snuggled against Micha as she struggled to catch her breath. Wow. That was the only word that captured the explosive pleasure that continued to pulse through her. It wasn't just the numerous climaxes that had clenched her body in ecstasy, although they had been spectacular, but the realization that Micha's feeding had mentally connected them. She couldn't read his mind, but she could sense his emotions. And for the first time since she'd crossed paths with the shockingly gorgeous male, she no longer doubted his utter commitment to her. It didn't matter that he had the power to command a Gyre with thousands of demons who called him master. Or that he was capable of causing earthquakes that could destroy entire cities. In fact, nothing about their mating made any sense at all, but fate had somehow chosen to put them together. And she intended to relish every single minute.

Smoothing his hand down the curve of her back, Micha propped himself on his elbow to stare down at her with a searching gaze.

"You're quiet," he murmured.

She smiled as a shiver of awareness raced through her. He was just so damned gorgeous. Even in the shadows of the cavern his raw beauty was like a punch to the gut. And then there was that sexy, naked body. Was it any wonder she was finding it hard to do more than melt against him in mindless joy?

"I'm savoring the moment," she admitted in a husky voice.

He dipped his head, pressing his lips against her curls. "Me too."

Skye tilted back her head, suddenly sensing a tension in the air that hadn't been there before.

"Are you?" she asked, a pang of unease tugging her heart as he grimaced. "Micha?"

"I want you to be happy here." The words were clipped, as if they'd burst out of him.

"I don't understand. I *am* happy."

"For now," he agreed, his expression suddenly troubled. "But this lair is remote and far away from your friends. And there are times when I'll have to be away for hours or even nights at a time to deal with the duties of the Gyre. I don't want you to become bored or lonely." His jaw tightened, as if he was clenching his fangs. "Or worse, feel like you've sacrificed your own life to be with me."

Skye reached up to cup his face in her hands. It seemed impossible to believe this male could doubt how much she adored him. Or that she would ever willingly walk away. But there was no mistaking the vulnerability that smoldered deep in his golden eyes.

"Micha, if I'm bored or lonely, I'm perfectly capable of finding a way to fill my days with projects that interest me. And I have every intention of traveling to Jersey to spend time with my friends, and hopefully, they'll come and stay here on a regular basis." She lifted her head off the pillow to brush a light kiss over his lips. "The only sacrifice would be if I had to exist without you."

He returned her kiss with a burning intensity, the hand on her lower back pressing her tight against his thickening erection.

"Never, never, never," he growled. "Nothing will ever come between us."

Readily melting into his kiss, Skye skimmed her fingers over his chiseled features. She was tracing the sharp line of his jaw when a random thought abruptly shattered the passion flaring between them.

"Micha." She pressed her hands against his chest, too distracted to appreciate his skillful touch. "Wait."

Micha lifted his head, regarding her with a sudden concern. "What's wrong?"

"I just remembered."

"Remembered what?"

"Where I've seen Lynx."

Micha arched his brows, but he didn't point out that it was an odd time for her to be thinking about other men.

"The fairy?" he asked in confusion.

She shook her head. "The original Lynx. The one who negotiated the Dragon Treaty."

His features instantly tightened, his fangs lengthening. He was still annoyed that the crystal had been snatched away by the mysterious creature. Skye didn't doubt it was an itch that wasn't going to be satisfied until they knew the full truth of who had appeared in the cavern.

"Tell me," he commanded.

"When we activated the memory spell that revealed the moment the Dragon Treaty was sealed I was certain there was something familiar about the original Lynx, but I couldn't pinpoint why," she reminded him.

"And now?"

"I saw a picture of a male who looked very similar."

"In one of my books?"

"No, in a photo that Peri and Valen found hidden at Wisdom Ranch."

"Wisdom Ranch." It took Micha a second to place the name. "That's the homestead in Wyoming where Peri's mother lived with her coven, right?"

"Yes," Skye agreed. The ranch had once been a remote, secretive area like Area 51. Now it was a beautiful vacation spot for children in need.

"Who was in the picture?"

"Supposedly Peri's dad. At least that's what her mother told her." Skye wrinkled her nose. Brenda Sanguis had been pathologically ambitious and willing to do whatever was necessary to gain power, including the murder of her own daughter. Which meant it would be foolish to believe anything she'd told Peri without verification. Still, for the moment, Skye was willing to accept that the male truly was related to her friend. "Peri never met him. Or had any contact that I know of, but she brought the pictures back to Jersey. That's when I saw them."

"And he looked like the original Lynx?"

"Not an exact copy, but they have to be related."

He nodded, his expression distant as he considered the implications of her revelation.

"Azra did mention there were several descendants spread around the world," he finally reminded her. "It wouldn't be a stretch to imagine Peri is a great-great-great-grandchild." He paused, as if carefully choosing his words. "And it would explain a few things."

Skye blinked. As far as she was concerned, the fact that Peri might be related to the mysterious creatures only added another layer to her confusion. "Explains what?"

"Her ability to tap into her wild magic." He held up a hand, as if he thought she might be angered by his words. "Not that I'm taking away from her enormous talent, but it's been endless centuries since any mage has been able to do more than skim a small fraction of that power. It's possible her ancestry gave her the unique ability to release the magic."

Skye couldn't argue with his logic. "It would also explain why the magic that Peri had loaded onto my charms reacted so strongly in the cavern," she murmured, recalling the thread of power that had led them past the lava and the ability to nearly destroy the crystal.

"True."

Skye pursed her lips as she considered the possibilities. She'd always suspected her friend was special. Unfortunately, they were no closer to the answers they needed.

"Even if she is related, it doesn't reveal the truth of who or what he was, or the identity of the male who appeared in the cavern to snatch Lynx and the crystal," she admitted, frustration bubbling through her.

"It's possible we could do some DNA testing."

Skye released a sharp laugh. "Are you kidding? You think Valen would allow you to start poking and prodding his mate?"

They shared a glance of dread at the mere thought of convincing the rabidly overprotective vampire to allow Peri to become a lab rat for the Cabal. Then, with a shake of his head, Micha visibly pushed aside the pending battle.

"A worry for later." His features softened as his fingers drifted over the curve of her hip. "For now..."

Skye's frustration was drowned beneath a wave of desire as she smoothed her palms over his chest, fascinated by the sculpted muscles that rippled beneath her touch.

"For now?" she prompted.

His cock pressed against her hip, his fangs fully extended. "I have a more interesting suggestion to pass the time."

Without warning, Skye pushed hard against his chest, tumbling him flat on his back. Not waiting for him to realize what she intended, she climbed on top of his sprawled body.

"It's my turn to decide how we pass the time," she informed him.

The candlelight flared and soft music filled the cavern as he gazed up at her in wonderment.

"Anything to please you, Skye Claremont," he softly promised. "Anything."

Epilogue

Maya stood back to study the Christmas ornaments and mugs of hot chocolate with candy canes that she'd painted on the front windows of the Witch's Brew. They weren't nearly as good as Skye's, but they were expected for the holiday season, so they would have to do.

Dropping her brush into the water bucket she'd set next to the palette of paints, Maya tilted back her head to study the thick clouds that obscured the sun. She'd spent the past weeks fretting over both Peri and Skye. Not only did she distrust leeches, but now they believed there was a connection between Peri and an ancient creature they knew nothing about, and Skye's brief but worrisome encounter with a dragon.

Today, however, was Sunday, and she'd promised herself that she was going to take care of the chores that had rapidly been piling up. Starting with the tedious paperwork that came with owning a business, followed by checking on Skye's friend, Madame Clarissa, who had come into an unexpected inheritance (that she had no idea came from Skye) and retired to a small house outside of the city. Then there were the order forms she needed to—

"How does it feel?"

Magic danced around Maya as she whirled around to discover Joe leaning against the nearby lamppost. Just for a second she held the spell that bubbled through her, longing to vent the irritation that had become her constant companion. She'd reached the limit of her patience when it came to this man sneaking around, spying on her, and hiding his true identity behind that ridiculous velour tracksuit and fishing hat.

It was only the knowledge that he was deliberately provoking her that forced her to release her magic and paste on a cool smile.

"How does what feel?" she demanded.

He jerked his head toward the shop. "Becoming an empty nester."

Lonely. The word whispered through her mind, but she kept her smile in place.

"It's not the first time I've run the shop by myself."

"True." Joe sucked air between his teeth, considering her with a gaze that threatened to pierce her very soul. "It won't be long, though. Soon enough you'll be on the search for your next stray mage to bring home."

Maya refused to react, even as she wanted to reach out and give the man a good shake. How had he known she'd already been searching for a suitable candidate?

"What does it matter to you?"

"The service in your coffee shop goes to hell when you're training someone new."

"Service?" Maya sent him a mocking glance. "Since when have you ordered, let alone paid, for anything in my shop?"

"Don't be a hater. I offer more than money."

"Really? What's that?"

He straightened from the pole, running his hands down his velour jacket. "I give the whole neighborhood its special vibe."

"Yeah, it's special all right." Maya folded her arms over her chest. It was that or striding forward and punching him in the nose. "And that's why you hang around here?"

"Why else?"

"That's a question I intend to answer." She deliberately paused. "With or without your help."

Joe snorted at the threat. "I admire your confidence. Even if you're doomed to failure." With a shrug he strolled down the sidewalk, pausing to whisper in her ear. "Enjoy the peace, Maya. It's not going to last."

She froze in place, the warning tingling down her spine. "Great. Just great."

Printed in the United States
by Baker & Taylor Publisher Services